A

REALM

OF

BLOOD

AND

MERCY

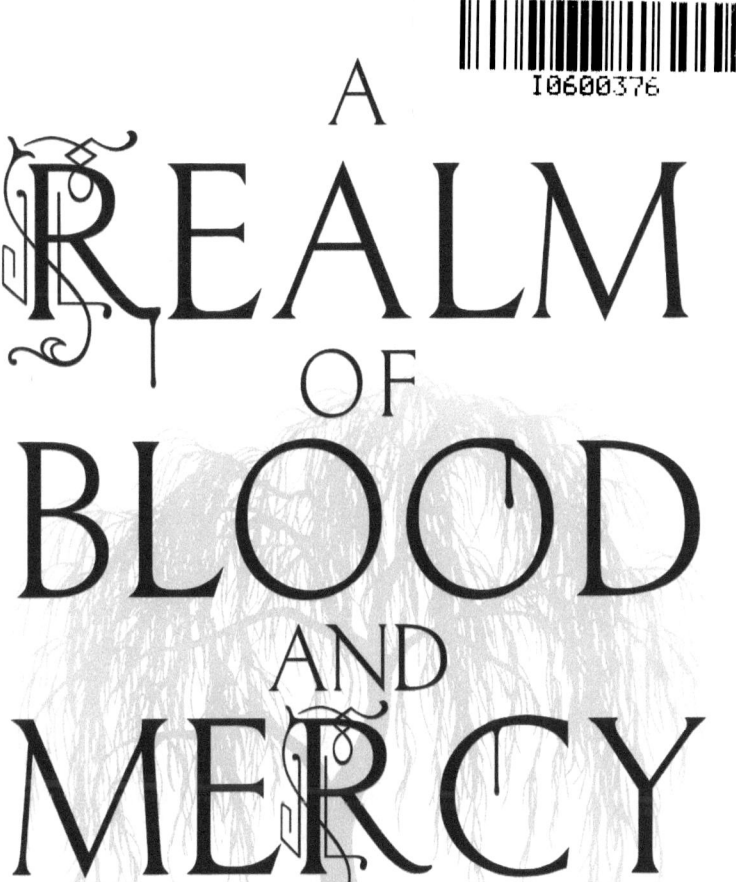

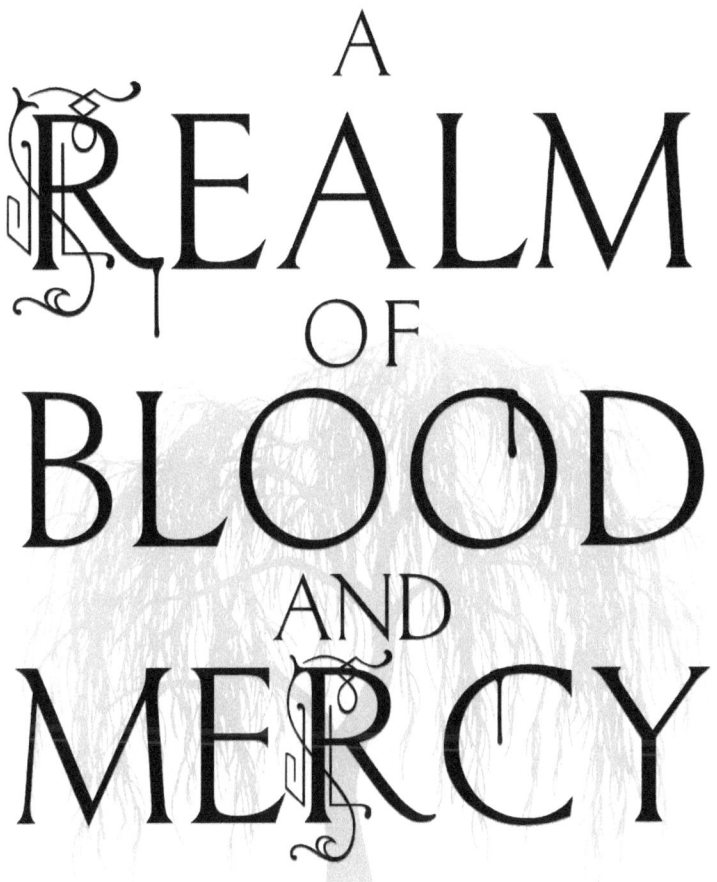

A REALM OF BLOOD AND MERCY

K. M. LAUMANN

WHIMSIQUILL BOOKS LLC

Published by WhimsiQuill Books LLC in Ohio.

Cover Design by Seventhstar Art
Map Illustrations created by "The Map Effects Fantasy Map Builder"
Map Designed by K. M. Laumann

Library of Congress Control Number: 2025916122

ISBN: 979-8-9992322-2-9 (paperback)
ISBN: 979-8-9992322-0-5 (Barnes and Noble paperback)
ISBN: 979-8-9992322-1-2 (ebook)

First Edition October 2025

*To the young girl who dreamed
and vowed never to give up.*

AUTHOR'S NOTE

A Realm of Blood and Mercy may be a fantasy romance, but there are some darker themes portrayed that may not be suitable for some readers. Swearing, blood and gore, death, violence, grief and loss, abuse, PTSD, torture, and sexual content are all depicted on the page. Your mental health matters. For readers who might be sensitive to some of these themes, please take note.

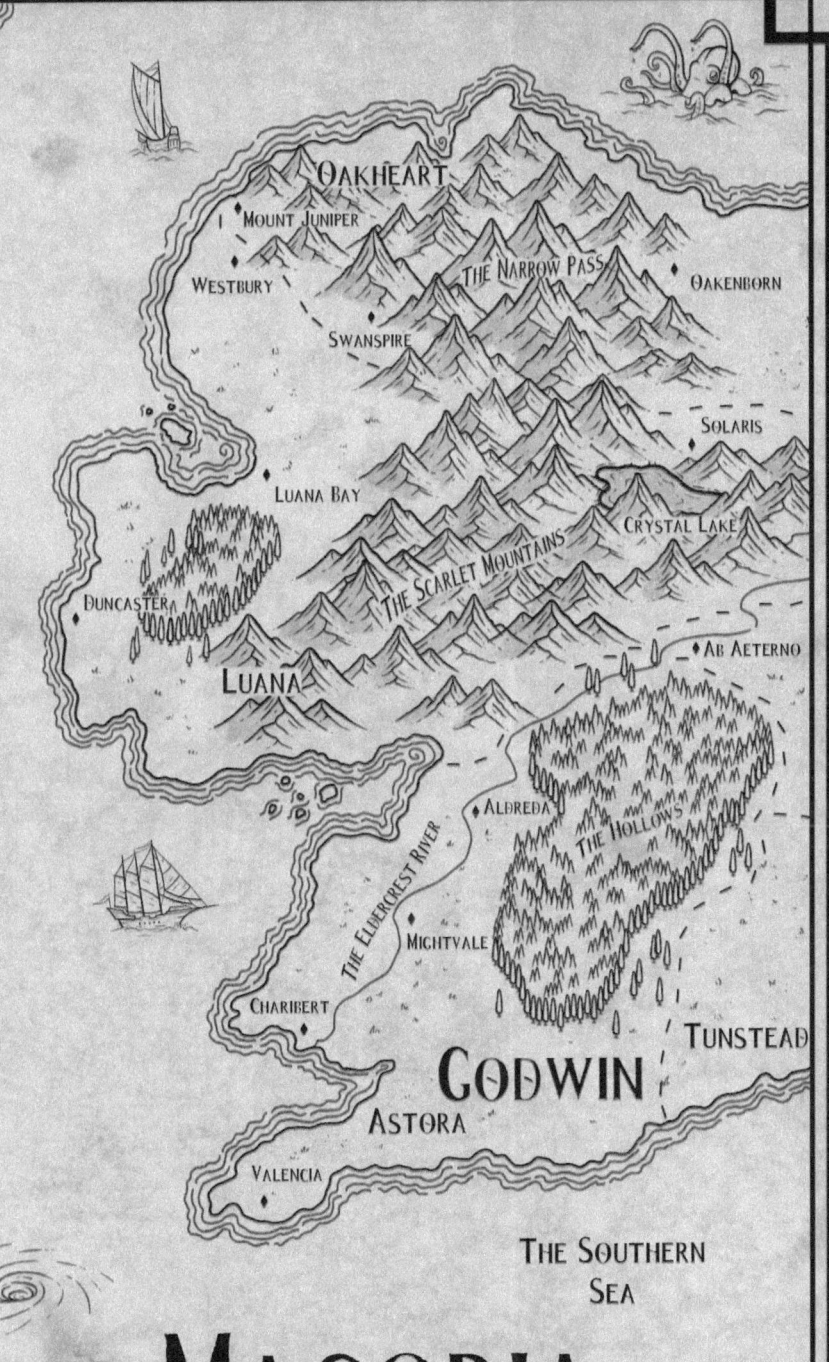

MAGORIA

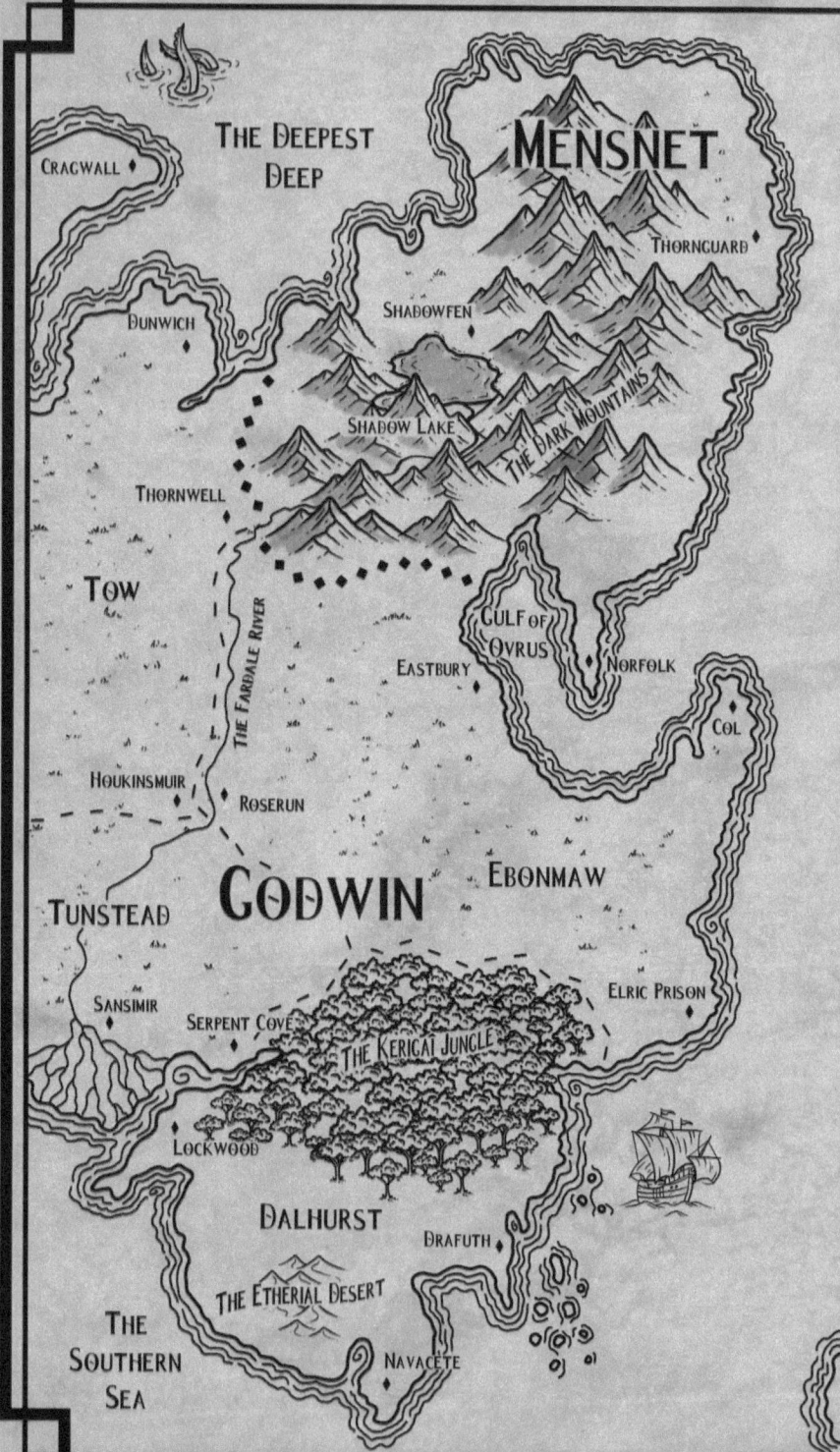

Vadhelle
Mosfelkov
Lungvik
N
The Nebulous Sea
Caesa
Thelona
Magoria
Hesana
The Djeri Jungle
Nekfu
Soyenia
The Demu Desert
Tashar

PROLOGUE

Freville

THE CLOTH BAG thrown over Freville's head threatened to suffocate him. He spied through the small holes at his surroundings, sniffing the woodsy air. His legs were cramping, and the rifle pushing at his back wasn't doing him any favors, nor were his bound hands.

Only hours ago, he thought he'd make it safely to Luana Bay. He'd been close, but his gnawing hunger had gotten the better of him. He'd managed to catch a silverling. It'd been his first kill without the assistance of one of his servants. Usually, he only hunted for sport, but he hadn't eaten in two days. Only small villages with whispering gossips littered the woods between Luana Bay and Duncaster, and he couldn't afford to be spotted within one of the local taverns or inns. As a lord, he would've been recognized immediately.

He'd been only a day's ride from Luana Bay, where he planned to seek refuge and warn the Duke of Luana, but they'd caught up to him. Days of riding through the woods had left Freville exhausted and careless. His fire had likely given away his position.

Freville took another step, the impact contorting his ankle. Pain shot up his leg, and he tumbled to the ground in a pitiful display of nobility. His frock coat was somewhere among the leaves and dirt back in Duncaster, and his waistcoat made of the finest silk from Soyenia was in ripped shambles. *What a miserable way to die.*

"Get up!" his captor barked.

The barrel of the man's rifle dug into the back of Freville's skull. A hoarse cough escaped him, built through the decades of smoking badaka and uppaway. He forced himself to stand.

After another hour, his captor grabbed him by the scruff of the neck and threw him into the dirt. His old knees protested, but he waited. The bag was ripped from his head and the waning hours of the sun cascaded an aura around the man standing with his rifle aimed at Freville's chest. He was a tall and lanky man with cinnamon-colored hair. Freville recognized him as one of Drauna's men who accompanied her in their last meeting. If only he could remember the man's name.

"Let's get this over with," he grumbled, lifting his rifle and closing a silver eye.

"Wait!" Freville begged, raising his hands and further chafing his wrists against the rope.

A rustle sent the hairs on the back of his neck to stand on end.

"Why should I bother giving you any more breath?"

It was her.

Drauna stepped from the dense foliage and planted a long, pointed nail on the end of the barrel. Her brunette locks were thrown in a wind-gusted braid, and her golden eyes bore holes into Freville's soul. He squirmed at her close proximity, but he felt a moment of reprieve when she forced her companion to lower his weapon.

"Please," he pleaded.

Drauna picked a bit of lint from her shoulder and flicked it into the leaf covered terrain, as if she were bored. "You crossed me."

"I'd never—"

"Then why were you running like a frightened lemchy with your tail between your legs?"

"I..." Freville stammered. "I'm headed to Luana Bay now."

Drauna kneeled before him, her red jacket spilling around her like a ceremonial gown. Streaks of black were embroidered in interconnected lines, rendering a lightning storm. She grabbed his chin with her nails, caressing his graying beard.

"He's lying," the man with the rifle spat.

Drauna smirked. "You don't think I know that?"

The temperature dropped, and Freville's ears popped. He gazed around the small clearing as the sky darkened and thunderclouds rolled in at an impossible speed. He gaped at the woman before him, but any words died in his throat.

"Here's what's going to happen," Drauna began. "Diggory is going to put a round ball in your heart, and maybe I'll let your family live. They can spend their days without your nuisance on your estate, drinking kusu in excess and relishing in your absence. How does that sound?"

The blood drained from his face. "Drauna, I promise you—"

"You're through making promises you can't keep. I've waited too long for a measly squirm like you to come along and ruin what I've spent years building." She tapped her nails down his neck as an echo to the beat of his hammering pulse.

Diggory grunted in approval and once again raised his rifle.

"What you ask is treason!"

"It's only treason if you're on the wrong side." She drew her nails over his skin, pressing until a trickle of blood seeped from the cut.

Freville squirmed. "Fastrada Manor is heavily guarded!"

Drauna rolled her eyes. "You lack perspective."

"Why her?"

Drauna quirked a brow before leaning in. "That's no longer your concern," she whispered in his ear. It was like a siren's song—beautiful, but deadly. "This is only the beginning. Something stirs within the realm of Magoria, but you won't be around to see it." She clamped down on his neck, sinking her claws into his arteries.

Freville choked and blood poured in a stream from his neck. With a single swipe, her nails cut through his windpipe and blood bubbled with a single gasp. He clawed at his throat, gurgling, but nothing could stop the drowning as he fell back and took in his last sight of Drauna licking the red from her claws.

CHAPTER 1

Amaris

AMARIS CARTER WAS no stranger to the silent whisper of death. It could clasp around her throat and choke her of her last breath, but she'd still welcome it. The raging fire surrounding her and Charlie was a testament to that. Charlie drenched the staircase in a shower of mist and rain, but the fire grew, feeding every last ember.

Amaris gripped the fire hose behind Charlie, feeding him more as he pushed up the stairs. She sucked in a breath, eating the beads of sweat pooling in the bottom of her mask. Each salty breath was a reminder. Her hands tightened, clinging to the last bit of hope as a wave of memories flooded her mind.

No longer were her gloved hands clasped around a fire hose, but a single piece of driftwood. The waves rolled over her face, threatening to suffocate her and drag her into their depths, along with the ship it'd claimed all those years ago.

"Amaris!" Charlie's scream pulled her from her memory.

Her eyes shot open, stinging in a murky haze from the sweat dripping from her brows.

"I've got a room here for you to search!"

Amaris blinked to clear the sweat. The fire hose sat between her gloved hands. She tracked the red hose, one of the few things visible in the heavy smoke surrounding them.

The fluorescent stripes on Charlie's gear and his panting breaths came from the top of the staircase. His helmet shifted, and a stream of light illuminated the cloud of gases, piercing Amaris's sensitive blue eyes. She faltered in his beam like a damn deer in headlights.

She took in a warm, stale breath and shut her mind to the morbid memory threatening to pull her from the fire. Bile filled her throat, but she swallowed it.

I need to keep my head in here. She couldn't allow herself to surrender to her grief. Since she'd been promoted to lieutenant, Charlie was more than her friend now—he was her responsibility.

It was dangerous to let the anxieties stirring in her stomach cloud her mind. A neighbor had seen the couple come home from a walk this morning. Amaris and Charlie had searched the entire downstairs with nothing to show for it but aching knees and waterlogged socks. As the officer in charge, she'd chosen to send them inside. She had to follow it through.

What if we're too late? She shook away the horrendous thought and climbed the stairs, pushing past Charlie. She eyed the shut bedroom door. Hopefully, it'd kept the smoke and fire from the room.

She entered, darkness overtaking her, and sprawled out onto her stomach, feeling for a wall nearby. Her only ally was the muscle memory and second sense she'd developed through grueling hours of training with her mask covered. She reached out, moving over the carpet until she smacked into a dresser. Groaning, she righted her face piece and checked she didn't have a mask leak. Her senses pulled her further—a lamp, a chair, but no human life.

She found the corner, marking her surroundings in her head, creating a map to lead her. Her hand slid along the wall until she met a large object, a bed. Lunging forward, she felt around and gripped a hand. Her heart lurched into her throat.

"I've got a victim!" She croaked, the acceleration of her heart seeping into her voice. *Calm down. You can do this.* A quick cough rid her mind of further anxieties, and she reached farther onto the bed. She met a tangle of limbs and grabbed under a pair of bony shoulders. They were light— *probably the wife.*

A rumbling of her face mask regulator startled her as she dragged the wife to the floor. How could she be at the end of her air bottle already? Her attention snapped across the room to Charlie. His hummed the same alert.

She took in a short breath, switching her breathing pattern to make her air last. She only needed a few more minutes.

Lunging for the bed again, she grabbed the husband. Her feet pushed off the bed frame to leverage his large body onto the floor.

An air horn blared from outside, pricking the hairs on the back of her neck. *No.*

A second blast followed and then a third, signaling them to exit the structure immediately.

She grabbed her webbing from her pocket, wrapping one around the husband and the other around the wife to get a better hold to drag them out. Her mind homed in. *I can make it.*

"Get out of here, Charlie!" she shouted. "I'll meet you outside!"

"No way!" Charlie hollered back, but his heavy breathing increased. He was probably exhausted after lugging the hose all over the house. "You can't drag them out by yourself!"

"I've got this!" she yelled back. "Get out! The roof might be collapsing!"

Why else would they sound the evacuation signal?

When they'd rolled up, the fire had been pushing out half of the windows on the second floor, and smoke had been puffing out from the eaves of the roof. A voice in her head had told her to make a defensive attack, that she shouldn't go inside, but she'd silenced it.

"I'm not leaving you!"

Amaris rolled her eyes. *Why does he have to be so fucking stubborn?*

With each step, her heavy SCBA on her back was a growing reminder of their limited time. She forced herself into a crawl, dragging the couple farther. A cough erupted from her lungs, but she resisted any urge to stop. She'd never pulled someone from a fire before. Training with a mannequin on the slippery floor of the truck bay was one thing, but two bodies was excruciating. It might have been only inch by inch, but she was getting them out of there. Charlie wasn't going to leave, but neither was she.

Steam burned against her skin, slick with sweat as Charlie whipped the stream of water in circles to douse the room. Her mask rattled off and on. She was nearing the end of her borrowed time, but she wasn't even halfway across the room. Charlie banged his hand against the floor, alerting her to his direction. The webbing pressed against her gloved hands, squeezing her fingers till they grew numb.

A gasp escaped her lips, but she kept pulling, dragging, barreling through the room. Whether it was her own darkening vision or the smoke pressing in on them, she was blind. She relied on her ears—the power of the hose as it blasted the ceiling and the final warning of her mask regulator.

She couldn't drag the couple down the stairs in time. She scanned the dark room, searching for any visible light. There had to be a window. They'd close the door to keep what smoke and fire they could out and flag down a crew outside to throw a ladder.

"Charlie, close the door! We'll get them out through a window!"

"I can't. We've got fire poking through the ceiling!"

Hope for their rescue plan evaporated as flames ate away the drywall over their heads and a deafening crack filled the room with hot smoke. It covered Amaris's mask and burned the tips of her ears. *Shit, shit, shit!*

"Amaris, what do we do?" Charlie shouted.

The couple hung limp, wrapped in the webbing, pulling the blood from her fingers.

"There's too much fire above us!" Charlie screamed, but his shouts were muffled by a high-pitched tinnitus piercing Amaris's eardrums.

I can't get them out. Each moment she'd spent training had been for nothing. She didn't have the strength to pull them out and couldn't even shout to Charlie to drop the hose and save himself.

Despite her hopelessness, her feet continued to try. They planted beneath her and made one more surge toward the door, but all Amaris could focus on were the grunts from Charlie as the hose sprayed sporadically around them.

This isn't how it's supposed to go. Amaris's mind reeled. *Hunt down the fire and put it out. Locate a victim, drag them out. We don't die.*

A hand gripped Amaris's shoulder, startling her from the endless ranting in her head.

"Get the hell out! I've got them," a familiar woman shouted.

Amaris needed to move, but her body froze. *How is Viv here?* The air horn went off. Viv should've been outside, but her strong arms wrapped around Amaris, pulling the webbing from her hands and gripping her SCBA. Viv shoved Amaris into the hallway.

"Get out before I kick you out," Viv yelled.

"Charlie?" Amaris called, attempting to get her feet beneath her.

"He's already headed downstairs," Viv said, handing one of the strings of webbing to her partner. "Follow him."

Amaris's dwindling air and her speeding heart ignited panic. *This should be me stuck here to drag them out, not her.* But as her mask sucked to her face, she found herself heeding Viv's orders.

She took one of the last few breaths from the air bottle growing heavier with each passing heartbeat. The rambling in her mind stilled. The fire ripping above her head was only a subtle warmth. Viv's grunts were only distant echoes. Amaris had trained for how long she could make her tank last, how many breaths she could suck down before she was out of air.

She took *one, two,* and another, *three.* Her feet buckled beneath her, *four*. Pressure built in her head, *five*. Her foot caught a hole gaping in the stairs, flipping her forward, *six*. She struggled to peer over her shoulder at her boot caught under the rise of the step, *seven*. She tugged, but her boot wouldn't give, *eight*. The light from the front door stretched to the bottom of the steps.

I can do this. It was right there, *nine*. She tried another breath but was out of air.

Another set of three air horn blasts sounded, sending her heart rate thundering in her ears. She pulled her foot from the boot, her sock the only thing protecting her skin from the heat. She leapt off the steps, slamming onto the front porch. The brim of her helmet smacked the concrete, and her chest burned for air. She ripped the regulator from her mask and sucked in a ragged breath.

Before she could take another one, someone latched onto her and dragged her down the steps. Shaky hands unfastened her helmet and chucked it across the grass. They ripped her mask from her face, pulling her braided hair tangled in the straps. She winced as strands of her hair tore from her skull.

She heaved the smoke from her lungs and wiped her mouth. Soot stained the back of her hand. She turned, and Charlie blocked any remnants of the afternoon sun. His big umber eyes were wide with terror as he gaped at her.

"That was close," she coughed.

§

AFTER CHARLIE STRIPPED Amaris of her SCBA and turnout coat, she fought him to the rehab area. He held tight to the collar of her drenched shirt, dragging her from the fire scene.

"I can walk on my own," she grumbled, but he was silent.

Amaris could've smiled at how well Charlie recognized her desire to jump back in, but not after that disaster. He refused to release her from his iron grip until he shoved her into a camping chair. He wasn't the biggest on the department, but he had an innate strength. It was the first reason her chief had thrown around the table when deciding whether to hire him two years back.

Her eyes were pinned to the front porch, her nails biting into the armrest. All her muscles tensed as she waited for her best friend to exit the house.

"Come on, Viv," she mumbled.

A plume of smoke billowed as the front door flew open. Viv and her partner tore through the opening with the victims wrapped in webbing. The newly arrived crews flocked to them, getting the victims onto stretchers.

Amaris sank into her chair, relief overcoming her as her limbs grew heavy. A water bottle landed in her lap, and Charlie stepped back and sprawled into the grass, drenching his beet-red and sweaty face with an entire water bottle. Amaris burrowed deeper into her chair and drank half the bottle in a single chug.

What just happened? she thought before taking a breath that was immediately sucked back out as Chief stomped toward her. His helmet skimmed above his scrunched eyebrows and his hazel eyes narrowed in on her.

"What the hell was that, *Lieutenant*?" His words were sharp, and he shook his head as he stalked closer.

"Chief, I—"

"You stayed in well past your low air alarms, you didn't exit after we sounded the evacuation signal, and you shouldn't have been in there in the first place!"

Amaris's stomach dropped as Chief's eyes trailed to Charlie's exhausted form taking root in the grass. "I know, but—"

"Nothing is more important than your safety! When you get back to the station, I want your ass in my office. Do you understand?"

She bit her tongue and her shame. "Yes, Chief," she replied, trying not to let her frustration seep through.

He returned to the fire and marched toward Lartondale's chief, likely to scream at him for sending Viv and her partner in. The house creaked, and the roof collapsed in on itself. Amaris leaned forward, pinching the bridge of her nose—*fuck*.

As she tore her hand away, Viv strode toward her. Wrapping her arms around Viv was all she wanted to do, but her body refused any notion of getting out of the chair.

Viv stripped herself of her gear, casting them aside in the yard as her ruby braid swished back and forth behind her. With Amaris's boot clutched tightly in her pale fingers, she narrowed her teal eyes.

"Do you have a death wish?" Viv asked, dropping her boot. The smell of burnt rubber overpowered Viv's rose-scented perfume.

"People were trapped," Amaris said, hauling the clunky boot over her foot.

Viv was a fierce woman standing at six-foot with an immense amount of muscle and strength. Folding her freckled arms, she gave Amaris a flat look before plopping in a chair beside her. Viv tapped her black nails along the armrest, eyeing the house as flames engulfed the upper story and the new crews manned the hose lines.

She returned her attention back to Amaris, her long braid falling over her shoulder. "Are you all right?"

"Yes," Amaris assured her, but she shifted her gaze to Chief, standing with a scowl lining his lips. Viv raised her brows. "Fine, I'm not. Why were you in there? The air horn—"

"You had a victim," she said. "You weren't going to evacuate."

"You can't risk your life like that."

"You can, but I can't?"

Amaris dropped her head in her hands. "That's not what I meant. You went in knowing full well the roof would collapse."

"I had my guardian angel at my back." Viv smirked.

Amaris ground her teeth. Viv may have believed in the protection of the supernatural universe, but Amaris never felt the presence of a positive energy or even a god when she was throwing her life on the line every day. "We were already upstairs."

"And you would be dead and out of air if I hadn't come to help you."

Amaris held back her frustration, sitting on her hands to cease their trembling as the adrenaline faded from her system.

"Fuck, Mar." Viv sighed, gripping the outer edges of her arms. "I'm sorry."

"I could've killed you all because I decided to go in," Amaris huffed, forcing back the sting in her eyes. "This was my first fire as a lieutenant, and I blew it."

Viv gripped her shoulder, pulling her in for a hug. "You should've taken off today."

Relief settled over Amaris with Viv's arms wrapped around her. She squelched the beginnings of a sob. She always took a vacation day on the anniversary of the shipwreck, but at twenty-five, shouldn't she have been able to stave off the heartache of her parents' deaths by now?

It's been seventeen years, she reminded herself, but no matter how much she wanted to forget that horrible day, she couldn't.

"I thought I could push through," she lied, thumbing the ruby in her silver engagement ring.

The thought of spending an entire day at home, mulling over her and her fiancé's fight threatened to boil her stomach. She asked for one thing from Derek, but apparently setting a wedding date was too much for him. She cringed as their argument from last night repeated in her head, spinning to the endless track of the longest engagement ever.

Viv eyed the paramedic walking toward them with the vitals monitor and lowered her voice. "We'll talk more later if you want. We all made it out. Don't forget that." With a flick of her braid, she was gone, directing the eager young man with the clunky monitor toward another pack of exhausted firefighters.

Amaris would forever be grateful for Viv, even if they bickered like siblings. She'd first met Viv at the fire academy. Viv had been loud and boisterous, everything Amaris wasn't at the time. She'd fit in regardless of what the other cadets had whispered about the two of them. *Hormonal misfits* had been a favorite insult murmured under their classmates' breaths. Being the only two women in their class, they'd automatically been roommates. Sharing their first box of tampons five years ago in that cramped dorm room had solidified their friendship.

Amaris sighed and picked her chair up, dropping it inches from Charlie's head. A few of his dark-brown strands clung to his forehead and others stuck out at odd angles. Sweat soaked the fibers of his navy shirt, leaving two thick lines where his bunker pants suspenders had been.

"How are you?" she asked.

"Exhausted." A short reply for a drained soul.

"I hope you're ready for round two. I sense a second fire in my bones tonight."

She bit her lip, balling her fists in anxious anticipation. They used to play a game of guessing what their next call would be. She hoped her attempt at humor could rally his spirits. At least one of them needed to not feel like shit about themselves.

"Yeah, whatever you say." He raised a trembling fist, his muscles fatigued.

A twinge twisted in her gut. A few months ago, he would've guessed an iguana stuck in a tree or some other ridiculous call. Now, with her promotion to lieutenant, he'd backed off on the jokes.

"I don't expect you to want two fires in one shift." Amaris guessed, if he was playing the role of firefighter, she should offer some kind of positive feedback as his superior officer. "I do appreciate the enthusiasm."

He rolled his head lazily to the side, raising a dark brow. "I knew what I was getting into when I applied for the job."

She picked at the chipped pink nail polish on the edge of her thumbnail. "What about a lieutenant who could've gotten you killed today?"

The guilt dropped on her shoulders like a load of bricks. It was one thing to risk her own life, but Charlie had stayed in with her.

He let out a sigh and sat, grasping his knees. "I've worked with you for two years, Amaris. I know you," he said. "You don't sit back and play it safe. That's the kind of leader I want to be someday."

That should've been a comfort, but it dropped another load of weights, sending her further recoiling into the chair. She was his lieutenant now, and it was her job to keep him safe.

"Don't ask me to leave you behind," he added. "I won't do it."

She remembered the mumbled gossip around the firehouse, constantly whispering about whether she was ready for the role or had what it took. *Maybe I don't,* she thought, but she forced a grin. She couldn't agree to any of it. Not to Charlie or Viv. They were her friends—she couldn't risk their lives.

CHAPTER 2

Theo

THEO FASTRADA SCANNED the docks of Duncaster, casting glances at the various ships with darting eyes as his hand wrapped tightly around his dagger still sheathed at his side. The hairs on the back of his neck pricked with each merchant, crewmen, or fishermen who passed along the docks, wafting the pungent odor of sailors who'd been at sea for far too long.

A bark grabbed his attention. A captain of a small schooner shouted his commands to his sailors as they ran through the docks with grins on their ruddy faces. They might have been late for their departure time, but they didn't seem to care with the waistbands of their trousers still loose and their shirts untucked.

Theo snorted and shifted his gaze to the galleon beginning its offloading. He watched carefully for the markings on the casks to identify their supplier. A barb-tailed ancient rugamon with its leather wings came into view. The markings of the famous kusu merchant from the nation of Jintaishu were a pleasant sight among the various ships coming to port from the Black Sea. Not only for their allegiance with the kingdom of Godwin but also the divine fermented beverage Theo would've given anything for a glass of at the moment.

He ran a hand through the black strands of his hair and turned to head toward the Trade House, running into a tall frame with a sinful smirk and wine-red hair. Theo's cousin eyed a Jin sailor winding her sleek-dark strands into a bun and slipping on her boots to begin her trek down the docks. A few snaps in Esaias's face turned his attention once again to Theo.

"Find anything menacing or out of the ordinary?" Esaias asked, his gaze once more lingering on the ivory-skinned woman helping her fellow sailors remove the casks. "Or even desirable?"

Theo slapped him on the back of the head as they made their way through the busy docks of Duncaster to the Trade House, where the rest of his squad resided. "Start thinking with this head instead of your other one."

"I merely meant precious and desirable cargo." Esaias flared his green eyes, a hallmark of the Burchard family, and dodged as Theo went to give him another smack.

"No, nothing out of the ordinary. A few grizzled-looking fishermen and eager merchants, but no one with sticky fingers or looking to pick a fight."

Theo hadn't expected to find proof of thievery on the docks or to spot suspicious activity, but he'd hoped for something other than normal operations. They'd been sent by his father to investigate the uptick in thievery and several fights bordering on riots breaking out within the streets.

As Duncaster was one of the largest cities in his father's province of Luana, it was vital they investigated the governor's extensive missives on the issues plaguing the city. He wrote of fights and protests over the tariff the King of Godwin imposed last year to help pay for the costs of the war. Theo had personally experienced the devastating effects of the short funds when he stood on the front lines for seasons, eating rations and scraps, but he hadn't anticipated having to deal with the aftermath upon returning home.

He'd been home for as little as three weeks before his father sent him on the journey to Duncaster, along with Chief Bennet, the leader of

Luana's forces. He hadn't worked under Bennet since Theo had left to fight in the Trade War three years ago, but their recent nights of meetings with his father and the five days journeying through the intense heat of Sunreign reminded Theo immediately that he was back under Bennet's command, not his own.

The bustling noise of the streets and shouting of merchants grew closer as they reached the end of the docks where the Trade House, run by a wealthy family in Duncaster, stood and housed several marketable goods within its warehouse. The Veduco family were the most influential investors in Duncaster's economy, and therefore Luana's, organizing shipments from the various islands, kingdoms, and nations located in the Black Sea and finding buyers throughout Godwin.

"Maybe the governor exaggerated the issues and this is nothing more than a fool's errand," Esaias muttered as he rolled up the sleeves of his taupe military coat. He'd already undone the brass buttons, opening his uniform to reveal the standard white shirt underneath. Esaias was never one to care about starched creases or displaying a neat presentation. No, he preferred the rugged appearance of a soldier, enticing to any women catching his eye.

Theo found himself wanting to do the same as the rising temperatures beaded his back with sweat, but instead he only tugged at his collar. "We can only hope." Theo couldn't afford to hope. He'd spent too many hours planning assaults, secret missions, and battle strategies to let himself hold on to the belief that all was well in the city.

He sensed the energy change. It was a lurking shadow he couldn't put his finger on. When he'd last visited Duncaster at twenty years of age, it'd been a boisterous and profitable trade city. Now, five years later, he recognized the shift in the atmosphere, the hesitant glances, and the watchful eyes, but saw nothing to warrant such behavior.

"Took you two long enough." Gris stood with her legs squared, arms crossed and a scowl lining her small lips. Her quiver of arrows peeked over her head, and her bow hung from her shoulder.

"We walked the entire length of the docks without a scuffle, while you stood in the shade all morning." Esaias wiped a bead of sweat from his brow and flung it at her.

"Remind me why your species exists?" Gris swatted him and wrinkled her thin eyebrows at Esaias, drawing her hazel eyes to narrow slits.

Not a single line of sweat dripped from her brow. It baffled Theo how she was able to wear the stuffy layers of their military uniform without ever showing any effects from the scorching sun.

"My species?" Esaias cut her a glare before turning to gain support from Alan standing beside Gris.

Alan raised a hand with a small wooden carving grasped within it to guard his light-blue eyes from the sun as he sent a smirk toward Esaias. His other hand flipped one of his long daggers he'd been using to whittle and returned it to the sheath at his thigh.

"Men," Gris lectured, throwing back her blonde hair with the sides braided back into a long ponytail. "While you spent your morning strolling by the water, we observed the trade dealings and spoke with the merchants. All we've got are people who apparently don't wish to keep their jobs. The man at the counter said he's lost three runners in the last two weeks. Said the boys didn't report back. Probably because he couldn't afford to pay them a living wage."

"That appears to be a theme around here," Alan jumped in. "A shopkeeper I spoke with said his best employee left without a word. She closed the shop one night and didn't return the next."

"And people are not happy with this tariff," Gris added.

As if her words commanded the realm of Magoria, a shouting match began at the nearby counter. Theo straightened his back and made his way through the crowd gathering with their papers and manifests in hand. A permeating smell of ocean water and fish was the odor Theo focused on instead of the unwashed bodies as he passed through the crowd.

"Outrage! Last year two percent, now five?"

Theo took in the burly man with dark skin and raven hair pulled into a leather tie. His common tongue of Akaric was broken, but Theo couldn't exactly place his accent over the shouting between him and the merchant at the counter.

"It's by order of King Edward. If you don't pay the five-percent tariff, then you'll have to find some other kingdom to do business with." The merchant at the counter ran a hand through his sweat-slicked and graying strands and flared his yellowing eyes at the sailor. "No pay fee, no sell goods!"

That was harsh. Theo stood beside the sailor and passed a glance to the old merchant behind the counter, who wasn't at all thrilled to be approached by another man double his size. "Can I be of service?"

Both faced Theo, and an unsettling feeling sharpened in his gut, one he'd get when he was close to drawing his sword. His hand twitched where it hung from his belt, but he forced his fingers around the hilt of his dagger instead. He dragged his thumb along the crest embedded in the metal: a crescent bay surrounding a fish with a sword piercing its heart. It'd become a nervous habit of his in the last few years, grasping to a single part of him that felt like home.

The merchant's eyes slid to Theo's shoulder where a patch of the same crest was sewn to mark his allegiance to Luana and then the gold bars on the front of his uniform noting his rank. "Lord Theodoric Fastrada!"

"It's Captain Theodoric Fastrada." Theo sighed and refrained from rolling his eyes, not one for titles unless it came from his military rank. His father may have been the Duke of Luana, but he didn't care for the courtesy title as a child of the duke. He was the second born anyways. While he would one day bear the rank of chief and oversee Luana's forces, his older brother, Luther, would bear the title of Duke of Luana.

"Captain?" The sailor's jaw feathered, and his hand slid to his side. He turned to the merchant. "Soldiers?"

"Yes, we are governed by the laws of the duke. If he should see fit to place soldiers along these docks, then he has every right."

A second sailor, with skin a shade darker and a height of at least three more inches, approached the first sailor and whispered in his ear.

"No business with soldiers." The first sailor turned his head and spat on Theo's boot. "*Fastida!*"

Bastard? Theo's hand slid from his dagger to his sword. Tendasy was a common language in the Black Sea but most prominently found in the enemy nations under the Deavonian Accords. If they were a part of the alliance sailing under Deavopan's banner, then they weren't welcome in Godwin.

"*Fangrallu gal tris fastida ied nil trid Tendasy?*" Theo said, relaying to the man how a bastard could ever come to speak Tendasy.

Both the sailors' faces leached of color. Tendasy wasn't a language taught in traditional Godwin schools, but by private tutors, ones who'd taught Theo since he'd been a boy at the behest of his father.

The first sailor reached for a dagger hidden in his waistband. Theo reacted on instinct, disarming him before he had a chance to brandish it. The distinct click of a pistol had Theo's eyes trained on the second sailor. He stood behind his friend and pointed the barrel straight at Theo's head.

Gods, he hated guns. They weren't standard issue for Godwin soldiers. Not that the kingdom could afford them.

"What in the realm is—" Esaias became speechless as he took in the scene.

"A little assistance." Theo raised his hands, backing away and dropping the dagger he'd taken at the sailor's feet. "I think they're of the Deavonian Accords."

Esaias palmed his sword, causing gasps as the crowd around them began pushing and shoving to pull back from the line of fire. Weapons were drawn, and pistols were loaded. The two sailors weren't the only ones of their crew in front of the Trade House.

It was in a single breath. A shot fired and the riot broke out. Blades crashed, and Theo had a second to drop before he got his head shot off by a pistol. He was on his feet and slammed into the first sailor, wrapping his arms around his middle as he brought him to the ground. It was a part of him, his instinct to attack. Theo had the man in a headlock and unconscious before he knew what his body was doing.

His sword was in his hand as the inner soldier took over his mind, meeting blades and disarming sailors. Theo ignored a cry ringing out and the sound of splintering wood and crashing carts. He didn't allow the burning of his nostrils from the gunpowder to cloud his head. He caught Esaias in his periphery guarding his other side and Gris firing from a safe distance above. Her arrows found homes in the thighs of her opponents.

Not to kill, Theo reminded himself. He switched his tactics, disarming the sailors who came at him and driving his elbow into the nose of a man ready to drive his dagger into Theo's gut.

"That's enough!" A sharp shout rang through the streets, and he knew Bennet had arrived with more soldiers.

The tall and burly sailor he'd knocked unconscious roused and sneaked off toward the docks. If enemy forces of the Accords had begun infiltrating the streets of Duncaster, then the problem had escalated to a deadly level. Theo ran after the sailor, dodging a sword made to take off his head. He rolled from the attack, turning only a brief second to find an arrow sticking out of the man's leg.

More soldiers flooded the streets—the ones he and Bennet had brought to station along the docks and the ones already under the governor's command. But the sailor was getting away. Theo raced after him, splitting from the fight. With his sword drawn and his chest heaving, he scanned the cobbled street. The sailor ran toward a brigantine already working their ropes and ready to set sail.

Theo sprinted for the ship. He needed to know if it was an isolated incident. What if it wasn't and the Accords were making moves against Godwin? Theo pushed away the internal strife and urged himself on.

His legs burned as they pounded against the planks. The crowds parted for him, gawking and gasping as he ran by. A fisherman fell into the water as he stumbled back.

He was gaining on the sailor, but the ship loomed closer. His comrades shouted to him, lowering a rope ladder. Theo picked up his pace, panting as he ran. Not another war. It ended now.

Someone stepped from the crowd, ramming into Theo and sending him tumbling to the deck. He rolled and struck a post. His vision blurred on the edges. He noticed a pair of boots with golden serpents before they scrambled away and disappeared into the swarm of bodies.

"Theo!" Gris's shout parted the crowd, and she kneeled at his side.

His head pounded, and his vision was still splotchy as Gris helped him to a seated position. She offered her water canteen, and he drank as the tunneling dispersed and Gris's concerned face came into sharp focus.

"He got away." Theo took another long swig.

"Yes, but Bennet and the others have already arrested the few stragglers. I can't believe all that was over a stupid tariff."

"They spoke Tendasy," Theo blurted.

Gris balked, grabbing her canteen. "You don't think—"

"We need to speak with the governor." He stood with a grimace, using the post that had attempted to knock him out to steady himself.

Theo slid his hand to his belt, fumbling for his dagger as his heart pounded. He wasn't ready for another war, especially not with the forces under the Accords' alliance. Pinching his eyes tight, he forced back the images threatening to leak through. He'd let the soldier within slip out. Theo threw a hand over the stitch in his mind. He wouldn't give in to it.

His trembling hand released his dagger and reached for his pouch, but he found only his belt. His eyes dropped to the empty space where his pouch once hung. He had to remind himself to breathe as he scanned the docks at his feet.

"What are you looking for?" Gris followed him as he retraced his steps and scoured the wooden planks for it.

"My pouch." A crack slipped into his voice, and he whirled on Gris as he tore his hands through his hair. "It's gone."

Her eyes were wide, and her gaze strayed to the locals staring at him like he was a raging lunatic. He couldn't lose control. His hand slid around the back of his sweaty and sun-scorched neck, and he blew out a breath. Overreacting was not an option. He was second-in-command and couldn't lose himself over a small memento.

He turned back to head toward the Trade House, but Gris caught him by the arm. Her eyes pleaded to let her in, but he couldn't. He waited for his heart to drop or a tear to fall, but there was nothing. It wasn't the silver or gold pieces within he cared for.

§

CHIEF BENNET RAPPED on the door of the governor's study, eliciting a muffled shriek from the other side. He squinted his caramel-colored eyes, enlarging his forehead already growing more prominent thanks to the receding hairline.

Theo stretched his spine, hoping to calm the screaming muscles of his back after his scrap from earlier. Once they'd procured a meeting with the governor, Bennet had assigned the soldiers to their posts on the docks, in the street market, and outside the Trade House.

The stifling heat of the cramped hallway dripped sweat under his shirt and rimmed it around his lips. He loved coming home to the warm weather, embracing it after spending years fighting in the north in the kingdom of Mosfelkov, where a warm breeze was a miracle, but this heat wave was excessive. He peeled away the drenched fabric of his uniform, attempting to air himself out as he waited for the governor to open the door.

"Will you quit wafting your stench in my direction?" Gris muttered to Theo, her feminine voice drawing a melodic tune.

"Would you prefer I fling my sweat instead?" Theo shot at her.

She shook her head, rolling her large hazel eyes as she suppressed a giggle. A short glance at the daggers and her bow surveyed the fierce warrior she was. But she had a gentle nature to her, reminding them all that humanity was still possible after what she'd been forced to do during the war.

As his sergeant for most of their time across the Nebulous Sea, she'd been by his side, commanding parts of their squad and overseeing training. With his father's approval, Theo had offered her a formal position as a lieutenant, but she'd denied him. He presumed she preferred the camaraderie of a soldier versus the loneliness often accompanying a commanding officer.

She bore no official rank as an officer but was still Theo's second. He preferred keeping Gris by his side, giving him another set of eyes and ears. She'd developed a great strength at recognizing when a person was lying and had attempted to teach Theo during the war, catching fidgets or small tweaks of facial muscles.

Gris crossed her arms and leaned against the wall, causing the quiver of arrows strapped across her back to jostle a painting of an abstract rendition of a silverling. Its fluffy silver tail was greatly exaggerated, and its pointed face was drawn into a vicious grin.

A pounding jostled them as Bennet again made the governor aware of their presence. Gerard's chortle was a low rumble as he swept back his dark hair with a leather tie. He, unfortunately, was a lieutenant and Bennet's right-hand man, a large man with a gut hanging over his waistline forming the bulk of his stature.

"This should be fun," Gerard whispered, elbowing Theo, who ignored his comment, shifting from his reach. "You receive a promotion during the war and now you can't join in the fun?" Gerard shook his arms free of his jacket and aired his sweaty pits.

When Godwin officially announced they were entering the Trade War and offering soldiers to assist Soyenia against Mosfelkov, Theo's father was more than happy to send reinforcements. Theo, Esaias, Gris, and a few of their other friends had departed to fight, but Gerard was one of the duke's soldiers who'd stayed behind. All of Bennet's inner circle had.

Theo bit his tongue, forcing himself to hold back. Gerard may have been a pain in the ass, but he was a decent fighter and damn good with a bow. Not as skilled as Gris, of course. She was the most talented archer in Godwin.

An enraged Bennet stared down the governor through the open door. At first glance, Bennet was stoic, but Theo knew his demeanor. He'd trained him for his entire life, and Theo had learned when his anger grew and how to evade the backlash. At least that much hadn't changed in three years. Bennet gripped his wrist behind his back, scrunching the cuff of his uniform. His widened stance with his leather belt strapped tightly around his waist with a sword and dagger showed his authority, and it worked as the governor cowered in his study.

The smell of musty books hit Theo as he crossed the threshold onto the red and gold rug, sending a familiar longing through him. Bennet followed him, passing cherry thistlewood shelves filled with various volumes of war, politics, and a few leisure reads Theo recognized would fit perfectly on his shelf along with his other adventure novels.

The governor raced frantically around his large desk, righting frames and shuffling piles of parchment. Bennet marched to the center of the room and stopped at the desk of the frightened dignitary. The governor slowed his frantic movements, and the whites of his eyes grew as he shrank before him.

Theo followed in his wake, feeling the shadow he was once again forced to hide in. Bennet wasn't pleased with the fight on the docks, but Theo hadn't had an opportunity to elaborate much beyond requesting a meeting with the governor.

It was strange working under Bennet again. Theo had led his own squad during the war and rarely had any other higher-ranking officer with him on missions. Only when Theo had been promoted to captain and became second-in-command of Thereus Company under Major Faylare had he worked with a commanding officer on a more routine basis.

Gerard took a place to Bennet's right, and Gris perched on the edge of a red fainting couch, crossing a leg over the other. Her movements were fluid and graceful. It was hard to believe she'd spent most of the last ten years as a soldier among many men who didn't share a single shred of her civility. She placed the tip of her extravagant bow at her feet and began spinning it in slow circles.

"Chief," the governor stammered, "I hope this is important. I was forced to push my meeting with—"

"Governor Risley," Bennet interrupted, narrowing his gaze as he gripped the back of an upholstered chair. "The fight on the docks this morning was intolerable." He threw a flared glance at Theo, who tightened his jaw but didn't interrupt.

"What happened on the docks was the direct result of an instigation by one of your officers," Risley growled.

The governor was a short and slender man with blond hair fixed into a slicked-back ponytail. Even in the intense heat, he still wore a red frock coat over a golden waistcoat. Theo scoffed at his comment, resulting in another glower from Bennet. Risley was the type of man bred for politics, not battle, or at least to look the part. He'd only won the election because he'd run unopposed.

"Which will be dealt with." Bennet ground his teeth. "But were you made aware of who else instigated this fight?"

The governor pulled a red handkerchief from his pocket to dab the beads of sweat crowning his forehead. "Chief, if you plan to insult me, you can stop right there. My soldiers contained these fights before they could turn into full-fledged riots and before your soldiers arrived." Risley shot Theo with a harrowing frown. "I've allowed this meeting, not to squabble over merchants and tariffs, but because I have a more pressing matter. I have too many reports of missing persons to cast them aside."

The missing runners and the shopkeeper's employee. Theo replayed Alan and Gris's comments from earlier. He wouldn't tolerate it. No one else would be ripped from their home.

Gris coughed beside him, and he glanced at her lazily leaning against the armrest, picking at a loose thread. She raised her brows as their eyes met. Theo flicked his gaze back to Risley, steadying his thoughts before they could ramble further. Somehow, she could always tell when they raced.

Bennet's voice was gruff as he asked, "What do you believe to be the cause?"

"The first reports coming in were of beggars who vanished, teenagers no longer scouring the docks for small jobs, but now they've escalated to esteemed members of society. Lord Freville and one of the Veduco boys has gone missing."

Theo contained his rage over the governor's naivete to dismiss the fight and his insults against his people. "Only with the absence of high-class members of society will you look into these disappearances?" Theo chastised, drawing a sharp look from Bennet. It was a waste of resources and time. Lord Freville was a pompous twat, and both Veduco brothers were well known for disappearing with a bottle of liquor in one hand and a woman on the other. "The men who *started* the fight this morning spoke Tendasy. Are you aware you now have ships docking from enemy territories?"

"Impossible!" Risley shouted, rising to his full height, which only came to Theo's shoulder. "Our enemies in the Black Sea wouldn't dare invade Godwin's waters. The king's armada stationed at Charibert would see to their demise instantly!"

"They could easily slip through a port of this magnitude," Theo replied callously. "Falsifying their documentation would be easy. What if they've brought their slave trade to Godwin?"

Bennet's hand gripped into a balled fist at his side, his knuckles burning white for Theo's outburst and insubordination. They didn't have time for Bennet's arrogance or the governor's naivete. If people were being taken, they'd need to put a stop to it.

The governor pressed his hands into the desk, but the color began slowly draining from his face. "What do you know of the ongoings of the Black Sea, Captain?" The inflection of his voice mocked his title.

Theo gripped the hilt of his dagger, running the thumb along the edge.

"You've been off fighting in the Nebulous Sea for the last three years in a ridiculous war that has wreaked havoc on trade in my port."

"Your port?" Theo yelled, releasing his dagger and slamming his hands against the desk. "Our armies are weakened, and our enemies know this. The slavers know this!"

"I will not entertain the ridiculous notions of a child," Risley ridiculed.

"That's enough," Bennet snapped, raising his hand to silence any further discussion. "We would be foolish to discount all theories. A ship possibly manned with our enemies made it into your port. We have brought more soldiers and stationed them along the docks. We'll leave them in your charge."

"More soldiers won't stop the issues," Risley replied.

"Do you wish for the duke to close the port?"

"That would ruin Duncaster."

"Duncaster might already be in ruin," Bennet snapped. "Until the issue with these missing persons is solved, every vessel wishing to trade will be searched before they are allowed to dock and after to be sure they're only carrying their stated cargo."

"This is how you wish to handle the situation? They won't agree to it."

Bennet pressed his hands against Risley's desk, leaning over the man as he retreated into his chair. "If they will not agree to pay or have their ships searched, then they won't be trading in Duncaster. Those are the duke's orders."

Bennet abruptly took to the hall, Gerard right behind him. The governor sat with his shoulders hunched and his mouth agape.

"Theodoric!" Bennet shouted.

Theo closed the door. *Madness. We discover tenants are missing, and Bennet wishes to lecture me now?* He shook off the sweltering anger clinging to every fiber of his body. The inner soldier threatened to break loose as he charged down the steps of the governor's office, but Theo shoved it down, shutting himself off from that part of him.

Once down the rickety steps and into the town center, Theo turned to Bennet. He forced his heart to slow and his breaths to remain steady. Learning to mask what emotions or thoughts spun within his mind was a useful skill he regretfully attained during the war, growing cold and numb.

"Missing tenants—" Theo began.

"Don't test me," Bennet said through gritted teeth, ushering them off the cobbled streets and into an alley between the governor's office and a butcher's shop. The smell of rotting meat hit Theo's nose instantly as they entered the filthy alley lined with rubbish and piss.

Bennet pinned Theo's shoulders against the building behind him. Theo could've pushed him away, shoved him back against the opposite wall, but he stifled his anger.

"You are only a captain here," Bennet snapped. "You'll do well to remember that. You spoke out of line and made us look like fools in front of the governor. Your actions were disgraceful. Two sailors and one civilian dead and three soldiers injured!"

Theo swallowed as Bennet spewed the results of their small battle from the morning. *One dead civilian.* The crimson overlay crept into his mind, bathing his vision in blood as he stood before Bennet. He may not have been the first one to attack, but he'd instigated the fight.

Bennet released his shoulder and began ranting about insubordination, but Theo could only hear the ringing in his ears. No one else would die for his actions. His breaths came quick and painful, like each one would be his last. *I fight and I live.* He repeated the chant, rubbing his thumb against the crest in his dagger's hilt.

He didn't know when Bennet stepped away or when Gerard cleared the alley, but his mind focused on Gris, who stood before him. The red slid away, and Theo found himself panting and staring down either end of the alley, but Bennet and Gerard were gone.

"Where did they go?"

"Back to the inn." Gris's voice was hesitant, but he pushed past her to head toward the inn they'd procured rooms at for the night.

They crossed the cobbled street and passed zooming carriages. Theo couldn't look her in the eye after his moment of weakness. What had come over him? What had Bennet said to him? He opened the door to the inn and rushed to his room before anyone could snag him.

He sat on the edge of the bed, gripping his temples between his calloused fingers and praying to his gods to keep his heart steady and his mind clear.

CHAPTER 3

Amaris

WITH HER DUFFEL bag hanging from her shoulder and a coffee spilling in her hand, Amaris fumbled with her key in the worn lock. The rickety porch squeaked as her feet finally shuffled into the house.

She was immediately hit with the smell of cinnamon rolls and a fresh brew of coffee. After the fire yesterday, she was ready to shove a fat cinnamon roll in her face and guzzle some piping hot coffee. She'd gotten her ass ripped by her chief, and if that hadn't been enough, Charlie had caught her bawling her eyes out in the utility closet. Thankfully, he'd stepped out and hadn't asked why, but he'd wanted to. His pleading eyes had given him away when he'd handed her a bowl of ice cream while they'd watched the television after dinner.

Amaris dropped her bag and shoes in the hall and leaned into the wall, picking at a spot of chipped off-white paint. No amount of ice cream or cinnamon rolls could take away the writhing in her chest. She'd played the scenario in her head all night, and no matter how terrible she'd felt, she wouldn't have done it any differently. They'd gotten the couple out, but whether they survived was a different story. She'd ignored the outcome report. Enough morbid thoughts had already consumed her mind.

She peeled herself from the wall, taking more paint with her with the elevated humidity plastered across her sweaty body. She rubbed at her sleepless eyes and the dark bags as her feet carried her through the living room and over the stained shag carpet toward the bittersweet smell beckoning her. Her legs were leaden from the fire as she stumbled to the kitchen.

She stopped before the swinging door, allowing the mask to settle over her, to harden like armor. It'd become routine now, bracing herself for which Derek she was about to get. With the stress of planning the wedding and work, his moods were growing unpredictable. Swallowing the lump in her throat each morning was growing more difficult, but cinnamon rolls were usually a good sign. She pushed open the door and was hit with an even stronger aroma.

"I'm glad I get to see you before work." Derek poured a thermos of coffee. "I made your favorite."

A smile flourished his features, capturing the perfection of his ensemble with his slicked-back, chestnut-colored hair and his button-down and slacks. She missed the police uniform he used to sport and the tight fit around his ass, but she didn't care as a weight released from the massive boulder sitting on her shoulders. She couldn't help her cheeks growing rosy at his peace offering.

He gestured to the folding table with the mismatched chairs they'd acquired through various garage sales. The counter creaked under his weight as he leaned against it and screwed the lid on his thermos.

"How was work? I was out of the station for most of the day and didn't hear anything," he said, further bearing his weight against the peeling white countertop.

"Fine," she began. Her teeth nibbled at the edge of her lip as she debated whether it was a good idea to mention the fire or not. "Just a normal day."

Derek didn't bat an eye as he plated her breakfast. She hated lying to him, to anyone. She was pathetic at it.

He laughed, sucking a bit of the icing from his thumb. "I'll never understand how any of you are willing to enter a stranger's house without a gun." His lips curled into a smirk as he patted the police-issued weapon strapped to his side.

Gainesville was a small department, which meant minimal staffing and cross training. Amaris wasn't only a firefighter but also a paramedic. She might have had the occasional combative patient or two, but no one had ever pulled a gun on her.

"They're usually not calling us because they want to hurt us," she said, sliding into a chair. "They want our help."

"So you say." The corners of his lips turned up, and he placed a plate of cinnamon rolls and a fresh cup of coffee in front of her.

"Thank you," she said, a plea for a truce.

Derek planted a kiss on the top of her head, stopping a moment before slithering over her neck to plant several wet kisses. Her hand slid into his hair as her pulse thrummed. The woodsy musk of his cologne filled her senses, relinquishing the hold the cinnamon rolls had. His arms slid around her body, embracing her in his warmth. His fingers twirled with the end of her ponytail as his lips nibbled at the edge of her ear.

"You know I only want you safe," he whispered. "I don't know what I'd ever do without you."

It was nice to enjoy a moment without arguing. His nose tickled her ear as he snuggled into her neck. Amaris couldn't help releasing a sigh, blowing out her anxiety for how the morning could've gone.

"I'm sorry about the other night. You know the scotch throws words into my mouth." He breathed into her neck, prickling the goose hairs down her spine.

"Let's forget about it."

His hand slid to her chin, grasping it between his fingers as he turned her to face him. His gray eyes gleamed against the fluorescent light overhead, and his prominent jaw angled forward as he slipped his thin lips over hers.

"That's why I love you, my beautiful Amaris," he whispered against her lips.

"I love you too."

She slid her arms around his neck and pulled him in for one more kiss. She wished every morning was like this. He was too charming for his own good, but he was right. The drunken fit had passed. He hadn't meant to say any of it, and she'd said things she wasn't proud of either. She sensed him smile as he pulled back, pressing his shirt of wrinkles and tending to a few stray hairs. She missed the shaggy mop he'd sported in high school. It'd made him more rugged, not as clean and put together.

She debated bringing up what was really on her mind, since it'd caused a fight the other night, but with his sober state, there was a chance he'd agree.

"How about you take a break from your cases for the night and we wedding plan instead?"

He cringed, his grin vanishing. "Now is not a good time to be planning a wedding."

She set her fork down. "Derek, we've been engaged for two years. How long are we going to keep pushing it off?"

"You know how busy I've been since I got promoted," Derek said. "I have to prove myself and at least close one of these missing persons cases. How can I call myself a detective if I haven't even solved one?"

"What about me? I got promoted and have more work than ever, but you don't see me stalling this wedding. Am I supposed to sit here and wait around for you to finally have a break in a case to buy a wedding dress?" she said as he grasped his temples, massaging the vein on his forehead. "Do you even want to marry me anymore?"

His face snapped toward her.

I shouldn't have said that. She gripped the edge of the table, waiting for him to clap back with something venomous.

"Of course I want to marry you. I love you, for fuck's sake, but I can't handle planning a stupid wedding while also juggling these cases. Doesn't the woman usually take care of everything anyways?"

Her heart plummeted with resignation into the knot claiming permanent residence in her stomach. Apparently, it was her job to plan alone what was supposed to be the start to the rest of their lives together. Forget that she'd spent years working her ass off too. She was just a helpless woman who couldn't perform her job without her fiancé worrying she'd be killed.

She wanted to make him realize what he was doing to her. Why couldn't he see it hurt, and he was pulling a piece of her heart each time he pushed the wedding off? She understood why he wanted to bring these people home, or at least give the family some resemblance of peace, but she couldn't take it anymore. She was here now. Why couldn't he see that?

"Can we talk about this later?" he said, grabbing his thermos. "I'm going to be late."

"Fine," she breathed, grabbing the ceramic mug and taking a swig of coffee like she was downing a shot of whiskey.

He leaned and pressed a kiss to the top of her head before running through the house. His footsteps carried him over the creaky wooden floors, over the ugly carpet, and out the front door.

Her hands wrapped around the mug. Its heat penetrated through the walls of the cup. *Was it selfish to want his time and to pull him from his cases?* She shouldn't have to battle it, begging for his affection one minute and working an extra shift to avoid him the next.

She dropped her head against the table, groaning as her fork bounced next to her. Derek hadn't remembered what yesterday was. She'd hoped for a text last night or something this morning, but he'd forgotten.

§

AMARIS WALKED THE same path as always, hopping the back fence leading to the park behind her neighborhood. She slipped through two large bushes and emerged onto the dirt trail, brushing off the twigs and leaves sticking to her shirt and jean shorts.

Each morning after shift, she took a trek through the woods, where she was free to be herself. Where she didn't have to wear a lieutenant's cap or a mask to hide her frustration or grief. She was free.

The discovery of the never-ending road had been a mystical moment when she'd raced after a rabbit in the backyard she'd grown up in. Gran and Grandad's old house was only a block from hers and Derek's. She'd been young then but had felt an instant sense of relief from whatever seemed to trouble a ten-year-old at the time.

She could never describe how walking the path lined with elms and dandelions cast the worries from her head. The dirt of the path kicked up around her and continued to coat her already worn sneakers in another layer of dust. She didn't mind it, though. It brought a small smile to her face.

The mundane path of towering trees flowed and bent until it came to a fork, and what lay between the differing paths was the large and beautiful willow tree. Its branches cast themselves in a canopy over the grass beneath and the trail beyond. It was a warm hug to be taken in by the arms of the weeping willow and swaddled in its cocoon.

Amaris gripped the lowest branch, hoisting her feet to wrap around it to hang and take in her upside-down surroundings. A squirrel skittered across the path and zoomed up a tree in the distance. She squeezed her thighs around the branch, closing her eyes as she released her arms to be free to flow through the air. It was a thrilling sensation of soaring with the security of her tree holding her tight. Her arms dangled, skimming the grass beneath her as she let out a frustrated shout.

For two years, she'd been trying to marry the man she loved, but something always got in the way. She curled herself up and scaled the rest of the way to the heart of the trunk, where she used a small indentation to nestle in and hide. She leaned into it and plopped one foot over the other, folding her hands behind her head and inhaling the drooping leaves dangling above her nose.

"I had my first fire as a lieutenant yesterday." She sighed, her words hovering in the branches around her, safe from the world. Her eyes burned as tears misted around the edges. "It was terrible. I almost got myself and Charlie killed." The image of Grandad jumping onto the fire engine popped into her head. When she'd been younger and a call had come in, Grandad had taken her to the station with him, and he'd even let her sit in the seat beside him sometimes. Amaris dragged her hands over her eyes. "Maybe I'm not cut out to be a lieutenant."

She pulled her hands back, shifting her gaze. She traced the initials she'd carved over the years, *AC* and *RC* for her parents and *GC* and *WC* for Gran and Grandad. Her father had never made the rank of lieutenant, but he'd still been a dedicated fireman; at least that was what Grandad had always said. A tear slid down her cheek as her fingers hovered over *WC*.

"I only want to make you proud."

The breeze rippling through the willow was her only reminder to breathe. She begged the flush in her cheeks to fade. Her hand fell away, and she allowed the memories to pass through her mind.

She combed her hands through the damp, dark-brown waves of her hair and began braiding it past her shoulder as a pair of what could only be combat boots came bursting down the path.

"Mar, you up there?" Viv's roaring laughter echoed as she slid to a halt at the base of the willow.

A small smile grazed Amaris's lips at Viv's upbeat voice. Her laugh was like thunder, loud and prominent. She was the only person Amaris had shared her sacred spot with. As best friends, they'd perched together in the willow, holding the other when life became unbearably lonesome. When Viv's mother had gone to jail last year, they'd spent an entire night listening to the violins of the crickets and the buzzing of cicadas.

"Maybe," Amaris mumbled back, wiping away the tears.

Viv's sigh was followed by the shaking of the branches. She climbed up, finding a seat across from Amaris, hugging her long legs to her chest. She leaned in and sniffed. "Do I smell cinnamon rolls?" Amaris could've sworn Viv had the senses of a bloodhound. "What did he do this time?"

Viv sipped from her thermos that read, *I survived the fire academy, come at me b*tch.* Her teal eyes shot like daggers over the rim with her cutting stare. She wielded her eyes like a weapon. One minute they were pleading and full of hope, and the next they were ripping your innards out.

"Nothing," Amaris groaned, "it was a stupid fight, and he apologized this morning." She didn't want to think about what Derek yelled at her each time they fought. It threatened to rip a hole in her chest.

"One word, Mar, and I'll rip his fucking head off," Viv said, biting into the wind.

Amaris admired her overprotective nature, but what she didn't want to see was Viv go toe-to-toe with Derek. No one would win that fight.

Amaris rolled her eyes and pulled out her phone as it buzzed against her leg. Notifications flashed on the screen. Seven unread texts about the fire and three missed calls—all from Derek.

Viv narrowed her eyes, but Amaris pulled the phone back from her prying daggers.

"For as clingy and controlling as he is, I'm surprised he cares," Viv said.

Viv hadn't been a fan of Derek ever since she found out they met when Amaris had been a freshman in high school and he'd been a senior. They hadn't dated until after she graduated, but Viv still refused to like him.

"He's stressed with work."

"But the arguing and the drinking, Mar? How long are you going to let this go on?"

Amaris dug her nails into her palms, fighting the anger simmering beneath. She didn't want to talk about it.

"Maybe it's time for—"

"For what?" Amaris shouted, throwing her arms out.

"A change." Viv held her stance, not shying away. "He didn't remember, did he?"

Amaris pulled her bottom lip between her teeth, fighting the urge to scream or cry—she didn't even know anymore. Derek had forgotten yesterday was the anniversary of the shipwreck and her parents' deaths.

"You're a successful and confident woman, and you've already lost so much."

That should've meant the world, hitting the sweet part of her chest and filling her with pride or at least reassurance, but Viv had hit a solid wall.

"I love him," she said. "Why don't you get it? Couples go through rough patches."

Amaris attempted to push her away, to send her words of love where her mind couldn't sink its claws into them. She clutched her cheeks and slumped against the tree trunk.

"Mar, please. You deserve—"

"Just drop it."

"But—"

"I'm fine," she snapped, but she was far from fine. Derek had called their wedding stupid, he'd forgotten about her parents, and he cared more about his cases than her. They hadn't been themselves, but there was still the hope it'd get better. Once he'd gotten a grip on his extra workload and slowed down on the drinking, they'd get back to the old them—*they had to.* He was still the Derek she'd taken midnight drives with and sneaked kisses with behind closed doors.

Viv leaned back, pressing her lips tight as Amaris threw her head back in a sigh. Viv's hand found hers and squeezed.

A breeze jingled the chimes above Amaris's head, attempting to pull the sweltering anger from her with its silver bells. Grandad had bought Gran a wind chime for each anniversary. When he'd died, Gran had tucked most of them away besides this one, their first wind chime. After Gran's death, Amaris had kept it and hung it here to always feel their presence.

Her mind raced—the heat of the fire pressing in, their low air alarms mixing with the air horn blasts, and the angry fights about setting a wedding date.

A breeze bristled the leaves. She knew it was only the summer air, but she wanted it to be them. All four of them, watching over her.

Why is everything falling apart? She was a paramedic. Healing and fixing things was her job. Why couldn't she mend what was falling apart between her and Derek? She prayed to the ghosts flying on the wind, hoping they would one day whisper back and answer her call.

CHAPTER 4

Theo

BLOOD WAS ALL Theo could see. It spread across his vision like paint on a canvas. He yanked his sword from the depths of his enemy's chest, taking the light from his eyes. The body slumped to the ground, limp and lifeless.

The throne room of Oystein Castle in Mosfelkov appeared before him, sending his heart into a frenzy as he moved without a notion of remorse or regret. The torches along the bleak walls blazed, spreading heat through the chamber.

Theo marched through the line of Mosfelkov forces, stepping over eviscerated bodies. Something was breaking in his mind, ripping a deep hole in his cavity. As his sword swung as an extension of his arm, he knew he was not the one in control.

Sucked into the deep hollow of his mind, he watched as he ripped through the masses of enemy soldiers. Where each one of his own soldiers had fallen, two of theirs sprawled on the bloody stones at his feet. Anger and his quest for revenge riddled through his bones. A monster was born.

He was mindless and thoughtless with no regard for his preservation or theirs. He dodged a shining sword, slicing the back of a heel as his momentum spun him. Theo's dagger found a throat before they had a chance to howl in pain.

His chest further tightened as he heaved himself up, grabbing a sword at his feet and lunging both blades into the belly of his next assailant. The intestines spilled as he swiped across his large abdomen. The soldier dropped to Theo's feet, begging for mercy. He didn't give it to him. No one deserved his mercy for what they'd done to him, his squad. They would pay with their own blood.

Theo's hand pressed into a gray column, a color so consumed by the cold it appeared blue. He wiped the sweat lining his brow, but the red still tainted his view. He wiped again, but his vision was consumed with the bodies, the blood, the death. The atrocity would forever be etched into his mind.

Through pursed lips, he forced what little was left of him down and pressed through the throne room. His soldiers were gone. Theo knew it was his last stand, nothing else mattered. He would take as many of them with him as he could. It didn't matter anymore that he'd been ripped from his home to serve in a war that wasn't his or that, before the dawn broke, his body would be among the masses scattered at his feet.

He dragged his sword behind him through the lifeless chamber, catching against the uneven stones and carving a line in his wake. They would remember him, the soldier who held the line and killed their friends. He spat on the bloody floor, stewing over the disgrace, the betrayal.

His feet carried him to the final door. The looping brass handle was ice against the warm blood clinging to his hands. Only yesterday, he'd been knee-deep in a blistering snowstorm. Now, he stood in the heart of Oystein Castle, where everything went wrong.

His heart pounded profusely against his chest, trying to find a way to escape one last time. The blood swarmed in his ears and beat against the drum. It banged louder than he ever thought it could. With each breath, he inched the door open. The symphony in his head grew as the darkness beyond stretched further from the light flowing behind him. His eyes beheld his last stance, and the breath caught in his chest. He held tight to his sword, angling the blade over his eyes, pushing down the last remnants of who he was.

Theo sat upright in his bed, gasping and reaching for his pounding heart. He swung the blanket off and pressed from the sweat-soaked sheets. He stumbled though the dark until his hand grasped the washroom door. Dropping to his knees against the wood, he began retching whatever resided in his stomach. The pain twisted into knots and cramped in his abdomen. He gripped the edge of the toilet and choked out the last of the bile.

He slumped against the sink cabinet, unable to close his eyes. He wanted to light a candle, to give himself more than the glow of the moon through the window, but he couldn't bear to see if a red shine reflected in his sight.

He flushed the vomit and showered his face with water from the sink. He was thankful the inn was profitable enough to provide internal plumbing and the ability for him to retch not in a chamber pot or bucket. He hadn't had a nightmare since they left Luana Bay days ago, which was odd since he'd had them every night after returning from the war. They flowed like the swiftness of the Eldercrest River. The few days of peace had given him hope he'd moved past them, but tonight's horrors had come in a smashing and vivid replay.

Theo threw on whatever clothes were beside his bed and slipped on his boots. Nothing could force him back into that bed tonight. He might not have had the ivory beaches of Luana Bay to bring him solace, but he didn't need the brush of the surf or the crash of a wave. He needed a miracle.

The streets of Duncaster were different at night, with the few candles within the streetlamps and the glow of the moon to his back. In the distance were the cheerful tunes of a tavern. How many of his companions resided within its stuffy walls, drinking ale in excess and living a life of complete bliss?

The road to Ateus's temple was barren, as the noise of Duncaster turned to whispers on the Sunreign breeze. Theo pressed open the large marble doors to find empty pews before the statue of the God of Miracles. A bright smile flourished on the god's face as his hands were displayed wide to offer gifts to his people. A pile of gold pieces sat in one hand and a loaf of bread in the other. Theo bypassed the pews and fell to his knees before the god.

Soyenia worshipped only one god, while Mosfelkov destroyed what was left of their dying religion. Theo hadn't been able to step inside a temple for years to offer his soul to his deities. He walked past the temple dozens of times in Luana Bay but couldn't step inside its hallowed grounds and taint it with the blood he carried.

But tonight, he needed to. What happened in Oystein Castle haunted him, and there was no one who could give him peace. He dropped his forehead against Ateus's feet and prayed. He didn't dare speak aloud, but he repeated again and again in his head. *Forgive me.*

A creak pulled Theo from his stance, and his hand slid around his dagger.

"You don't need that in here," came a raspy voice. A short woman with a hunched back waddled from behind the statue. Her cane echoed off the coffered ceilings, and her small eyes narrowed as she gazed through the dimly lit temple.

"My apologies, High Priestess." Theo bowed his head for the woman who seated herself in the first pew.

The single mark of Ateus with raised hands sat upon her brow. She tapped Theo's leg with her cane and pointed to the seat beside her. "Sit."

Theo did as she commanded. She was the high priestess after all.

"You ask for forgiveness."

Theo's eyes trailed to where he'd once kneeled and wondered if he'd accidentally spoken aloud.

"You don't need to say what's in your heart for the gods to know." She patted Theo's hand as it rested against his thigh. "You are a soldier who has seen battle."

Theo's eyes now lingered on his clothes. In the dark, he'd thrown on a rumpled blue shirt and black trousers, nothing resembling his uniform.

"That dagger has seen many battles in the hand of a Fastrada, Captain." Her smile was warm, and it allowed Theo to release the tension in his shoulders he hadn't even realized he'd been holding. "I presume you are Theodoric. I doubt Luther has grown this strong." She poked Theo's bicep. "And you are no Adelaide or the young Jeremiah."

"You know my siblings?"

"As high priestess of Ateus, it is my duty to bless our duke and his family, and I see my prayers have been answered." She leaned back and rested her cane against the bench. "I hear Jeremiah is acting more like you every day. Adelaide is a miracle in herself. Your stepmother and father have miraculously arranged a betrothal for Luther, and you, my dear, have come home to us."

Theo should've felt elated, but the idea of his older brother's Conjugation to celebrate his betrothal in the Crimsonreign season threatened nausea, and any thoughts of Adelaide and Jeremiah were still heavy. The hardest part of coming home had been the anticipation of seeing his younger siblings and whether they'd accept who he'd become. Jeremiah had grown at least a foot. Adelaide had been standing in the foyer waiting for him when he'd arrived, but his sister had forgone her youth and become a woman. She walked with radiating confidence. For three years he'd left them.

There were many nights when he thought he'd never see Luana Bay again or hear his siblings' laughter. Theo wished for a welling in his chest or emotion to flood him, but there was nothing where his heart should've been. It beat, but for what, he didn't know anymore.

The priestess leaned closer and rested her hand against his forehead. Theo closed his eyes, receiving her blessing like he had from the high priestess who resided in Luana Bay before he left for the war. She murmured, and Theo dared open his eyes to see her wrinkly features pressed tightly together in a cringe.

"The suffering you carry upon your shoulders would kill a king."

Theo jumped from the pew, knocking over an iron candle holder. It crashed to the ground and further raced his heart. "How would you know that?"

She merely sighed and stood, wobbling without her cane as she pointed it at him. "You will crumble under its pressure. One day, you will have to decide your fate, one not even the great Ovrus, God of Destiny, can predict."

Theo's breath quickened before the frail priestess. "My fate is already decided—"

"No one's fate is certain. You may have lived through this war, but will you survive the next?" She turned, the echo of her cane bouncing off the stone walls.

Theo couldn't speak. *Another war?* He couldn't live through another one. The sheer agony of the loss alone would bring him to his knees.

Before she disappeared into the dark, she took one last look at him. "Pray for your miracle, Theodoric. It might be closer than you think."

He didn't wait for her to retreat before he took off through the temple and threw open the doors. Huffing, he leaned into one of the stone pillars to ground himself. What had she meant by another war? Were the sailors on the docks the beginning?

"That was longer than expected."

Theo whirled. Esaias seated himself on the stone monument marking Ateus's temple with his leather boots caked in mud dangling off the side. He raised his brows and smirked.

"That is sacred." Theo pointed to the slab of stone Esaias was defiling with his close proximity.

Esaias gazed down at the stone and shrugged before he hopped off. He didn't sway, nor did he have a permeating smell of alcohol.

"You weren't at the tavern?"

"Taverns are for celebrating. We discovered members of the Accords on our waters, and three of our soldiers have been sent to Duncaster's mystique for healing, who I hear is inexperienced and lacks the proper training."

"At least they have a mystique," Theo countered.

Luana's old mystique had traveled with them across the waters to aid in treating the wounded, but he hadn't been among the people who'd returned. He'd been killed two years in, when Mosfelkov forces hit an infirmary. It'd been disgraceful, but Theo had known they were merciless.

"Is that who you went to pray for? Old Cornelius Wellins?"

"You know that's not who I prayed for." Theo's hand trembled at the thought of whose name he'd muttered at the god's feet. He grasped his shaking hand and attempted to massage the muscles to keep Esaias from noticing. He failed.

"You don't have to hide it from me. We do share a bedchamber wall back home."

Theo turned from him. Esaias was the only one who knew about the nightmares, but not out of choice. He'd been at Theo's side when they first flooded his mind in the infirmary during the war. Esaias had witnessed his screams, but Theo couldn't bring himself to tell him what happened in Oystein Castle. Theo had failed as an officer. He would take it to his grave, as should've happened that night.

"I've heard you a few nights since you've been home. When did they come back?"

A long period of time had gone by when sleep had been scarce and, with it, the nightmares. He'd assumed it'd been easier to stuff down any lurking worries with Gris and Esaias by his side when he returned to the fighting after he'd been healed. By the time the war had ended, Theo could count on one hand the number of dreams he'd had. Luana's forces had come back to Godwin in a trickle. Esaias had seen the walls of their home a season before Theo had, but the first thing Esaias had uttered to Theo upon his return was *How are you doing*? Theo had assured his cousin he was well and ready to come home, but that night, a nightmare had woken him from a restless sleep.

Theo returned his gaze to Esaias, but there wasn't a glower or a tap of a foot waiting for his response. "A few weeks ago," he confessed.

Esaias leaned against the monument and rubbed a thumb along his shadowed jaw. "It's different now. It doesn't feel like it used to three years ago."

No, it doesn't. It felt an eternity and only a few moments had passed all in one, but he knew Esaias didn't mean Duncaster. Luana Bay had been Theo's home for all his life and Esaias's for most Sunreign seasons until he turned eighteen and moved there permanently. That had been eight years ago, but Theo still had the catch of breath when the season changed and feared Esaias would leave with the warm weather.

"Do you ever wonder if it was worth it?" Esaias asked.

Theo stared at his cousin. He was a strong warrior with years of sparring and training to build his strength. The years of war rations had trimmed a bit of his childhood fat, but it only added to the number of women flocking to him at night.

"It wasn't," Theo whispered coldly.

"I'm not ready for another war," Esaias blurted out.

"There won't be one." It felt like a lie after what the high priestess had said, but Theo couldn't afford to believe her ramblings.

He spotted something glowing on the edge of the towering buildings. He narrowed his gaze to a person shrouded in a dark cloak, with serpents wrapping their boots. His hand slid to his empty belt where his pouch had once hung. *The thief.* His pouch had been secured tightly and wouldn't have fallen off in the tumble. They'd cut it off.

"What are you looking at?"

"I think I found the person who stole my pouch," Theo whispered.

He stepped off the path to avoid the detection of the streetlamps and slipped through the darkness. The thief was short and nimble, hiding in the shadows of a cask or crate. Esaias slipped his dagger into his hand as they made their approach. Theo motioned for Esaias to circle around to cut off an escape before he palmed his own dagger. He took a deep breath and followed the thief.

Periodically, they glanced over their shoulder, but they were unaware of Theo's presence. He lurked closer, getting a better view of the scoundrel as he followed them into an alley. The clattering of a rubbish bin startled Theo, and a silverling jumped from the bin and took off down the alley. Theo tracked its silver movements until his eyes caught sight of the thief as they stared back at him before taking off.

Theo raced after them, splashing through puddles as he turned down a back alley between the tight buildings. His breath was warm, but the air was hotter and burned his lungs. A coppery taste seeped into his mouth as he raced faster.

The thief was light on their feet, shifting into various forms as the light of streetlamps and backdoors came into view and shunned them to the shadows. They vanished once again into the darkness, but Theo heard a clattering and continued his pursuit. The thief climbed over a pile of crates and jumped over a tall wooden fence.

Theo didn't think twice before he scaled the fence and hurtled himself to the other side to continue his pursuit. The thief looked back and accelerated.

Theo rounded the corner, but only a single circle of luminescence stood in the alley. He took a moment to catch his breath, but a stifled scream raised the hair on his arms. Esaias pulled the thief from the shadows with his arm wrapped around their neck and his dagger pressed against their abdomen.

Their hood slipped. The thief was a woman who couldn't have been any older than them. She revealed a youthful face, with black hair pulled into double braids and freckles scattering her sunburnt cheeks below golden eyes. Not a hint of fear hid behind her gaze. Her eyes navigated to the dagger in Theo's hand, raising a brow. Something within her eyes brought a sense of déjà vu over him.

"I suggest giving him his pouch back." Esaias's voice had lost all its humor and was laced with lethal warning.

"How do you know I have it?" she snapped. Esaias strengthened the grip his arm held, and she winced. "Alright!" She reached into her cloak.

Theo raised his dagger, but she only retrieved his pouch, tossing it at his feet.

Theo pushed the woman's glare from his mind and squatted to grab the pouch without taking his eyes off her. A quick glance showed not a single hilt or glimmer of a sword poking out from underneath her cloak, but it didn't mean a dagger wasn't hidden somewhere on her person.

"Are you going to arrest me?" she asked, struggling in Esaias's hold.

Theo rifled through the pouch, not bothering to count the silver and gold pieces but to feel his hand grasp around the small painting at the bottom. Relieved, he stood and gripped the buckle of his belt.

"Depends," Esaias said.

"On what?" the stranger asked.

"You help us, and we'll help you."

Theo shot Esaias a piercing glare. What could she offer them?

Esaias released his hold around her neck, leaving her standing between them and two solid brick walls. She would have to take one of them down to escape.

The woman crossed her arms and flashed a scowl. "I don't need your help."

"Our help will be keeping you out of prison. How does that sound?" Esaias gloated, swirling his dagger in the air as he pointed it at her.

The thief gritted her teeth, her eyes turning to small slits. "Fine."

"Smart," Esaias said. "What can you tell us about these disappearances?"

Her rebellious demeanor faltered, but she quickly regained her control. "I haven't a clue what you mean."

Well, if that isn't obvious.

"Why did you steal from him?" Esaias asked. "And why stop him on the docks?"

"You're not from here, are you?" she asked, exchanging glances with both of them.

"No," Esaias admitted, but a smirk crossed his features.

Theo shook his head.

"What's your name, gorgeous?"

She rolled her eyes. "Isabel."

"Esaias." He extended a hand, but Isabel didn't take it. She glared at the gesture. Flattery wasn't going to get him anywhere. "Well, Isabel, I'm sure you've heard ramblings about what's going on in Duncaster. Everyone else has."

Steady, Esaias. Theo internalized his caution, but they couldn't incite panic by divulging what they knew about the incident on the docks.

"I don't care to take part in gossip."

Theo's hand rubbed at the stubble along his chin, watching the break in Isabel's solid expression. Her left eye twitched, her fingers dug into the crook of her elbow.

Esaias cocked his head, narrowing his gaze. "You know." His fingers coiled tighter around the hilt of his dagger. "What's happening to the tenants going missing?"

"I don't know what you're talking about," Isabel sputtered.

Esaias took a step closer. "Oh, I think you do. Tell us, or we can't help you."

Isabel's eyes wandered, glimpsing the darkness surrounding them and their daggers trained on her. "What's in it for me?" She eyed the pouch now strapped tightly to Theo's belt.

Theo could barely contain his shock. *She robbed me and now wants a cut of my silver?* He opened his mouth to protest, but Esaias beat him to it.

"Not going to happen."

"Then I can't help you." She crossed her arms and turned her nose up at him. "Besides, I'd never help *fastida* nobles."

"Careful what you say," Theo warned, stepping closer.

"The big man does speak." She grinned. "Do I look or sound like I hail from Deavopan or Bazrath?"

Theo knew she was right. Her fair skin wouldn't fare well in the tropical climates, but it didn't mean her allegiances hadn't transferred elsewhere.

"How do you know we're—"

"You wear the dagger of a Fastrada noble." She eyed Theo, then turned back to Esaias. "And your physique is far too impressive to have come from anywhere near here with our starving bellies." She rubbed her flat stomach and gave them a mocking smile. "Duncaster is struggling, and soon we'll be set to ruin while you fancy nobles live your life of luxury."

Esaias gripped her arm and began dragging her back to the street.

"What are you doing?"

"You don't plan on helping us, so I'm only doing my duty as a *fancy noble* and escorting you to your new quarters." His own mockery of a smirk rivaled Isabel's.

Theo followed closely behind, in case she had any ideas and tried to break free. They reached the town center, and Theo and Esaias dragged Isabel, kicking, into the jail housing five cells, all but two occupied. A fellow soldier came to their side. He shackled her wrists as she fought against their hold.

"You'll regret this," Isabel spat.

Esaias wiped her spit from his cheek and shoved her into the first cell. "It would seem there are a few obstacles in your way now."

"*Aslorn per de eclahard!*" Isabel screamed, grasping the bars in her desperate attempt to hurtle herself at Esaias.

"Careful which tongue you throw around. Wouldn't want you to further incriminate yourself." Esaias turned to the soldier filling out her forms. "What is the punishment for treason? Still hanging? Sorry, I've been away fighting in the war. We didn't have time for trials."

Isabel's face paled and her hands slid from the bars.

Aslorn per de eclahard. The phrase sounded familiar to Theo, but it wasn't Tendasy. Was she fluent in multiple languages? It could've been Gorrin, the old language of Godwin spoken mostly in song or in private dwellings, but it also could've been one of the dozens of languages scattering the Black Sea. Theo had studied many, but there were always phrases or words that were ancient and hardly used in everyday vocabulary.

Esaias set to signing the forms of Isabel's arrest while she sat in the corner of her cell and hugged her knees to her chest. Theo couldn't help but see Adelaide in her. She was probably a few years older than his sister, maybe someone else's sister. He wished she would pick her head up so he could catch another glimpse of her eyes, but she remained with her forehead pressed to her knees as she mumbled in prayer.

They left with a nod to the soldier and in the direction of the inn, but Theo knew he wouldn't sleep the rest of the night. An uneasiness settled over him at leaving her in that cell, but she'd stolen from him. As a soldier of Luana, it was his duty to enforce the laws.

She wouldn't be tried for treason for stealing, but her use of Tendasy when she'd called him a bastard was dangerous after the circumstances of the morning. Then again, it was likely no one knew the reason for the fight. Whoever knew the language could still speak it without having committed any crime.

Still, she'd taken one of the few possessions he truly cared for, and he didn't know what would've come over him if he'd never seen it again.

CHAPTER 5

Amaris

AMARIS SLAMMED HER shoulder into the stuck lock of their stupid front door. After Viv had finally stopped pestering her, they'd gone shopping at the mall and spent the evening at their favorite hangout. The Boiling Pantry was a tarot shop and lounge Viv loved dragging Amaris to.

Now, with her body reeking of incense and her keys stuck, she winced and gazed up at the porch light flickering beside her. Grunting, she kicked at the door, but it refused to budge.

She leaned her head against the cool metal. She hated this door. She hated this house. *Fuck*, she swore, *I hate today.*

She stepped back, braced for impact, and charged for the door. It swung open, and her feet slipped against the hall rug as she fell into Derek's arms. *Intoxicated* wasn't a strong enough word to describe the smell smacking her in the face. His breath, his body, everything reeked of his cheap scotch.

"You know the door likes to swell in the humidity," he grumbled, shouldering it to get it to shut.

"I know," Amaris said, wiping her tennis shoes on the rug as she pushed further into the house.

She kicked off her shoes and stepped onto the cold floorboards. She veered toward the kitchen to assess the level of the scotch bottle on the counter. A thud and curse erupted behind her. The hairs along her neck spiked. With her heart caught in her throat, she turned to see Derek collapsed on the floor. Her shoes flew into the living room.

"What the hell, Amaris?" he thundered. "You leave your shit anywhere."

Her eyes threatened to mist with the familiar burning sensation. "I'm sorry," she whimpered.

No, not again. She took cautious steps toward him and offered a hand. He pushed her gesture aside, pressing against the wall instead. His staggering gait swayed as he took his first step. Her instincts made her reach to steady him.

"I'm fine," he spat, brushing past her toward the kitchen.

She followed him but paused at the swinging kitchen door. She needed to hold it together. For one night, she wanted to make it through without shouting or breaking down and crying.

Her hand trembled against the white wood, but she forced it to surrender. Derek poured another glass of scotch. She grabbed a beer from the fridge and hopped onto the counter beside him.

"How was work?" She gripped her beer tight to keep her hands from shaking.

"Shitty," he uttered, swirling the scotch in the bottom of his glass. "You didn't call me about that fire you had." He set the glass on the counter with a deafening ring.

She lifted her gaze, her heart torn. Part of her wanted to melt at the sight of him, and the other wanted to cower and lock herself in the bathroom. He looked the same as when he'd dropped on one knee with his denim jeans, black baggy shirt, and a backward baseball cap. It was the same one she'd given him when they'd first started dating.

"There's nothing to talk about," she said, fixing her attention to the sweat dripping down her beer. "I did my job."

"You almost got yourself killed." He gripped the counter, his power and strength building beneath.

"I'm fine."

"But I'm not," he began. "Why did I have to hear about your reckless stunt from one of your captains?"

"It wasn't reckless," she said under her breath.

"What was that?" he growled, releasing the tension he held on the counter and turning to her. He leaned in, his scotch breath drowning her senses like her head was being run under a garden hose.

"Nothing," she choked, fighting the lump in her throat.

"Why do you do this to me?"

"It's my job." Taking note of her sudden rise in volume, she bit her tongue. If things were ever going to change, she couldn't feed into his anger and retaliate with her own.

"Your job?" he shouted. "Your job is to keep yourself and your crew safe."

"Don't bring Charlie into this," she demanded.

"Why? You didn't care when you dragged him along in that fire."

Amaris set her beer on the counter and gripped the outer edges of her arms. "Derek, stop it."

"No. Why did you hide this from me? Is it because you knew what you did was stupid and careless?"

"Why does everyone keep berating me? I gave them a chance," she choked. "When I took my oath to serve and protect, I knew it meant putting my life on the line. That's what I did, and I'll gladly do it again."

Jumping from the counter, she stomped out of the kitchen before her meltdown could consume her. She ran to the bathroom, slamming the door behind her. The cool water from the faucet drew a breath from her as she splashed it against her flushed cheeks.

Why can't anyone understand me? She took a handful to fill her mouth, swallowing everything she wanted to say to him, to everyone.

"Amaris, open the door."

Gripping the edges of the sink, she let out a frustrated grunt to keep him from hearing a scream. Her throat ached as it ripped through her, one of anger and torment, one coming from the burning within. The reflection she saw in the mirror was of a coward. A woman afraid of herself and her life. A woman who had allowed everything to spiral into a pit of darkness. She punched the image glaring back at her.

Pulsing pain surged through her knuckles. She pulled her balled fist instantly to her chest, gaping at the shards of the mirror embedded in her skin and the bones along her hand shooting with pain. *What's wrong with me?*

The door rattled. "Amaris, what's going on in there?"

"Nothing," she shouted back.

"Open the door!"

She tore through the mangled mirror cabinet, but there was nothing. No rubbing alcohol or hydrogen peroxide, not even a fucking bandage. Some paramedic she was. The blood oozed from her cuts, dripping into the porcelain sink. She tried wiggling her fingers, but each movement was excruciating.

Glimpsing at the jagged reflection, she didn't recognize the woman staring back at her. Her hair fell from its bun, the chocolate waves draping past her shoulders to the middle of her back. She ran her good fingers through it, trying to untangle the knots that had formed throughout the day. It was all she could do, untangle the mess of her life one strand at a time.

When she'd been younger, the top had shone with a golden tint from the constant rays of sunshine on the beach, and the waves would curl from the salt of the water. She wished she could go back, to have her parents there to tell her what to do. But she couldn't, and now her hair remained its natural dark tint, and the loose waves hung limp.

She pulled her phone out and shot a text to Viv as the key turned in the lock. The door burst open, and the glass crunched under Derek's shoes.

"What is this?"

Amaris pushed past him, but Derek grabbed her arm.

"Are you fucking crazy?"

"I'm not crazy." She yanked her arm away.

"Normal people don't go around smashing mirrors when they're upset."

Flinching, she rallied whatever bravery she had, grabbed her duffel bag and work boots from the hall, and shuffled into the bedroom. She couldn't do it. She needed a moment to breathe.

"Amaris, I'm talking to you."

She pretended to ignore him as she fought back the tears. Viv would be there in minutes. She stuffed as much as she could into her duffel.

"What are you doing?"

"Packing," she mumbled. "I'm staying at Viv's tonight."

"The hell you are," he shot at her, nabbing the strap of her duffel.

"Yes. I. Am," she seethed, ripping it from his hand.

"You're not going." His gray eyes darkened as his jaw clenched.

"You can't tell me what to do." She kneeled between the bed and the wall, rummaging through the drawer underneath. She needed to breathe. Viv's apartment was just down the block, but Derek stood between Amaris and the door with his chest puffed out and his hands gripped into fists. She slid her work boots on. "I can't do this right now."

"No, we're going to talk about this, because I'm tired of this hero complex you've built."

"Hero complex? Do you hear yourself?" she snapped. "What if someone pulled a gun on you at work? Wouldn't you take that bullet, do what you signed up for?"

"Amaris, it's different, and you know it." His teeth ground together as he took a step closer, guarding both the window and door as he pressed her into the corner.

"No, Derek, it's not! We both could be killed. Why does it only matter when it comes to me?"

"Because I can't lose you. What would happen if you died?"

"If I died, you'd all move on without me. The world would keep spinning."

"Are you trying to get yourself killed? Am I not enough for you? Have I not done enough to show you I love you? I work my ass off to put a roof over our heads. I bake you breakfast. I clean up after you."

His insults roared through her mind, igniting a fire to spark within her. "You forgot, Derek!" she shouted, her duffel dropping to the floor. "Yesterday marked seventeen years since my parents died. You know I need you then."

He hesitated, and for a moment, she believed the shadows painting his features would lift, but he was consumed by the scotch. "Yeah, seventeen years. Don't you think you should be past this by now?"

"I'm spending the night at Viv's."

I can't believe he said that. Her mind and body were numb. She moved to step past him, but he grabbed her by the arm, his fingernails digging into her skin.

"Let me go," she snapped, trying to grab his wrist, but her right hand was useless.

"You're not going anywhere. You're not running out on us. You don't get to do that."

"I'm not running out on us," she shot back.

His grip tightened, and a whimper slipped through. Fear swelled, begging her to bend and cower.

"Looks like you are to me, running to that bitch's house."

She stared him dead in the eyes. She allowed the tears to fall, no longer caring if they made her look weak. "Never speak about Viv like that ever again."

Derek yanked her arm, pulling her closer to his noxious stench. "Why do you protect her? She doesn't deserve it."

"Let go of me, you asshole!"

Derek released her arm, but before she could jump for the door, the back of his hand smacked the side of her face. Her body slammed against the bed. Her hand shot to her cheek stained in tears and blood.

His eyes bore into the cut dug into her cheekbone by his class ring. "Amaris—"

She raised her hand, choking on the tears she couldn't stop from falling. "It was an accident. You know I would never do anything to hurt you."

A knock filled the house, and Amaris's phone chirped in her pocket—*Viv*. Derek's eyes were once again filled with menacing anger as another chirp rang through the deathly quiet room. "Who's that?"

Amaris jumped from the bed, but he beat her to the door. He shut it behind him. Her fingers curled around the knob, but it wouldn't turn.

"This is for your own good, Amaris."

She shoved her hip against it, but it wouldn't budge. *How did he lock me in?* Her breaths grew erratic as she slid down the door.

"Where is she?" came Viv's muffled voice.

"She's not leaving," Derek sneered at her.

"Mar?" Viv shouted.

Amaris wanted to scream for her, but her lips were sealed, frozen shut.

"She isn't going with you, and she's never going to see you again. You're a piece of trailer trash that belongs with your mother behind bars."

"What the fuck is wrong with you?" Viv shouted back at him.

Amaris's chest heaved with every agonizing breath.

"Get off my property." His voice was lethal.

Get out of here, Viv, Amaris pleaded. *Don't push him.*

"Not until I talk to Mar," Viv snapped back at him. "Where is she?"

"This doesn't concern you," he said before slamming the door.

His bounding footsteps woke Amaris from her stupor. She lunged for the window and slid it open. Her leg slipped over the sill as the doorknob turned. She jumped the rest of the way and sprinted toward the edge of the yard. Her name was only a distant echo as she hopped the back fence and didn't look back.

Amaris ran the trail, wiping raindrops from her face. Everything and nothing at all raced through her mind, but one word came into focus.

Safety. A safe spot to hide. The one place she kept hidden, to herself. The one place she'd never shared with Derek.

She sprinted past the drooping dandelions, and she swore the trees bowed in remorse. Her feet carried her to the willow, but she stopped and assessed her hand against the trail lights. Blood leaked around the shards of glass.

What have I done? She clenched her teeth between her knuckles and fished out a large piece. A cry leaked through her gritted teeth. A twig snapped behind her. She choked back her sobs and turned to face the protective covering of the canopy.

Without another thought, she jumped, grabbing the branch with both hands. She bit her tongue to suppress her muffled scream, the coppery taste of blood spilling between her teeth. She swung her legs and swallowed her cries with a mouthful of the fabric of her shirt.

Her foot slipped on the wet bark, her heart skipping a beat. She reached for the nearest branch, latching on with her fingers like talons. A thud sounded below. Her phone illuminated as she watched it slip into the mud. Her chest heaved with the short release of adrenaline. Tears spilled as she climbed the last branch and nestled into her safe spot, hugging her legs to her chest.

He hit me. Her thoughts were distant, and she settled her head on her knees. *Derek actually hit me.*

She prodded at the blood on her cheek, wincing at the delicate touch. Sobs escaped her, and she traced a small crevice she'd dug out years ago. Pulling out her knife, she wedged it into the slit to pry free a plastic bag. She pressed it against her thighs, revealing the hidden drawing she kept within. All their faces smiled back at her. Grandad, Gran, and her parents. She hadn't drawn anything in the last year past a doodle. It was like everything had been sucked away from her—drawing, Derek, her mental stability.

Footsteps bounded below, but with the mud, she couldn't tell whose they were. She slipped the bag into a pocket in her boot and drew her legs closer.

She wanted it to be Derek, for him to run down the path and apologize, to say he wanted to start the night over again, but she knew he wouldn't.

A snap echoed behind her. She froze.

She felt around the branch, assessing for cracks. There was no way she was falling from this height. One drop and she'd break her neck. Swallowing her fear, she scooted back toward the trunk, or at least where the trunk should've been. Amaris flipped backward, but she didn't fall to her death. She dangled *within* the hollow of the tree.

What the hell?

Darkness consumed her, all but the single opening within the trunk she'd fallen into. The glow of the trail lights flickered through the hole. Her fingernails bled from her death grip. She tried grabbing anything with her other hand, but it gave out. Then she heard her name. Viv's voice came from below.

"Viv!" Amaris shouted before her hand slipped, and she fell into the dark void of the tree.

CHAPTER 6

Amaris

STRIKING BLUE STARS danced around Amaris, blocking out the darkness as she fell. The light was blinding, absorbing everything, even her screams. She hit the ground hard, grasping the back of her head.

"Viv!" she called, but not a single sound came from down the path.

What just happened?

Amaris pushed off the ground, teetering as her vision threatened to blur around her—at least the few feet she could see. The trail lights must have been out from the storm, but not a single raindrop pelted her head. Reaching out, she waited for the water to puddle in her palm, but she was only met with a gentle summer-night breeze. She furrowed her brows at the clouds. It must have been a quick storm.

She sucked in a breath of woods but startled when she got a subtle whiff of salt. *How hard did I hit my head?* A frustrated groan slipped out as she dropped her head into her hands. She needed to find Viv.

The woods were pitch-black, and each branch threatened to be a hand reaching out to smack her in the face again. Guilt spread through her with each flinch. Her steps were methodical to avoid tripping and falling off the path. She attempted to study her hand, but it was useless.

Her heart still pounded against her ribcage. She leaned against a tree, fighting the urge to cry as her hand grazed the edge of her jaw where the blood crusted. He'd never hit her before. A few times in the last year she'd stepped back, fearful he might, but he'd never actually done it.

He couldn't have meant to, she tried to convince herself. *It was an accident.* She forced herself to keep moving, to prevent her mind from spinning. She couldn't stay out here forever. She had to face reality eventually.

A few more steps carried her forward until she smacked her boot against something solid and careened forward. Pain shot up her arm in her attempt to catch herself. She dropped to her side, screaming as she sprawled in a patch of grass.

Amaris couldn't fathom how her night could get any worse. She threw her good hand out, feeling for the edge of the path, but her hand traced along the mossy covering of a log. *No.* An actual tree. Her boot nudged it, but it didn't budge. She crawled over it, spreading her arm out to feel for the path, but all she found was more grass—*shit.*

The woods weren't that big. If she kept walking, she'd eventually come up on the edge of town or one of the county roads. Maybe a longer walk would help to slow her thundering heart. She'd sleep the fight off at Viv's, and she and Derek could fix everything tomorrow after shift. He'd have time to simmer down, and she'd distract herself with other people's problems for a while. They'd figure it out. They had to.

A horde of flies pulled Amaris from her dreaded thoughts. Their buzzing whizzed past her ear. She dodged and swatted at the annoying pests, stumbling through a dense group of bushes to outmaneuver them. But their presence only grew when she stepped from the foliage into a small clearing. Her next step carried her into a puddle, and a warm and gooey substance splashed up her leg. Her muscles stiffened. She'd stepped in a deer carcass once while hunting with Grandad as a kid.

She leaned down to confirm what was seeping into her boot, and the coppery scent of blood wrapped around her. Her stomach lurched, and she gagged, spitting up a few chunks of her burger from dinner. She pulled her foot back as the clouds shifted overhead and the moon cast its glow around her.

Her feet tangled beneath her and sent her falling into a butchered body. Blood spurted into her face and soaked her shirt. A frantic screech escaped her throat. She pushed off his severed flesh and propelled herself back, shoving her boots against anything to push herself from the pile of bones, skin, and organs.

She wiped at her shirt, her hand becoming stained in his blood. She wedged her fingers through a hole in her shirt and pinched something squishy in her bra. Another scream escaped her lips as she tossed a maggot toward the other side of the clearing.

The body wasn't recognizable covered in slashes, and his face appeared mauled. A snap of a twig stalled her heart. She scrambled back into the bushes behind her, obscuring herself as something crept through the dense foliage on the other side of the clearing. She bit her bottom lip as it drew closer, waiting for a coyote or some other predator to come lurking.

A man stepped into the clearing. She heaved a sigh.

"For realm's sake," he muttered, dragging his hand through his jet-black hair.

Amaris paused. *What did he say?*

The stranger examined the body, squatting to lift the dead man's arm. A cough rippled from his chest as he dropped the limb. He eyed the abdomen, cocking his head to the side as he took in the gashes.

Something wasn't settling well with Amaris. She shifted her gaze from the body to a glittering bit of metal at the man's side. It reflected the moon, and she squinted to see it more clearly. *Is that a sword?* She pressed a hand into the dirt, leaning closer to get a better look at him.

He couldn't have been much older than her, with a stubbled beard covering most of his tanned face. He wore a loose white top tucked into a criminal shade of taupe-colored pants fitting tightly to his thighs and tall riding boots. She should've relinquished herself from her hiding place to speak with him regarding the animal attack, but something about that sword made her hesitate.

"Theo, it doesn't take this long to piss," a woman said.

"Over here, Gris," he hollered back, but refused to avert his gaze from the body.

Amaris sat back on her heels. They weren't from Gainesville, but she couldn't place their accents.

"What are you..." the woman named Gris said as she stood beside her companion. "Holy realm. Is that—"

"I thought I heard something and came to investigate," the man named Theo answered.

Gris stepped toward the body, further illuminating herself against the moon's light. Her attire was the same awful taupe, only cut tighter to the curve of her hips. It looked almost like a military uniform, but a sword didn't drape her side like Theo. Several small hilts poked out from sheaths at her thighs, and she clutched a bow in her hand.

A small voice screamed in Amaris's head to turn around and run, and it sounded a lot like Viv's. But her stubborn feet planted her firmly in place.

Gris bent down, searching the man's pockets and eyeing his abdomen.

"Is it him?" Theo asked, kneeling beside her and choking on another breath.

Gris pulled out a blood-stained paper from the man's jacket and sighed. "Lord Freville isn't missing anymore."

"Do you think it was an animal attack?"

"Possibly." She turned her head to study the markings on his abdomen. Her complexion paled with a swallow, her eyes widening as she leaned in.

"What?" Theo followed her gaze and the tilt of her head.

"The markings," she breathed, hovering her fingers over the abdomen.

"They're sawed through with a dagger, not a claw."

Amaris swallowed as her heart threatened to climb up her throat. Her hand shook as she slid it over her lips. *Sawed through?*

"Are you suggesting he was murdered?"

Amaris gasped, then clamped her hand tight to her face. Their conversation ceased. Gris stood, her eyes darting around the clearing. Tears spilled from Amaris's eyes as she fought to hold her breath.

"I'll grab Bennet. He'll want to see this." Gris was wary as she turned and sprinted back the way she came.

Amaris recoiled. Their suprise was the only reason she wasn't sprinting, but that small voice begged her to get out of there. Staying low, she took crouched steps back but bumped into a pair of leather boots. Her head snapped up to face a menacing grin covered in brown stubble as the man beamed down at her. He snatched her arm, yanking her to her feet and shoving her into the clearing.

"And who might you be?" He smirked.

Forget demons with their beady black eyes. His striking light-blue ones threatened to slice her open.

"Get your hands off me!" Amaris shouted as he tossed her beside the body. She landed against her right hand, immense pain searing into her bottom lip as she bit back her scream.

"Looks like I found our murderer."

Her eyes stopped on the long knives strapped to his thighs and his pale fingers hovering over them. Her heart beat rapidly as he leaned down, narrowing his face into a wicked smile.

"No..." Amaris stammered, but her tongue twisted at the sight of his weapons within a moment's grasp.

"What do we have here?"

Amaris snapped her head. A man with a receding hairline of sandy-blond locks entered the clearing sporting a similar variation of their uniform. She'd never felt claustrophobic before, not after years of training in tight spaces, but the trees hanging above their heads pressed against her shoulders.

"She was hiding in the bushes," the snitch said.

The sandy-haired man dropped beside Amaris, and instantly, she was fighting back nausea. She'd take the stench of blood over his pungent body odor. He seemed to be the type of person to always wear a scowl or never see a bar of soap. He furrowed his brow, and his lips scrunched together. The moon on his face illuminated a scar draping his chin. It followed his scowl, starting at the corner of his mouth and ending on his neck beside his carotid artery.

Amaris startled and shuffled back as he pulled a knife from his boot. "I'm not a murderer!"

"You're covered in the man's blood," he said, pointing his knife at her. It was too long to be a simple pocketknife. It must have been military issue.

Amaris's gaze bounced across all their faces, their rage settling around her. Gris returned, her jog slowing as she eyed Amaris. Her blonde brows raised as she stared back and forth between all of them.

Amaris looked to Theo, who hadn't moved an inch, his expression stone-faced and cold. His first movement was his hand as he gripped the knife dangling from his waist. He was incredibly tall, far taller than Derek, at least. It was an unsettling thought as he stood with his hand wrapped around his weapon. He combed back his hair and revealed the brightest green eyes Amaris had ever seen, but what could've been beautiful were encased in dark storms.

The sandy-haired man regained Amaris's attention when he took the tip of his knife and settled it on her cheek where Derek's ring had cut her. "Why did you kill him?"

"I didn't," she protested, her eyes darting around, meeting their hollowed expressions. "You have to believe me." Their faces remained unfazed. "Call the cops. My fiancé is a detective. He'll sort this out." She panted, attempting to catch her breath, even though she was sitting and barely doing anything besides trying to focus on what the hell was happening.

"Sounds like the words of a rambling fool," the man with the long knives said. He had one pulled and resting against the outer edge of his crossed arms.

"Rambling?" Amaris breathed. Everything shuffled in her brain.

The morose man grabbed her right hand, and her eyes instantly watered at the pain. Gris and Theo both startled at her cry.

"Please." Amaris tried to pull back her hand.

He prodded at her swollen and smashed knuckles, dragging his dirty thumb over the glass still embedded in her skin. Her vision darkened as he pulled her to her feet.

"Sunrise is nearly upon us. We'll take her back with us and determine what is to be done," he said.

"What?" Amaris shouted, but the man who'd caught her grabbed her arms and started shoving against her back. He forced her toward a small camp. "Let go of me!" She tried wiggling out of his iron-like grip.

Fight! Viv's voice flooded her mind. Viv had always said, *If someone tries to kidnap you, you either get on all fours and bark and chase after them, or you run like hell.*

"Alan, keep hold of her for now. She'll ride with Gris." Theo gave his order, and Alan's hand coiled tighter around Amaris's arm.

More people were scattered around a dying fire with bleary eyes straining against its little light. They had long, matted hair and grizzled beards. None of them were wearing anything suggestive of the current century. Their mumblings immediately silenced as Alan dragged her over.

"Please, someone help me!" she screamed.

No one got up, but whispers erupted around them.

Alan whipped her arm back and pulled against her shoulder. "There's no one here to help, you murderous scum," he spat.

She yanked against his hold, but he shoved her elbow deeper into her back. Her shoulder burned as it strained. She forced a breath and waited several seconds. *What would Viv do?*

She summoned all her courage. Now was the moment. When Alan released the pinch of her shoulder, she turned and drove her leg up into a groin kick. She took off running and didn't look to see if he shriveled up on the ground or if anyone was running after her. The faint echoes of a curse and the gasps from his friends followed her. She thought someone even laughed, but she couldn't stop. She should've grabbed her phone. She needed to call the police, to call Derek.

What in the actual fuck is happening? Her mind spun like the county fair spinning strawberries. *Why are these people kidnapping me? Why aren't they calling the police?*

She raced through the woods, her ankles threatening to roll while using the moonlight to avoid running into a tree. Her hand burned as she pumped her arms and pushed branches out of her way. She shouldn't have punched that stupid mirror. Anger found its way into her heart, for them, for Derek, for this whole situation, but mostly her own stupidity.

When she leapt over a log, her foot slipped, and she fell forward. Her momentum carried her down the hill in a series of somersaults that twisted her stomach. A sudden stop drove a sharp pain in her side. She fell back, panting as she expelled air from her lungs. She turned her head, and her vision narrowed on the tall and burly figure sauntering down the hill toward her.

CHAPTER 7

Theo

THEO WATCHED AS she toppled down the hill, knowing better than to chase after her and risk following in her tragic pursuit. She collided with a fallen tree and collapsed on her back, heaving to collect her breath.

It was important to play everything carefully. As he approached her, he eyed her legs and waist but found no traces of weapons. That was strange, considering she'd come from a murder scene, but the real oddity was her appearance. The woman looked absolutely terrible. The sleeves of her entirely too-thin shirt were ripped off, and her odd trousers were cut to her rump. He'd never seen clothes like hers.

Theo squatted down, his knee hovering over her chest. Her blue eyes grew wide, but her attempt to speak caused a cough to ripple through her.

He leaned in, lightly pressing his knee onto her chest to keep her pinned as he bent his head and whispered in her ear, "In a moment, I'm going to remove my knee, and you're going to get up and follow me."

If she continued to run, she would only further incriminate herself, and Bennet or Alan wouldn't be far behind them. Theo studied her hand as she grabbed her head, and her eyes crinkled together. Blood caked every part of her body, but her hand appeared to have more than traces of the man's blood.

He took hold of it, and she let out a muffled cry. Her knuckles were smashed and puffy, but when he went to set her hand back on her chest, something sparkled, reflecting the waning hours of moonlight.

"Is that glass?"

"Mirror." She groaned and tried to pull it back, but Theo refused to relinquish his grip.

"What did you do? Punch it?"

The subtle twitch of her eye gave her away. There wasn't a village for miles. How could she have punched a mirror? He pinched a shard between his fingers and pried it from her flesh. Sure enough, it reflected what little he could see. She bit her bottom lip and squirmed beneath him.

"When?" he whispered more harshly than he intended as he dug another piece from her hand.

She winced as he prodded at a piece of glass between her first two knuckles. "Maybe thirty minutes ago," she squeaked. "Stop touching it."

He allowed her to pull her hand from his grasp. He would've expected her injury to be from a punch to a jaw, not a mirror. There was no pus or signs of inflammation. She was telling the truth.

As Theo contemplated the situation, an irksome thought occurred to him. *Would she have been able to take a man of Lord Freville's size?* He may have been older, but Freville had been a decently sized man, and where they were camped, they should've heard the fight. She appeared strong, but Theo doubted she would've had the strength with her fingers in that state. Lord Freville's body was cut beyond recognition, and their fight would've been loud and brutal. It wasn't possible she killed him in the last several hours.

"Are you going to get off me?" She eyed his knee still pressed to her chest.

Theo hesitated for another moment as all the information jumbled in his head. Something wasn't adding up.

He lifted his knee and stood. "Are you—"

Cutting him off, she rolled and kicked his legs out from under him. She tried to jump and make a run for it, but Theo grabbed hold of her ankle and brought her to the ground. She was strong as she kicked and fought him. Her nails scratched at his arms, and she attempted to knee him several times in the groin. He grappled with her, finding one wrist and then the other. He pinned them above her head and settled on top of her as she screamed and raged against him, but he restrained himself from an overbearing grip. He couldn't allow the monster within him to escape, the man he was during the war. He had no idea who she was. She could be running from a slaver or caught up in something entirely unrelated for all he knew.

"Let me go, you prick!" She spat in his face, but he kept her arms pinned.

He leaned closer and allowed his voice to deepen. "I don't think you quite understand your situation. We found you at the scene of a brutal murder."

"I didn't do it!"

"Then quit fighting me."

"You're the one trying to kidnap me!" She bit back the choking in her throat.

Kidnap her? Did she not recognize their uniforms?

"I'm Captain Theodoric Fastrada. I'm not kidnapping you. I'm arresting you."

She blinked, and her heavy panting slowed. Theo let go of her hands.

"You're what?" Her shoulders released their tension, but it was only a diversion. Her fist collided with Theo's mouth, and he rolled over, grasping his jaw.

Her hand slid along his belt. Before he could draw a weapon, she was standing over him with his dagger pointed at his chest. He couldn't reach for his sword. She would attack before he had the chance to draw it. Theo raised his hands in surrender.

"What do you mean arrest me? Are you some private militia?" Her voice cracked as she stumbled over her words.

Theo's dagger shook in her hands, but he focused on her rose-tinted lips and the accent escaping them. It was an interesting drawl he couldn't place. He could easily take her down, kick her legs out from under her. But he wanted to see what she would do, what she was capable of.

"We're no militia. We're soldiers in the king's army, Luana's forces."

She sputtered incomprehensibly, but he made out "king" and "shit."

"Are you a tenant of Luana?"

Her chest heaved, and her hand wrapped tighter around his dagger. She shook her head.

"A subject of Godwin?"

"Godwin?" Her muscles stiffened as Theo sat up. "Don't come any closer."

"What's your name?"

"What's my name? You're fucking crazy."

"I'm not the one covered in a lord's blood and holding a weapon against a soldier." Theo had enough of her stammering and swept her legs out from under her. His dagger slipped from her fingers, and he caught it, brandishing it across her neck as he straddled her. "If you're not from Godwin, where are you from? I hear your accent. Do you reside under the Deavonian Accords?"

Tears leaked from her eyes. "I'm from Gainesville. I don't know what you're talking about."

An uneasiness fell over him at the sight of the tears rolling down the sides of her face and the strange town name she'd uttered. What if she truly wasn't from Godwin or Deavopan or even Bazrath? What if she was running from a slaver?

"Who were you running from?"

She sucked in a gulp of air, but before she could speak, Alan came jogging down the steep slope with Gris in tow behind him.

"Did you catch her?"

The woman's gaze shifted to Gris and Alan. "This isn't real," she muttered.

Theo lifted himself off her and grabbed her by the arm, hauling her to her feet. Her muscles were rigid, but she didn't meet his gaze. In fact, he couldn't see where her eyes focused. He tugged her onward, and it was as if a trance had fallen over her as her feet fell in line beside him. He waited for the second she'd snap out of it and pull some stunt to rip her arm free, but she stared forward and didn't utter a single word until he got her to Gris's horse.

Theo removed the hold on her arm and slid his hands to her waist to assist her up, but she froze and clutched his hands.

"Don't touch me!" she shouted, and Theo released her instantly.

Gris flashed expansive eyes between him and the strange woman who wrapped her arms around herself.

"I can get on by myself."

Theo allowed her to seat herself in the saddle. As Gris pulled her reins, kicking her horse to get them moving, he watched as the woman's hand hovered over the small cut along her cheek.

"What do you think?" Bennet's voice startled Theo and had him whirling around to meet his menacing scowl.

Theo didn't know what he thought. Only moments ago, he was bent on capturing her and hauling her to the dungeons beneath Fastrada Manor, but now, as he watched her and Gris disappear down the trail, a question filled his head. *What if she's innocent?*

"Something doesn't feel right about this," he said.

"We'll see if she's willing to confess to your father. Stay back with Gris and keep an eye on her."

Bennet mounted his horse and trotted to lead their party. Theo found his hand trailing to his swollen lip where her fist had collided. She had a strong punch.

"Daydreaming?" Esaias mused behind him. He had the misfortune of carrying Lord Freville's body wrapped in a blanket.

Theo could already begin to smell the rotting reek of decay. "Only thinking." He mounted Bear and rubbed his horse's mane. Thankfully, they had a long enough journey that he could begin deciphering the chaotic situation and maybe get the mysterious woman to explain herself before they reached Luana Bay.

Esaias pulled ahead and found a spot beside Alan, most likely to pester him with the wretched smell. Theo pulled behind Gris, keeping one hand on the reins and the other wrapped around his dagger as his eyes trailed through the shadows under the trees.

The first few hours of their journey were silent, but as the sun began poking over the trees to their backs, it was like a new breath had been released with the morning breeze.

"What's your name?" Gris's voice finally cut through the silence, but only the three of them were around to hear it as they trotted down the river path. The others had gained distance and pulled ahead, leaving them alone with the rush of the river beside them.

The woman blinked as if woken from her stupor. "Who are you people?"

Theo raised an inquisitive brow.

"I asked you first," Gris threw at her.

"Amaris," she said with a small sigh.

"Griselda, but you can call me Gris."

Amaris pinned her gaze to Theo, narrowing her eyes. "Alright, Gris and *Captain Theodoric Fastrada*—"

"Theodoric is fine," he grumbled, his blood heating from her mocking tone.

Amaris straightened up. "Who are you people, and why are you kidnapping me? I'm not buying into the kingdom, soldiers, and arresting crap. Are you some kind of cult, or are you planning to ransom me?"

Theo gaped in confusion. It was as if she were plucked from a small island in the sea and thrown into their path. She had to be acting. No one was this oblivious of the realm.

"Excuse me?" Gris snapped.

"Theodoric here claims to be a soldier in this mighty king's army. I call bullshit. You're the ones who attacked, chased, and kidnapped me."

"We're not the ones who killed a man."

"I'm a paramedic. I save lives, not take them."

What in the realm is a paramedic? Theo questioned. *She saves lives?*

"Look, I stumbled on that body a few moments before you all did," Amaris said. "I hid because I thought you were an animal or something."

"Why are you covered in his blood?" Gris asked.

Amaris had the audacity to roll her eyes. "I fell on top of him. Besides, I couldn't have killed him. He was dead long before I found him." Gone was the frightened demeanor, replaced by a sharp tongue that sent Theo's blood curdling. It was going to be a long ride. "Did you not see the maggots?"

Theo sharpened his gaze. *Maggots?*

"If you're not some cult or group looking for money, then what are you playing at? Are you overly dramatic role-players? Or a traveling reenactment group getting off on kidnapping people?"

Theo's cheeks reddened to her offensive language. Amaris continued her tirade at a faster cadence than a trotting horse, but he questioned everything. She was either playing them and was deadly or she was the key to understanding what was happening in Luana.

"If you didn't kill him, then why were you in the woods?" Theo asked. "There isn't a town for miles, and we found nothing to suggest you had provisions or a camp."

"I...I was..."

What was she hiding? Theo narrowed his gaze on her, but Bear jerked under him.

"Easy, Bear!"

His eyes darted around them. Maybe a silverling had spooked him. Bear whinnied and stood on his hind legs. Theo's thighs squeezed, keeping him in the saddle. He pulled at the reins, the leather digging into his fingers. Bear slammed his hooves into the dirt, and a jaded gecko skittered back into the brush, its navy scales reflecting the sun.

"Theo, are you—"

"I'm fine, Gris," Theo said through gritted teeth, keeping from shouting to further spook him, but Bear continued to buck. Theo's right foot slipped from the stirrup, and he braced harder to keep his seat. Theo's left foot slipped. He gripped lower on the reins, but Bear edged toward the river. The roaring current no longer had a calming effect as it loomed closer.

Bear screamed and bucked. Theo couldn't hold on any longer and flipped over his head. He landed against the steep edge of the riverbank, smacking his forehead as he rolled off into the stream.

CHAPTER 8

Amaris

ALL THOUGHTS OF questioning whether her reality was real or not evaporated from Amaris's mind as Gris leapt from the horse. She didn't even bother with Amaris as she rushed toward the steep river's edge.

"Theo!" Gris screamed, scanning the water.

With the pace of the current, he had to be farther downstream. Amaris slid from the saddle, biting back the pain in her hand. She shoved it away and headed toward Gris's cries of distress.

"Theo!" Gris yelled again.

"Can you swim?" Amaris asked.

She turned to Amaris, the whites of her eyes growing into porcelain saucers. "I...I can't."

Amaris stepped closer to the edge. It was a five-foot drop, but the water had to be deep without a single sign of Theodoric floating above the surface. Her boots kicked off with ease. She only wished she could be jumping into her bunker pants instead of a river. Amaris stepped back a few paces, released a breath, and jumped.

The cold water shocked her. *Shit! What the hell am I doing?* Her legs kicked furiously as she treaded water, and the river washed over her face. *Did I just jump in for this asshole?* She choked out a breath, refusing to swallow the nasty river water. The current swept her downstream before she could even assess how deep it was.

"Theo!" Gris screamed from the edge of the river.

Amaris righted herself, getting her feet behind her to propel herself forward. Apparently, someone cared for the prick. He had to be here somewhere, but a hard lump in her throat formed. She didn't see his head or any part of his clothing poking out.

"Ride farther down and let me know if you see him!" she shouted to Gris.

Gris jumped on her horse and forced the creature to a sprint.

I'll find him. Amaris swam faster, kicking her feet and dragging her arms over her head one after the other. It was entirely too natural for her body to adjust to the water again. She'd begged Gran to put her in swim classes as a child, fearful what happened to her parents in the shipwreck would repeat itself. Her hand sliced through the water's surface, but a river was different than a swimming pool.

"He's down here!" Gris shouted.

All Amaris could see along the river's edge were trees as they extended over the water. She swam faster, her legs burning with each kick.

"Over here!" Gris pointed across the river.

A moss-covered tree had fallen across the water. Her eyes peered closer, and hanging along the edge of a branch, looking like it could break any second, was a belt.

Amaris fought against the current, trying to veer toward him, but it swept her up and smacked her into the tree. It shifted, and the branch creaked with the thud. Her nails dug against the tree, trying to gain leverage. The bark bit into her fingertips as she inched toward him.

Lucky bastard. If it hadn't been for his belt, they never would've found him. Unfortunately for him though, his belt was also holding him beneath the tree.

Amaris reached out, a cry of agony escaping her lips as the current snapped her hand back. She needed to push through. She couldn't move her fingers, but she could feel for his head and cradle it around her wrist. Her legs were leaden, threatening to get sucked underneath.

She reached again, feeling down his shirt until his hair was brushing against her hand. Her fingers tried to open to grab him, but they wouldn't move. She fought the tears of pain surging through her. Wrapping her wrist around his head, she tried again to pull him back, but the current was too strong against the weakness growing in her hand.

She forced a breath, frustration overcoming her. She needed a different strategy. The belt caught her eye, and she instead slung her arm around it, wedging it into the crook of her elbow. Painfully, her swollen hand wound around the leather. She slid her other hand down the slippery surface of the tree, feeling for his head again. She was so damn close but couldn't reach him.

She knew what she needed to do but she didn't like it. *Why did I have to punch that stupid mirror?* Holding her breath, she dove under the water. The current tried to take hold of her, dragging her under.

She further twisted her hand around the belt, hooking her wrist. She opened her eyes, fighting the sting of the murky water and the tunneling vision from the pain radiating up her arm. She couldn't pass out. Her lungs burned, but she wrapped her legs around his torso and pulled his body closer to hers. She reached into the murky darkness, feeling for something to pull his head up. She wiggled her fingers, and her hand slid to the back of his head.

Theodoric's face breached the surface, but there wasn't a gasp for air. Amaris shifted herself behind him, allowing his head to cradle against her shoulder.

"Theo!" Gris shouted as she came running down the tree. The weight of her feet caused it to shift. They almost slipped from the branch, but Amaris held Theodoric tightly with her legs wrapped around his waist and his back pressing against her chest.

She placed a finger on his neck as she waited for Gris to reach them. A pulse beat beneath her fingers—*thank God*. His head rolled toward her neck, but she didn't feel a shallow breath or even see the rise of his chest. She pinched his nose and forced a breath into his lungs—*gross!* She'd never done actual mouth-to-mouth since they carried masks, but if she didn't, he was going to die.

Gris dropped into a crouch and leaned over. Her feet shifted, keeping her balance as she tried grabbing underneath Theodoric's arms. She couldn't possibly pull him up herself. He was too big.

"Get his belt off the branch, and I'll grab him," Gris said, readying herself.

"Can you—"

"Yes," Gris insisted, and Amaris unwound her hand and jimmied the belt off the branch. "Let go of him. I've got it from here."

Amaris studied her. Gris's muscles flexed and strained as she fought his dead weight. Amaris unwrapped her legs but was ready for when he slipped from Gris's hold.

No way she does it. Amaris took a breath to dive to the bottom and push off the river floor to give Gris any bit of help, but she grunted and stood, deadlifting Theodoric out of the water. *Holy shit!*

Gris grabbed Amaris's arm and hurtled her onto the fallen tree. Seizing under his arms again, she dragged him toward the shore. Amaris froze, draped over the tree. She'd never seen anything like it. Gris was pretty much her size with the strength of Viv.

"Let's go!" Gris shouted to her.

The rushing current looked all too appealing to make a quick escape, but Gris fought her sobs as she dragged Theodoric down the moss-covered tree.

I'm going to regret this. Amaris swung her legs over and got her feet underneath her. Her muscles were riddled with fatigue, and her legs burned with each step. Gris hauled Theodoric off the tree, sprawling him on his back in the grass. He still wasn't breathing.

Amaris flailed her arms, fighting her balance against the slippery moss as she ran the last few paces. Jumping down, she rushed toward his head. She bent down and gave him another rescue breath, ignoring his bad breath.

Jeez, brush your teeth lately?

Theodoric's chest rose but settled as Amaris removed her lips. She took her left hand and began compressing on his chest.

"Do you have your cell phone? Call nine-one-one," Amaris said.

Gris stood with her arms pinned at her sides. Her eyes trained on Amaris pressing against Theodoric's chest.

"Give me your cell phone." Amaris could understand her shock. Most family members would be hysterical.

Gris furrowed her brow, and the question she uttered was airy. "Cell phone?"

"If you don't call for an ambulance right now, he could die!"

"What in the realm is an ambulance?"

"Go get the others," Amaris demanded as her thoughts began to spin. *A cell phone...an ambulance...is she seriously this clueless?* An icy chill shot down Amaris's spine as she pulled back her hand and leaned over to give Theodoric another breath. She considered their matching clothes and the possibility they could be part of a cult that didn't give them access to the world.

She brushed her lips against his as she gave another breath and resumed compressions. She tried not to focus on his chapped lips but what was unraveling around her. Maybe it was all a vivid hallucination from being doped up on morphine while she lay in a hospital bed with a broken neck. She kept compressing.

Maybe I'm not, she considered. Her hand wouldn't hurt this bad if she was, or maybe her mind had a sick way of dealing with its subconscious. She gave another breath and concluded, *This is just a desperate nightmare.*

She wished she had her ambulance, her airway equipment, her automated vent. She brushed bits of moss off Theodoric's cheek for a breath and resumed pumping against his chest. She wished she had Viv and Charlie here to run the call with her, for her vitals monitor and drug box. Sweat and water mixed along her forehead, trickling off the bridge of her nose as she used her entire body to power her compressions. One handed wasn't sustainable. He needed to start breathing, or she needed a damn ambulance.

She leaned down and forced one more breath. He lurched forward, smacking his head into hers. She fell back, groaning and gripping at her skull. *Fuck, he has a hard-ass head.*

Theodoric rolled over, vomiting and coughing up the water from his lungs. Short gasps followed a coughing fit. He rolled over and tried to sit up.

"Hold up. Catch your breath first," Amaris said, reaching for him.

He whipped back his arm, swatting her hand away as another cough spewed more water from his chest. His fingers dug into the dirt, his body sucking in whatever air it could. He tried to stand, but his leg buckled as he planted one foot beneath himself.

Amaris shoved her shoulder into his chest, keeping him from face-planting. "Will you sit here for a minute? Gris went to get the others for help. We need to get you to a hospital."

"A...what?" he breathed.

Her eyes snapped up to meet his. He didn't know what she was talking about either. She brushed back the hair clinging to his forehead. A massive gash sat above his brows, fresh blood leaking from the cut. Maybe he was concussed.

Theodoric pushed her hand away with a wince and sat back on his heels. She gripped his shoulder, refusing to let go and risk him falling and further adding to the head trauma. He dragged his head up. Those stupid bright eyes had small bits of gold catching the sun, but they shifted, and Amaris turned to the men following closely behind Gris.

Immediately, Amaris's body trembled with furious anger. *They fucking kidnapped me.* But she didn't release her grip on his shoulder. She could've gotten away, but she'd saved him.

"What happened?" the sandy-haired man burst out, running toward them. He gruffly took Theodoric's face in his hand, brushing back his hair to examine the cut oozing blood down the bridge of his nose.

"I'm fine, Bennet," Theodoric whined, pulling his head free from the man's grasp.

Bennet turned to Amaris, ripping his knife from its sheath. He pinned her to the ground and pressed the blade against her neck. His teeth bared and spit flung from his mouth. "Did you try to kill him!"

"No, she helped," Gris said, wrapping her hands around Bennet's forearm.

I did a little more than help, Amaris thought.

"Please," Gris pleaded.

Bennet's glare shot back and forth between them, but he pulled back and sheathed his knife. "Let's get moving. We're already at a pace to reach Luana Bay well past sunset."

"No, he needs medical attention," Amaris snapped, standing to face Bennet. Her face may have only reached that puffed-out chest of his, but she couldn't let that stop her. Theodoric needed a doctor.

"He'll get what care we have when we return home," Bennet barked as he stepped closer, his chest inches from touching her nose. He turned to Theodoric. "Can you ride?"

"I can," Theodoric said, struggling to stand as Gris draped one of his arms around her shoulders. A tall redhead slid under his other arm.

"No, you can't," Amaris interjected. "You almost drowned. You could pass out and fall off your horse."

"I'll be fine."

She ground her teeth, forcing herself to keep from screaming at him, but she couldn't force him to go to the hospital. Those were the patients she hated the most, when they continuously refused and thought they knew better.

"Only if I ride with you," she demanded, crossing her arms. There was no point in fighting it. If she ran, they'd find her and drag her along anyways.

"No," Theodoric said.

"If you pass out, you're going to fall off and break your neck. I'm riding with you whether you like it or not."

She turned to grab his menacing horse, but the damn beast had already found its way toward them. Its black coat fit its evil personality. She swore it mocked her as if it were waiting for her to get on its back to buck her off too.

"Are you a mystique?" Gris asked, helping Theodoric with the other man's assistance toward the creature.

"She's a murderer, not a mystique," Bennet snapped beside Amaris.

"First of all, I'm not a murderer. Secondly, I'm a paramedic."

"A para-what?" Alan cut in from nowhere, coming to stand beside her. Probably to make sure she didn't run off.

Amaris digested his words. None of them had any idea what she was talking about. They'd never heard the terms *paramedic, ambulance,* or *cell phone.* A shiver crept down her back, and she had the strangest feeling she was no longer in Gainesville. Amaris took in the morning sprouting around them.

"What year is it?" she asked, daring a glance at Bennet as he glared back at her, his eyes narrowing in.

"Six thousand, fifty-six, why?" Alan asked.

She sucked in a breath. *Time travel is a definite no.* She shook the ridiculous thought from her head. She was in a coma in a hospital. No other logical explanation existed.

They managed to get Theodoric on his horse, but his face leached of color. Exhaustion settled over him, and she wondered if he'd plummet to the ground at any moment.

Bennet snatched Amaris and whispered, "If you try anything, you'll be begging for death." He jerked her arm, flinging her forward.

Gris pulled Amaris's boots from her saddle bag and tossed them to her. At least she had the decency not to let her walk around in mushy socks for the remainder of their journey.

Amaris's adrenaline was fading, and a bout of nausea was around the corner. She allowed a single boost from Gris to mount the horse. She awkwardly swung her leg over to avoid roundhouse kicking Theodoric in the head as she settled in front of him.

She conjured up a smile toward Gris, not that she deserved it. She might have had immense physical strength and even persuaded Bennet to pull the knife off her neck, but she was still part of the band of criminals. Gris stared but didn't offer a smile back. A muscle in her jaw feathered before she turned for her own horse. *All right, maybe she is like the others.*

Theodoric gripped the leather reins and got them moving. He hunched forward, his breaths trailing down the back of Amaris's neck. Of all the things to dream about. She expected her mind to come up with something more exciting, like a car chase or a superhero coming to her rescue, but it was settling on vivid and oddly detailed Renaissance fair people.

As they rode, she attempted to shift her dream to something other than Theodoric's monstrous form leaning against her, but with each passing minute, she felt the weight of him growing heavier. He shouldn't have been riding this long and would probably collapse before they made it to their destination. He'd aspirated water and might have had a lung injury. Amaris needed to convince him to see a doctor before he could develop pneumonia or worse. It might have been some stupid dream, but on the off chance that it wasn't, she needed to get him to a doctor.

"You need to get help," she whispered. "You almost drowned and—"

"I'll be fine," he muttered, his arms dropping against her thighs.

He wouldn't make it the next twenty minutes. Amaris shifted in the saddle to catch Gris behind them. Maybe she could convince him. He perked for a moment, drawing back his broad shoulders—*his incredibly sculpted shoulders.* Amaris swallowed and stared at the bear of a man and how he completely blocked any line of sight of Gris.

"You need medical attention."

"Are you suggesting I see a mystique?"

"Look, I don't know what religion you people follow or who you go to for medical advice, but I suggest a legit hospital. Getting antibiotics and being admitted for observation."

"Are you sure you weren't the one to hit your head? Your words are daft."

"Are you calling me stupid?" She narrowed her eyes.

"I said your words were. There is a difference."

She scoffed. *What a prick.* She'd saved his ass, and instead of thanking her, he insulted her.

CHAPTER 9

Amaris

THE GRUELING HOURS of riding took them well into the night. Amaris had contemplated jumping off several times, but her instincts to protect her patient overpowered the tiny voice screaming at her to run. She'd never abandoned a patient before and wouldn't start now.

Along with the internal anger, she was kicking herself for not snatching her duffel before she fled her house. She would have given anything for a sweatshirt with the breeze brushing against her damp clothes, and Theodoric wasn't any help in the matter with his own shivering.

With another twitch of his thigh and the rubbing together of his hands, dread filled her. *I'm the worst paramedic ever.* She got him breathing again only to kill him from hypothermia. She should've thought of it sooner.

"Are we almost there?"

"Soon," Theodoric whispered.

Every insult and snarky comment riddled through her head, but before she selected her slight, Theodoric draped something over them. It was a cloak. Its dark nature blended against the horse, but a gold stitching along the edge drew the light from the moon. She hugged the edges, getting an interesting scent of leather clinging to the cotton fabric.

A rush of warmth spread across her cheeks. Embarrassment, anger, confusion. Everything gnawed at her stomach. She'd been about to sling every curse word she knew at him, but his cloak was a surprising anomaly.

They kidnapped me, she reminded herself. What she needed was a hospital for his lungs and her hand, not a damn cloak. She'd removed the glass from her skin, but she worried about a possible infection.

"Back on the riverbank..." he spoke, then hesitated. Maybe he was considering letting her go. "Did you bring me back?"

Amaris peered over her shoulder, disbelief settling over her. His face resembled a chiseled stone statue. He might have had an immaculate jawline, but not a hint of emotion lingered in his eyes. He was serious.

"You weren't dead." Amaris's eyes skimmed the canopy above them. "You may have had one foot in the grave, but your heart was still beating. You *almost* drowned."

"But..." he stammered, the first break against his brick wall of a face, "I was at the gates of After."

After? She contemplated his interesting version of an afterlife before saying, "I don't know what you think happened, but you weren't—"

"I was gone."

Amaris scoffed at him. If he didn't know what a phone or ambulance was, then he certainly wouldn't understand basic CPR. Returning her attention to the woods in front of her, her heart leapt as the shadowy forest came to an end. She'd grown accustomed to the steady breaths of the horses and the chirping of insects. It startled her when the clacking of hooves clicked through the air. A cobblestone path sat beneath them, not pavement or asphalt, but actual cobblestone.

She leaned over the horse, squinting to get a better look at the city emerging before her. A list formed in her mind of every surrounding town, but none of them matched what befell her eyes. A main road spiraled through the medieval-styled city, winding and twisting with shops and their darkened windows.

Smaller avenues flowed beyond. Amaris cranked her neck to set eyes on the small wooden and stone houses. The strangest part, though, was the lack of electricity. The only signs of illumination were the candles within the streetlamps.

What is this place? That same tingling sensation seeped down her spine as she took in the few people they passed. She was hoping for someone to save her from her kidnappers, but everyone either waved in greeting or bowed their heads. But the greatest oddity was what they were wearing. Long dresses, knee-length frock coats, tunics, and billowing shirts dressed the occupants of the city. It was as if the laws of societal dress code were gone, and everyone dropped back decades or even centuries.

Amaris was caught in an overload, taking in the scene unfolding around her. It wasn't possible. No town existed within miles of Gainesville with similar architecture, but by the end of the road she could no longer contain her shock. Her jaw dropped. An elaborate castle stood, etched in gray stone with towers narrowing to points.

She pinched her eyes tight, praying it was all a mirage from the lack of sustenance and water or even a dream, but everything was still there. They trotted through a stone archway lined with torches in a wall built around the castle, wrapping around it like a fortress. Candlelit lanterns scattered the yard, casting the grass in a swarm of shadows. Everything was dark, and Amaris found herself missing her flickery porch light.

They veered to the side instead of the front where stone steps protruded from a set of wooden doors with iron swirls running along it like vines of ivy. No, they ventured toward the side entrance with steps leading down into the dark.

Theodoric slid from the horse, holding onto the reins as he grasped at his temples. He raised his hands, ready to grab hold of her waist.

"I can get off myself," Amaris sneered. He would've dropped her anyways. She slid onto her belly and plummeted to the ground, the momentum carrying her back as shockwaves traveled up her shins.

"Put her there for the night, and we'll deal with her in the morning," Bennet grumbled, gesturing to Alan.

Technically, now that Theodoric was home, Amaris wouldn't be abandoning her patient if she escaped. At least that was what she tried to convince herself of, because there was no way she was going into that rat-infested hole.

As Alan approached her, she recalled all Viv had taught her about self-defense, which was minimal since Amaris declined most of her offers to join her classes she taught to women. She was kicking herself now. Alan would see the kick to the groin coming—she needed something different. He grasped her arm, but his grip was nothing compared to before. He was tired. She allowed him to pull her toward the basement-like catacomb, shifting her gaze to each of the figures beginning their trek home.

With the others' attention set to their warm beds, she waited until Alan was at the edge of the steps before she struck. She ripped free from his grasp and drove her knee into his stomach. He hunched forward, moaning in agony.

She took off. The uneven ground threatened to roll her ankles, but she needed to get away, to hide in the forest or maybe somewhere in town. She raced for the arch. Two of their cronies chased after her, darting to cut off her path, but she was too far ahead. She panted and pumped her arms as she pounded her feet into the ground. She was going to make it.

Passing into the city, she tore down the cobbled street, ignoring the shouts behind her. An alley caught her eye, but before she could escape to freedom, an arm snatched her around the waist, and they tumbled in a mass of limbs and grunts. Strong arms wrapped around her as they rolled and skidded across the street. They came to an abrupt halt in the alley, smacking into some kind of cart. She couldn't breathe. Not because the wind was ripped from her lungs, but whoever caught her now had their knee compressed against her chest.

"Don't...make this harder...for yourself." Theodoric panted, attempting to catch his own breath.

"Fuck...off," she gasped. She was growing tired of this specific encounter.

Theodoric fell forward, his hand slamming beside Amaris's head, catching himself before his massive form crushed her.

"How are you not dead or passed out by now?"

Theodoric regained his strength as he leaned forward, further pressing his knee into her ribcage. "I don't have the patience for this tonight." A bead of what she was hoping was only water trickled down his nose and splashed against her cheek. "Get up before I drag you back."

Some concussion. Apparently, Theodoric turned into an asshole when he had a headache.

"Like you have the strength right now to even stand."

"Have it your way," he grumbled, sending vibrations down his knee and through her chest. He scooped her up in a single movement and threw her over his shoulder like a sack of potatoes.

"Now you have the strength? Where was this when you kept falling asleep and drooling on my shoulder?" Amaris kicked her legs and beat her single fist against his back, but he seemed entirely recovered as he restrained her legs and carried her toward the dark stairwell.

The creak of an iron gate had her sinking her nails into his shirt, but he didn't flinch. They descended the stairs into a dark and dreary basement. *Scratch that, dungeon.* Doors lined the walls, each one with a small window blocked by iron bars. He took her to the far end and set her in the back of the cell, locking the door behind him as he slipped out.

"Let me out of here, you bastard!"

Blatantly ignoring her, he slammed the gate at the top of the stairs behind him. Amaris was left alone with the only company being a small flame in the lantern of the even smaller cell. Stone walls kept her in. Her body was defeated and her hand throbbed as she hugged it to her chest. A wave of nausea passed over her.

She couldn't believe it was all a dream. They weren't supposed to be gut-wrenching and painful, but any alternative was unbelievable. None of them knew what she was talking about, and a castle sure as hell wasn't within miles of Gainesville.

The smell of mold and damp stones and that subtle hint of salt wafted through the air. Regret was her new companion as she milled through her thoughts. She should have left instead of saving his ungrateful ass. She curled on her side, the cold, dirt floor sending a shiver through her chilled body. Her eyes flashed to the bedroom when Derek had smacked her across the face. It was as if she could still feel the sting of his backhand. Did he feel guilty? Did he even miss her?

Her gut tightened. She couldn't tunnel herself into despair, not now. Scanning the cell, she looked for the makings of an escape plan attempting to form in her exhausted brain. A pile of hay sat in the corner and a pot resided by the door.

She managed to get to her feet, feeling the gritty stones disintegrate between her fingers. Pain burned in her hand, causing her vision to narrow. She leaned into the wall, fighting the darkness as she let out a few long breaths to clear her vision. She might have dug out all the shards of glass, but it'd done nothing for the pain. The river had likely increased her risk for an infection, and having Theodoric dig his grubby hands into her skin to fish out a few pieces hadn't helped either. Tearing a strip at the end of her shirt, she fashioned a bandage.

She slid her other hand through the bars of the small window set in the door and felt for the lock. The metal hole and locking mechanism seemed simple. As a firefighter, she'd broken into her own fair share of buildings, but sometimes the simplest-looking locks were the absolute worst.

She didn't have lock picks or any of her other tools, but she had her knife. She dug into her boot, her chest fluttering as she grasped the hilt. It wasn't retractable like a pocketknife, but it was one of the few possessions from her parents she'd kept. Her hand tightened around the ribbed hilt. The black blade practically glowed in the candlelight, begging to be used.

She sent a silent prayer to her parents and an apology to hopefully not mess up the knife they'd left her. She wedged it in and began her work.

Learning how to pick locks had been a dreadful experience, but she couldn't bust down every door. The department used to have an old locksmith who volunteered with them. He found amusement in locking them in his homemade-lock-breaking-training contraption. Amaris may have cursed each time she'd been locked in there, but she was thankful now. After another minute or two, the mechanism turned, and the door shifted. A single push swung it open.

With her knife in hand, she approached the steps, prepared to battle her way out. The moon's light was her guide, allowing her vision to adjust to the darkness as she crept up the stairs and through the gate. The wind bristled through her hair, the clouds moving at a rapid speed, guarding and revealing the moon in bursts, but her eyes caught above. What should've been a dark sky with only a few stars was a beautiful arrangement of constellations and a vividly bright moon. She rubbed her eyes. Not a single crater marked its surface.

Her heart sped up. She leaned against the wall, digging her nails into the stone to fend off the panic. Nothing about the last twenty-four hours made a lick of sense, but she couldn't stay and attempt to decipher the shit fest.

With her back to the wall, she moved around the corner. The wind continued to blow a scent she hadn't experienced in years. It brought a swarm of memories to light—her father standing her on a surfboard and her mother in the light of a campfire.

Propelling herself forward, she lunged into a full sprint. Her breaths were loud, coming in short bursts as her legs burned and a coppery taste seeped into her mouth. She was exhausted but couldn't let it stop her. A force drove her forward, whether it be adrenaline or fear, but she kept running. She sprinted through the arch. No one chased after her, but she careened forward and toppled into the sand.

She brushed the particles from her face, rubbing the grit between her fingertips. It wasn't the same arch. With the castle to her back, she peered out into the vast darkness. A wide expanse of long grass grew in the sand around her. She went to turn back, but the rolling of the surf was a chorus in her ears.

It couldn't be. The distinct crashing of waves was no stranger to her. It pulled at her chest, calling her to the beach. The next wave hit. The warm pull within her chest grew, and it was as if the sand latched onto her feet and tugged her closer.

She returned her knife to the confines of her boot and squished her fingers through the granules. A single breath held back her hesitation. Amaris hadn't stepped foot in the ocean since she'd been rescued on a nearby shore the night of the shipwreck.

She didn't know how it was possible, but the ocean was here. A louder crash erupted, and a force had her stepping toward the powerful and turbulent current rolling up the shore. She dragged her hand down her face. What if she wasn't in a hospital bed? What would that mean? She sucked in a breath and dared a step closer to the powerful body of water before her. She needed to see it with her own eyes, to feel that it wasn't an anomaly. A wave misted her face. She paused but licked the salt from her lips. It was real.

Amaris took one more step, but before another wave could send its droplets over her, arms wrapped around her neck. Her nails dug into her assailant's leather coat, but they only brought her to the ground and strengthened their grip.

Pinned in the sand, breathless, and on the verge of losing consciousness, Amaris took one more look at the ocean coming up to meet her before she passed out.

CHAPTER 10

Theo

THEO SAT WITH his knees spread on either side of the toilet as his stomach heaved again, the contents climbing his throat. Wiping the edge of his lip with the back of his hand, he sat back on his heels.

He hung his head, praying to the gods to rid him of the nightmares, the torment, or at least his headache. His fingers brushed against the cut on his forehead. Thankfully, it'd scabbed over in the night. He draped the short strands over it and leaned back over the toilet as another bout of nausea churned in his stomach.

There was a knock on the washroom door. His shoulders sagged as he eyed the latch secured in place.

"Theo," Gris called from the other side, "you've ignored two summonses from servants. We're going to be late."

Theo flushed the evidence of his dread. He lifted the latch and cracked the door. "I'll be out in a moment."

"Did you not wash your hands?" She crossed her arms, settling her gaze on the dry porcelain sink.

He rolled his eyes and let out an exaggerated groan as he turned on the faucet and eyed her through the crack, showing her the hard scrubbing of his fingers. Gris wasn't satisfied. She never was. Theo opened the door completely and stepped into his room in nothing but his undershorts and a lose sleep shirt. Gris had seen him hundreds of times in this manner during the war, but even though her tastes lay elsewhere, he still scoured the floor desperately looking for a clean shirt.

Gris drew the navy-blue curtains open to flourish the room in its natural light. Theo averted his eyes from the sun attempting to blind him as he went about his room and assessed the cleanliness level of various shirts and trousers to pick something appropriate for the meeting with his father.

Now that he was home, he could sport what he wished to. After wearing nothing but his uniform for years, he was eager for something else. They all were. Gris even wore a pair of black leather trousers and a matching vest.

"Here." Gris stood with a cotton shirt hanging from her finger. "You could try grabbing one hanging in the wardrobe."

Theo snatched the clean shirt from her and stepped into the washroom to change. He peeled off his sweat-soaked sleep shirt and let it fall in a heap on the floor. The chill of a breeze pricked the hairs along his back. He was exposed. He hastily dressed before returning to his bedchamber to secure his sword and dagger at his hip.

Yesterday's events played in his mind, but each thought brought a stronger pound to his head. He settled on the edge of his bed, pulling back his covers to hide the sweat line seeping into his sheets.

"Why does it smell like musty socks in here?"

Gris wrinkled her nose and began tossing dirty clothes in a small basket set beside his wardrobe. He eyed his disaster of a room. Slowly, he was turning into Adelaide. His sister had the messiest bedchamber, with clothes discarded across every piece of furniture and her blankets rumpled under her bed.

He used to take pride in keeping the space tidy, but it was a chore to keep it up. He'd banned any servant from entering his room since he returned from the war, but apparently, they were well-needed. His desk was piled with old battle plans and letters he'd yet to return. Even his personal bookshelf was bursting and spilling its contents onto the floor. Stacks of books piled around the bookshelf, and smaller tomes were shoved into nooks and crannies.

"Must be my species." He sent Gris a flat smirk, but she wasn't impressed and instead sauntered toward the door.

"Let's go before your father and Bennet have a fit."

Theo followed her through the manor. The servants were active and moving with exuberant energy. He didn't want to think about why, but his brother's Conjugation was in a few weeks, and his stepmother would no doubt begin pestering him about escorts.

The dark-green curtains were pulled back, casting rays of light through the halls and the paintings lining them. The vaulted ceilings always were a breath of fresh air, keeping the space from feeling as if it were pressing in on him. But today was different.

Theo had spent hours replaying the events with Amaris but had come to no natural conclusion. He'd even pondered Isabel's words, *aslorn per de eclahard,* but he hadn't had the energy to take a walk to the library and scour the shelves for an answer. He knew Pricilla, one of the librarians, would help aid in his search for the phrase, but he hadn't wished to bother her last night.

Upon his return, Pricilla had handed him a list of books she'd made while he'd been away. Before he'd left, they'd shared their favorite titles with one another, recommending their latest reads. She had interesting tastes, but she'd never failed to pique Theo's interests.

They rounded the next corner, and he felt the ceiling shrink as they grew closer to his father's study. He wished for a moment to breathe, to hide in one of the alcoves or find a space to retreat in the library. He didn't want to think about the threat looming over Duncaster or the new nightmare plaguing his mind from last night.

The God of Death's talons scratched along the edge of his mind, whispering judgment in his ear. He'd been there. Kedes's claws had wrapped around his soul, digging out all he'd done.

Theo released a hot breath as Gris stopped at the door. She turned to look over her shoulder, and her hazel eyes shone back at him. He couldn't tell what she meant to convey in that single glance, whether it was a plea or simply an apology for what they were about to endure.

When they entered his father's study, Bennet was already seated before his father in a heated discussion, and Gerard had taken up a space beside a bookcase with a gold clock set into the wood. Gris slid to the back corner, crossing her arms and legs as she leaned into the wood paneling.

Theo approached his father, who gave him a disdainful look as he settled in the seat beside Bennet. Brushing his hands through his hair, he attempted to look somewhat presentable, but he knew his father tracked every wrinkle.

A small bouquet of snowdrops with drooping white pedals sat upon the desk and seemed far more interesting to Theo than his father's glare. A beautiful flower able to be grown even under the coldest of conditions. Theo had once picked snowdrops every week with his mother to set them in that very vase.

Theo remembered a particular time when the crisp bite of Whitereign was settling upon Luana and, with it, the foreshadowing of a disastrous Darkreign with heavy snowstorms.

Do you know why we plant snowdrops? his mother had asked him. Theo, only a child at the time, had grinned as she wrapped him in his cloak and slid mittens over his small hands. *Because Father loves them.*

He'd beamed with a half-toothy smile. He'd lost a tooth the night prior, after sneaking a piece of hard sweets from Ms. Borstad in the kitchen.

His mother had laughed and flourished her radiant smile at him, throwing her own cloak over her shoulders. She'd kneeled beside Theo and placed her hands against his rosy cheeks. *Your father only loves them because I do. I want you to remember, Theo, when you find that special someone, remember every single detail about her. Write down her favorite flower, the way she takes her tea, the crinkle of her features when she laughs.*

That's a lot to remember, Mama.

Yes, it is, but it will show her you care. His mother had stood and braced her newly showing pregnant belly as she took his hand and led him into the cold.

"Not only are tenants disappearing," Bennet said, pulling Theo back into the stifling heat of his father's study, "but we came upon Lord Freville on our travels back. He was murdered."

Theo's muscles stiffened. Hearing it again was all too real. He expected to come home from the war and spend the next few years training to take Bennet's place, not dealing with the beginnings of another fight.

"She was standing over the body and everything," Gerard said, smirking from his spot against the bookcase.

Theo couldn't understand how Gerard managed to wiggle his way into Bennet's graces. More superior men would've made a fine second. Theo wasn't sure how he became a lieutenant either.

His father leaned back in his chair, running his hands along the edge of his graying beard. Rings of purple sat above his sun-spotted cheeks, making his mismatched eyes more menacing. His eyes used to both be the dark brown his left one was, but an unfortunate scar marred the right side of his face, taking with it the vision and color of his right eye.

"Where is this supposed murderer?" his father asked.

"In the dungeons. We attempted brief questioning, but the woman was spouting lies and nonsense," Bennet answered.

Theo felt his father's gaze fall to him, and when Theo raised his head, he narrowed his dark eye at him.

"What did you discover?"

"She's adamant she didn't murder Lord Freville, and I don't know if she possessed the strength to—"

"Of course she does," Bennet interrupted. "Randolf, this woman is a lying wench who played into her dramatics. She was covered in Freville's blood with no other explanation for the scene we found."

"We are sure she's the murderer?" his father asked.

"No," Gris interrupted, pulling herself from the wall before Theo got a chance to speak.

Theo whipped his head in her direction as she strode to Bennet's other side. Bennet gripped the edge of the chair, his nails digging into the armrests. Crinkles set in above his father's brows at Gris's disrespect for the chain of command, but Theo bit his tongue.

Where is she going with this?

"Of course she is," Bennet clapped back.

"No, she's not," Gris snipped. "Did you see her hand or the wounds in Freville's body? She couldn't have had the strength to do that much damage. We also didn't find a single weapon."

Theo eyed Gris but still refused to step in. Her logic seemed reasonable.

"What makes you say this, Sergeant Salter?" Theo's father asked, giving her the floor.

"She has a broken hand, and there were squirms in the body. I assessed it when we returned, and parts of it were covered in them. He had to have been dead at least a day for them to gather."

"But the body hadn't been touched by a scourge or other ravenous creatures," Bennet cut in. "It was a fresh killing."

"No, it wasn't," Gris said through gritted teeth.

"Quiet," Theo's father shouted. "A heinous crime has been committed on Fastrada land, and the one responsible will pay the consequences."

"Randolf, I request to interrogate her for information. We need to learn what she knows regarding these disappearances," Bennet said.

Theo's attention snapped to Bennet. To keep the laws of morality, the law didn't allow for torture unless the accused was, without a doubt, conspiring against the kingdom or in extreme cases.

If his father granted an interrogation, Bennet would drag Theo along with him. Gris's wife, Sephardi, was their usual interrogator, having performed many during the war with Theo at her side, but he hadn't checked if she'd returned yet.

Theo's hand grasped the hilt of his dagger. During the war, he'd been taught to break someone to pieces but never how to pick up his humanity afterwards. Sephardi had told him to remind himself why they interrogated, for their safety, the people they loved, but Theo didn't think he'd be able to do it, to hear Amaris's screams as he pried information from her.

His father inhaled deeply, taking in both Gris's and Bennet's outbursts. Theo pulled himself from his daunting thoughts and watched Gris as she sent her eyes flaring at Bennet.

"We can't interrogate her nor keep her locked in a cell without sufficient evidence," Theo blurted out, ignoring Bennet's heated glare as he faced his father. There was a subtle raise of his brow, and Theo knew his father wasn't pleased.

"I have every right to protect my people," his father began. "What other evidence do we have against the woman?"

Theo gripped the small strands of his hair tickling the nape of his neck. They had nothing. It was hard, either way, to pin the murder on her or absolve her completely from any wrongdoing. She'd taken his dagger and aimed it at him.

"What we've presented is enough—"

"Bennet, we'll hold off any interrogations for now. I wish to have an audience with her before I make a decision."

"But, Randolf—" Bennet began.

"You're dismissed," his father said, waving his hand toward the door.

Never once had Theo seen his father dismiss Bennet in such a manner.

Bennet stormed from the room with Gerard in tow, and it slammed with a thunderous jolt.

His father reclined back, resting his hands upon his abdomen. A simple position one would believe to be of respect or informal, but with him, nothing was without power.

"Sergeant Salter, is there anything else you wish to tell me regarding the situation?"

Gris opened her lips but paused. Her finger coiled the end of her hair, but she shook her head.

"Then you're dismissed as well."

Gris retreated from the study, but not before Theo spotted the tightening of her jaw and clenching of her fists. It seemed neither of them could feel a moment of resolve in his presence.

His father relinquished the safety of his desk to take a casual stance by the window. Almost every room had expansive windows lining the walls to allow the natural light to bathe the room in brightness, but not here. A single window centered in the wall was all the study held. All the dukes before his father shared the office, and Theo always wondered why such a small view of the bay was taken for the prize office of the leader of Luana.

His father slid off his pristine frock coat, the golden buttons reflecting the sunlight. Underneath he wore a matching brown waistcoat. He was always a man to dress well—being the duke brought that out in him. His shoes were always shined, not by him of course, and his hair was never tousled like Theo's but slicked back with a leather tie.

"How are you?"

Theo's shoulders released their tension, having prepared for the snapping of his tongue, but that might have been far worse. "I'm well." Theo shifted in his chair, crossing his arms over his chest. A simple lie, but he saw no reason to be spilling what haunted his thoughts or had his head pounding.

His father's gaze remained fixed out the window, but it was beyond

Theo's comprehension what he was even staring at. The charged atmosphere between them was more enticing than anything outside that window.

"We have yet to discuss your time overseas, but I was kept updated throughout the war. It devastated all of us to hear you went missing after your first several seasons of service."

Theo forced his mind shut to the vivid images attempting to leak through. Maybe it devastated Adelaide, Jeremiah, or even Genevieve, but Theo doubted his father would've shed a tear for anyone. Theo had been avoiding him since he'd returned home, and then the issues in Duncaster further pushed their discussion of the war.

"I don't see that as a pressing matter," Theo said. "More important things are worth discussing."

"Lord Freville's murder."

"I presume Bennet explained our situation?" Theo asked.

His father relinquished his attention from the bay beyond the window and offered a single nod.

"When the sailors in Duncaster discovered I was a soldier, they despised the idea of our presence. Then the fight broke out, and some of them got away on their ship. They spoke Tendasy. It can't be a coincidence that the city is struggling, and we discover an enemy ship within our docks."

"It's not uncommon to find Tendasy speakers outside of a tutoring session." His father returned to his desk.

"If their language isn't incriminating, the pistol aimed at my head was surely enough."

His father's even breaths faltered, but he resumed the steady cadence of an old man's breath.

"They can't be the only ship coming to Duncaster's port. If it were, that would be some luck we had," Theo began. "No, I believe these disappearances are due to slavers."

"Theodoric—"

"Think about it, Father. First, it's beggars and poor boys, who might not be missed—"

"What about Philip Veduco and Lord Freville? I doubt slavers would kill their cargo."

Theo still felt the unease at the lack of respect given to the common people, but he wanted his father on his side and would play his game. "Phillip Veduco is still missing, but what if Lord Freville's death was completely unrelated? He was known for his gambling debts. We must also focus our efforts on the other missing tenants, not only Lord Freville. I fear, with the vulnerabilities from the war, slavers have begun infiltrating our cities."

"What about these traders who spoke Tendasy? What was their cargo?"

"We checked their manifest they left with the clerk but didn't have the opportunity to search their ship. They were spice traders, and their papers said they were from the Vukubua Islands, but they could easily forge their documentation." Theo dragged his hand down his face, feeling exhaustion settling in his bones and the steady beating against his skull.

"What of this woman you found in the woods? Does she reside in Godwin?"

Theo forced himself to sit taller in his chair. He would get one chance to speak his thoughts on the matter, even though they still jumbled around and switched sides with each passing heartbeat. "The woman we found speaks Akaric well, but I don't recognize her accent. Her allegiances are unknown, but she said she was from *Gainesville*."

His father tested the word, playing with the way it slipped off his tongue. "I've never heard of it."

"Neither have I. She could be deranged for all we know or traumatized."

"Traumatized?"

"As Gris had said, Freville had been killed long before we found her, but with the state of her injuries, she was in an attack."

"If she's injured, is it possible she obtained these from the assault? What are the state of her injuries?"

"An injured hand and scrapes across her body, but what has me questioning is how she injured it. She punched a mirror, and I found shards of it still embedded in her skin."

A silence settled over them as they both thought over what Theo set before his father. The tick of the clock behind Theo grew louder, and his heart beat to each strike of its hand.

"Do you believe her to be dangerous?"

After what Theo experienced during the war, he believed anyone had the capability to be dangerous, but something still didn't sit well with him regarding Amaris or their entire situation. Isabel again passed through his head and her words. *Aslorn per de eclahard.*

"I don't know what I believe of her." Theo leaned back and slid his hand through his hair.

"Where did you get that?"

Theo hesitated before re-covering the gash on his forehead. "It's nothing." He wanted to ignore his father's momentary attempt to be a decent father for once in his miserable life.

His father leaned back and smoothed down his beard as he sighed. "I want to keep this woman close. Regardless of whether she is to be incriminated as Lord Freville's murderer or not, she might have insight into these nefarious deeds plaguing Duncaster."

"Do you intend to keep her in the dungeons until her identity is irrefutable?"

"I'm not sure what her fate will be. I will assess after I've spoken with her myself."

Theo released a breath, but it was immediately sucked back in as the door was thrown open. Theo stood and spun on his heels, his hand ready on his sword.

"You may drop the theatrics. It's only me," Luther said, waving his hand toward Theo's weapon.

His older brother had a knack for intruding in others' conversations.

He was the closest resemblance to their father out of the Fastrada children, showing the predominant features of light-brown hair and dark eyes. His hair was even pulled back like their father's.

"What are you doing here?" Theo asked, dropping his tense stance. He'd shifted himself in front of his father, but even as he settled on the corner of his father's desk, his heart still pounded.

Luther was finely dressed, straightening his brown shirt, pressed free of wrinkles, and fussing with his golden waistcoat, embroidered with vines. He always preferred attire to make a statement rather than for function.

"I hear you've returned from your extended journey with a murderer," Luther answered, his lips drawing into a grin. "I would much like to meet him."

"Her," Theo corrected, refraining from snapping as he dug his fingers into the fabric of his trousers, attempting to calm his quick pulse.

"Excuse me?" Luther responded in his pompous voice.

"The alleged murderer is a woman."

"Alleged?" Luther tapped his long, pale finger against his chin. "Interesting, that isn't what I heard Gerard and Bennet grumbling about."

"Enough," their father barked. "We've already been over this. Theodoric, see to your duties. Luther, we have business to discuss."

Luther flashed his smirk at Theo, his dark-brown eyes matching their father's in every way possible. It was only fitting Luther was to assume their father's title. It suited his arrogant ass.

Theo nodded his head to both before making a hasty exit into the hall. The door closed behind him, but his feet were like Ms. Borstad's evening stew, threatening to puddle beneath him as his heart continued to speed. He settled into a small alcove, hiding behind one of those ugly curtains.

His hand brushed the pommel of his sword. He was in his own home. He was safe. He slammed a hand over the talons threatening to claw at the edge of his mind. Kedes waited for him. He evaded him not once, but twice.

Theo opened his eyes and trained them across the wall. He stared at the grout between the stones, tracing it along the wall. His breaths came in short pants as he pushed the memory away. In all the books he'd read, the hymns his mother had sung, all of them had one conclusion. No one had ever lived after crossing a god.

CHAPTER 11

Amaris

AMARIS GRIPPED HER temples, wincing as a massive headache ensued. She begrudgingly rolled over as she reached for her pillow, but her hand scraped against stone. Her eyes shot open, and her hand reached for her throat. She was back in the cell.

She dragged herself to her knees, scraping dust from the wall as she stood. All her pain was real. The dungeon wasn't a dream. She wasn't lying in a hospital bed with sweat dripping down her ass crack. They weren't some back-country cult, either. The ocean outside discounted that theory. Amaris raked a hand through her hair, accepting the brief moment of numbness coursing through her right hand.

The reality caved in her chest. Before she could attempt another escape, the iron gate at the top of the steps flew open, the metal rattling against the wall. Their steps grew louder, or maybe it was the beating of her pulse in her ear. The lock clicked and the door swung open.

"You can't keep me here," she demanded for what felt the hundredth time. "I have rights!"

Alan stepped into the cell, his light-blue eyes striking a piercing glare as he strode toward her. He bent over, snarling in her face. "I don't care what you think you have."

Amaris recoiled, but he grabbed her arm, pulling her to her feet.

She struggled. *What was he told to do if I resist?* Every moment of defense for her self-preservation proved futile. Maybe she couldn't fight it.

"Where are you taking me?" She tried to bring a bit of oomph to her words, but they fell flat.

"You've won the favor of being presented to the duke." He grinned menacingly. "Now, let's go."

Where was she that she was being presented to a duke? Amaris recalled what Theo had said yesterday, but she thought he'd been crazy when he'd mentioned being a soldier in some kingdom.

Her thighs ached from riding, and she was starving, but she willed her body forward like every day at the fire academy, when all she wanted to do was stay down and curl into a ball. She glared up at Alan, unable to throw up her mask and keep the peace. He dug his fingers against her skin, pinching bits of flesh as he made for a fast pace up the stairs. She should've torn her arm from his hold and shoved him down the stairs, but with her luck, it would've only pissed him off.

They emerged into the daylight. Amaris had to squint against the blinding rays of what should've been beautiful sunlight, but all she wanted was the cover of darkness. They rounded the corner. It was a massive stone fortress. She was torn between the stunning beauty and the rage that filled her.

How is this place possible? That shivering ripple returned as it snaked down her spine. She couldn't be in Gainesville anymore, let alone Indiana.

As Alan dragged her up the elaborate steps, she thought about every impossible reality. She tripped at the top, and his only response was to grip her arm tighter and yank her forward. She shot him a menacing glare. He was wearing a billowing, maroon shirt rolled to his forearms. At least he was more presentable than the last time she'd seen him, but gone was his uniform. His square jaw was clean-shaven, and his ash-brown hair had seen a brush.

He threw open the doors, their loud boom emanating into the hollow space around them and swaying a candlelit chandelier made of brass loops hanging above their heads. "This way," he grunted, not that it mattered since he was still dragging her along.

They trekked down a hallway stretching with floor-length windows draped in forest-green, velvet curtains. Gray stones composed every wall around them, and the interior walls were decorated with paintings of creatures, vivid landscapes, and portraits. Her eyes lingered briefly on the faces, settling on one particularly familiar one, and she scoffed. The painting, however dreadful, did nothing to capture the true essence of Theodoric's eyes. They bordered more on dull and gray than the vibrant shade of green.

Alan dragged her down more hallways, getting her completely lost by the fourth turn. They didn't pass a single soul for how huge the place was. He wasn't as tall as Bennet or Theodoric, but his long strides were still annoying. She didn't know where she was, but she already hated this place, Alan, and most certainly, whoever the duke was.

They finally came to a halt in front of a set of exceedingly tall doors. They were decorated with carvings of elaborate battles instead of iron vines, and above the arching entrance was an arrangement of symbols. They swung open on creaking hinges, as if their mere presence willed them open. Alan forced her over the threshold and into a throne room. A pit grew in her stomach, along with the crushing reality that something unworldly had happened to her.

The slamming of the doors behind her brought her back to reality. Soldiers scattered the sides, parting for them and leaning against dark Gothic pillars. All the curtains were pulled shut and shrouded the room in an intimidating darkness. If they were trying to scare her, it was working. The only sounds were the jingling of the zippers on her boots, the crackling of the fire within the torches hanging from the walls, and Alan's heavy breaths in her ear.

Ahead was a dais and a large throne with vines wrapping around the armrests like snakes and a crescent adoring the high back of the wooden chair. She couldn't make out the rest with the man seated on it, but the blood drained from her face. Every part of Amaris's being screamed for her to rip her arm from Alan's hold and run.

She shifted her gaze from the throne as the soldiers grunted and sneered, their viciousness visible by their grips on the pommels of their swords. Everyone's stares were soulless, their eyes only beholding what they wanted to see, a murderer. Amaris was slowly regretting staying by Theodoric's side instead of letting him pass out so she could run for her freedom.

Her worry only dissipated for a moment when her eyes latched on to the one face among all the rest, the only one not drawn into a snarl. A single head poked out from behind one of the curtains. She had a square face with high cheekbones sitting below her green eyes, ones Amaris had become all too familiar with. Her black hair was Theodoric's, too, but where his had small waves, hers was sleek and pulled back into a long ponytail. Her skin was a complete contrast to his. Theodoric's had a tan glow, and hers was paler than Amaris's, with signs of sunburn along the bridge of her nose and cheeks.

Her eyes met Amaris's, but there wasn't shock or the twitch of her jaw. She stared at her, studying her. Alan shoved against her back, reminding her she wasn't in a staring contest with the floating head peeking out from the curtain. Amaris took a short breath, watching out of the corner of her eye, but the woman was gone.

Alan forced Amaris to her knees at the edge of the dais. She bit back what felt like the hundredth scream as she hit the floor. Her head dropped, her chin resting on her chest as she fought back the urge to cry. She needed to compose herself.

Someone before her cleared their throat, and several steps echoed to her right. A pair of black boots stood a few paces at the foot of the dais.

She hadn't prepared anything. Should she scream and demand to be let go or cry and plead it was all some misunderstanding?

Alan gripped her hair, pulling several strands out as he lifted her face. Amaris refused to make eye contact with the supposed duke, but her eyes snapped up to meet Theodoric's instead. He stood before the dais with his hand resting on the hilt of his knife, as if he were ready to strike her down. He rubbed a thumb along the edge, most likely contemplating whether to cut her head off or bleed her dry. He was a guardian, a soldier to the duke, but why was his portrait hanging on the wall?

Her throat constricted with the sandy-haired man standing behind the throne, but she forced her eyes from his taunting glare and finally acknowledged the duke. His jaw was hidden behind a light-brown and graying beard, but his defined cheekbones were a sharp contrast to the purple bags sitting below his mismatched eyes. One was a dark shade of shit brown that pierced her soul, while the other was a bleached white and threatened to pin her to the floorboards. A scar started from his right temple and ran through the eye, stopping short of his lip.

The man on the throne broke the deafening silence. "What's your name?"

Amaris held her lips tight. *No immediate proclamation of my death or torturing information out of me?*

The duke inclined his head to pierce through her silence with his beady eye. In the few seconds she had, she attempted to piece together everything she'd learned. Derek had always said to keep her eyes and ears open, taking in everything. She should've paid more attention instead of discounting everything as a dream.

"Your name," he bellowed.

Her anxiety-ridden thoughts were going to get her into further trouble. Her silence was definitely a cut to this guy's ego.

"Alan." The duke motioned with a simple wave, and Alan tugged harder at her hair, eliciting a short yelp. "This is your only chance to defend yourself, and you wish to throw it in my face. You can rot in the dungeons for all I care. I am at least giving you the decency of a trial."

"You call this a trial?" Jury, judge, and executioner all rolled into one.

"One I hope you take seriously before there are graver consequences," he threatened, grimacing.

Theodoric's grip tightened around his knife.

"You'd kill me?" Amaris looked to Theodoric, her voice cracking like she was some pubescent teen.

"My son will do what he must to protect Luana Bay. If that means ridding Magoria of a murderer, then so be it," the duke raged.

His son? Luana Bay? Magoria? A tightness in her chest overcame her breaths, as if a rubber band squeezed around her, taking every bit of life from her soul. *Where the hell am I?*

"Who are you?" Amaris was certain she was about to discover the biggest disaster of her life.

"If I give you the common courtesy of answering your question, will you answer mine?" he asked, and she nodded. "I'm Randolf Fastrada, Duke of Luana."

"Amaris Carter." She held strong against the fear she grappled with and pulled from Alan's grasp to hold her own head high. Keeping the bite from her words was going to prove difficult, but she stifled the rage settling beneath. It was routine, throwing up her mask to prevent a fight. She released a breath and allowed her mask to settle over her features. It would keep her alive for now.

"I was informed you were found at the scene of Lord Freville's brutal murder," the duke said.

"I didn't kill him," Amaris began. "It was dark, and I fell—"

The duke raised his hand, and Amaris pursed her lips. If she followed along, maybe she could get out of it. He shifted on his throne, eyeing the sandy-haired man behind him. "Chief Bennet."

"Lord Freville's blood taints your hands," Bennet began, descending the dais.

Amaris fought an eye roll for his dramatic display but immediately reminded herself she wasn't in a dream. She'd been kidnapped, and these people were dangerous.

"You were covered in it as you leered over his body, watching us and waiting to kill us next."

"I tripped," Amaris cut in. "I couldn't see a thing."

"Liar!" Bennet snapped.

Amaris recoiled against his intimidation as he took a last daunting step and kneeled before her. "Please," she begged, feeling her mask slipping away. "I want to go home." She didn't care about their fight or whether Derek would be drunk or sober. She wanted him, his protection.

She stiffened as Bennet's hand reached for her face, but Alan was behind her, holding her shoulder still.

"What a beautiful mark," he whispered only to her, the tip of his finger dragging down her cheek.

Her hand twitched as he slid his finger over the cut from Derek's ring, forever etched into her mind. *No, it was an accident.*

A dull ache spread across her skin as he pinched her cheeks and shifted her face to examine the cut and what felt like a bruise.

She tore her face from his grasp and her mask slipped. "Don't touch me." Fiery hatred swarmed her skin, prickling along the surface, but she forced it down again as Bennet sneered. She would only make matters worse for herself, but every muscle in her body wanted to fight. It was what Viv would want her to do.

"You're going to tell us why you're here and why you killed a member of noble birth," Bennet said, "before I slit your throat here and now."

The duke coughed, and Bennet's grip tightened around his dagger. Bennet stood and took up a stance beside Theodoric with his knife still firmly clutched in his hand and a vein bulging in his forehead.

Amaris returned her attention to the duke, who said, "I would like to hear your side of the story—how you came to Luana and how you came upon Lord Freville."

Amaris couldn't piece together the situation in her head, let alone explain it to anyone else. "I..." The words hung in the back of her throat as Bennet's eyes homed in. "I'm not sure what happened. One minute I was home and..."

The blue stars. Her mind emptied.

The duke cleared his throat, pulling Amaris back into the torch-lit throne room, encasing them in dark and looming shadows.

"I couldn't see a thing." She would contemplate the celestial anomalies later. "I stumbled on him, like you all did."

Theodoric raised an inquisitive eye at her before wincing and gripping the bridge of his nose. Amaris narrowed in on the squinting of his features and the clenching of his fist, but she quickly shifted her attention to the duke. "I couldn't kill anyone."

"You were covered in his blood and have the injuries of a fresh fight. No one else was in those woods," Bennet snapped.

"I ran away."

She immediately wanted to suck the words back in. She was expecting them to be a lie, but the cringe inside her when she told even the tiniest of lies was absent. She *had* run away. She'd run out on Derek.

"Where were you running from?" the duke asked. "From what my soldiers describe, there wasn't a city or village for miles."

Every thought evaporated. Theodoric had asked her who she was running from in those woods, and she'd almost said the truth, but she couldn't bring herself to say it now. It was an accident. Derek didn't mean to hit her, and she shouldn't have run out on him.

"Where were you running from?" The duke's voice carried through the room, silencing the even breaths of everyone around her.

Gainesville was on the tip of her tongue. Would they believe her? Theodoric had spouted all sorts of places Amaris had never heard of, and he didn't seem to recognize it when she told him the other night. What if it didn't exist to them?

Panicking, she looked to Theodoric, but he didn't acknowledge her as his eyes pinned to the floor, and he gave his head a slight shake.

The duke raised a suspicious brow. "Are you a slave?"

"What?"

"If you're not a slave and you claim you weren't the one behind this attack, we will need proof of your innocence."

Amaris tried to keep her focus on the duke, but Theodoric continued to pull her gaze as he rubbed the back of his neck, and his chest moved at a swift pace.

Proof? Amaris didn't have any evidence. She was still proving to herself what the hell happened. The room began to shrink in on her. "I don't have anything."

A murmur went through the crowd, but the duke didn't silence them. Amaris studied his stony face, not a single bit of emotion crossing his features.

"As you are unable to provide evidence to the accusations against you—"

"Wait—"

"Do not interrupt me!" the duke roared.

Bennet's eyes flared with excitement, but there wasn't rage in Theodoric's gaze. He didn't even appear to be listening anymore.

"I will have no choice—"

"What about what happened in the river?"

The crowd silenced. The tapping of the duke's ringed finger was the only sound emanating through the throne room. Her one stupid act of pure instinct could possibly be her only mercy.

"I saved him."

Theodoric's face snapped up to meet hers, finally pulled back into the conversation, but his face was draining of color. Amaris kept a hesitant eye on him.

"What do you mean you saved him?" the duke asked, but the slight flicker of anger within his features wasn't aimed at her but at Theodoric.

"His horse bucked him off into the river. I'm the one who jumped in and got his head out of the water." Amaris bit back against the words she wanted to fling at the duke and forced herself to be reasonable. If she continued to fight back, she would end up spending the rest of her life locked in that cell. "Would a murderer have rescued your son, jumped into a dangerous river, risked their own life?"

Theodoric stiffened as she hooked him. He gripped the hilt of his dagger and opened his lips as if to say something, but he closed them.

The duke stroked his beard, pulling at the edges. "How did you come to possess such talents?"

"I'm trained," Amaris uttered. Likely no one here would know what a paramedic was either.

"You're a mystique then?"

Gris had asked her that. Was that their version of a medical professional?

The duke leaned forward, interlacing his hands as he rested them upon his knees. His white eye glared at her like it was reading her thoughts.

"I'm trained in the medical field well enough to know your son has a severe concussion and has been struggling with a headache ever since the incident."

Theodoric's stoic expression broke with the widening of his eyes. The duke turned sharply to him, but Theodoric trained his focus on Amaris.

"How do you know that?" he asked, his words coming out quick with his breaths.

"As I said, well-versed in the medical field." Amaris sharpened her eyes, attempting to give him that soul-piercing glare his father was immaculate at.

"Is anyone able to corroborate Miss Carter's story?" the duke shouted.

Gris hadn't told them about the river or that Amaris had given up multiple opportunities to escape. She scanned the crowd, but Gris was nowhere to be seen.

"She's lying," Bennet snapped. "Gris pulled him from the river."

Amaris glared at Theodoric, begging him to remember something and stand up for her, but his cheeks were stark white, and he widened his stance. *Is he going to faint?* Amaris tried to stand and lunge for him, but Alan slammed against her shoulders and forced her back to the ground.

"Captain," the duke barked, "can you attest to any of this?"

Theodoric jerked his gaze from his father, back to Amaris, but his eyes were wide, and his chest heaved. He rapidly blinked as his fingers released the hold on his dagger and twitched. Her gut tightened. He staggered and reached for his head. She struggled once more to run toward him, but she was too late. Theodoric collapsed.

A gasp hung over the crowd, but Amaris was out of Alan's reach and kneeling over Theodoric before the duke was out of his seat. She dropped her cheek to his face and slipped her finger over his pulse. Thankfully, he was breathing, and his heart was beating. A crowd gathered behind her and a hand gripped her wrist.

"Step back!" Bennet seethed.

"Let her," the duke ordered, kneeling on Theodoric's other side.

Amaris didn't stop to question him. She opened Theodoric's eyes and checked his pupils, but neither of them seemed larger than the other. Her hands brushed the sides of his face, but he didn't feel feverish. Why had he passed out? She fussed with the tie around his collar, opening the top of his shirt. Maybe his concussion was worse than she expected.

She reached for his wrist to check his heart rate, but her hand felt a warm substance. Blood seeped from small crescent moons in his palm and stained his fingernails red. *What if it's not the concussion?* She rubbed her knuckles into his sternum. He needed a hospital, or at least more than whatever a mystique was, but what if a hospital didn't exist?

Theodoric grimaced and squirmed beneath her hand. His eyes fluttered open, and Amaris sank back on her heels. His stunned gaze jumped to the faces crowded around him as he pushed up to his elbows.

The duke settled his hand on his shoulder. "Are you all right?"

Theodoric ripped his arm from his father's touch, and he stood. He swayed for a moment, and Amaris gripped his arm to steady him. His eyes bore into her, and she quickly pulled back.

The chatter of the room stilled as Theodoric headed toward the main doors.

"I have a proposition," the duke announced, and Theodoric stopped short. "You can prove your innocence as Luana Bay's mystique."

How would that prove anything? "But I'm innocent!"

"That is still to be seen," the duke roared. "You'll remain here and provide care as you have my son to the people of Luana. In time, you will either prove your allegiance, and therefore innocence, or"—the word was a threat in itself—"if you prove to be a murderer...well, I have no problem with my son spilling your blood on this very floor."

Amaris swallowed. His threat was almost like a promise that, one day, he would personally fulfill. It filled her with dread. The doors slammed open and startled her as Theodoric stormed into the hall, fuming.

CHAPTER 12

Theo

WHY DID SHE save me? Again, Theo had been spared from death when he didn't deserve it. The Goddess of Life laughed at him, as if Kata pulled the imaginary strings of his life. His fate might have been in her hands, but he didn't want to cheat death anymore.

He wiped the blood leaking from his palm against his trousers and stormed through the halls. Theo couldn't breathe, couldn't think. He needed to know how he'd survived after being thrown from his horse. He threw open the training room doors. His eyes fastened on Gris. Her leather-clad legs were drawn tight to her chest as she ducked behind a rigged barricade of chairs. Her breath halted, but she didn't acknowledge his presence until her fingers released her bow, and her arrow landed in the center of the target.

"What happened in the river?"

Gris met Theo's furious glare with her lips scrunched and a knowing glance in her eyes. She relinquished herself from her hideout and settled on the edge of the archery platform, her feet skimming the ground. "Who brought it up?"

"Amaris." Theo couldn't control his anger or whatever else was swirling beneath. He crossed his arms to keep his fingers from drawing more blood.

Gris's shoulders dropped, and she sighed. "I figured you'd find out sooner or later."

"What happened?"

What had been so dreadful that Gris kept it from him? He knew he'd gone into the river but hadn't had time nor the desire to ponder the exact details of the situation. No, he was more concerned with Kedes attempting to drag him into the cracks of the realm.

"Theo, are you sure you want to—"

"Now."

She hung her head. "After you went over the edge, I... Theo, you know I can't swim. Amaris didn't stop to think before she jumped." Gris spread her fingers over her thighs. "When we found you, your belt was caught around a branch."

Theo listened, but something was still missing. Something else happened.

"Theo, you weren't breathing."

Theo dropped beside Gris, all his thoughts lost to him.

"We pulled you out, but I was delirious. I'm so sorry. I was useless and stood there like a fool, but Amaris was calm. I first thought she was crazy when she leaned in to kiss you, but she was trying to breathe for you or something. Then she began pressing on your chest. I'm not sure what I saw, but it worked. When I came back with the others, you were alive."

Theo couldn't respond. *First, she kissed me? Second, she saved me?* Not only did she jump into a river, but she brought him back to life. The grim talons of Kedes weren't a dream. Her skillset must be extraordinary to be capable of performing such a miracle. Was that why she was running, to protect herself? With her skills, she would be worth a fortune, but she'd discounted his initial thought of slavery. Who was she running from? What else was Amaris hiding?

"What in the crack in the realm was that?"

Sephardi and Esaias charged through the doors and pulled Theo from his daunting thoughts. Sephardi crossed the room with her hands balled into fists and her brown eyes wide.

"Nothing," he shot back. To prove his health, he stood from the archery platform and crossed the room toward the wall of windows bathing the room in the afternoon sun. The heat was a needed warmth as it wrapped the room in a sauna.

"That wasn't nothing." The black swirls inked across Sephardi's tawny Soyenian skin stretched as she folded her arms across her muscular chest. She was daunting, to say the least, with her tall stature and strong legs. "You passed out in the throne room."

Gris whirled on him, but he shot her a glare. She had no room to talk after keeping what really happened in the river from him.

"I hadn't eaten is all," Theo lied, rubbing at his temples. His headache was growing inconvenient and further persisted with nothing to ease the ache. He was cornered but wouldn't allow his friends to bully him into revealing what really happened in the throne room.

"If you say you're fine, then how about a duel?" Esaias grinned.

Sephardi shoved him to the side. "This is not the time for—"

"Fine." Theo drew his sword, and a smirk crossed Esaias's face as they both entered the ring set in the center of the training room.

Theo kicked a battle-axe discarded on the floor. Sephardi stopped its slide with her brown leather boot. He would deal with her gritting teeth after he proved how fine he was. A good swing around the training room was precisely what he needed, not to be coddled. He cracked his neck and readied his stance.

"Are you sure about this?" Esaias asked.

Theo didn't wait for Esaias to get into position before he lunged at him. His blade was barely a weight in his hand as he wielded it against his cousin. Esaias met his blow, and the clashing of swords rang out through the room.

Each of Theo's moves was quick and calculated. He allowed his inner soldier to seep through the cracks in his mind and slide around his hand.

Where Theo struck, Esaias parried.

"If you wish to move to more pleasing topics than whatever that was, then we can gladly discuss the Conjugation." Esaias raised his brows as their blades pressed against each other.

Theo grunted and pushed off Esaias's sword, hurtling his attacks one after the other. The last thing he wanted to discuss was his brother's Conjugation. He'd avoided his stepmother earlier and her nagging to select an escort.

Esaias laughed and set to his own series of offensive moves. "You're still planning to seclude yourself up in your room with a book instead of a woman?"

It was easy for Esaias. He won the affection of every woman he passed, with his charismatic smile and bright-green eyes always on the prowl for his next nightly companion. Theo, however, didn't wish to attend a party with another noble his stepmother would attempt to betroth him to.

"Watch your weak side, Theo," Sephardi shouted over Esaias's games.

Theo grumbled, but he drew his dagger and blocked the next blow. Esaias had the uncanny ability to half pay attention in a fight and still win.

"I have an idea." Esaias smiled.

"Nothing brilliant comes when you say that."

Theo's anger began fading away with Esaias's quick jabs and laughs as he danced around him. Esaias had always been a skilled fighter, hailing from Mount Juniper. They were known for crafting legendary warriors. A smile curled on Esaias's lips as he guarded Theo's next blow and the next and the next.

"Hear me out," Esaias began, stepping back to allow them both a few breaths. He cocked his head and grinned. "Twins."

Theo rolled his eyes. "No."

Esaias groaned, dropping to the floor and making to kick Theo's legs out from under him. Theo jumped over his foot and rolled across the ring. Esaias whirled around, dropping his sword and readying his fists.

"How about you quit toying with each other and actually fight?" Sephardi cut in.

"Come on. You already have a date to the Conjugation."

"You mean my wife?" She cast her gaze to Gris, who smiled at her and blew a kiss from across the ring.

"How about a go, Sephardi?" Esaias grinned.

Sephardi rolled her eyes but stepped into the ring and popped her knuckles. Before Theo even stood, Sephardi sent a jab straight into Esaias's nose. Blood sprayed across the floor.

"Fuck off," Esaias shouted at her.

"Make me," she taunted.

Esaias lunged for her, but she rolled past him, coming to a crouch behind him while he stumbled forward. She shot up and sent her foot straight into his ass. He toppled out of the ring.

Gris jumped and shouted, "Kick his ass, love!" Her small hooray was extinguished as she caught Theo's icy glare.

He may have felt a bit of relief from his small tumble with Esaias, but he was still angry she hid the events of the river from him. He had a right to know the truth.

Esaias sank to the floor, grabbing a strip of linen from the wicker basket to dab at his nose. He winced as he stanched the bleeding.

"You could have spared him a broken nose," Theo shot at Sephardi.

She only shrugged her bare shoulders and unwound the brown wrappings from around her hands.

Gris extended a cloth to her to dry her hands of Esaias's blood. "How did your supply run go?"

Theo had instructed Sephardi to start stocking up on various supplies. After they returned from the war, he felt the need to stockpile Ms. Borstad's pantry and their shelves of herbs. He needed to be prepared for whatever troubled Duncaster. During the war, supplies became scarce. It pained him to think he may have been right and a threat could be waiting in the Black Sea.

"I've procured the extra herbs Pricilla listed. The rations were a little harder to come by, but Ms. Borstad is storing them as we speak," Sephardi said. "Next time, I'd like to accompany you to Duncaster instead of running around doing your errands." She raised a brow, but it wasn't a demand, only a request. Sephardi was one of the most loyal soldiers Theo had ever known. If he asked her to follow him to their deaths, she'd pick up a sword and guard his weaker side. "Gris updated me on the possibility of Deavopan's slave trade coming to Duncaster. Do you suspect they may find themselves in our harbor?"

Luana Bay wasn't an illustrious port city like Duncaster, but their docks were still crowded with fishing vessels and some merchants. With the chaos of the last few days, Theo hadn't thought much regarding Luana Bay's harbor and whether slavers would move along the coast trapping innocents.

"We can't be sure," Theo began. "Fortifying our coastal border and adding more patrols to the docks wouldn't be a terrible idea."

"I can start on a new sentry duty schedule," Sephardi suggested. "We'll run double shifts."

"Extra shifts won't be necessary yet."

"Is a guard rotation needed for Amaris?" Sephardi asked.

All their eyes snapped to Theo, pressing against the weight already threatening to shorten his spine. He hadn't stopped to think about what would become of her now. His father appointed her as the mystique, but she was still under investigation. It was a precarious situation, and one he'd never dealt with.

"I volunteer." Esaias grinned. "Does she need a guard in her bedchamber as well? I promise not to fall asleep. There are far too many activities to keep us occupied."

Theo didn't bother entertaining him with an eye roll or a remark. Of course, Esaias would be the one to attempt to woo a suspected murderer.

"Exclude Esaias." He attempted to protest, but Theo raised a hand. "Stay as far away from Amaris as possible and rotate with Alan with his watch by the stables."

"No fun," he groaned like a child.

"We'll start a rotation for Amaris, but I'll see how my father wishes to proceed."

Theo wasn't sure what his father's intentions were. He expected a decision to be made, but now they'd likely be playing nursemaid while Amaris went about her duties as the new mystique.

Sephardi nodded, watching him as he dragged his thumb along the hilt of his dagger. She wasn't only strong but also analytical, honing her mind like her own sword. Something wasn't sitting right with her.

"What is it, Sephardi?" Theo asked.

Esaias had given up on redeeming his pride and retreated to the table by the door, where a basin of water sat for him to wash the blood from his face. Gris again found herself perched on the edge of the platform, but she kept her distance from Theo. A silence sat between them.

"Do you think she did it?"

Theo prodded at his lip that still had a slight puffiness to it. He didn't know what to think. She'd punched him in the face, held his dagger to his heart, but also saved his life. Would a woman who murdered and butchered a man have risked her life for his?

"Time will tell," Theo mumbled before picking up his sword and taking a reprieve from her interrogation.

He needed to breathe, to examine everything out before him. His enemy no longer wore a breast plate with a yonedu pressed on the front, with its snarling jaw and color-shifting scales. No, his enemy waited in secret and milled through the same crowds he walked daily.

The high priestess's warning came to him. Godwin would rage a war in a heartbeat against Deavopan or even the entire Accords if their slavers crossed into their waters. If there was to be another war, Theo wasn't sure if he'd be able to pick up his sword again, to watch as he drained the life from another set of eyes.

CHAPTER 13

Amaris

THE WOMAN WHO had hidden in the back of the throne room raced after Amaris and Alan, grabbing him by the arm and whisking them up a back stairwell. They whispered back and forth, but even with Alan keeping a firm grip on Amaris's arm, her attempts at eavesdropping were futile. Their echoes turned to muffled speech as they bounced off the walls of the narrow passage.

She pondered the mystery within the throne room—Theodoric's widened gaze and his quick recovery as he sped into the hall. She'd wanted to chase after him, but Alan had held her back. The duke demanded Alan take her to be cleaned up and see her to her chambers, which Amaris understood, bars or not, was still another prison.

With Alan's hand wrapped tightly around her limb, she knew she wasn't simply a visitor or their mystique. She was a prisoner and would be carted around the castle like one. Her muscles clenched as she waited for Alan or the woman to slap iron chains around her, but they stopped at single door.

The woman whispered to Alan, "You better explain yourself later." She gave Amaris a side-eye. "It would seem you were sparse with your details."

Alan released Amaris's arm, drawing closer to the woman as he whispered, "I didn't know."

She eyed Amaris over Alan's shoulder, then leaned close and whispered something in his ear. He ground his teeth, pushing into the room. She didn't follow him but instead leaned into the frame, crossing her arms as she dragged her eyes over Amaris.

"What did you do to your hand?" she asked, grabbing Amaris's forearm.

Here we go. She waited for a shackle to latch on to her arm, but the woman released her grip.

"Accident," Amaris breathed.

Confidence radiated from the woman. A long leather jacket framed her shoulders and hugged her toned arms as it draped down to her knees. There was no denying that she must have been related to Theodoric. She was a third his size and barely old enough to drink a beer, but she still looked like she could kick his ass.

"Must have been one crack in the realm of an accident," she said, nodding for Amaris to follow her into the room.

Amaris stepped over the threshold into the biggest disaster ever. Not only had her life crashed in a matter of seconds, but she stumbled into the woman's room. With her slicked-back ponytail and neat presentation, Amaris expected her room to be pristine, with her comforter tucked and pressed like a military cot, but this was chaos.

A large four-poster bed with black drapes sat in the center and appeared to not have been made in days, with her comforter half on the floor and her top sheet poking out from under the bed. Off to the side sat a black-marble fireplace with red velvet chairs surrounding it. It was the only part of her room not covered in clothes.

The woman, too, struggled to cross the treacherous floor, tripping over a pile of rolled up shirts. The clanking of metal rattled as she kicked it under her bed. She relinquished her jacket, tossing it onto the mattress. Without a single care, she fell into a chair and draped her legs over the side.

"You can wash in there," she said, pointing to a small bathroom.

Amaris's legs anchored themselves to the floor. She shifted uncomfortably as they both studied her, but the woman's eyes didn't relinquish their focus from Amaris's hand.

"Do you have some rubbing alcohol and a bandage?" Amaris asked, raising her hand in a plea.

"Rubbing alcohol? Like rum?" the woman asked, turning to Alan, who leaned against the mantel with his hands hovering over those long knives.

"No," Amaris started. Whatever this place was, she hoped it didn't follow the rules of medieval medical practices. She didn't want to fend off critics trying to use mercury and bloodletting. "Something to clean it."

"Using alcohol instead of herbs? Is that a new medicinal practice?" The woman shrugged but continued before Amaris could get a word out. "I'm sure Pricilla will have something for you when she acquaints you with your duties."

"What about clothes?" Amaris folded her arms across her chest as she spotted her bra poking out from a rip in her shirt.

"I'll have something for you after you've bathed. The others returned reeking of horse dung and horrid body odor." Her gaze drifted to Alan as she inclined a brow.

Amaris refrained from smelling her armpit. Whether she smelled or not was the last thing on her mind. *Escape, run, get help.* She sucked in her lips, giving a wry smile as she tiptoed across the room and closed the door to the bathroom. A breath escaped her. She'd survived another encounter in this hell. Her eyelids squeezed tight, and she held her breath, counting to four before releasing it in a slow exhale. She had to stay calm. If she got worked up, there was no telling what they would say to the duke.

What if they kill me? Amaris remembered the hate-filled words spit back and forth between her and Derek. She held back the emotions climbing her throat. How was she supposed to prove herself when she didn't know where she was or how to be whatever a mystique was? Escape was her only option, but first a fresh pair of clothes, something to eat, and a decent bandage.

She took in the immaculate bathroom, a far contrast from the rest of the bedroom. She brushed her hand along the edge of a brass tub. A black-marbled vanity and sink sat to the side, and a toilet was posted in the corner. At least indoor plumbing existed. Her eyes caught a glimpse at her reflection in the vanity mirror. She kept her distance, not wishing another mirror to suffer under her wrath, or to see the cut and bruise marking her cheek. She turned from the mirror, fending off an emotional outburst. As warm water spilled from the spout, she tore off her clothes and slid into the tub.

Amaris couldn't even begin to fathom what had happened in the last forty-eight hours. The only explanation was she was in some other world. She'd never been one to believe in wormholes or alternate dimensions, but nothing explained the behavior of the soldiers, the kingdom, or even the ocean.

The ripped and bloody excuse for a bandage fell apart when she began unwinding it. Her hand was swollen and red around the small cuts. Biting her lip, she dared to touch one. Instant pain. She dipped her hand beneath the water, needing to do whatever she could to clean it. She expected to flinch or pass out from the soap, but it was a different sensation of pins and needles skittering up her fingers,

Am I trapped here? She didn't even know how she got here, let alone how she'd go about finding a way back home. *Bathe, clothes, bandage, food. Escape later.* After scrubbing the last remnants of her weary journey, she stepped from the tub. Her body may have been clean, but she still felt tainted as she caught another glance in the mirror. No matter how hard she tried, she couldn't wipe away the bruise on her cheek.

Learning all she could about Luana Bay and its inhabitants was her top priority. They all seemed hell-bent on incriminating her. If she wanted to get back and fix things with Derek, she needed to find a way to escape first, which meant doing a little interrogating of her own. Whoever this woman was, she wasn't welcome in the throne room. *Why else would she hide behind a curtain?*

Amaris wrapped herself in a thin towel and peeked into the bedroom. The woman still sat in her chair, twirling a blade between her fingers as she bickered with Alan. She wore a black blouse under her leather vest with rolled sleeves to reveal small, white scars scattered across her arms.

She looked the part of a warrior, but without a uniform or a sword or knife attached to her hip, Amaris questioned whether she, too, was one of these soldiers. With Alan's and Theodoric's lack of uniform today, maybe not everyone bore their weapons or their rank for the world to see. They certainly hadn't searched Amaris, but maybe they didn't expect her to be carrying an old heirloom in her boot.

The woman sprung from the chair as Amaris slid through the crack in the door. "I presume you prefer trousers, judging by what's left of your ripped garments, but I also laid out an assortment of dresses, skirts, and tunics. I have an older pair of trousers, but I question whether they'll fit you. Your curves are more prominent than mine."

Amaris slinked toward the bed, sifting through the pile of clothes. The material was odd, not cheap fabric, but sturdy and without any elastic. "Thank you..."

"Adelaide." Her tone was short but lacked the callous inflection Theodoric's held. "I also found these for you."

Adelaide handed Amaris a small wooden box filled with linen squares and a roll of cloth. Amaris wasn't sure if they were sterile, but she'd deal with that when she spoke with Pricilla. The soap and water would have to hold her over until then, but an aching feeling spread up her arm.

Amaris placed several of the linen squares over her knuckles, but Adelaide must have sensed her awkward struggle to hold her towel in place, along with the squares, while she wound the bandage around her arm. Adelaide reached for the bandage, but Amaris's towel slipped from the small corner she tucked underneath her armpit. Amaris snatched it off the floor, hauling it over her naked body. The inflamed cheeks on Alan's face were a match to her own as the flush spread up her neck.

Adelaide quirked a brow and tilted her head, flashing Alan a smirk. "A body is a body." Her glare persisted as he shifted uncomfortably, angling himself to face a different direction.

The towel remained wrapped around Amaris with Adelaide's assistance while she finished binding her hand, keeping sure to secure her fingers together as best she could. Amaris didn't want to risk further injuring them or, *God forbid, an infection.* Amaris grabbed the only pair of pants among the mass of clothes and a navy blouse before heading for the bathroom.

"You forgot this." Adelaide tossed Amaris a rigid black corset. "You'll need it." She placed her hands on her own chest and eyed Amaris's breasts attempting to spill from her towel.

What a confidence boost. Not only did Adelaide imply Amaris's butt was too big for her pants, but now she thought a corset was needed to keep the girls from dangling to her knees.

The pants were worn around the edges and barely fit, but Amaris managed to squeeze her *fat ass* into them. Luckily, they weren't leather, like Adelaide's current ones, but they were a strange material. Amaris squatted and hoped the seam of her ass remained intact.

Her fingers fumbled for several long minutes with the corset. Now she could begin to blend in, pretending she belonged while she deciphered where she was and how to get out of here. She contemplated the thought of revealing her true origin, but would they believe her? Bennet and the duke hadn't accepted a single word she said, but Adelaide seemed different. She hadn't once attempted to question her.

Amaris zipped up her boots. It barely crossed the boundary of normal, but it felt more like her. The pants, the dark colors, her work boots—all were her—a medieval replica of her work uniform.

Amaris pulled open the bathroom door. Alan had disappeared. Her body went rigid, scanning the room, on high alert.

"He left to scrounge something up from the kitchen. I would be famished if I were you," Adelaide said.

Adelaide tossed her a comb and plopped onto the bed, stretching her hands behind her head and crossing her boots. Her demeanor was the complete opposite of how Amaris thought her treatment would go. Her lax position didn't scream that she saw her as a threat, or maybe she was confident in her abilities to catch Amaris if she tried to escape.

She had to decide carefully whether she planned to tell the truth and to whom. They could think she was crazy. If someone had claimed to be from a different world back home, they would've been carted off to a government facility.

Alan returned with a red bottle and a few pieces of bread and cheese. Amaris's mouth watered at the sight. He poured himself and Adelaide a glass before retreating silently to his place by the mantel, while Adelaide returned to her chair. She rolled her eyes at Alan and poured a glass for Amaris, who gave it a good sniff and then again as it lured her in. It was divine, like strawberries. She took a sip and wanted to sink to the floor.

"What on earth is this stuff? It's delicious!"

"'What on earth'? What a foolish phrase," Adelaide whispered to herself and then completely dismissed it altogether.

Oh shit.

"Kusu. The duke likes to keep a steady supply from Jintaishu."

Amaris took another sip, savoring the kusu and pretending Adelaide's comment didn't short-circuit her brain.

"Most prisoners dine on stale bread and water. You should count yourself lucky."

"Lucky?" Amaris wiped the liquor spilling down her chin. "I'd hardly call being a prisoner in any form lucky."

"It could've gone differently," Adelaide insisted, raising her brows as she drank from her glass.

"How could it have gone any worse?"

"Watch your tone," Alan seethed, his fingers twitching as they hovered over his knives.

Amaris ignored his taunt, but the hairs along her arms spiked at the proximity of his weapons. "I'm not a murderer. This is all a big misunderstanding."

Alan scoffed, and Amaris refrained from ripping her boot off and chucking it at him.

She set her drink down and sat in the chair beside Adelaide, hiding her hand balling into a fist. "What gives him the authority to decide my fate?"

"He is the duke," Adelaide said as her gaze panned to her jacket upon the bed.

Amaris caught the subtle caress of her arm and the scratch of her thumb against one of her scars. Adelaide didn't wear any weapons for others to see, but she had those marks and bruised knuckles. She was a fighter, that was for sure, but why had she been hiding in the throne room?

Amaris thumbed her engagement ring and took a stab in the dark. "He's your father, isn't he?" Amaris waited in the silence, knowing she hit her mark when Adelaide blinked and swallowed her drink.

"Not many people catch that minor detail."

"After your father announced Theodoric as his son, it made sense. You two must be related with your black hair and green eyes."

"Our mother's." Adelaide smiled, swishing her kusu in a circle. "Beautiful traits from the Burchard side of the family."

"If he's your father, why were you hiding behind the curtain?"

Alan stopped mid-sip, his eyes shooting to Adelaide as she draped her arm over the back of her chair and prodded at the inside of her cheek with her tongue.

"Why did you run away?" Adelaide threw at Amaris.

She felt the unease as Adelaide studied her, but she tracked her eyes set on her engagement ring.

"Does it have anything to do with the rock on your finger?"

"No," Amaris lied, sliding her hand under her thigh. "Are you a soldier like your brother?"

Adelaide's fingers tapped against the back of the chair, her eyes shifting to the window as she took another drink. "No."

Even with her short reply, she'd offered Amaris more than anyone else. Her daddy issues were apparent, and she was young. She wasn't a soldier but looked well-versed in a fighting ring, which meant she was rebellious. If anyone here would go against the duke to help her, it would probably be her.

"You look like one," Amaris began, concocting the beginnings of her plan of flattery to befriend her. "Your attire is similar, and you look tough with your scars."

Adelaide's jaw clenched.

"I'd mind your words carefully," Alan seethed, resting his cup on the mantel.

Interesting.

Adelaide cleared her throat and rolled her sleeves down. "You're observant, but how I dress is no one's concern but my own."

Amaris was observant because she needed to be. One shift in the wind could send a fire crawling down the wrong hallway. One single symptom could be the deciding factor to give a medication. But now her life depended on it.

"My mistake," Amaris said, attempting to recover. "I thought, as the daughter of the duke, you'd have a similar position as Theodoric."

"You thought wrong," Alan grunted.

"Alan," Adelaide snapped.

Amaris's attempt at friendship would be a whole lot easier without

Alan interjecting his commentary.

"She is a lady of Luana. You'd be wise to speak with respect in the presence of nobility," Alan snipped.

Jut into my convo with one more word, pretty boy. I dare you. Amaris released the tension in her shoulders and straightened her back. "What about you? You don't seem to be much of a *noble*. If I didn't know any better, I'd say you're just an errand boy."

Alan's blades were in his hands, and he was across the space. Amaris's heart leapt. She didn't have a chance to raise her arms in defense, but Adelaide flung her knife through the air, colliding with both of Alan's with a simple clink. All the blades scattered across the room.

"Not a single drop of blood," Adelaide sneered. She reclined back in her chair, like attacking someone with a knife was an everyday occurrence.

Amaris dug her nails into her palm, staving off the attempt her heart was making to jump from her chest.

§

AFTER THE NEAR assault with his daggers, Alan took Amaris to a room, where she'd been locked up since. He'd smiled as he bolted the door behind him. He was going to be a pain in her ass. The room was a step above the cell, with a bed, a decent pillow, and a dresser. Alan informed her a washroom was down the hall. Apparently, her bathroom privileges were on their time as well.

Amaris laid on the bed, her head still pounding, since she didn't have access to ibuprofen or coffee. She'd already checked out the floor-length windows, and they opened, but she'd be scaling down a steep thirty or forty feet. As Amaris had leaned over the edge, her stomach had grown queasy. That was going to be her last line of escape.

A knock on the door pulled her from her planning, and Alan appeared in the doorway. "Supper time," he snipped, crossing his arms. "I'll be escorting you to the main hall."

Amaris refrained from groaning since she was starving and followed him, but also because she would need him on her side until she could get her hand looked at. Over the course of the last hour, the pain had intensified, and her fingers poking through the linen were now swollen tight and bruised.

Amaris cleared her throat as they walked the halls. "Can I speak with Pricilla?"

"Tomorrow."

"If I don't take care of my hand soon, it could get infected." It probably already had with how much it throbbed.

"You should have thought of that beforehand. Someone will fetch you in the morning to begin your duties."

"It won't always be you?" Her shoulders dropped. A small offering from the universe.

"I have more important duties to attend to than watching over you."

"Yeah, because running messages around is so important," Amaris muttered, skimming the ceiling with her eye roll.

He gripped her shoulder, pinning her against the wall. "Adelaide may have taken a liking to you, but I most certainly don't care for your tongue. A mystique hardly needs one to perform their duties. I suggest you keep whatever comments you have to yourself, if you prefer to keep your tongue intact."

If Adelaide saving her from Alan earlier wasn't enough, he confirmed Amaris's suspicions. Adelaide liked her.

"Fine," she mumbled.

Alan pulled back, satisfied from his power trip, and remained silent the remainder of their walk to the main hall.

Dining room was too small to describe it, and *cafeteria* didn't do it justice. Two long tables sat on either side of the room, with a path leading up to a fifth one. The duke was seated beside a woman who Amaris presumed was the duchess. She had deep, fiery hair so similar to Viv's that it hurt. Several others, who must have been important figures, sat on either side of the couple.

A small hand shot in the air and waved Alan over. He grasped Amaris's arm and tried leading her the other way, but most of the seats were already taken. He released a sigh and headed toward the older woman.

She was a petite lady with icy-blue eyes and blonde curls on the verge of turning silver. She wiped her hands on her apron and pointed to empty seats near her. "Alan, introduce me to your friend." The woman smirked. Her accent was different than the others, deeper and thicker.

"This is Miss Carter. She's to be the new mystique," he answered, but his tone was far from polite.

She raised an impressive brow at Amaris, and the corner of her lips turned up. "Been time since old mystique died. I'm Ms. Borstad, keeper of manor. Hope ready for position. Highly esteemed role."

Alan inclined a brow at Amaris, but Ms. Borstad was too busy fussing with the centerpiece to notice.

"I am." Amaris faked a grin for Alan to bear witness to her attempts at playing nice as he rounded the table and took the seat across from her. "Your accent is different. Are you from...err...here?" Amaris had already forgotten the name of the kingdom.

"Not from Godwin," Ms. Borstad exclaimed. "Immigrated from Mosfelkov long before war. Don't worry, not enemy traitor looking to stab heart in middle of night."

Amaris let out a nervous laugh. At least not everyone knew she was being accused of murder or Ms. Borstad *would* stab her in her sleep.

Amaris gazed into the clay bowl. Chunks of meat, potatoes, and vegetables swam in a broth. It reminded her of Derek's pot roast, as the scent of rosemary filled her senses, causing her tastebuds to salivate at the comfort. She sank deeper into her chair and took her first bite. It sure wasn't beef floating around, but Amaris was no stranger to gamey meat. With another bite, she closed her eyes and savored the delicacy, not taking notice as the seats around them filled.

"We'll discuss that later."

Amaris's eyes snapped open to see Theodoric seated beside her. She should've known with his daunting presence. A battle raged within her to ask of his health or ignore him after he'd thrown her in that cell.

Her spoon dug into her palm, but she turned and sighed. "How are you feeling?"

The side glance and short raise of his brow was all she needed for her blood to boil. He took a sip from his drink and returned to his conversation.

"Esaias, do you plan to visit your father now that we're home?"

Fuck him.

"Are you joking?" Esaias asked.

Amaris recognized him as one of her fellow kidnappers.

"You can't avoid your family forever."

"Watch me. My nieces and nephews will cling to every limb, begging me to stay. My father will have a line of curses to spew, and we won't even speak of how my mother will react."

Esaias's hair was a match for Viv's, too, and it made Amaris's stomach churn again. His deep-red hue was neatly cut above his ears. His skin however was vastly different from a normal ginger's. Where Viv was pale with freckles, Esaias had the same tan skin as Theodoric and not a single freckle marring it.

"Stupid boy," mumbled Ms. Borstad so only Amaris could hear. "Give up life for women and swords."

"Theo!" A scrawny boy with gangly legs, far from proportional to the rest of him, ran through the doors. Russet locks fell from their tie and flopped to his shoulders in a wavy mess. A bright smile flourished his cheeks, and his green eyes were wide with excitement.

Theodoric turned, and the child who couldn't have been any older than nine or ten slammed into him and wrapped his arms around his neck. "Don't ever leave me again!"

Theodoric let out a laugh, a real laugh, as he hugged him and pulled the child back to gaze at his face.

Another sibling? Amaris watched as Theodoric smiled at the boy. She didn't think he was capable of such a thing.

"It's good to see you, Jeremiah," Theodoric said, ruffling his hair. "I haven't had a chance to ask how your season in Oakheart was."

Jeremiah rolled his eyes. "Warin is bossy, and all Kaz and Lina wanted to play was *Afgiga*." His nose scrunched up, and he crossed his arms over his chest. "When I asked for them to teach me, they laughed and said it wasn't a game for *dowmi*."

"If calling you a fish was the worst of their insults, I'd say be happy and swim on." Esaias added with a smile, but Jeremiah stuck his tongue out at him. He returned the gesture.

Jeremiah slid into the seat beside Theodoric and dragged the bowl and utensils closer, immediately devouring the dish.

Esaias looked down the table, and his gaze landed on Amaris. He raised a seductive brow, causing his bright-green eyes to light up. They weren't like Theodoric's or Adelaide's but were similar to fresh blades of grass. His smirk sent her stomach to further turn to boiling knots. He turned his attention back to Theodoric and Jeremiah, his heated gaze not registering with anyone else.

Who the hell does he think he is?

"My family can wait another season, or even a year, before my next visit. Their last letter stated they would ponder attending the Conjugation. Colette is pregnant with her and Ricard's fourth child and isn't able to travel. Apparently, if one of them isn't able to, none of them are," Esaias rambled, leaning back in his chair and swirling his kusu in his silver goblet. He coughed before taking a sip.

Amaris grasped her own, downing half the glass in a single gulp. She could bathe in the stuff, but she'd settle for the aid with the increasing pain in her hand. Her thumb traced the design crafted into the silver. A bay with a fish in the center being stabbed with a knife.

"Must we continue with talk of the Conjugation?" Theodoric droned.

Conjugation? Amaris pondered the affair but thought better than to trouble her mind with anything other than gathering information for her escape. She pulled from their discussion, searching the main hall for Adelaide, but she wasn't seated at the head table, or anywhere else for that matter.

"Your looks are wasted on you," Esaias said. "You could have any woman as your escort, but you're going to choose some wrinkly old—"

Amaris dropped her spoon and choked on a piece of meat. She coughed and smacked against her chest, attempting to clear the blockage. Theodoric thumped her on the back, and the meat flew into her mouth. She turned away, spitting the contents into her napkin.

Esaias coughed. "I was going to say book, my dear, but I love where your head is at. Also, you must learn to swallow properly. I find spitting to be impolite." He smirked, taking a long drink of his kusu and refusing to avert his eyes from Amaris.

Her jaw dropped at his audacity. She gripped her spoon and thrust it in his direction. "Well, I find your vulgarity repulsive. I should take this spoon and shove it down your throat. We'll see who's gagging and spitting then."

The few around them fell silent as their eyes trained on Amaris with her spoon poised to attack. Theodoric's hand slid around hers and the spoon, lowering them to the table.

"I suggest a different piece of cutlery if there will be any throat-gagging or even slashing." He waited to release her hand until she let go of the utensil.

Amaris's cheeks flushed, the room growing stifling hot, even as goosebumps raised on her skin. She was done with them. She refused to be someone's eye candy while also being belittled and degraded.

"If you wish to threaten me with your spoon by assessing my gag reflex," Esaias began, grinning like a fiend, "it's only fair I retaliate with similar action."

"Esaias, enough of your witty antics," Theodoric said, grasping Jeremiah's ears. He gave Theodoric an annoyed side eye but must have believed appeasing his stomach was more important and continued to scarf down his food.

"Witty antics?" Amaris seethed. "Witty?" Her hand darted for the spoon, but Theodoric was quicker, snatching it off the table. "Fuck both of you."

"At the same time?" Esaias mused.

"You both are insufferable." She pushed out her chair, slamming her hands onto the table as she stood. A gasp escaped her as searing pain burned up her arm.

Alan's chair tipped back, but Theodoric shot him a look. Amaris's foot gave out beneath her as her vision began to tunnel. She caught herself at the expense of her hand when her elbow slammed into the table.

Theodoric leaned in. "What's the matter with you?"

"I'm fine," she snapped. "Sound familiar?"

Her eyesight returned with vivid and blotchy colors outlining Theodoric's face. She made for the door, gripping the backs of chairs as she passed through the main hall to make sure she didn't faint. What a spectacle that would be. Two fainters in one day.

She stopped a few feet outside the door, forcing a few breaths. Her vision was returning, but the pain still lingered. Each throb of her heart was an agonizing pulse through her bones. She unwound the makeshift bandage, and an all-too-familiar aroma leaked from the cloth. A rush of nausea washed over her. Where the glass pierced her skin, yellow pus now leaked. The rest of it was either bruised, red, or swollen with infection.

Heavy shoes followed behind her. She was almost thankful for Alan. She could officially demand to see Pricilla and maybe spew a line of curses at him for not taking her seriously. She turned around, but it wasn't Alan. Theodoric stepped closer, his eyes darting to her wound.

"Ugh, why you?" Amaris groaned.

"Has no one tended to your hand?" he asked.

"No," she shot back, "and I don't need anyone to. I can do it myself."

She tried to walk away, but he grabbed her arm. He brushed the back of his hand over her forehead, dragging it down her cheeks.

"You're overcome with fever."

"No, I'm not," she muttered, pushing away from him. "I'd know if I had a fever, and I'm certainly not taking your word for it."

"We must see your hand is tended to," he said, ushering her down another hallway.

"I don't need your help. Point me to Pricilla."

He scoffed, "And allow you to roam the manor alone?"

"I have an infected hand. I'm not running away in this condition." She ripped free of his hold.

"Do you plan to run later then?"

He sped in front of her, and Amaris slammed into him at his abrupt stop. Another surge climbed up her arm. Her vision narrowed again, and he gripped her shoulder to keep her standing.

"No," she lied, "and stop manhandling me."

"You can barely stand by yourself," he retorted.

"You aren't even allowing me to try."

He released both hands, but her legs gave out. She dropped to her knees and breathed through the pain rippling up her arm.

"Do you want my assistance or not?" He took a step back, likely to mock her fragile state.

What an asshole. Amaris stood, but the blood drained from her face at the fast movement, and her vision went black.

CHAPTER 14

Theo

THEO DOVE FORWARD to catch Amaris. She was agonizingly stubborn. The pressure in his head grew as he heaved her up. She was heavier in his arms than he expected, with more muscles than soft curves. With his head pounding, he hadn't noticed the other night when he'd thrown her over his shoulder.

In a short time, she'd already started to get on his nerves, won Esaias's affections, and managed to piss off most of the army. The audience with his father had been a disaster. If she didn't have such a sharp tongue, he would've felt more inclined to side with her against the allegations made of her.

The sweet smell of vanilla wafted from her hair as her head bobbed against his chest. A few groans slipped past her lips as he carried her through the empty halls. The curtains had been drawn for the night, and the servants were going around lighting the torches. The few they passed paid them no attention as he lugged her through the darkened halls toward the library.

His eyes skimmed the portraits outlined in golden frames. His mother always hated this wing. She used to say she was being watched by the beady eyes of the portraits gazing down on her. Theo had never taken issue with them before, but since he'd returned, their eyes followed him, knowing, taunting.

He forced open the door. It didn't need to be decorated in vines or elaborate renditions of past battles to stand out among all the rest. In fact, he preferred the simple nature of the solid wood with brass handles. His mother may have hated walking down the hall of piercing glances, but she'd always said it was worth it to reach the treasures at the end of the hall. She would've spent her entire life behind the library's doors if she could've.

Theo was greeted with the lovely scent of old leather, musty books, and candle wax. All the librarians were either still eating or had gone home for the night, but one woman always stayed later after supper than anyone else. Along with being a librarian, Pricilla was capable of healing small ailments and had begged to take over the duties of the mystique until a new one came along.

Her fascination for the mystique world had always baffled Theo, and the old mystique spent a great deal of time shooing her away. She wasn't much older than Theo, but with the number of books she digested, she was one of the smartest people in Luana Bay. It was a good thing Amaris was unconscious. Not only was Pricilla intelligent, but she was also the sweetest and most gentle creature he'd ever met. Amaris would've eaten her alive.

He followed the fortress of towering bookshelves leading to the mystique tower at the back of the library. He found it hard to believe anyone other than an accomplished reader wouldn't get lost in here. In the center of the library, a frosted-glass ceiling overlooked a wide gallery of the librarians' desks and other tables. Theo used to find home at a small table shoved at the back near a shelf of books on sailing adventures.

He hefted Amaris tighter to his chest and continued his trek through the endless rows of stories and adventures to the back staircase. He approached the open arch, but scaling the tight spiral staircase would prove to be a challenge with Amaris in his arms. He moved slowly, using the tip of his boot to feel each step with the light of the few torches lining the walls. It didn't make sense to place the infirmary five stories up, but the manor was several hundred years old and hadn't been built with that in mind.

The door was already open, with candles illuminating the center of the room. He stopped in the doorway, clearing his throat. Pricilla stood nose deep in a book perched on the worktable.

She lifted her head of snowy-white hair, smiling sheepishly as a glassy daze settled over her violet eyes. At the sight of Amaris, her smile faded, and her eyes were alert and fixed on her, cradled in Theo's arms. "What happened?" she asked in her light and airy voice.

"She fainted, but her hand is what concerns me." Theo placed Amaris on the small bed by the hearth, her figure crinkling the pressed white linen.

A fire glowed beside him, sending the aroma of a campfire to settle through the room. The popping and cracking of embers sounded in his ear as he kneeled beside her to brush a clump of hair clinging to her lips.

Pricilla kneeled beside him, bowing her head with a graceful nod before she studied Amaris's bandaged hand. Her fingers moved in slow, fluid movements as she unraveled the loose linen. A yellow substance seeped from the wounds on her knuckles, and her fingers were red and swollen with bruising. He should've been more attentive to her injury.

"Do we know what caused this?" Pricilla studied her hand gingerly as she turned it over to assess the swelling of her fingers.

"A mirror."

"Who is she?" Pricilla didn't lift her gaze as she dragged her thumb over a cut, leaning closer to analyze it.

"Amaris."

The only people allowed in the throne room had been soldiers, and they'd been given a direct order to keep the accusations against her within the confines of the army. No one was to know of her identity until his father was satisfied and made his decision. She would be under guard at all hours of the day and locked in her room at night. Bennet disagreed, but his father provided a valid point. If the people of Luana Bay believed the new mystique was being investigated for murder, they wouldn't seek her out for medical attention.

"She is to be the new mystique," Theo added.

Pricilla released a deep sigh. "I knew this was only temporary, but I didn't think the duke would find a replacement so soon. I haven't even had time to organize Cornelius's possessions."

Theo gazed around the filthy room and the large pile of chests and bins yet to been cleaned out. Cornelius had never been one to care about the cleanliness of his study, and upon his death, the room further fell into disarray.

"Her wound has festered. I can use the yuxiway leaves and assess as she heals," she said, pulling back his attention.

"Will she lose her hand?" Theo had had a soldier under his charge who'd been shot with a rifle. The injury had become inflamed, and they'd been behind enemy lines and without proper herbs to tend to it or the ability to remove the musket ball. He'd ended up losing part of his leg when they'd returned to camp.

Pricilla offered a gentle smile. "It's always a possibility, but I wouldn't think so." She strode to the wall of shelves with jars upon jars of herbs.

Theo left her to collect the necessary items. He didn't know how to begin identifying herbs. He was only familiar with fade chicory and its ability to stanch bleeding. It'd been the only herb they carried with them on missions.

Theo took a seat in one of the upholstered chairs by the hearth, across from Amaris. He studied her hand but found his eyes wandering to her face with the cut and bruise on her cheek. Initially, the cut had appeared like the other scrapes across her arms, but with the newly sprouted bruise, it told a different tale. *A strike to the face?* He cocked his head and further studied the cut. *Maybe from a ring.*

"Crack in the realm," Pricilla muttered from across the room.

"What is it?" Theo shot from the chair.

"I'm out of ude stalk." She planted her hands on her hips, shifting the white dress spilling to her shins and marking her as a servant. With a sigh, she grabbed a bowl off the counter and placed it under his chin. "Spit into this."

"You want me to do what?" The bowl was filled with crushed-up leaves resembling a small pile of dirt.

"I don't have any more ude stalk to give the leaves the consistency I need."

"Why don't you do it?" He threw back at her.

She thinned her lips and eyed a glass bowl on the worktable.

"Is your throat dry from smoking uppaway, Pricilla?" Theo teased.

She scoffed, "If I'm not mistaken, it used to be a fun pastime of yours."

Theo dipped his chin and spat into the bowl. Pricilla narrowed her eyes, and at this distance, a thin red ring lined her irises. She whisked the bowl away and blended the concoction furiously.

"Grab the linen from the table," she ordered.

As she knelt beside Amaris and began rubbing the mixture onto her hand, Theo crossed the room to the worktable. He smiled at the rolled leaf resting in the glass tray, long since extinguished. After he officially became a soldier, he'd elected to avoid the herb to keep a clear head at all times. He found the small cloth squares set in a basket with several rolls of linen, but his eyes stopped on her book.

"What are you reading?" he asked, admiring the large text with vivid colors.

"A bit of light reading," Pricilla said without a glance over her shoulder.

Theo would hardly call the massive book *light*. A beautiful ocean was painted across both pages, with a small vessel floating on the surface.

He went to turn the page, but his eyes caught a smaller tome open on the edge of the worktable. It was written in the old Gorrin language. He skimmed the open page but stopped on the phrase *aslorn per cuitnun*. Isabel had been speaking Gorrin. He recognized *per cuitnun*. It meant "for cover," but *aslorn* remained a mystery.

"Pricilla, what does *aslorn* mean?"

"Brace."

"Brace for cover?"

"Captain, quit reading and bring me the bandages," she huffed.

Theo gave her a shrewd look. She'd never once referred to him by name, preferring his title, as she was a servant of the manor.

She brushed off his look. "Hold her arm steady."

He took Amaris's hand in his own, holding her puffy fingers and forearm as if they were made of glass. Pricilla began wrapping the linen around it.

"Have you ever heard the phrase *aslorn per de eclahard*?"

"I thought you were taught Gorrin by your fancy tutors?" Pricilla smiled and tied off the end of the bandage. As her adoptive mother was the head librarian, Pricilla had run around the library as a child and had often thrown folded paper at him when he'd been at a desk studying. "Brace for her something, but I don't know what *eclahard* means. It sounds like one of the older Gorrin terms. It probably died before the language itself was put to rest."

At the dead end, Theo sighed and returned his attention to Amaris. She slept with her lips slightly parted, and the air whistled as it swept through them. His fingers hovered over the scab on her cheekbone and the ugly bruise tainting it. Something didn't sit right, and he doubted the injury was from Freville.

"From the same incident?" Pricilla asked, standing and striding for the worktable.

"If I were to guess." He refrained from further questioning aloud the possible origins of such an injury. Amaris hadn't said anything about another altercation. With the freshness of the bruise and her hand, though, they couldn't have been that far apart.

His eyes slid down her arm to where her left hand draped across the bed. A ring sparkled off the flames. Theo kneeled beside her and examined it. *She's married?* Amaris's story was certainly growing more perplexing. Why hadn't she come forward with that information? His father could've sent for her husband to speak on her behalf. *Unless he's the one she's running from.*

"I'll look after her," Pricilla said, turning a page in her large book.

"Are you sure?" Theo glanced at the small clock resting upon the mantel. It was growing rather late, and exhaustion was setting in. Amaris would sleep through the night, and hopefully well into tomorrow. A guard wouldn't be necessary.

"See to your duties. I'm sure you're busy."

His headache flared between his eyes. Amaris had known from the few interactions what had been ailing him, whatever she called it.

He turned back to Pricilla. "Do you have a remedy for headaches?"

She inclined a brow, and her eyes wandered to where the cut was likely peeking through his parted hair. Her smile was a friendly reminder that not everything within the walls would add to his aching mind. She rifled through a cabinet, pulling out a vial with a dark-blue tonic.

"Take this when you feel it begin to start up again."

"What if it's never gone away?" Theo took the vial and smelled the contents. It was potent and smelled of soil.

"Then I'd be concerned, depending on how long you've had it. Try this, and if it doesn't work, I'm sure Amaris will have a better option."

"Thank you, Pricilla." He offered her what he could of a smile and turned down the stairs.

Hopefully, it would work, and he wouldn't be asking Amaris for any assistance. With her skills, she'd have a remedy for the pounding in his head, but he feared she'd be the top contributor to any future pains his mind was to endure.

Once he was back within the library, he couldn't help himself as he passed several intriguing titles. He collected several books and pulled others out, so as to easily spot them later when he finished the first few. Most of the librarians knew to leave them sticking out, as he was bound to grab them within a day or two.

With his small stack, he grabbed a lantern off a table and set himself up in the back corner behind an empty cart. He sneezed and dust flew up around him. Squeezing his nose, he waited for it to settle before cracking the first spine.

He slid his finger across the page and whispered the Gorrin words, testing them on his tongue. Even if he couldn't find the meaning of *eclahard*, he'd derive it from its root. He couldn't put to words why he needed to know, but something within him craved to decipher Isabel's secret. Besides, it kept his mind from wandering to the twist of his stomach at the idea of who Amaris could've been running from.

CHAPTER 15

Theo

TWO DAYS THEO had sat by Amaris's side while she slept. He'd read through several books, attempting to decipher Isabel's message, but came up short. Amaris hadn't woken since Pricilla bandaged her hand. She checked on her morning and night to confirm she wasn't developing a fever. Theo was thankful for the recess from her foul language and irritating personality, but he was beginning to worry for her wellbeing. Not that he should have. The confusion was unsettling, but without further knowledge of who she was and what had happened, it only grew.

Solace had always found him on Luana's beach. He trudged through the sand and dropped down beside the largest rock, which had never once been a terrible companion, and slid his book across his lap. He gave himself a break from the Gorrin texts. The stray piece of parchment he'd grabbed as a placeholder for his novel slipped from the page. It had a few scribbles of an old battle plan.

He leaned back and tried to read the first few lines of the chapter using the light of his lantern. He spent every spare moment devouring any book he could get his hands on, but as his eyes shifted over the text, nothing imprinted in his mind. He'd come out here to allow the sound of the surf to calm the ever-growing need for a breath. For a moment, he didn't want to think about Amaris, his nightmares, or his discussion before supper with his stepmother.

Genevieve was adamant about assisting him in selecting an escort for the Conjugation. Theo had managed to spare himself for now, but she'd handed him a list of eligible women and demanded he picked one within the coming weeks.

"Pondering life's greatest mysteries or hiding?" Adelaide's voice drifted from up the path.

Theo closed the book and shifted his gaze to his sister jogging toward him with flushed cheeks and beads of sweat trickling down her face. Her sword and dagger dangled from her hip.

"Thinking," Theo answered, but hiding was more like it. Hiding from Bennet, his father, Genevieve, anyone threatening to send his head into a deeper spiral.

Adelaide drew her sword, twisting it in the moonlight. Her hand rotated the blade, twirling it like an extension of her arm. She flipped her long black ponytail off her shoulder and lunged, striking her invisible opponent. It was incredible how long her hair had grown in what felt to Theo like only a short period of time. Her resemblance to their mother was growing more prominent with her years. Especially with those eyes they'd shared with her.

She dropped the tip of her sword and leaned into the hilt. "Looks more like brooding to me. I'm surprised you're not in bed, snuggling up with your pillow and muffling words of longing as you drool across your sheets." Sibling mockery enveloped her laugh in a warmth Theo couldn't reciprocate.

Gods, I missed her laughter. Before he'd left, it'd carried through the halls, and every single person within the manor had felt its contagious warmth.

"I'm not brooding." He wished he laid in bed dreaming of a woman, or anything other than the war. A peaceful night's rest was precisely what he needed.

Her giggles ceased. She inclined her head and raised a suspicious brow, her eyes glittering with silver specks. "I know you, Theo." He gave her an incredulous look, but she only raised her brow further. "You are aware I can find out whatever information I desire, or have you forgotten my cunning abilities already?"

Theo moved before she could react, kicking her legs out from under her. Her sword fell several feet away, and she landed in the sand with a sharp grunt. "How can I forget your incessant need to ramble during your training?"

A spark ignited in Adelaide's eyes as she rolled back on her hands and propelled herself up. She took her fighting stance, lifting her fists. With his headache, Theo questioned if he'd be able to beat her in a fight, but with the waves crashing against the rocks, there was no better distraction.

She swung her leg out, making to collide with his head. He rolled to the side, getting his feet under him. A blow to the head in his condition would be a short end to their sparring, and he didn't need Adelaide asking why he wasn't himself.

"You've lost weight," she said, cocking her head as she began her circling. "You're quicker." She faked a jab to his face, but he caught her attempt to open his stance and blocked her as she sent her fist toward his stomach.

"I see your first move is still to fake your opponent out."

She charged, hurtling a series of punches and kicks. Theo focused his attention on her attempts at sending her fist into his skull, but he failed to block her kick to his chest. His lungs burned for air, but he didn't keel over. He panted through pursed lips, keeping his arms up.

"What happened in the throne room?" she asked.

Theo threw a punch, but she blocked it, dodging out of the way as his arm sailed past her head. She gripped his arm, bending it at an odd angle as she drove her knee into his abdomen. This time, he pitched forward, grasping at his stomach as his body sucked in whatever air it could.

"Tell me!" she demanded.

Theo barely knew what happened in the throne room. One moment he'd been thinking about the issues of Duncaster, and the next his head had spun with Amaris's story. Hiding anything from Adelaide was futile, though. She often discovered any information she wanted to know, but Theo couldn't bring himself to tell her.

"What happened in the throne room was a mix of dehydration and lack of sustenance. What really matters is what we discovered in Duncaster."

She released his arm but didn't send another punch or even a kick his way. Instead, she folded her arms and prodded at the inside of her cheek. "I already heard all about it. Fights, Deavonian Accords, slavers."

"But Freville?"

Adelaide wasn't impressed and cocked a hip. "You think she did it?"

"No, maybe." Theo groaned, cupping the back of his neck. "I don't know."

"Did she tell you who she's married to?"

He narrowed his eyes at her. "How do—"

She raised her hand, silencing his words. "I know everything, Theo, remember that."

He released an annoyed breath.

"Are you jealous?" Adelaide teased.

"Why would I be jealous?"

"Because she's pretty."

Theo rolled his eyes. Why did every person within these walls wish to discuss the mating of the sexes?

She went on. "Well, if you're not jealous, are you at least as infuriated as I am? I don't know about you, but that is a nasty bruise across her face, and the cut on her cheekbone"—Adelaide shook her head and tsked— "probably from her counterpart's wedding ring."

158

"Are you saying you think her husband hit her?"

"You've been thinking the same thing. It's probably why you're out here brooding."

"I'm not brooding."

Adelaide shrugged off her long leather jacket and discarded it onto the rock. She wore black trousers and a matching vest over her shirt. She looked the part of a warrior. Theo only wished she could carry her sword in the daylight as she did now.

Adelaide bent down to pick up her sword and held her stance, pointing her weapon at him. He pulled his own from its sheath. She gawked at the silver blade, admiring the serpent hilt.

"New sword?" she asked, her eyes fixating on the jewel for its eye.

"One good thing needed to come from the war," he said, but a smile never reached his lips. An invisible layer of blood coated the blade. No matter the amount of scrubbing he'd done, he would always see their faces. Losing his old sword, the one piece of home he'd brought and promised he'd cherish, had been a disgrace. The only reason he still had this one was because it'd been a gift from Cris.

Adelaide yelped, and their blades collided. Her feet moved in a swift rhythm, carrying her over the sand with each of her strikes.

"I see your footwork has improved," Theo said.

Her blade met his, and she pressed against it. "As I spend my time training instead of reading silly little novels, I would hope so."

She pulled back, but then she surged, and he was forced to move at a speed he hadn't used since the war. With her smaller stature, he'd taught her to use it to her advantage. Wear her opponent down and move with quick strikes. She stepped back as she began circling to catch her breath.

"If you read more, you'd find they aren't silly at all, but rather thrilling adventures." Theo smiled, pleased with the shift in conversation.

"A thrilling adventure would be to sail the Nebulous Sea to war or travel to Duncaster. Those are real adventures, ones you get to live yourself." Adelaide pulled a hidden dagger from her boot and angled both blades before him.

He released a sigh. As much as he wanted her to become a soldier, he didn't wish to shift to this conversation right now.

"Not all travels are adventures. You must not mistake them for reckless danger." Theo drew his dagger as she lunged at him. Their swords met with a piercing ring that made him wince. Adelaide pulled back, but he shook it off before she had a chance to notice.

"At least you saw combat." She readied herself for another strike.

"War isn't glorious, Adelaide."

Theo didn't wait for her to attack. He stepped forward and unleashed his own series of moves. She didn't balk or stumble in her steps. Her arm moved in a fluid motion as it blocked each of his slashes. She ground her teeth together and moved before he sensed it. She kicked his hand, sending his dagger into the sand.

"Why do you get to run off and fight while I'm left here?"

Her scream pulled at his heart.

"You weren't old enough," he reminded her. She'd only been seventeen when he left, too young to experience any of it. If it'd been his decision, she would've accompanied them to Duncaster, but it hadn't been up to him.

"Screw being of age," she sneered with a vengeance as she sailed into another attack. "I'm almost twenty-one. I should have gone to Duncaster with you."

"Father wouldn't have allowed it."

She let out a frustrated grunt, pulling back and sheathing her sword. "It's always the duke won't allow it, or the duke says to stay put, or the duke says I'm not to train. Why won't he let me?" Her face turned a bright shade of crimson as she trembled with furious anger. She stomped around the beach, throwing rocks into the crashing surf and kicking at large piles of sand.

"Will you compose yourself?"

"No," she snapped, kicking up more sand.

He shielded himself against the particles flying at him in her tantrum. The same conversation had been held between them years ago, but now she could throw heavier rocks and with better aim. She hadn't been born into the life she deserved. Because of circumstances far beyond her control of heredity, she hadn't been allowed to train. Unfortunately, she resembled their mother too much—not that their father would ever reveal to Adelaide that that was his reason for holding her back.

Adelaide squatted down, lifting a rock she had no business attempting to pick up. She cradled it between her arms and wound herself up. She threw it into the surf with a large crash. Theo took a step back as she went for an even larger one, and the muscles of her arms pressed against her shirt. Wailing, she flung it even farther than the last. Apparently, she hadn't only increased in skill in the last three years but also strength.

There was no sense in trying to bring hope to her desires. Theo still hadn't figured out how he could help her. Luther would uphold their father's wishes when he took his place as the next duke. Theo only hoped, with his influence as future chief, he could find ways to assist her, to give her a chance at the life she wanted.

"For how many years? Eleven? Twelve?" Adelaide began. "I've trained for years on this beach, Theo. For so many fucking years, and what do I get for it?"

"Adelaide—"

"You don't get it. You never will. As soon as you were old enough to hold a sword, Bennet trained you."

"Need I remind you that none of us have a choice of what becomes of our lives?" He sheathed his sword and dared to grasp her shoulders as she heaved a rock over her head. It slipped from her fingers and fell behind her with a thud. "I applaud your strength and will continue to train you. It'll be more valuable in your life than you know."

"But I'll never get to use it as a soldier, will I?" she asked. "For years, you trained me, but it was all for nothing."

"It's not all for nothing."

"Why do you hate it?" She ripped her arms free, and her eyes grew darker with the anger swelling beneath.

"Being a soldier is more than glory." Theo turned from her, from the defeat on her face.

"I don't care about glory. I want to serve my people. I want to stand beside you, Alan, Esaias. I'm not meant to wear dresses and sip tea while chatting about politics."

"You can still have an influence. You don't need to pick up a sword to serve your people."

As the third born, Adelaide didn't have a duty to live up to. In most noble families, that would've given one the freedom to pursue what they desired, such as soldiering, or even marrying who they chose, but not theirs. Adelaide wasn't to become a soldier, and she wouldn't marry for herself but to continue the noble bloodline.

"What happened, Theo?"

He stiffened but forced himself to brush the feeling aside. He refused to tell Adelaide the truth. She'd never understand from a mere story. The real gravity came with the experience, which he hoped she'd never have the burden of carrying.

He didn't answer her.

"We all see it," she said, reaching for her weapons.

Theo grabbed his book and headed toward the path. He took a long breath, hoping emotion would flood his veins so he could shed a single tear.

"You've changed," she breathed.

Bristling, he didn't have to turn to see the darkness in her eyes, but he heard the swipe of her sword through the air. He drew his, meeting her blade before she had a chance to slice his back open.

"You'd stab me in the back?"

"What happened to the man ready to jump into the fight, who begged to go overseas?"

"He wasn't a man but a boy!" His tone caused her to stumble, but he didn't strike. She could have the victory, because she deserved them all. She deserved to wear a sword in the daylight, to train not under the cover of darkness, and to call herself a soldier.

Her sword slid down his blade, and she grabbed his arm, rotating as she disarmed him of his weapon. She kicked it away and thrust hers against his neck, stopping before the point could nick his skin. Her smirk tore at his heart.

"Enjoy this time," he breathed. "If we're right and slavers are entering our waters, you'll get the fight you want." His fingers brushed aside the blade as her shoulders slackened and her smirk faded.

CHAPTER 16

Amaris

AMARIS'S HEAD WAS groggy, and all her thoughts were shrouded in mist. Awake with her eyes still closed, she attempted to piece together the fragments of the night and decipher reality from her feverish dreams.

"You're awake."

Her eyes snapped open, and she bolted upright. Seated in a chair across from her was a woman with two pistols strapped to her sides. Amaris stiffened. The woman looked the part of a menacing soldier with tattoo sleeves and thighs that looked like they coudl crush a watermelon. She sat with her foot propped on her knee, and she stared at Amaris with sharp brown eyes.

"Who are you?" Amaris's throat felt like she'd gargled sand.

"Sephardi," she said, brushing back the short strands of her dusty brown pixie cut.

Amaris assessed her hand wrapped in a thick bandage. Wiggling her fingers would probably be excruciating, but she gave it a try. She tensed her muscles to prepare for the pain, but they moved with only a small ache and minor stiffness. She balled her hand into a fist, then pressed against her knuckles, bending her wrist back and forth.

"Holy shit," she muttered to herself.

"How are you faring?" Sephardi asked, leaning closer to examine Amaris's hand as she turned it in circles.

Amaris unraveled the linen to reveal her disgusting-looking hand. All the swelling was gone, but scabs ran along her fingers and spread across her knuckles. She turned her hand over and clenched and extended her fingers again. Pressing into the cushions of the cot caused little pain as she swung her legs over the side. She hadn't a clue where she was or even the time, judging by the dreary light coming from the single window.

"How long was I out?"

"Three days."

That's all it's been?

Amaris took in the room. Several misshapen and differently sized candles scattered a cluttered worktable, and the walls were lined with shelves of dusty books and a ton of jars of who knew what.

She left the sweltering heat of the cot perched near a crackling fire, wiping a trail of sweat from her forehead. Stacks of books and pieces of paper scattered the worktable. They must have had miracle medicine to heal her hand in only three days. A small book was propped open. It contained various wonders of anatomy, herbal recipes, and some haunting material regarding the grinding of bones into fine powders.

"Are you here to...watch me?" She may have still been groggy from the three days of straight sleep, but one piece of her memory was clear. She was a prisoner.

"It's only a precaution."

She returned to the book and skimmed a formula labeled *lizard's breath*. At least she didn't have Theodoric or Alan breathing down her neck. She prodded at the inside of her cheek, taking in the rest of the room. It wasn't much. The worktable took up most of the space, along with the single bed. One corner housed stacks of dusty trunks and crates, making the room feel even smaller.

"Where are we?"

"The mystique tower."

Amaris headed for the single window, and sure enough, it was a tower, with an exceptional view of the bay. The ocean spread far into the horizon, spilling off the edge of the earth—*or whatever this place was called.*

"What now?" Amaris raised her arms and gestured to the room around them. "Am I going to be locked up here in this tower?"

How ironic. She'd never cared much for fairytales. Her mother had read her bedtime stories as a child, but it was an absurd idea to call down from a window, begging for a man to come and rescue you.

"There isn't a lock on the door."

Sephardi was right, only a spiral iron handle. That meant, every night, she'd be locked up in that bedroom, while each morning she'd be carted off like a prisoner to the tower.

"What if there aren't any patients to help?"

"I hope you enjoy reading." Sephardi grinned, grabbed a book from a pile on the floor, and waved it.

Amaris groaned, plopping back onto the cot. She would call it a bed, but with how thin the mattress was, it reminded her more of the cot in the back of her ambulance. Did her friends and coworkers miss her or even know she was gone? She hoped Derek had the entire police department out looking for her. She slammed her head back. The tower stretched into a single point at the top. She bet it would be drafty in the wintertime.

Wait, winter? Amaris needed to be home before then. Maybe her disappearance would frighten Derek enough that the fighting would finally come to an end. They'd have a peaceful night where he made her cinnamon rolls in the morning, not out of sorrow, but because he wanted to. Her stomach growled for the gooey drip of icing and the bite of the spice.

"Are you hungry?"

Amaris lifted her head. Sephardi was at the door. She followed her, not bothering to question any bit of her kindness. The spiral stairs were poorly illuminated with torches on each landing. She slid her hand along the wall. *Had they ever heard of a railing?* Amaris felt each step with her foot to keep from following the increase of her heart rate and speeding off the edge to tumble forward. Only a week ago, the greatest oddity in her life was how a zit had continued to pop up every other week. Now, she had to worry about watching her back to make sure Alan wasn't there with his threats or Bennet with his knife across her throat.

Emerging into a grand library, her jaw fell open. Bookcases towered high above her head and spanned far beyond, looking miniature in the distance. Each shelf she passed, her fingers trailed against the soft and rigid bindings, the leather scent freshly wafting her nose. Her fingers stopped on a single book pulled from the perfect row. She stroked her hand over the cover. It flopped open, and she pinched the edges, fanning her face with the pages. She adored the musty smell accompanying old and withered leather-bound books.

Sephardi continued as she stopped and read a random page. Amaris blushed at the provocative scene and slammed it shut, placing the book back on the shelf. Viv loved romance novels, but Amaris could never seem to get through reading a sex scene without laughing or growing beet red in the face.

"Can I help you?"

Amaris jumped as the meek voice came from the silence. A woman stepped from the dark and into the sparkling light of the nearest candle. Her violet eyes drew Amaris's attention, stars gazing through her skull. Platinum blonde hair fell in large waves and grazed her hips. Her skin was fair and partially hidden beneath a simple white dress and beige apron.

"No," Amaris stammered, hoping the woman had no clue what she'd been reading. "I'm on my way to get some food."

"How lovely. I'll join you."

Amaris's head jolted, but the woman smiled and fell in step beside her.

Sephardi gazed over her shoulder, smirking as the woman hummed beside Amaris.

"Who are you?" Amaris asked, hesitant.

"Oh, how silly of me," she laughed. "I'm Pricilla." She stopped and outstretched her hand.

"Amaris."

Pricilla's handshake was firm, but not a single callous lined her palm. Her small giggle illuminated her innocent smile.

"You're the one who's going to be showing me the ropes?"

"When I've finished with my duties around the library, I'll acquaint you with your workspace and your tools. Well, I presume you've already seen the workspace."

"Was this you?" Amaris asked, holding up her hand.

Pricilla's eyes widened, and she took Amaris's hand in hers, dragging her fingers over the scabs. "Incredible," she muttered. "How are you feeling? Any pain?"

"Only stiff from not moving it. I thought it would've taken longer to heal."

Pricilla was gentle as she went down each finger, assessing their condition. Amaris tapped her foot as Pricilla held her hand for far longer than necessary, but eventually, she pulled back and rubbed at her small chin.

"Do you mind if I jot something down before we eat? I wish to record this."

"Sure."

Normally at the sign of strangers, Amaris would've turned the opposite direction and shoved her hands into her pockets, but as Pricilla seemed one of the few who didn't want to kill her, maybe she could be helpful too. At the sound of Amaris's name, Pricilla hadn't startled or exclaimed, "Murderer." With Ms. Borstad's reaction, and now hers, maybe not everyone knew.

Pricilla hummed while they walked, her feet moving in rhythm with her tune. Sephardi was several paces ahead of them but didn't turn back to keep a watchful eye.

"You said you have duties in the library. Does that mean you're a librarian?"

"I am." Pricilla beamed. "If you should ever have need to escape within the realms of the pages, allow me to be your guide."

"Librarian and mystique?"

Pricilla smiled, but her enthusiasm faded. "Only a librarian. I'm not formally trained as a mystique. I've read a great deal on the subject and offered my services until the duke found a replacement."

Pricilla pulled them from the labyrinth of bookcases and stepped into a wide mezzanine. People scattered around tables with their noses glued to books. Iron candles sat at each desk, but they weren't necessary, as Amaris squinted from the frosted-glass ceiling over their heads. Pricilla grinned and turned her face up as they walked into the burning light beginning to pass through the glass.

"I love the morning light," she sighed, wrapping a strand of her hair behind her ear. Pricilla led Amaris to a messy desk with scrolls littered across it and ink-smudged parchments scattering the floor. She pulled out a quill and began jotting a scribble of cursive down as she muttered to herself. "Any itching?"

"No. I'm also not feeling bad either. No fever, nausea, dizziness. I'm as healthy as I was a few days ago." Pricilla's head lifted as Amaris's stomach protested. "Starving, but healthy."

Pricilla made a few more notes before tossing her quill aside and shoving the piece of parchment into a drawer.

"What did you do to my hand?" Amaris reclined against the desk, assessing her strength as she pressed her weight against it. The scabs pulled as her skin stretched, but the stiffness was waning.

"Yuxiway leaves."

"How do they work?" They sounded like a plant. Judging by the limited equipment in the tower, Amaris didn't think they had an advanced medical system. However, with results like this, she was intrigued to learn more.

"Mixing the leaves with saliva creates a paste that fights inflammation and festering." Pricilla grinned at Amaris's face of disgust. "You can also add them to ude stalk."

Sephardi offered a laugh that had Amaris smiling.

"Will you be filling the position permanently?" Pricilla asked.

Amaris gripped the edge of the table and shot a look toward Sephardi as she stood with a smile on her lips and her arms folded across her chest.

"For a time," Sephardi added.

"Are you a traveler? I do adore your accent. I wish I could see the realm beyond these walls."

"I...no."

Pricilla took Amaris's arm in hers. "Not many have the luxury. I wish to travel to every corner of Magoria one day. I want to learn about the different cultures, especially their myths and legends."

"Do you have a fascination for the occult?" Amaris was oddly growing used to it over the years, with Viv attempting to read her future through tarot cards and wafting sage in her direction every time she said she was with Derek.

Pricilla furrowed her brow and played with the word, exaggerating it and repeating it.

"It means believing in supernatural things—palm readings, spells, that kind of stuff."

Amaris tapped her fingers against her thigh. Her healed hand brought a whole new level of possibilities. She could try to escape tonight if she wanted to, but there was still the impending question of where to go.

"I most certainly do then. I adore learning all things about magic."

Amaris stumbled but smiled as she attempted to keep herself from face-planting. Did Pricilla mean tarot and séance magic or magic-magic?

"Magic doesn't exist," Sephardi cut in. "They're only fascinating tales to tell your children at night."

Pricilla extended a gracious smile, but a hint of annoyance lurked in her eyes as a muscle in her cheek twitched. "It's said Magoria was once filled with magic. The people and the ground we stand on subsisted on it."

Sephardi rolled her eyes, scoffing as she returned her attention ahead of them.

"Then what happened to it?" Amaris asked, wondering if magic wasn't as far gone as Pricilla thought. Maybe magic still existed. How else would she have found her way here? Science couldn't explain it.

"Lost to the realm."

"How do you know magic existed?"

"Stories passed through the generations. Some had the ingenuity to write it down in the folktales and various myths. Why would they bother to if it wasn't real?"

Hope fleeted away. Pricilla's belief in magic was no different than believing in dragons or unicorns in Amaris's world.

"Where do you think you're going?" A towering presence blocked their path, and Amaris rolled her eyes as Theodoric stepped closer from the shadows of the bookcases. Her shoulders tensed as he furrowed his brows, his eyes glaring at her.

"Captain," Pricilla greeted, inclining her head in a small curtsy.

Are you kidding me? Amaris wasn't going to curtsy for this jerk.

"Food. I'm hungry," Amaris said, crossing her arms.

"I'll be taking over from here. Sephardi, see to it Miss Carter's breakfast is brought up to her tower," Theodoric ordered.

Amaris released Pricilla's arm, clenching her hands into fists. Her cheeks flushed as Pricilla's gaze swept between them. Pricilla might believe in fairy tales, but she could be a key to escaping, and he was ruining it.

"Miss Carter?" Amaris sneered.

"A formality," he stated, a twinge in his jaw, making her further narrow her gaze at him.

"Then what should I call you?"

"Theodoric will do fine." His voice was crisp and irritating.

"I was thinking more along the lines of prick or jackass. Which would you prefer?"

Pricilla gasped. Amaris didn't care if he was her boss. He wasn't getting away with acting like a jerk.

"Let's go." He grasped Amaris's arm and urged her toward the tower.

Pricilla shuffled away, darting behind the nearest bookcase.

"What was that?"

"You're to remain in the tower, not parade around, doing as you please," he answered.

"I wasn't," she shouted. "Sephardi was there. I haven't eaten a solid meal in days. Do you want me to starve?"

He didn't bother to answer, only allowing a short burst of breath through his nostrils like he was a beast snarling at her.

"Do you have any idea how to be a normal human being?"

He released her arm, catapulting her several steps ahead of him. "Keep going."

Amaris stormed through the arched threshold of the stairs and stomped like she would when Gran would send her to bed without dinner for back-talking. She threw open the door, the boom echoing through the cramped space. Theodoric appeared through the darkness and took Sephardi's spot by the fire.

"You never even thanked me."

"What in the realm do I have you to thank for?" he asked.

If he hadn't had a knife and sword within reach, Amaris would've sent a fist flying into that smug and perfect jawline.

"I don't know," she began, sarcasm lacing each syllable, "maybe because I saved your life. I could've died in that river!"

His shoulders tensed. "How did you?"

"How? No *thank you for saving me and not leaving me to drown* or an apology for taking me fucking prisoner?"

Amaris's chest tightened as the coursing of her blood flooded her veins and the speed of her breaths grew erratic. She was losing her shit. She could only take so much before she finally snapped and began spouting off. It's why her and Derek fought almost every night. She couldn't drop it, no matter how hard she clung to her mask—she had to fight back.

"You're a prisoner here because you haven't been forthcoming with information. There wasn't a village for miles, and you haven't once revealed who you were running from."

Amaris's cheeks flushed, feeling trapped. She couldn't go to the gym, cry her frustration away with Viv, or pick up an extra shift at work. "It's none of your business."

"It is my business. We found you—"

"Oh my God, give it up already. We've heard this a million times!" She waved wildly. "You found me when I was lost and trying to get away but stumbled on that poor man."

"Get away from whom? Your husband?"

Amaris froze. "I don't have a husband."

"Then why do you wear a wedding ring?"

She twisted the band of metal. "It's an engagement ring. I'm not married yet."

"You're betrothed then?"

"Yes, but why do you care? It's not like he can help me. You idiots can't put two and two together. You couldn't figure out how I ended up in the middle of the woods, so the only logical explanation you had was I'm a murderer!" His jaw tightened, but she continued her rant. "It's all you want to see. You don't have answers for what you found, so your tiny-ass brain did all it could and connected two completely different situations."

"Why are you enraged? If your betrothed is truly missing you, wouldn't he be looking for you? Or are you lying and you know you're trapped now?"

"You're a bastard, you know that? He's searching for me and won't be happy when he finds out what you've done."

"What will he think of what you've done? I wouldn't take too kindly to my betrothed running away. Do you think he'll even come for you now?"

Amaris knocked over a jar of herbs as she stumbled back into the worktable. The shattering of glass was deafening. "Get out," she croaked, fighting tears.

"Not going to happen."

"There's only one way in or out. Go sit at the bottom of the steps if you need to guard me." Amaris hid her face, holding back a scream from ripping through her throat.

He dropped his head in his hands, dragging his hair back as he sighed. "I don't like this situation any more than you do, but we're stuck with each other. Let's at least make the most of it."

"You get to act like a complete asshole, but I have to play nice?" Amaris blew out a breath, but it did nothing to mask her fury. "Fuck you."

"You're the one who started this arguing."

"You want me to apologize because your daddy is the duke? Let me guess. You're used to getting everything you want? Once someone shows you a bit of disrespect, you demand for them to grovel at your feet and kiss your boots? I don't care if you're a lord or a goddamn prince. I won't let you or anyone else treat me like I'm someone less than. He'll come for me because he loves me."

Amaris turned her back on him. Clenching the edge of the worktable, she stared at the jagged edges of the broken jar. He had no right to say anything about Derek. Her chest sharpened as her heart beat like a stampede. She wasn't even sure Derek *could* come to her rescue, let alone if it was even possible for her to get back.

The door shut behind her. It wasn't a slam, but it rang louder in her ears than if he'd unleashed all his anger into the wood and splintered it.

CHAPTER 17

Theo

THEO'S FATHER MOTIONED for him to enter his study. Theo took a casual position, resting upon the corner of the large, wooden desk while his father stood by the window. He rubbed his hand along his temples, bracing his mind between his fingers. Theo hoped the summons would be short and without emotional outbursts from either party. He still prayed to the gods that was the case.

"Who have the gods cursed upon us?" his father muttered.

"I hardly see the gods deeming us of any worth to burden us with Amaris."

"Alan, will you fetch something stronger than tea?"

"Oh course, Your Grace," Alan answered before exiting through the hidden servants' door.

Many years ago, they'd all used the servants' passageways as a means for adventure. Adelaide had stumbled upon the door and insisted on using the secret entrance for their own mischief. Their father hadn't thought it amusing at all when he entered to find forty-nine chickokees squawking about and discarding their droppings on his desk. They'd planned to unleash fifty, but Adelaide had insisted on one for a pet.

"Theodoric," he began.

Theo's body stiffened at his call. Whether he started a conversation with *Theo* or *Theodoric* usually dictated the course of their meetings.

"What do you think of Miss Carter?"

Theo was tired of the question. He took a deep breath and rested his hands upon his belt. "She's stubborn and annoying, but with those qualities, she'll fit in perfectly."

The scrunching of his father's brows and drop of his eyelids were enough to show his displeasure at Theo's attempt at humor. Describing what was reeling through his mind was impossible. He didn't have the courage to break the deafening silence between them. Theo had intended to rile Amaris last week to see who she was running from, but he'd lost it when she spoke of her betrothed. She was emotional, but she'd defended him. Maybe Theo was wrong, and her injuries weren't related.

Theo's father pondered carefully. He was a strong leader. Theo would give him that much.

"Do you trust what she had to say?"

"In which regard?"

"She claimed to have pulled you from the river."

Theo paused. Only Theo, Amaris, and Gris knew what happened that day. He'd already made a fool of himself when he'd fainted in the throne room and didn't want his father believing Amaris had summoned him back from the dead. "I spoke with Gris, and she vouched for Amaris's story. She was the one who jumped in, not Gris. I believe she's telling the truth about running away too."

Theo held back the new information regarding her betrothed. He wanted to learn more before he told his father. She was still hiding something, and Theo was going to learn what it was. Maybe it would clear her of the allegations.

"Indeed. I want this to continue to remain within the army. I don't want a single word escaping these walls about how we have allowed a possible murderer to parade around as the mystique."

"Why present the position to her?"

"She's proven valuable, has she not?"

Theo ignored his father's attempt to bring up his collapse in the throne room. "You wish to exploit her for her skills?"

"A time will come when her identity is revealed. She'll either prove herself by working here for a time or slip up. Regardless, however long it takes is our opportunity to learn what skills she possesses."

"Aren't you afraid she'll cause further harm or kill someone in the role?" If he truly believed her to be dangerous, it didn't make sense to offer a role to her that held life delicately in one's hands.

"She rushed and tended to you without a thought in the throne room. It's said amongst the mystique community that selflessness is the first trait of value to a powerful healer. Miss Carter may not be forthcoming with who she really is, but her instincts are to act."

Theo was thrown into the war again, forced to discern who his enemies were and what they were planning. He missed the few weeks of peace, where the only worry was whether he'd wake from a nightmare needing to vomit.

"You think she'll put other's safety before her own?" Theo asked.

"With patients, yes." His father leaned further into the sill, the sun casting him in a bright aura, a massive contrast to the darkness he emanated. "I wish for her not only to be under guard but for someone to infiltrate her life."

"I'm not sure I follow."

His father's face scrunched up as he took a seat in a leather chair beside the window. "Have you learned nothing while you were away?"

Theo took a deep breath, forcing himself to surrender to his calm demeanor. "Is a guard not enough to gather information?"

"You of all people should understand that's not enough. I want

177

someone to gain her attention, become her ally."

"You wish for someone to earn her trust and spy on her?"

"If given the opportunity to befriend, I believe she may open up. People sometimes have loose tongues around those they're comfortable with."

"She won't appreciate our deception."

"She'll be none the wiser. They'll keep their mission secretive."

"Would Adelaide suffice?"

She seemed to have taken a liking for Amaris, even though he couldn't imagine why.

"Adelaide," he said through a raspy breath, "is to do nothing of the sort. She may run about the manor pretending she is a soldier, but she hasn't the skill for a task such as this."

Theo loosed a breath and shoved away the beginnings of an outburst. It wasn't the time for that fight. "You wish for a soldier to gain her trust, then? I can delegate the mission to Sephardi or Gris?"

"No."

"Amaris might be more willing to reveal her identity to another woman," Theo countered.

"Sergeant Salter has already shown her true colors regarding what she believes of Miss Carter. She'll be harder to control. Corporal Salter will no doubt side with her wife."

"Who do you suggest then?" Theo had several more than qualified soldiers at his disposal for such a task. His arms folded across his chest. He waited for his father to say Alan or even Esaias, but after the near attack with her spoon, Theo would suggest anyone other than Esaias.

"I've grown tired of your lack of care for the loss of Lord Freville. He was a nobleman of Luana and deserves our respect. *You* will do it."

"Me?" Theo questioned. "I have more than enough duties—"

"You will be the one to earn her trust. As you have become infatuated with the nefarious possibilities of the Black Sea. It's only fitting she is your responsibility.

"My responsibility?" Theo scoffed.

"You're to be her guard and earn her trust."

Theo's nostrils flared. "I can't," he protested. The idea of parading around with Amaris on guard duty was insulting, and the thought of befriending her sent his teeth clenching. "I'm a captain."

"You're a soldier." His father pressed his hands into the chair's arms and rose. His presence towered over Theo, but he was already in the stages of falling from his prime. He may have had a couple of inches on him, but Theo was still stronger. "You don't get to deny an order."

"This is an order then, not a request?"

"This will be the last of this conversation. Delegate your investigation into Duncaster to one of your soldiers. I want you focused on earning her trust and learning who Miss Carter is. Is that clear?"

Theo's body acted of its own accord, rising from the desk and interlacing his hands behind his back. "Yes, sir." He was a captain and should've been spending every moment investigating the Duncaster disappearances, not trading stories with Amaris.

"Your people are depending on you. We've invited a viper into our midst, and we must be prepared."

My people. Everything their family did was for the people of Luana, not for themselves, but the people his father cared for held titles or had enough gold that their pockets dragged against the floor. Theo had brief bouts of jealousy of Esaias and his strength to step away from the life of nobility when he moved to Luana to be a soldier. Now was certainly one of those moments.

"What am I to do when I discover she isn't the murderer?"

"Are you certain she isn't?"

Theo's weight shifted beneath him. He hardly knew her, but she'd saved his life. His mind was swallowed by the grim memory of standing outside After's gates and Kedes's claws reaching out. He shuddered, gripping the hilt of his dagger.

His father went on. "Don't go into this believing she's innocent. Believe the worst until she proves otherwise. I'm certain with what I heard during the war, you'll have no trouble extracting the truth from her."

His father's taste for power and control was overwhelming. He knew more about the war than Theo believed him to. He turned, reaching for the door.

"Do whatever is necessary to earn her trust. I only ask, Theodoric, that you remain professional and refrain from procreating. We don't need a bastard staining the Fastrada bloodline."

Theo flung the door open, wishing it would snap from its hinges as he stepped into the hall. He ignored his father's disapproving grunt as a servant came racing toward him with flushed cheeks and panting breaths.

What is it now?

§

THEO MOVED SWIFTLY down the hall, not caring that he was sending paintings to turn on end or passing servants at an alarming rate. He raced toward Esaias's room, stopping and pounding on the door.

A muffled sound came from the other side. Theo grasped the handle and entered the bedchamber. Esaias was in bed with his golden quilt pulled up to his chin. Onika was at his side, pressing a compress to his forehead. She turned her head and offered a weak smile. She pulled a stray strand of her dark curls and wound it tightly behind her ear.

"Can we have a moment, Onika?" Theo asked.

She raised a brow but dropped the rag in the basin of water. As a servant of the manor, she wore the same white dress and beige apron as all the rest, but a gold necklace could always be seen poking out at the back of her neck. Theo always wondered why she hid it instead of displaying it over her dress. Maybe it was family heirloom.

She stood, brushing her umber-colored hands across her apron. She stopped at Theo's side, her head barely coming to his shoulder.

"He was fine the last few days, hardly more than a cough—" Theo began.

"He's caught a fever and hasn't thrown a single insult at me," she said, which, when it came to Onika and Esaias, that was grim news. "I found him unconscious in the stables last night. He hadn't been able to stay awake for more than a few minutes at a time throughout the night."

"Did he catch something in Duncaster? Has anyone else fallen ill?"

"I'm not sure where he caught it, but I haven't heard of any other cases."

"Thank you."

Onika nodded, and Theo hardly heard her leave or the familiar click of the latch when she closed the door. The ceiling pressed against his shoulders. He went to Esaias's side and sat in the small chair beside his bed.

"Esaias," Theo whispered.

Esaias answered him with a moan. His skin was pale, and beads of sweat trickled down his forehead. Theo grabbed the rag, wringing it out and dragging it across his brow.

"Theo," he wheezed.

"I thought you only attracted women, not a plague," Theo said.

Esaias attempted a laugh, but he erupted into a coughing fit. He tried to sit up. The quilt fell from his chest, revealing the beginnings of black lines running like veins across his chest.

"Esaias." Theo's voice was breathless.

He dropped back to the bed, his hand reaching for his heaving chest. "I know," he whispered. "Scrying fever."

"How is that possible? There hasn't been a case in Godwin for years." Theo pulled his shirt over his face and stepped back. The only cases of scrying fever he'd ever encountered were in Mosfelkov during the war when it wiped out half a company.

"Theo, I need you to do something for me."

"Don't talk like that," Theo shot at him. "You're not dying."

"Please," he whispered, his voice raspy. Esaias turned away, coughing into his elbow.

"Why has no one sent for Amaris? Why was Onika even in here?"

"I tried to throw her out, but she wouldn't listen to me."

Onika wasn't one to take risks. She may have sailed with them during the war to assist the mystiques and perform other duties, such as cleaning and cooking in the camps, but she was often far from the fighting.

"What can be done?"

"Nothing," Esaias said.

"There can't be nothing. What about Cornelius's journal? Has Onika looked in there?"

He'd attempted to find a treatment during the war and spent countless hours concocting various tonics.

"I'm not sure."

Theo sat back, running his hands through the strands of his hair. He couldn't lose Esaias. No one else, never again. "Amaris must know something. She saved me for realm's sake."

"It's useless," Esaias mumbled. "Burn my body, and all my possessions while you're at it, to keep it from spreading."

Rather than argue, Theo ran out the door and headed toward the library.

CHAPTER 18

Amaris

AMARIS WAS ATTEMPTING to keep count of the days with small tally marks she'd dug into one of the legs of the worktable, but with getting knocked out and forgetting here and there, it was hard to tell. *Nine or ten days? Maybe more?*

Pricilla didn't seem to understand personal space when she visited Amaris almost every day to go over the various herbs and where to go about finding things around the tower. Her company, however, was better than Theodoric's. Amaris refused to utter a word to him, and he retaliated with beastly grunts the few times they'd run into each other.

Sephardi was the one who picked her up from her room to grab breakfast each morning before settling her into the mystique tower. Amaris had first thought Sephardi was going to be like the rest of them, but she had an interesting nature about her as she smirked and sat in one of the chairs by the fireplace. She wasn't one for conversation, though, as she shuffled through various pieces of parchment.

An echo of heeled boots rang through the stairwell, and Amaris and Sephardi both turned to find Adelaide with a large wicker basket resting on her hip. "More herbs for you."

Adelaide gave her a funny expression, likely because Amaris was staring at her as if she were a figment of her imagination. She hadn't seen her since that first time, and since she wasn't a soldier, Amaris had lost faith she'd help her escape.

Sephardi offered Adelaide a quick nod as she plopped the basket on the worktable and whistled, taking in the room. "You cleaned."

"There isn't much else for me to do."

"Besides argue with my brother."

Amaris didn't bother entertaining her comment as she began sifting through the basket of new herbs. She hadn't recognized a single one in all her cleaning, but with Pricilla's help, maybe she would find a good place for them.

"Theo isn't much for talking these days," Adelaide continued.

Amaris groaned. "Even if your brother wanted to talk to me, I'd have nothing to say to that ungrateful jackass."

Adelaide smirked, but a stifled laugh sounded from Sephardi before she cleared her throat and continued her work.

Turning to avoid prying ears, Adelaide leaned closer. "It isn't that he's ungrateful," she whispered.

"What are you saying?"

"I know my brother better than anyone, and even I've felt he's pushed me away. I don't think he wanted you to save him."

Amaris placed a jar of herbs on a shelf, her mouth going dry. "You think he wanted to die?"

Adelaide nodded toward Sephardi and stepped closer, whispering in Amaris's ear. "Theo's been gone for three years, fighting in the Trade War. My family received word during his first year that he went missing behind enemy lines for two seasons. He came back different."

"What happened to him?" Amaris shouldn't have cared to learn what he went through. It didn't change how he'd treated her or how he'd implied Derek didn't want to be with her anymore.

"I don't know."

Amaris eyed Sephardi but continued to flip through her pages. "Was he captured or lost?"

"Again, I don't know." Adelaide's voice was soft, and Amaris strained to hear her. Adelaide seemed to be well-versed in the art of whispering. "My guess is captured, but even Esaias won't say."

"Esaias was there too?"

How many more of them had been in the war? Had Alan or Sephardi been there too? Maybe that was why Alan was such a brute.

"Not when Theodoric and his squad went missing, but they were all under the same company."

"Why are you telling me this?" Adelaide hardly knew Amaris but didn't seem to care that she was throwing her brother's deepest secrets at her.

"He'll never tell you why he snaps at you or says something rude, but I thought maybe if you knew, it wouldn't be so bad."

A life preserver. That was what she'd thrown out, but Amaris wasn't sure if it was for Theodoric or her.

"Theo is caring. Try appealing to that side of him."

Amaris scoffed, "Believe me, I tried that the first day I met him."

"If he would only set his duty aside and get Bennet out of his ear, he would see what I do," she said.

"And what do you see?" Amaris filled her arms with more jars. Even if she didn't know their properties, she could at least alphabetize them.

"You didn't kill Lord Freville," she whispered.

Amaris almost dropped the jars, leaning into the counter to catch them.

"The duke believes what he does is for the good of the province. I, however, believe he only cares about building his reputation. I suggest, if you want to walk out of here, you play their games."

"I tried playing, but it didn't work," Amaris muttered, hanging her head. "Bennet wants to kill me, the duke thinks I'm lying, and soldiers like Alan think they can treat me however they like."

Adelaide tapped her chin. "Alan carries many faces—"

"He threatened to cut out my tongue," Amaris snapped.

Adelaide met her with silence, obviously not surprised.

"I noticed how close you are. Are you two—"

"Together?" She smirked. "No, it's not like that at all. Alan may be protective, but we don't fancy each other. Besides, I have no plans for marriage."

Amaris lifted her head. "You don't?"

"Why would I?" she growled low. "Shackled to a single person for the rest of my life isn't exactly what I envision for my future."

A twinge sharpened in Amaris's chest. Was that how some people envisioned marriage? She thumbed the inside of her engagement ring. They may have had their disagreements, but Amaris wanted to be with Derek forever, or at least however long they could get in their lifetimes.

"Is that why you ran away?" Adelaide asked.

Amaris held her breath. It was a blow each time one of them mentioned it.

"No." Amaris nibbled the edge of her lip.

"What's his name?"

Amaris contemplated giving up her weakness, but if she was stuck here, then they likely couldn't find him and use him against her. "Derek."

"What an odd name."

"What do you want out of life if marriage isn't on the table?" Amaris brushed back her hair and leaned against the worktable. She missed the caress of his hands across her arms and the kiss of his lips on her neck.

"To fight." Adelaide didn't hesitate with Sephardi in the room as she drew her shoulders back. "I want to serve in the King's Guard one day."

"How can you?"

"That's the problem," she breathed. "I don't know yet."

A cough echoed in the tower and Amaris shot her gaze to the tower door.

Theodoric braced a hand on the frame, his cheeks flushed and sweat beading his brows. "What are you doing here?" His eyes settled on Adelaide.

"Leaving," Adelaide threw at him without turning his way. She offered

Amaris a smirk before she ran past her brother down the steps.

Amaris folded her arms, raising an inquisitive eye. "What do you want?"

"I have a patient who needs your help."

Finally. Before her feet even moved, her hands were already fussing with her hair to braid it out of her face. "Lead the way."

"I must warn you, it's scrying fever."

Sephardi faltered with her shuffling papers and sighed.

"What's scrying fever?" Amaris asked.

"I thought you were a mystique?" he snipped.

"I am"—Amaris bit her lip—"but it doesn't mean I've heard of everything. What is it?"

"It's a deadly fever that gives someone a haunting rash," Sephardi said, her voice losing all its warmth.

"A fever and a rash?" Amaris raised a brow. "Doesn't sound that deadly to me."

"Hardly anyone has survived it. I know of one person," Theodoric said.

Amaris gulped, her fingers slowing as they neared the end of her braid. "How contagious is it?"

"It killed over a hundred soldiers during the war."

Amaris didn't have masks, but she sure as hell wasn't catching some deadly disease and dying before she got a chance to escape. She scanned the room and grabbed a few pieces of linen. Amaris began down the stairs, not bothering to wait for him. Jumping the last few steps, she took off at a quick pace through the library. She wrapped the linen around her neck and let it drape loosely over her chest.

Amaris threw Theodoric the other piece. "Tie it around your nose and mouth when we're near them. If it's as deadly as you say it is, we don't need anyone else contracting it."

She pushed through the library doors and turned, but he grabbed the collar of her shirt and pulled her the other way. "This way," he said, taking the lead.

"Who's the patient?"

"My cousin, Esaias," he answered, his voice cracking.

Amaris stumbled at the break in his tough demeanor, but she didn't stop as she chased after him.

He halted outside his cousin's door with his hand wrapped around the handle.

"What are you waiting for?" Amaris blurted out, needing to see the scrying fever for herself.

"You must prepare yourself for what you're about to see. It can be shocking," he whispered.

"Oh, please." She waved him off. "I've seen worse."

She likely had, but she was curious if it was about to be some new disease or if it was something as simple as the chickenpox.

She tugged the cloth over her mouth and nose as Theodoric pushed open the door. Even through the thick piece of linen, the all-too-familiar smell of sickness hit her. The one where someone had been lying in bed with a nonstop fever and a hint of puke. She didn't feel the need to wrinkle her nose, though, or gag at the familiar stench.

A woman with rich umber skin sat by his side. Her dark hair ran down her back in tight curls and fell over her shoulder as she leaned and muttered into Esaias's ear.

"What do you want now, Onika?" he groaned.

Onika narrowed her honey-colored eyes at him, but their parallel to the sweet nectar stopped there with her glower. She pulled the damp compress from his forehead, which earned her a begrudging grunt.

"He's been awake since you left," Onika said, standing and striding through the room. She stopped and leaned closer to whisper before she departed. "But I think it's spreading."

"What's spreading?" Amaris asked.

"Who's that?" Esaias attempted to sit up. He smiled as he caught sight of Amaris but winced with the little effort and fell back to the bed. "At least I can gaze upon a beautiful sight before I die."

"What are your symptoms?" Amaris ignored his pathetic excuse for flirting and pulled back the covers. She gasped.

"That," Esaias coughed.

"And a nasty cough," Amaris added.

Esaias's wheeze at the end of it meant the small passages in his lungs were starting to tighten. That might have been the least of his worries though. Amaris couldn't avert her eyes from the black streaks spreading across his body like arcs of electricity.

"The rash, I assume?"

Esaias snatched the blanket from her grasp and hugged it up to his chin. "I'm freezing."

Amaris moved to his wall of expansive windows, drawing back the golden curtains.

"What are you doing?" Esaias groaned, pulling the blanket over his face.

"Fresh air." Amaris felt around the sill for the mechanism and unlatched the window. It was identical to the ones in her room.

Theodoric gave her a side-eye. "You figured that out quickly."

Amaris returned a nefarious grin with a shoulder shrug.

"What will that do?" Esaias coughed.

"First of all, it'll bring fresh air for you in this stifling room with that wretched cough," she said before striding to the door.

"Where are you going?" Theodoric asked.

"There's nothing in here that'll help me cure him. I need supplies." Amaris's gaze shifted to Esaias, who was now having a coughing fit.

"What you need," he gasped, "is the mystique's—"

"The what?"

"The—" Esaias tried again, but his cough overtook him.

Theodoric sighed. "The old mystique kept a journal of everything he encountered. When he was stationed with us during the war, he would've recorded the cases of scrying fever."

"Alright, where's this journal then?"

"I'm assuming with all his belongings."

Amaris cringed at the remembrance of the stacks of crates and chests she'd dreaded touching. "I might know someone who can help." She removed the cloth from her face and headed back to the library. "I expect privileges if I'm going to be curing this deadly disease."

Theodoric lowered his makeshift mask. "What sort of privileges?"

She stumbled forward, having thought he was going to flat-out deny her. Now she had to think of something, but what kind of privileges could he even offer? It wasn't like she could ask for free time when he wasn't there breathing the same air.

"First, I want an apology."

"An apology?"

"Yes." Amaris shifted her focus forward, turning her nose up. "You owe me."

He stopped, but his gaze swept to an open window, his thumb swirling along the hilt of his dagger.

"Why do you do that?"

"What?" he asked, pulling from his trance, his eyes narrowing after their moment of glassiness.

"You hold your knife and rub your thumb along the edge of it."

"A habit," he whispered, resuming the trek toward the library.

Amaris ran past him, stopping as his chest slammed into her. He clenched his teeth, flaring his nostrils.

"As you said, we're stuck with each other, so how about, instead of you being—"

"Will you quit insulting me?" he grumbled, and Amaris pulled back. "You have done nothing but spew hate at me, calling me all sorts of horrendous names."

"You..." she stammered. "You kidnapped me! What am I supposed to call you, Mr. Ray of Sunshine?"

He turned away. "I'm sorry! Is that what you want to hear?" he shouted. "You have no idea what it's like having to deal with all of this!" He stepped over and leaned into the wall, pinching his nose as his eyes squeezed together.

"Are you still dealing with headaches?"

"Yes," he said, hunching forward.

"Why didn't you tell me?" she scolded, cocking a hip and folding her arms. "I could have given you something." She was surprised he was still dealing with the concussion, but it wasn't uncommon for symptoms to persist, especially with the severity he had.

"I can handle it myself."

"Obviously not," she scoffed. "You should be resting. All this stress is making it worse."

He let out a small bit of laughter, but it wasn't the happy kind, more like a creepy laugh that pricked the hairs on her arms. "There is a murderer within Luana's borders, and you're telling me I need to rest?"

A tough guy who thought he didn't need to take a break. Amaris hated these types. "You're no good if your headaches keep getting worse. A concussion is a serious head injury."

"Good thing we have the best mystique," he said sarcastically. "Tell me, how do you do it?"

"Do what?"

"Save people who are on the edge of death."

"Is this seriously about what happened in the river?"

"Why are you so adamant about hiding your secret?"

"It's not a secret," she huffed. "I... Why would I bother giving you the answers you want? Have you ever been ripped from your family and unable to get back? You kidnapped me because I was in the wrong place at the wrong time and have treated me like I'm a piece of gum on the bottom of your shoe."

His hand slipped from the hilt of his dagger.

"You all assumed I was the murderer in that clearing and didn't bother to believe anything I said or to even look for evidence of someone else. I'm sorry if you're all too terrified, but I have a home and people waiting for me. I don't care about this murderer, this place, or what your father says. I want to go home."

"You're right," he whispered. "I don't think you're a murderer."

"Your damn rig— Wait." Amaris's breath ceased. "You don't think it was me."

He shook his head.

"Then why am I still a prisoner?"

"I hold no authority over my father or Bennet."

"I'm stuck here until they decide otherwise?" An ache rattled in her chest. She breathed, blinking back tears.

"Is anyone looking for you?"

"I'm not a murderer," she choked.

"Where's your family?"

My family. Amaris didn't know what to call what she and Derek were. *Family* didn't settle well on the tip of her tongue, but what even was a family? Viv certainly felt like a sister, but an ache stretched a hole inside her that she didn't know who could fill anymore.

"I have no idea," she cried, dropping her face into her hands.

"Why were you in the woods?"

Tears spilled between her fingers, salty beads of shame for what she'd done. "We had a stupid fight, and I ran." Her legs gave beneath her, and her knees hit the floor.

"Do you think they're looking for you?"

"They have to be," she said through the tears. "But...I don't think they'll be able to find me."

Theodoric kneeled beside her, his eyes darting around them as he leaned in and whispered, "My father will only release you when he's satisfied or if someone comes to speak on your behalf."

Amaris choked, attempting to pause her sobs to speak. "What happens if no one comes or he isn't satisfied?"

He dipped his chin and rounded his shoulders. She'd learned they were the same age, but the sunken nature of his cheeks and the dark circles under his eyes added years to his face. Adelaide had said he'd changed. Did he once have a pink tinge to his cheeks? Did a smile once flourish on his lips every morning?

"Will he actually kill me?" she breathed, finally controlling her sobs.

He swallowed, and for a moment, she saw a boy kneeling before her. A young boy uncertain of the world, maybe even fearful. "I don't know. Your skills as a mystique are valuable. I can't see him giving that up."

"What can I do?" Her eyes were puffy, and she wiped a bit of snot dripping from her nose.

"Use your skills and prove to my father you're more valuable alive."

It was no longer a fight for her freedom but her life. If she didn't wow the duke, she was dead. How was she supposed to be a great mystique when she barely knew what she was doing?

"What changed your mind?" she asked as he offered a hand and pulled her to her feet.

"You jumped into a river with an injured hand to save me," he whispered. "Someone you didn't know and who treated you so poorly."

Amaris gazed at his hand slipping from hers and settling along his belt as he sidestepped her, continuing toward the library. She paused, running a thumb over her palm and watching as his figure shrank, and he once again transformed into that small boy. She silently followed him, passing through the halls that all looked the same, down the grand staircase, and through the hall, where every portrait stared down at her.

He braced his hand on the plain doors and pushed them open. Amaris would never get used to it. Instantly, the smell of old books hit her, and it was a small bit of beauty in this prison. She wasn't one to read much, but she understood it was an art, much like her drawings.

"Who are we looking for?" Theodoric asked.

"Pricilla."

He took the lead. They made several weird turns, getting them completely lost by her standards, until they came to a small alcove. It was a dead end about ten feet wide and circular in shape, with bookshelves lining the entire wall. A single desk sat with scrolls pinned down on top of it. A few red velvet chairs and a matching couch were among the hanging lanterns scattered about. For a place tucked away, it seemed to be used frequently, with the worn couch cushions and books piled on the floor.

Standing on her tiptoes across the room, reaching for a book on the top shelf, was Pricilla. Theodoric strode over and grabbed the book for her.

"Thank you, Captain." She smiled, then turned to meet Amaris. Her lips spread into a large grin, but Theodoric pulled back her attention.

"We need the mystique's journal." He eyed Pricilla as one might a child who'd done something wrong.

"You think I have it?" Pricilla balked.

"I thought you'd be able to help me find it," Amaris interjected, "being the mystique's replacement for a while." She wanted her help, not to get her in trouble, but Theodoric didn't pay Amaris a second glance as he eyed Pricilla.

"If I recall, Cornelius was certain a few of his anatomy tomes had gone missing over the years," Theodoric said.

"All right," Pricilla said, her voice airy. "I may have found it." She skipped to an empty part of the floor and pressed on a wooden plank, gripping it as it came flying up to meet her. She withdrew a leather-bound journal and tossed it to Theodoric. "I was going to return it after I finished recording everything. Cornelius always kept all his books to himself."

"As we have a new mystique, I think she might allow you access to her collection," he said, licking his thumb and shuffling through the pages. "Here it is."

"What does it say?" Amaris asked.

"He lists the ingredients for his scrying fever tonic."

Pricilla's eyes turned wild. She brushed her shoulders and turned in a circle. "Why are you looking that up?" she asked in alarm. Maybe it was a way of warding off bad energy.

"Esaias has contracted it. It's likely he brought it back from Duncaster," he answered.

"I'm so sorry," she began. "If I'd known—"

"You couldn't have," Theodoric said, grasping her shoulder.

A single tear rolled down her cheek. Amaris imagined he'd pull back or shy away, but he wiped it, giving her a wry smile. He threw the book to Amaris.

She shuffled through the pages until she found *scrying fever* written across the top of one. She skimmed through the chicken scratch. *Had he ever heard of good penmanship?* She fanned a few pages, reviewing the contents. It was her own set of protocols, like the ones at work. It listed everything from tonic recipes to descriptions of his patients' injuries and illnesses.

"Let's get what we need." Amaris continued reading. The old mystique's descriptions weren't encouraging that the cure worked, but there was one account of a patient who survived the disease. She forced a swallow. What if the tonic was useless and that one patient was just a lucky break? What would happen if she couldn't cure Esaias?

Theodoric gave Pricilla a reassuring nod, and Amaris offered what smile she could before they were off and headed toward the tower.

"Have you ever heard of bufomom?" Amaris's eyes were glued to the journal. She giggled to herself thinking of how, back home, someone at the station would've tried to crack a mom joke, but she refrained from letting Theodoric hear her. The disease was scarier than she initially thought.

"I'm not familiar," he answered flatly.

"It says it's the main ingredient in the tonic."

"What does it look like?"

Amaris shoved the journal in his face, pointing to the small yellow flowers sketched on the page. She flipped through the book, perusing the various pictures and recipes. Her eyes stopped on a description of the best method to suture a cut to the abdomen. A knot twisted in her gut. A mystique wasn't some ordinary medical professional or even the level of a paramedic. They were physicians.

She stepped into the nearly pristine tower, ignoring the stacks of crates to her right. The wall of shelves looked perfectly symmetrical after her constant organizing. She set about pulling them down, reading the labels, and comparing the flowers to the picture in the journal.

"Can you grab those for me?" she asked Theodoric. He reached up and pulled down several jars with specks of yellow on the leaves. He set them beside her, then leaned against the counter and waited for his next order in silence.

"You said you lost the mystique in the war. You were there?" she pried.

His thumb brushed what appeared to be a drawing etched into his knife's hilt, circling the worn carving.

So that little habit has to do with the war.

"Yes," he finally answered. He slid up his sleeve and scratched his arm, but the faintest glimpse of a jagged scar began on his upper forearm and disappeared under his shirt.

Amaris averted her gaze. "Where were you stationed?"

"Fort Berland in Lungvik," he answered sharply. "Have you found it yet?"

Startled at his tone, she dropped the flowers, and they scattered across the wooden counter. "I believe these are it," she said, swallowing her breath.

"You believe?"

"Okay, yes." She dragged her finger across the label. "But we'll need more ingredients. It says we need pygmy peppermint and thorn marjoram. I don't remember seeing those when I organized everything."

"They're common kitchen herbs. Ms. Borstad will have them in the garden."

He pulled from the counter, his belt jingling and his steps heavy as he started toward the stairs. Amaris paused before following him, pinching a bufomom flower between her fingers. Its petals were like velvet, its color a vibrant yellow. She dropped the flower back into the jar and caressed the shiny, white scars scattering her knuckles, Theodoric's thick scar still prevalent in her mind.

§

AMARIS KNEELED BEFORE the planter and dug her fingers into the dirt. The fresh breeze ruffled through her hair, and her fingers embraced the cool soil. Theodoric was perched on a short stone wall on the edge of the garden. His complexity was an understatement. She'd spent the entire trek examining how he walked, the way his hands clenched, and how his eyes cleared each door he passed.

The paramedic within her couldn't help analyzing him. He rubbed his shoulders, attempting to massage the strained muscles. It was hard to believe he was so young and had been to an actual war.

"Good, he's letting you out for some fresh air." Adelaide grinned, plopping beside Theodoric.

He gave her a gentle smile, breaking the crust he held firm in his jaw. She kicked her legs against the gray stones, knocking the sand from her boots.

"We're creating a tonic," Amaris announced, still digging up the thorn marjoram. It was a tricky root, burrowed in the ground. She planned to gather as much as she could, especially since the disease seemed to be highly contagious. She needed her strength to be alert. If eyes were watching her every moment, she wanted to be prepared.

"What for?"

"Scrying fever," Amaris said, ripping up one of the roots. Dirt flew everywhere as she collapsed back. She cringed as the back of her head smacked the ground.

"Good one." Adelaide laughed. "Next you're going to tell me nether madness is running rampant." She folded over in laughter, only ceasing when she saw Amaris's muscles stiffen as she laid still in the grass. "You're serious?"

"What's nether madness?" Amaris hoped it wasn't something else she had to deal with.

"Nothing we'll ever have to worry about here," Theodoric cut in.

"It's a disease that makes you go crazy till you..." Adelaide slid her hand across her throat, crossing her eyes and sticking out her tongue.

"You die from delirium?"

"Or you kill yourself, whichever comes first." Adelaide smirked and smacked Theodoric on the back. "Like he said, not around here. But please indulge me. Who in the realm has scrying fever?"

"Esaias," Theodoric said gruffly.

Adelaide lost all matter of her joking demeanor. "Has anyone else come down with it?"

"Thankfully no," he answered.

The whinny of a horse grabbed Amaris's attention. Neither of them seemed to notice, but her eyes darted over her shoulder and scanned the grounds. The wall engulfed the manor, only slowly receding until it stopped at the beach.

She squinted, and along the edge of the wall she could make out what looked to be a barn or some stables. Her heart lifted, a plan forming. She'd only pondered how to slip away from her guards, not what she would do once she did. Would Theodoric help her now?

"Amaris?" Adelaide's voice beckoned her back to the conversation. "I said, tell me about Derek. I find it hard to believe that a woman as fierce as you would settle for any ordinary man."

Amaris raised her brows and passed a glance to Theodoric, who had previously been busy nudging the toe of his boot at a rock. Now his awareness was keenly set on her. She wished she hadn't heard Adelaide and Theodoric hadn't either. Adelaide was either baiting her or wasn't one to

keep secrets.

Amaris sat up, brushing the dirt wedged between the lines of her palms. "We've been friends for so long it's hard to pick a few things to describe him."

"What's the worst part of relationships?"

"Adelaide," Theodoric snipped.

She waved him off, furrowing her brow as she implored for Amaris to go on.

What was the worst part? For Amaris and Derek, it was the fighting, and for what? Most of their fights were stupid bickering matches. A few weeks ago, they'd fought over who'd left the toaster unplugged. She hated it—the person she'd become and what his job had turned him into. Before his promotion, he'd never raised his voice at her.

Amaris found her hand trailing across her cheek, her nails caressing where the bruise once sat, but she instantly dropped her hand, hoping neither of them noticed. She'd studied it every morning during her bath to assess the discoloration.

"Sharing food." She nibbled at the corner of her lip, and a subtle shift of her gaze caught Theodoric's eyes trained on her. "Derek loves to swipe food off my plate."

"How rude." Adelaide gawked. "If a man ever tries to grab from my plate, I'll pin his hand to the table."

"With what daggers?" Theodoric asked, his eyes growing wide.

Adelaide sent him a narrowed gaze. It was probably a sibling thing. "With a fork. It'll hurt more."

Amaris went back to the pesky roots within the garden box, but Theodoric's eyes were like magnets. She refused to meet his eye contact but knew it was there, burning through her skin. He couldn't have pieced it together. She could've been scratching an itch for all he knew.

CHAPTER 19

Theo

AFTER PROCURING THE necessary herbs, Amaris had set to making the tonic. It'd taken hours of measuring, boiling, and her frustrated grunts, but she'd finished the first couple of doses late last night. Theo hadn't been able to sleep until he'd known they had a tonic in hand for Esaias in the morning.

Gris had been the only person during the war who'd survived the disease, and she'd been delirious for most of the time. Cornelius had healed her, but it'd taken weeks for her to fully recover. Even with the tonic, it'd been a miracle that she'd survived, but it had worked once and would do the same for Esaias.

After the discussion with his father, he relinquished his investigation into Freville's death and the other disappearances to Gris. As she'd taken it upon herself to examine the body in the first place, she was best suited for the task.

That left Theo to spend what time he could helping Amaris with the tonic. Unfortunately, bufomom hadn't been on Pricilla's list of herbs for Sephardi to track down on her supply run. Cornelius had once told Theo of a shop he frequented to procure rare herbs and other curious items.

He lifted his hand to knock on the washroom door to check on Amaris, but it swung open, and she wore a navy-blue dress hugging her every curve and flowing barely past her knees. It left her legs bare with nothing to be imagined. She'd even parted with her strange boots, exchanging them for a pair of silk slippers.

"Impatient, are we?" she huffed, inclining a brow.

Theo felt like he was sixteen again and about to fumble over his words at the slightest glance of a woman.

"Laundry day," she added, noticing Theo's eyes lingering on her dress.

She stepped past him and headed for the main staircase. Theo shook the unnatural feeling of seeing her in anything other than her usual blouse and trousers. Her hand slid down the banister as a hop overtook her steps. She was lighter on her feet, bouncing instead of dragging her jingling boots behind her. Perhaps she was hopeful the tonic would work, and she had a sparkle in her eye. Theo had seen it last night as she stood scribbling in the journal and counting and weighing the herbs. Cornelius had had a similar look about him when he dove into his work. Maybe she was no different.

If she could remain sure in the face of the frightening disease, then maybe Theo could too. He forced Esaias's pale and sweaty face from his mind. Amaris had given Esaias the first dose of the tonic that morning, but Theo had been forced to hold his mouth shut after he'd attempted to spit it out.

"What's this shop called?" Amaris asked.

"The Merry Sheridan." Theo followed in step beside her as they descended the stairs leading to the city.

She paused before the wall surrounding the manor, staring up at the sentries posted for the day. Her swallow was audible, but they took no heed of her as Theo offered each of them a curt nod.

"Am I allowed—"

"As the mystique, it's customary to see you milling through the city. If you weren't, the people would think you were imaginary."

"Oh." She sighed and raked a hand though her hair. It'd started curling around her crown, and the ends had begun to form small ringlets, as if remembering a time where it'd once held voluminous tendrils.

Her home grew more perplexing as her story began to unravel, especially as her hair appeared to not have felt a salty breeze in years. Her accent wasn't of Godwin, but it wasn't likely she came from an island in the Black Sea. Asking where she was from had been on the tip of his tongue, along with further questioning her regarding her betrothed. The small caress of her finger over her cheek when she'd spoken of him told more than she would ever reveal, and it heated Theo's blood.

Their stroll drew them closer to the bustling streets of the city. She gaped at the cobbled road and darted her gaze around at the towering buildings around them. Her lips parted as her head whipped back and forth, eyeing the glass-windowed shops and the open windows above with families chattering. Laundry lines were strung up, and blankets and garments flapped as a briny breeze swept in from the bay.

They pushed deeper through the beginnings of the city, and Amaris's eyes grew larger with each step. It was the look of someone who'd never set eyes on Luana Bay, and a part of Theo felt a certain elation to be the one to show her. He'd always been proud to hail from here, not because of his birthright but because of the people.

Rounding the corner to pass through the open street market, she gasped at the crowd. Tents of varying colors lined the cobbled street filled with vendor carts, some wobbly and sagging, while others were robust. The tenants swarmed the carts, their chatter catching Theo's ear as they went about their daily shopping.

Amaris's hand latched on to his arm. His eyes drifted to the white knuckles of her fingers digging into his forearm.

"Are you not accustomed to busy towns?" Theo hollered over the shouting and haggling of the street merchants.

The space between them tightened as she attempted to avoid getting swept up in the crowd. "No, I've been to busy cities, but when I first saw it...it isn't at all what I thought it would be."

"What did you picture it to be in the daytime?"

"I don't know. Maybe less normal shopping and more..." It seemed she couldn't even bring herself to express what she thought.

"Well, I can assure you that Luana Bay is as normal as it comes."

The corners of her lips turned up, but Theo averted his face instead of returning a smile of his own. Her fingers loosened their grip around his arm, but she still clung to his shirt as he dragged her through the crowd. She watched with great intensity the business of the street vendors. As they had doses for the next two days and weren't in the greatest hurry, he allowed her to stop at several booths to see what they were selling.

She was continually astonished, like she'd never seen the vibrant life of a market either. Even her toes kept catching on the uneven cobblestones beneath their feet, as if unaccustomed to the everyday road structure. Some villages and towns, such as Westbury, were still supported with dirt roads.

What if she was betrothed to a Grant and had traveled from Westbury? It was a different direction than Duncaster, but if she'd been running from him, he could've followed her. Her haste could have sent her into the woods. His father could protect her if she were being harmed. No woman had ever come forward from Westbury, but they heard rumors of the ongoings behind closed doors.

They stopped at a painter's booth after Amaris requested to see each piece of art. Her eyes locked on a painting of the night sky, her fingers hovering over the stars, as if she were trying to make out the constellations. Unfortunately, only Edgar's Shield was depicted. What could've been a beautiful sight was tainted with its focus on the God of War. Amaris sighed as she moved to the next landscape canvas.

"Do you admire art?" Theo asked.

"I love it," she admitted. "I used to draw but not much anymore."

"How come?"

She gave Theo a thin smile, shrugging. "Life got in the way." She perked up at the lively cadence of a fiddle. "Is that music?"

A small band was set up outside The Merry Sheridan, bustling a Gorrin tune. She tapped her foot and held her arms. Something attempted to break through her grim mask. The lines around her eyes creased, and a single dimple poked into her cheek. Not long ago, Theo thought he'd never see anyone with a look like that ever again, a genuine smile.

Something dropped in his chest, and he rubbed at his sternum as he took shelter beneath the canopy of the shop. It was heavy and began wrapping around him. It was similar to the moment in the throne room. For so long, he'd been feeling nothing besides the hilt of his dagger in his palm or the anger constantly skimming the surface of his skin. He took a deep breath, attempting to push whatever it was away.

He forced several deep breaths as he focused his eyes on Amaris clapping and humming along. With each next beat, it slowly receded. When the song finished and his chest felt as normal as it could be, he gestured with a nod to the shop door. Amaris headed in first, sending a chime to ring through the room as the door swung open.

"Feel free to look around. I'll be with you in a moment." A woman's voice carried as a distant echo.

Amaris paused beside the front counter, gawking at the wall of herbs, the antiques displayed in glass cases, and the other oddities. She assessed her surroundings and stepped deeper into the shop.

Theo rubbed at his chest as he turned to a glass case with a small replica of a ship floating over a stormy sea. Its sails were black, and a serpent protruded from the bow with a forked tongue. He'd read about the pirate ship once called the *Serpent*. It was a deadly vessel, leaving no survivors, and had been rumored to sail as the flagship of the Pirate Queen's armada. Theo settled his hand over his mouth as he read the label.

Epchatet. Bimpa monom per ditsa wafshom. Aslorn per de eclahard.

His eyes widened as he read it again. The *Serpent*. A deadly ship for a disastrous captain. *Brace for her what?*

Theo pulled away before more confusion settled over him. Amaris had moved to the back of the shop, and she stood with her lips parted as she admired a black crystal chandelier with dozens of candles glowing above her head.

If he was ever going to get her to open up to him, he needed to offer something in return. While he'd watched her work in the tower last night, he had the realization. She was a woman who sought justice. She wouldn't divulge her secrets to just anyone, let alone someone she frequently called names and screamed at. Theo hoped the moment in the hallway had since changed their dynamic and that her desire to help heal Esaias wasn't only because she knew it was her duty. His father had asked him to get to know her, but it wasn't about attaining information for him. She wasn't a murderer. No, it was for her protection.

Theo had spent most of the time waiting for her to bathe deciding what to share with her. It'd seemed a deep level of understanding was needed for her to reveal her abusive betrothed. The war was, unfortunately, the rawest information Theo felt even compared to what she went through.

"It's miraculous, isn't it?" Theo stepped toward her as she still gaped at the chandelier.

"Do you think they have to replace all those candles each day?" she asked.

Theo blinked, waiting for her to burst into laughter, but her gaze remained twisted in a puzzling expression. "You're serious?"

"Well, yeah. That's a shit ton of candles."

"I would imagine so." Theo took a moment before he spoke further. "A luxury like candlelight was one thing I took for granted during the war. We lived by the sun most days, which, in some parts of Mosfelkov, doesn't shine all parts of the year, due to the intense snowstorms."

"Wasn't it dangerous to make you go in the winter?"

"Winter?" Theo asked.

Amaris sucked in her lips, her eyes darting to the shelves. "The cold...I mean, snow and stuff."

How odd. Theo continued. "Most of Mosfelkov experiences bitter cold practically year-round. Only a few parts along the southern coast have limited snowfall and experience the full nature of the seasons like we do. We didn't do most of the fighting during Whitereign or Darkreign, though, but it was still freezing within the confines of our camps and the fortress we held."

"It wasn't that long ago?" she breathed, shifting her gaze to the abstract paintings along the wall as she tilted her head to study them.

"No," Theo sighed. "I returned at the end of Bloomreign only a few weeks before we journeyed to Duncaster."

"How do you forget about it? Move on like nothing happened?" she asked, her fingers tapping her thigh as her eyes stared at Theo. Those blue things attempted to pierce through every wall he'd built.

His body tensed, and he forced a deep inhale, needing to push himself to say something of value, to offer her something. He hadn't moved on. He couldn't. What happened in Oystein Castle would forever be etched in his mind, the atrocities committed, the horror he'd seen.

"Theodoric..."

His vision grew red around the edges. The room became shrouded in a bloody hue. *Not again.* He gripped the hilt of his dagger, praying to any god to pull back the red, to pull him from his head, to release him from the panic.

"Are you—"

Theo's chest instantly released. A woman with a dirty rag in her hands, wiping the grime from her fingers, ducked her head beneath a banner and came to the front of the store. Theo attempted to shove the memory within the small crack of his mind.

"What can I do for you?" Her deep-set, silver eyes landed on Amaris leaning against the wall of herbs.

"I need bufomom," Amaris answered. "Lots of it." She pulled her attention from Theo.

"Bufomom?" the woman asked, chuckling. "What do you plan to do with that?"

"This is Amaris Carter," Theo cut in, clearing his throat. "She is Luana's new mystique and is preparing to bolster her stock. We've procured most herbs for her, but this is a rare one."

Amaris shot Theo a questioning look, but he gave a brief shake of his head. Growing word of scrying fever would be as grim as the disease itself spreading through the city. Panic in the streets was something Theo didn't wish to deal with, as he could barely grapple it in his own head.

"I see." The shopkeeper placed the rag on a nearby shelf and came to stand beside Amaris. She pulled her ebony hair back into a knot at the nape of her neck. "The old man who used to reside in your tower took a liking to this shop. He frequented here often, asking for rare items and herbs. Can I hope for the same business from you?"

Before Amaris could turn her head and give the shopkeeper any reason to question why she would need to ask for permission, Theo pinched the back of her arm out of the shopkeeper's gaze. Amaris flinched and jabbed her elbow into Theo's ribcage with a laugh.

"Of course," Amaris said, "I don't see why not."

"Perfect!" The woman smiled, turning to the wall of shelves to gather several jars.

Amaris stepped back to give her room, purposely finding the toe of Theo's boot. She further leaned back, and Theo forced his lips tight before he snapped at her.

"For the four jars, it'll be four silver pieces. Will you be paying up front, or would you like to open a line of credit?"

This time, Amaris did stare at Theo, and he remembered Amaris didn't have the same luxuries as other servants of the manor with steady pay.

"Up front," Theo interjected, reaching into his pouch to fish out the silver.

The shopkeeper wrapped the jars in cloth, placing them into a satchel. Amaris slung it over her head. "Thank you..."

"Brelynn," the shopkeeper finished, "but my customers call me Brela."

"Brela?" Theo questioned. "As in the Goddess of Trickery?"

"My parents chose a ridiculous name, so I went about using an even more absurd nickname. It's quite fitting, though, for the oddity of this shop, and I suppose the people who frequent here as well."

Before Brela could retreat behind her banner, Theo stopped her. "The ship in the case over there...what does '*aslorn per de eclahard*' mean?"

She inclined a brow and smirked. "Brace for her storm." She waved them off and retreated to her back room.

Theo stepped out onto the cobbled streets. *Brace for her storm.* What could Isabel have meant by that? What storm?

Theo turned to Amaris, who looked all too inclined to ask what had happened in there. "Are you hungry?" he hastily asked.

"I'm fine," she lied, while her stomach growled.

"Too bad, because I am." Theo whisked her off before she could ask her question. He took her to his favorite tavern and ordered two silver rolls.

"What's this?" she asked, poking the silverling meat. She must have been truly sheltered.

"It's best to eat and not ask what's in it. But if you must know, it's my favorite dish," he said through a mouthful.

"Why do you bring up the war if you don't want to talk about it?" Her blue eyes cut through his shield, threatening to pull apart the mended stitch in his mind.

The muscles of his neck tensed, and he waited for the blood to taint the dimly lit tavern and the panic to lay siege to his heart. Maybe it was something within that food-packed smile, or his prayer was answered by the gods, but the panic didn't take hold of him.

"It bothers you." She lowered her voice, drawing out a whispering note.

"I presume you assessed that in the shop."

"It's part of my job to see that stuff too. You had this far-off look in your eyes," she said, sucking the silverling juices off her fingers. "And you grabbed your dagger."

Theo fought the urge to grab for it now.

"Is that what happened in the throne room?"

Theo ignored her and asked, "There are things that bother you, but you wish not to speak of them?"

"Sure," she harrumphed, turning her nose up. For a woman no taller than a few inches past five feet, she had the ability to stifle the size of any opponent to bring them to her level.

"I lost good people," Theo confessed. He fought back the heaviness in his chest. Their names on the tip of his tongue.

Stopping mid-bite, she recoiled deeper into the bench. "I'm sorry," she murmured. "Is that where you got that?" She pointed to where the scar hid underneath his sleeve.

He paused but couldn't bring himself to continue. "A story for another time," he breathed. "We should get back to the manor and begin the next set of doses."

He stood from the table, slithering through the afternoon rush. The tavern door closed as a fiddle struck its first tune, but he began the trek back to the manor with Amaris hurrying in step to catch up.

CHAPTER 20

Amaris

"THE MYSTIQUE'S JOURNAL says, if it works, it'll take at least another few days for the rash to disappear," Amaris shouted over her shoulder at Theodoric.

The worktable, stained yellow from crafting the tonic with the bufomom flower, had become Amaris's permanent residence. She scratched at her nails, grimy with its pollen, as she stuck her nose deeper into the spine of the mystique journal. Astounding, descriptive, maybe even lucky. She had an entire outline of how to be a mystique within her possession. What Amaris didn't know yet whether it was her new burden of responsibility or her saving grace.

Her own notes scattered the margins, written in an awful penmanship from the messy quill. She'd set about making comparisons from the drugs she knew on Earth to the properties of the herbs the mystique wrote about. So far, only a few were outrageous. One herb ate a person's flesh. Amaris scoured the tower for it the moment she read the words *imminent death* and placed it on the top shelf, out of any possible hands. She'd only seen a few children running around, but she had no plans to be sent to her death for them being eaten alive by void caraway.

"Esaias has taken the tonic for five days now. When can we expect to see improvements?" Theodoric slammed his book shut.

It'd only been five days, but he was already on his third novel. Amaris tried sneaking a peek at the cover that morning, but he'd casually slid his hand over the binding. She amused herself with the idea that he snuggled up at night reading romance novels. For his burly and masculine personality, she thought it fun to imagine he had a soft, romantic side. Teasing words hung in her head, but she considered how he could sit with a straight face and without a boner.

Her eyes peeled from the journal, but she shot them back down as her cheeks heated. Did she seriously poke her head up to check to see if he had one?

"This dose is the last." Amaris grabbed at her collar, the stifling heat increasing at a rapid rate. "Then it's a waiting game."

She'd been trying to be optimistic for Theodoric's sake, but Esaias was still confined to his bed. The bit of hope she clung to was that he'd survived the last five days. The journal's recounting of the late mystique's many patients overseas had an average mortality rate of two or three days.

After their venture into the city, she'd chastised herself for happily perusing paintings and eating mystery meat instead of slipping away into the crowded streets. She'd then felt a knot in her stomach and reminded herself, *You're a paramedic. You're giving Esaias a chance.*

Amaris had taken on, not only Esaias as her patient, but also Theodoric...not that he knew about it. Twice she'd watched his breathing grow erratic and his eyes glass over. She'd seen it before in patients with panic attacks, but until he approached her about it, she felt helpless to do anything. But the paramedic within her felt compelled to act. Watching him rub at his dagger without a thought while he read had her antsy and needing to do something to help him.

Her best idea had been to throw whatever she could into saving Esaias, and that had also meant postponing her escape attempt until the last tonic. As much as it'd pained her to wait, Theodoric's growing impatience and fear held her at bay the last few days when he'd left regularly to check on Esaias or asked constantly about the progress of his condition. He was grasping at straws that Amaris could perform some miracle, like she'd done with basic CPR after the river.

Theodoric sauntered toward her, pinching the small vial between his fingers. "I'm going to give him the last tonic. I'll be back to escort you to your bedchambers."

"You could let me walk there myself." She didn't look up, still feeling the burning sensation in her cheeks.

Ever since he'd told her that he didn't believe her to be a cold-blooded killer, she'd begun testing her boundaries for when she was ready to make her mad escape. Sephardi no longer hung around in his absence. He escorted her to and from her room, but when he visited Esaias or trained, she was left alone.

"I'm not giving anyone any leverage to think the worst of you. I'll see you to your chambers." He closed the tower door behind him, his steps silent as he made his way down the stairwell. He was good at that, creeping around.

Amaris watched the clock sitting atop the sagging mantel, waiting a good ten minutes until she made her move. Her gut tightened as she descended the stairs. With her door locked every night, her only window to escape would be when Theodoric trusted her enough to leave her in the tower. She considered asking for his help in her escape, but she wasn't prepared to answer the questions regarding where she was from or the possibility he would refuse. Yesterday had been a trial run, and she'd made it as far as the mezzanine before she ran into Pricilla.

With the last dose of the tonic on its way to Esaias, she could escape any day now, but not tonight. Anxiety had her fingers clinging to the stairwell walls. She needed to have her escape planned and set before Esaias's condition worsened. Without any improvements, his state had grown stagnant, which further sent jitters through her. If Esaias didn't make it, she'd need to be ready, because the duke likely wouldn't let her live to see another day.

As she stepped into the library, she couldn't fathom what Derek was going through. She'd be hysterical. Throughout her planning, she'd begun to wonder what Derek would do or say first. A plate of cinnamon rolls, a dozen kisses, and a sincere apology were what she needed, but a daunting thought lingered in her mind. *What if Derek thinks I left him?*

Her only hope was that Viv knew she'd disappeared and had Derek using all his resources within the police department to find her.

Each step through the library felt criminal. It was well past dinnertime, meaning the librarians were gone for the night. The eerie shadows of dim lanterns unsettled her as she tiptoed through the bookcases. Upon reaching a corner, Amaris heard it. It was either a faint hum, or someone had left a window cracked.

She stuck her head around the corner, but the path was empty. Her shoulders sagged, and she pressed on, ignoring the spike of her heartbeat. She sidestepped a ladder, but something landed on the top of her head and sent her flying to her back. Slightly dazed, she spotted Pricilla perched on the top rung with her leg locked around it and a mountain of books stacked in one arm.

Pricilla's humming ceased, and her eyes widened. Discarding the remainder of the books on an empty shelf, she slid down the rails without a single grunt or hiss. "I'm dreadfully sorry. Are you alright?" Pricilla reached down and hauled Amaris to her feet. "Sometimes I get lost in my head up there." Laughing briefly to herself, she leaned into the ladder. "Why are you up so late?"

"I could ask you the same thing." Amaris rubbed the top of her head. She was going to have a bruise everywhere by the time she got home.

"I got caught up with a good book. I need to put away that stack before I leave for the night or Talitha won't be pleased."

"Talitha?"

"The head librarian." Pricilla said, then added, "Well, and my mother."

"Ladies," Ms. Borstad called from down the aisle. Her hands fanned her flushed cheeks as she marched toward them. She dragged her sleeve over her wrinkled forehead. "I thought I heard lovely voices."

Pricilla smiled, but Amaris inclined a brow. She'd never seen Ms. Borstad outside the kitchen or the main hall. Thankfully, she was still among the population clueless to the actual reason for Amaris's extended stay.

"I need assistance with preparations for Conjugation."

"Of course!" Pricilla said. "I would be delighted to."

Amaris recalled Theodoric and Esaias discussing the same topic weeks ago. "What's a Conjugation?"

"They're splendid," Pricilla began. "This will be my first!"

"You think Conjugation mighty? Try Mosfelkov Veil of Vows. Weeklong party of trials and celebrating," Ms. Borstad added, wiping her sweaty hands on her apron.

"I wish to live a life as full as yours, Ms. Borstad." Pricilla tipped her head back and smiled as she sighed.

"What's a Conjugation?" Amaris repeated, feeling she'd been shunned to the shadows like the discarded books with layers of dust.

"To announce union. Luther to be wed to the Honorable Petra Godfrey," Ms. Borstad said. "Lovely woman. We all know Luther needs woman with head on right and not stupid girl."

"It's a wedding?" Amaris asked.

"Oh no," Pricilla added. "The wedding is a simple and formal affair that'll take place when they're ready. The Conjugation is a mass celebration. I'm surprised you've never heard of one."

Amaris imagined a sparkling disco ball and everyone hopping in tune to a popular line dance, but she doubted the Conjugation would resemble anything close to her senior prom. Magoria seemed more sophisticated than acne-covered teenagers sneaking swigs of slipped booze in the middle of the dance floor.

"I add both you to list of hands," Ms. Borstad said before scurrying away.

"When is this fancy party?" Amaris asked, turning to Pricilla.

"Only a few weeks away!" Pricilla said, shaking with excitement.

Amaris almost found herself missing the chance to attend such an elaborate affair, but she knew she wouldn't be here long enough to attend the Conjugation.

"I'll leave you to your books." Amaris turned to head back to the tower. Another failed mission, due to Pricilla's love for late-night reading.

"I have all night to put those away. Join me for a bit?" Pricilla latched on to her arm, whisking her away. "I want to show you this extraordinary book I've been flipping through."

If Pricilla moved any faster, Amaris would've found her legs flailing behind her as they sped toward her recess at the back of the library. Pricilla's excitement was an interesting contrast to Viv's brute honesty, punchy quips, and vulgar stories. Amaris clung to the image of her best friend: Viv's black jeans, combat boots, and leather jacket. A screech ripped the picture from Amaris's mind as Pricilla shoved one of the worn chairs to post up beside her desk.

As usual, a large scroll was held down with whatever Pricilla seemed to get her hands on. Tonight, it was a brass candle holder, a blue slipper, and two books on the other corners. Amaris's finger skimmed the text, but it was in a script of different symbols.

"What language is this?" Amaris asked.

Pricilla threw her slipper over her shoulder and let the scroll roll up. "Gorrin." She replaced the scroll with a large book. Dust billowed around them and flew up Amaris's sinuses. "This is Hofati."

"Can you read them?" Amaris asked, her eyes watering as she pinched her nose.

"Gorrin, yes, but I'm still learning to read Hofati. It's a dead language and not many scholars or tutors teach it anymore." Pricilla opened the book, thumbing the edges until she came to a marked page and shoved the book in Amaris's face. "What I wanted to show you are the paintings."

"How...? Did Theodoric tell you?" He'd been the only person she confided in about her love for art.

"He may have mentioned it. What do you think?"

Amaris returned her attention to the page. It was more a work of art than a book, with bright yellows and oranges jumping out. Amaris traced the gold painted edge of a sunset. "Is this gold?"

"Many rulers had their important texts or pages transcribed with the material." Pricilla caressed the page, her dainty hands brushing against the shimmering symbols before she flipped to the front. The entire first page was a long paragraph of the decorative markings.

Amaris pulled from the book and wandered toward the wall of shelves to discover her own treasure. What if there was something that could help with her situation? Her finger slid across the bindings while she tilted her head to read each of the spines.

"Over there, you'll mainly find legends, mythology, and magic."

Her fingers stopped. "Magic, you say?"

"Would you think I'm crazy if I told you I believe magic still exists?" Pricilla lowered her voice, as if the books had ears and were likely to mock her.

"Maybe."

"Many find the idea repulsive, but you seemed intrigued to learn more when I first met you." Pricilla jumped from the desk chair and ran her hand over the tomes filling her space with mystery and wonder. "The myths speak of a time before the Necrotic Ages blessed with magic."

Necrotic Ages? Amaris pondered this, then said, "But they're just myths, right? Not real history?"

"Myths are history," she snorted. "The stories might be different, but they all speak of the same thing...magic. One depicts ancient beings with everlasting life, another people with the ability to take on another form."

Amaris pictured Pricilla's bedroom with a hidden corkboard and red strings running from each title and the exact line adding to her suspicions.

"What makes you think magic still exists?"

"You know when you just have this feeling that something's there?"

"I think I know what you mean," Amaris said.

Pricilla picked up the rolled scroll, looking defeated, with her shoulders hunched forward.

"What kind of magic was there?"

Pricilla gazed at the rolled piece of parchment in her hand. "I assume people had magic that allowed them to do things to make mundane tasks easier."

"It doesn't say?"

"Not exactly. It speaks of magic running through the veins of Magoria and people accomplishing the extraordinary, but there aren't specific details. A few stories tell of people with gifts, like wielding fire or water, but that must be taken with a grain of salt, like this." Pricilla skipped over to her loose plank, retrieving a brown leather journal and tossing it to Amaris. For being a librarian, she seemed to let books fall wherever she pleased. "I found that a few years ago but don't know what to make of it."

Amaris's palms grew sweaty as she anticipated what she was about to unleash. She hoped she wasn't about to read about blood magic or voodoo. At the top of the first journal entry was scribbled *1994*.

"What do you think?"

Amaris barely had the ability to form a single line of thought, let alone speak. According to Alan, Magoria was well off into the six thousand years already. Her mouth dried as she read the first entry.

I've found myself in the most precarious of circumstances. I tried to hide who I was to protect myself, but there wasn't anything I could do when the anger ripped through me. I couldn't stop the transformation, so I fled. It'd been years since I slipped up, and I'd prayed to Izmir that I could once again build a new life.

I ran to the edge of Charibert, hoping I'd fall into the Black Sea and finally be swept up into the rocks to meet my final demise. Alas, the realm had other plans for me. I scaled the nearest tree, narrowly avoiding the man with his sword drawn and a piercing gleam in his eyes.

I thought it would finally be the end to my life. I felt as though I'd lived a hundred lifetimes and was prepared to give it all away. I neither felt the pain nor remembered anything beyond that. I fell from the tree, but instead of meeting the blade of the man, I was sprawled on a rough terrain so unlike the cobblestone streets.

The realm around me buzzed with activity. Loud wails and triumphant calls pounded against my ears. People were everywhere. I was hardly able to stand without being trampled in the process. The structures around me towered far into the clouds. They were taller than any building I'd ever seen in Godwin.

Amaris's reread the entry to be sure she hadn't imagined it.

"I presume you're as baffled as I was when I read it."

"Yeah," Amaris whispered. She went to flip to the next entry, when a shadow caught her eye. Amaris stretched her neck to gaze down the aisle and spotted Theodoric passing by. *Crap.*

Pricilla loomed over her shoulder. "What are we looking at?"

"Theodoric." Amaris found herself grumbling his name.

"What about him?"

Amaris rolled her eyes.

"I'm all ears if you need to talk," Pricilla offered. "If you're worried I might tell anyone, I promise you, most of my friends are leather-bound and crinkly."

It's not like she hated the man anymore. He'd quit treating her like she was the last kid picked for dodgeball, but before she could stop herself, she blurted out, "He's so closed off."

"I picked up there aren't entirely positive feelings."

Amaris planted her face into a palm. "He's insufferable sometimes."

Maybe she was a little upset about her limited freedom to even go to the bathroom by herself.

"He's been like that since he's been back." Pricilla sat and pulled her knee under her. "He only came back last season, and he...well...he wasn't so happy anymore."

Amaris jabbed a finger over her shoulder. "That man, happy?"

"Believe it or not, he used to be quite boisterous," she sighed. "Arrogant at times, but he also loved to laugh."

Standing, Amaris gripped the journal to her chest. She needed to run back up the stairs before he thought she'd actually tried to escape. "Did he want to go?"

"They all did back then," Pricilla whispered, her expression further fading to sorrow.

Amaris wanted to stay and console her, but she had to go. "Can I borrow this?"

Pricilla nodded, and Amaris was jogging down the aisle of books, hoping she'd catch up to Theodoric before he had a temper tantrum. She ran toward the tower and bounded up the steps, barely taking notice of the darkness as the torches burned out. She rounded the next landing and smacked into the wall.

Nope, scratch that. Theodoric's ridiculously muscular chest. She stumbled back, her feet sliding off the edge of the steps. He grasped her shoulders, keeping her from meeting an untimely demise.

"Do you ever skip chest day?" Amaris groaned, rubbing her nose, which had gotten the brunt of his impenetrable force.

"What are you doing? I said I was coming back to escort you."

"I know. I was talking with Pricilla," she muttered, gripping her nose until the burning subsided.

Maybe she'd be like him and have a concussion, lasting her weeks. He'd finally allowed her to make him something the other day, after she grew tired of him wincing and groaning about it. Her exact words had been,

Let me make you a tonic, or I'm making good on your father's accusations and smothering you with one of Pricilla's stained couch cushions. He hadn't complained since.

"You must be careful—"

"Oh please, Pricilla is likely the last person who would spout off to your father about me. She keeps to those books of hers."

"I'm well aware that she's a wallflower, but there are others who enjoy the privacy of the library at night."

Amaris squinted, attempting to make out whatever details of his face she could. With Pricilla's grief-stricken expression, she wondered if there was more to their relationship. It was odd, she referred to him as *Captain*, but he'd brushed her tear away the other day.

"Have you and Pricilla ever...?"

"Excuse me?"

"You know?" Amaris muttered, combing through her hair. Asking about his relationships seemed too personal, but her lips kept going. "Knocking boots, bedroom rodeo, doing squat thrusts in the cucumber patch?" *I hang out with Viv too much.*

"Are you attempting to ask if Pricilla and I have ever had intimate relations?" Annoyance seeped from him.

"I was going to say bumping uglies, but if you want to be all sophisticated, then yeah." Amaris smiled, feeling completely stupid.

"No, Pricilla and I are—"

"No judgment if you two—"

"Don't even finish that sentence," he groaned.

"I was going to say if you're childhood friends, that's cool too. Don't get your panties in a twist." She couldn't see the expression he gave her, but she knew it wasn't a smile. She was thankful he couldn't see her face either, or the embarrassment spreading across her cheeks.

"As we both have a love for books, we've become acquainted with one another."

"Acquainted?" Amaris questioned. "Seriously, you can't say the word *friends*? Do you even have those?"

"I do have friends, but she prefers to refer to me by my title. As a servant of the manor, she has declined an official friendship."

Amaris let out a long and exaggerated groan, brushing his hold on her arms. "That sounds like formal garbage. Why can't you be normal?"

"I'm of noble blood. There's no such thing as normal."

Amaris raised her nose in the air, brushing the end as she spoke with a nasally voice. "I'm a snobby noble. All look upon me in shame."

"You're ridiculous," he whispered, pushing past her to descend the steps.

"Hey, I'm not the one with blood of gold coursing through my veins. Do you shit diamonds and wipe your ass with dollar bills too?"

"How does anyone tolerate you?"

They stepped out into the library, and Amaris held the journal tight to her chest. Her mind begged to devour the rest of the entries. Whoever the journal belonged to, they had a lot of explaining to do.

"I'm an absolute hoot back home."

He didn't even let out a tiny laugh, but Amaris's was an awkward chuckle. She tried to picture him smiling and hunching forward in laughter. She even eyed him in her periphery to see if he had crow's feet around his eyes. Of all the people who could've believed she wasn't a murderer, it had to be him. The giant with a face of stone, who no longer had an ounce of humor in his body.

CHAPTER 21

Amaris

THEODORIC LOCKED THE door behind Amaris. She leapt onto her bed, setting the book on her lap. For a second, she stared at the cracked leather, tracing her finger down the largest one. In her hands she held what was either the worst trick in the universe or a clue to learning what happened to her. It couldn't have been a coincidence that the man wrote of falling from a tree to end up on some other poor forsaken planet— *world, realm*?

Amaris breathed, settling her shaking hands and fidgeting knees. She could do it. All she had to do was open the page. *I've experienced one outrageous anomaly. What's another?*

She flipped to the next entry. Hours passed, or minutes, maybe even seconds. Time was nonexistent as Amaris read and deciphered the scribbled mess. Each turn was a new boost of adrenaline shooting through her veins. She'd never been this on edge before. Her feet fluttered as she absorbed each morsel of information.

The man was named Valentine Wineman, and he'd recorded his journey. He'd even described the same blue stars that had swallowed

Amaris whole. As she read further, she learned their stories were reversed. He was from Magoria. Based on the entry dates, Wineman had traveled to New York and stayed for two years, meeting a woman named Sarah, before heading out west. He rambled on about her beautiful features and gushed about her striking personality.

Amaris's fingers skimmed over the words of love, wanting there to be a journal stashed somewhere in their house where Derek poured his heart out. He'd always been caring, but had never offered a love letter, nor been overly affectionate. Derek was a private person.

Amaris read on, her heart heavy as his tone grew angrier and frustration bled from his words. He didn't say what was bothering him, but he felt an overwhelming burden affecting his relationship.

As the pages grew scarce, her heart hammered. She tucked her legs in to keep her nervous energy from sending her pacing about the room. Was there enough ink left to give her the truth on how to get back? Amaris turned the last page, begging he'd written the answers on the back, but it was blank. Her finger dragged along the binding. Pages had been torn out. She slammed the book shut and tossed it across the room.

"That's it?" She pulled at her hair and screamed.

The universe was laughing at her, giving her a bit of hope and then ripping it from her grasp. He'd grown discontent in life, like every other fool, and never made it back. Amaris hugged her knees, staring into the void darkness of the room, her tiny prison.

Is this going to be the rest of my life? She was going to be forced to remain the duke's prisoner, acting as his mystique, but how long could she keep it up? When would he decide he'd waited long enough or that she was inadequate? Theodoric said to make herself valuable, indispensable, but she couldn't. She wasn't a mystique and didn't belong here.

Amaris crawled from the bed, fishing the journal off the floor. It was surprisingly sturdy; not a single piece of paper slipped from the binding. *A sturdy journal indeed.* The pages of the journal were worn, but their initial color of white showed through. There were no ink blots but cursive lines drawn with a ballpoint pen. It wasn't of Magoria. Wineman had made it back. Her shoulders sagged. *Of course he made it back.* How else would the journal with his adventure have found Pricilla? Unless the tree could transport only books, he'd returned from Earth.

Amaris flipped back through the pages, noting the differences in their stories. She'd completely dismissed the old willow, but seeing it was likely her way home, she felt her cheeks heat with embarrassment. Was the way home only a day's ride into the woods? What about Charibert?

Wineman had mentioned the city in his first entry. Amaris hadn't heard of it before, but it was possible there were multiple trees leading to different locations. *Or I'm screwed and now have to find this Charibert.* What if there was only one tree that spit the person out wherever it pleased? She could work with New York. Calling Derek from a pay phone or contacting the authorities to get a hold of him would be easy. Wineman may not have known if there was a tree in Luana Bay, but he'd traveled through the one in Charibert. She could scour the forest in Luana and if she couldn't track down the willow, she'd find a way to Charibert. She owed it to Derek and Viv to try. If they were using their time to search for her, then she could do it.

She grabbed the empty satchel from her visit to The Merry Sheridan and threw the journal inside. Her hands trembled as they wrapped around the strap. She was going to do it. It was too late for anyone to be up. She would sneak into the library, steal a map, and be gone before daylight.

She unlatched the window. A breeze caught it, dragging it open with a slam, tensing her muscles. Seconds passed, but there wasn't a cry of alarm or the shouting of a mob armed with torches and pitchforks. She was only a few stories up, but it was still higher than most standards.

In high school, Amaris had challenged the ultimate feat on a weekend basis and snuck out a window and scaled down the downspout to meet up with Derek. One time, she'd slipped from the window and miraculously didn't wake Gran. She only hoped that wasn't to be repeated. There weren't bushes below to catch her fall now.

She slid her feet out first, finding a rock to brace herself. She shimmied off the windowsill and began her methodical trek to scale down the wall. She'd go to the library and then head out to the stables. The journal had found her for a reason. Esaias had taken the last tonic. She needed to quit being afraid and do something about it. Tonight was it.

She jumped the last two feet and landed near the garden. Unease warped her stomach. Why did it feel wrong? She was going home. She'd gone into the river to save Theodoric, and now she'd done all she could for Esaias. Hunched forward and following the shadows, she found the kitchen doors. The loudest creak ever erupted through the massive kitchen, but Ms. Borstad wasn't around. She'd said she wasn't looking to stab her in the heart, but if Amaris snuck up on her, she didn't want to learn what the old lady was capable of.

She moved swiftly through the halls, stopping at each corner to make sure she didn't face-plant into anyone. Even if only soldiers knew of the accusations against her, she couldn't risk being spotted. The last hallway sent shivers through her. She swore the portraits were haunted. The frames' occupants were waiting for a single soul like her to show their ghostly forms. Her feet sped along, her eyes focused on the floor until she slipped safely through the library doors. She brushed a line of cold sweat beading her forehead.

She hadn't ventured much farther than the mystique tower or Pricilla's little alcove, but it couldn't be that difficult to find a map. The challenge would come with trying to find one that would fit in her satchel. Pricilla's ancient scrolls were at least three feet wide.

The jingling of her boots' zippers was the only sound ringing through the library. There wasn't the hum of Pricilla or the deafening flip of pages. She skidded to a halt as the moon passed over the frosted glass overhead in the mezzanine.

A large shelf in the back was filled with scrolls of parchment. She began pulling them from their nooks and crannies, rolling them open and peering at the contents. Most were ledgers with various amounts of silver and gold listed beside names. Moving down the line, her eyes caught a thicker scroll tucked into the bottom shelf. She dragged it out, but it was at least two feet long. As she rolled it out, it expanded to five feet.

It was a map, at least—a map of all of Magoria. She grabbed a few books left on the table behind her and began laying them along the edges. Mosfelkov and the city Lungvik near the southern part of the continent drew her attention. How long had Theodoric been stationed there? Did they engage in battles on a constant basis? Amaris grabbed the journal and a quill and ink from a nearby desk. It didn't matter where he'd been stationed or what happened to him. She was leaving and would never see him again.

Her hand moved, tracing the outline of the continent. In the case she couldn't find the tree in Luana, she needed a backup plan. She wouldn't be coming back. Luana was in the northwest. She scavenged the map for Charibert, finding it on the west coast, south of the Scarlet Mountains. Of course, it was miles away, but at least it was on the same land mass. Based on what she'd gathered, it took about five days to get to Duncaster. She eyed the distance between Luana Bay and Duncaster, measuring with her finger and attempting to gauge how far it would be to travel by land.

"That's a lot of fingers," she groaned.

It would take weeks, maybe months. She had no food or money. She rolled the scroll back up and shoved it on the shelf, fighting the defeat sinking into her shoulders. There was still the possibility a tree grew in Luana's woods. She wouldn't let herself be discouraged yet.

She pulled her hair out of her eyes, braiding it down her back. She had to try. Already, she felt the burden of leaving. If she stayed any longer, something could happen, and the duke would have her head. She was sure Bennet was waiting for her to slip up. *And Derek.* Her chest ached. They hadn't been apart for this long since the academy.

She hid any traces of her perusing and made for the door, slipping into the hall. Rounding the corner, she stopped dead. Adelaide whipped to face her, her eyes growing in alarm. Both remained frozen in place, but Adelaide wrapped her hand around something at her side. A sword. She pulled it closer, her hand trembling as she slid it further under her jacket.

"Are you alright?" Amaris asked, taking a step toward her to break the stalemate.

Sweat dripped past Adelaide's temple. Her knuckles were white against the hilt of her blade. "Fine," she blurted out. "What are you doing out here?"

"Moonlight stroll?" Amaris offered, but Adelaide narrowed her gaze, eyeing Amaris's satchel. Nothing got past her, but Amaris had her own tricks. She knew Adelaide wasn't a soldier, but she hid a dagger or two. Never a sword though. "What are you doing out here with a sword?"

Adelaide stiffened. "Nothing, I was—"

"Training?" Amaris asked.

Adelaide's green eyes, once lined with flakes of silver, faded to darkness. It didn't matter to Amaris what she did in her free time. As the duke's only daughter, she imagined Adelaide was allowed to do about anything she pleased.

Amaris clung tighter to the strap of her satchel. "I won't say a word." She knew what Adelaide thought of her, but she was also a wild card. Adelaide rarely frequented dinner, slept past lunch, and often had Amaris questioning what she did when no one saw her for hours at a time.

Before either of them could run or get another word in, footsteps announced they were no longer alone. Adelaide shoved Amaris into a curtain. She waited for the blunt hit of the wall but instead slipped through and crashed into a hidden alcove. She slid back and forced herself into the dark corner. The footsteps grew louder, and their owner's shadow cast itself under the edge of the curtain.

CHAPTER 22

Theo

THEO SCREAMED, JUMPING up, his dagger's hilt embedding into his palm. His chest heaved, his pulse throbbing against his skin, waiting for the enemy to strike. He turned in the darkness, listening for the crunch of snow, the clink of metal, or the click of a rifle.

He placed his hand over his mouth, knowing he had to silence his ragged breaths. It only intensified the sound. He bit down on his tongue until he tasted blood. If he got them caught and his squad killed, he deserved a fate worse than a swift death.

No, my squad is dead. I failed them.

His eyes adjusted to the darkness around him as he rapidly tried to blink and remember where he was. Flashes of white snow. The snowflakes burned as they settled against his skin, like an iron rod branding his flesh. He screamed.

"Theo!" Esaias shouted, but Theo couldn't see him. He tried to call for him, but it was a gargle of lost letters in his mouth. "Damn it!" The splintering of wood rang in the distance. That was it, they were spotted, and it was all because of him.

Arms barreled around him, holding him tight. "Theo, it's me!" Esaias pinned Theo's arms to his chest and pried the dagger from his fingers. It clanked against solid ground.

Theo opened his eyes, trying to adjust to the darkness. Wine-red hair loomed over him.

"You're home."

"Home," Theo coughed.

"Yes, home," Esaias said, holding him on the bed.

He swallowed a breath, turning his head in the darkness as the furniture of his room formed around him. He made out the shape of the wingback chair beside the cold hearth and the outline of his wardrobe. His breaths were loud and quick.

"Esaias." Theo's voice was hoarse.

Esaias leaned back, releasing him from his hold. Theo sprang from the bed, his stomach twisting into writhing serpents. His fingers fumbled for the washroom handle. The bile crept up his throat. He landed in front of the toilet just in time, as a single cough spewed chunks of his supper.

"Would you like me to get you anything?" Esaias was behind him, fighting to catch his breath.

How does he have the strength? The last Theo saw of him, he was still lying in bed. Theo felt another surge from his stomach and gripped the rim of the bowl.

"I'm fine," he managed to say, his voice echoing. His throat felt as though he'd swallowed a needle. He didn't know how many more nights he could wake in a fit and find his head leaning over the porcelain rim. His throat ached, and his stomach cramped. "How are you feeling?"

Esaias leaned against the doorframe, a cough ripping through his throat. "Sure you are, but I'm feeling better. After that last dose, I felt my fever break."

"It's only been five days. How is it possible?"

"I'm not sure. Maybe Amaris truly has a gifted skill set."

Theo sat back and rubbed his eyes with the heels of his hands. The familiar grip of the lever as he flushed the toilet pulled his mind from the residual effects of his dream. Amaris had followed Cornelius's instructions. Theo thought she'd followed the recipe, at least, but maybe she'd added something. He welcomed the cool water dripping down his face and slid his hand under the faucet to cup a handful to his mouth. He didn't care that it sprinkled his night shirt in more droplets of water; he was already drenched in sweat.

He gripped the edges of the sink, staring into the drain as the water swirled into its vortex and disappeared. He couldn't lift his head to meet the reflection. A monster would be the one to glare back at him. A burning crept behind his eyes.

"What's causing them?"

Theo turned, and a sharp pain shot through his jaw. Esaias only sported his undershorts, but it gave Theo a relieving visual to see the rash had resolved itself. He wanted to say it was the stress, but it wasn't. With Esaias's illness, he hadn't heard when Theo screamed, not that it happened with every nightmare. Sometimes he was silent, staring into oblivion.

He'd been haunted by the spirits of the people he'd killed or who he failed to save. Ever since he took Amaris into the city, she'd wiggled her way into his dreams too. His hand pressed against her throat as she writhed beneath him, begging for her life, but he was consumed by the monster wanting only vengeance.

When she cried before Theo, dropping to her knees as she sobbed, it broke something within him. He knew all too well what it was like to be ripped from his family. A part of him fractured, and from that fissure bled his shame and guilt, but grief was the hardest to bear of them all. He had yet to mourn their deaths or speak with their families, and Amaris's imprisonment sat in his mind. She didn't deserve it. He felt indebted to her for saving his life in the river and now for giving him back Esaias.

Theo dared lift his head to see his hollowed cheeks and sunken eyes.

A welling began in his chest, the heaviness that overcame him in the city. It was a relief to feel the first burn of a tear. He rested his arms against the sink and wept.

§

THEO SULKED DOWN the hall. The only place he'd find solace tonight was with a book. Sometimes he found his way to the training room, but not tonight. He should have felt elated to see Esaias standing and with a bit of color coming back to his cheeks. Not only would Esaias survive, but it meant Amaris had accomplished a miraculous feat, and his father would have to see that for something. But Theo could only feel helpless as his nightmare lingered.

He was ashamed for surviving that night and the hundreds of nights that followed. For being a coward and hiding within the walls of his home instead of asking for forgiveness. Their families deserved the truth instead of redacted missives. What would they say when they learned it was his fault?

A heaviness clung to his heart, but his feet continued their silent trek through his childhood home. Where he'd grown up beside his siblings and friends, smiled and laughed. He breathed, holding back another round of sobs.

He'd finally discovered the meaning of Isabel's warning, hoping it would lead him to a resolution, an answer for Duncaster, for Amaris. It was a dead end. An old phrase uttered by a helpless woman, who'd taunted them with the last bit of her anger.

Theo rounded the corner to find Adelaide heading to the beach for a training session. With the extra duties of keeping a watchful eye on Amaris, he hadn't been able to accompany her. He'd been too exhausted to resume where they'd left off.

"Heading out?" he asked, not bothering to fake a smile. She would've spotted it instantly, but the prideful grin usually painting her lips when she set out into the night was absent. Maybe she sensed his agony.

"Yes," she said, her tone short.

He eyed her sword reflecting off the torch between them. It was the first one he'd ever been gifted as a boy. The leather had been dyed and woven into gold and navy plaits. It looked perfect at home by her side. He only wished she could always wear it, having the protection with her.

"I would accompany you tonight, but—"

"Will you walk me out at least?" Adelaide didn't wait for his response. She latched onto his arm and spun him away from the library.

Out of the corner of his eye, he caught a breeze ruffling the curtain of the hidden recess known to house a secret or two. He hid his suspicious glance. If Adelaide was running around at night with a man, he didn't want to know about it. Partially because he'd kill any man who even looked at her in lust, but mainly he wanted her to have some form of normalcy. She'd never shown an interest in anyone, rejecting the idea of marriage for as long as he could remember. Maybe whoever was hiding behind that curtain would help her see the idea of sharing her life with someone wasn't all terrible.

"How's your training progressing?" Theo asked.

"I've hit a standstill. I've knocked Alan on his ass more times than I can count. I need my old teacher back." A subtle plea. Her jaw didn't tighten, nor did her shoulders slouch. She remained firm and squared her stance.

Theo sighed. "I know. I'm trying to make time for it, but with Duncaster and Esaias—"

"And Amaris," she cut in. "You've been spending the majority of your time with her."

"You know why."

"I know it's to guard her, but you and I both know she's not a murderer, so why do you continue to do it?"

"Do you really think Father has given me a choice?"

Her attempt at a stoic demeanor fizzled, and she rolled those large green eyes. "Who cares what the duke says?"

"It isn't a matter I can cast aside. He's ordered me to."

"You should be looking for the real murderer. Why set you on guard duty? Is he punishing you?"

"Why do you suspect that?"

Adelaide pinned her arms across her chest. "Remember, I know everything."

She was cunning in her ability to gather information, but Theo and his father's discussions were held behind closed doors.

"Maybe because I've been avoiding him." He brushed aside his sister's curious abilities for now. "That's not all he's asked me to do."

She inclined a brow. "What has he asked of you?"

Maybe she didn't know everything. "He wants me to get to know Amaris on a personal level, learn who she really is."

"Why does he care? Does he have nothing better to do?"

Theo grabbed Adelaide's arm, pulling her down the hall. Whoever was behind that curtain had no business eavesdropping in their formal affairs. It was one thing for her to disrespect their father's name in the confines of her bedchamber or on the beach where no one could hear over the cresting of a wave, but not out in the open.

"I'm not going to tell him anything."

Her brows knitted together. "What do you mean?"

"I said I'd learn who she is. The problem is, the more I learn, the greater desire I have to hold her secrets."

"What has she told you?"

"Her life outside of here is still a mystery," Theo began. "I was hoping she'd at least have knowledge of where her family was so we could send for them, but she doesn't know."

"What else?"

"Why do *you* care so much?" Theo shot at her. He appreciated her desire to help but hated bringing her into it. Going against their father was dangerous, and he didn't want her to get wrapped up in his burdens. Besides, she needed to occupy herself with training. If she ever wanted to rid herself of her current life and become a soldier, she needed to prove herself. "You've known the woman for all of a couple of weeks."

She balled her hands into fists, pulling back her shoulders. "She's... It's..." For once, she was at a loss. "She ran from her old life. She's courageous and stands up to the duke and Bennet."

"You admire her."

"And you don't? We need to protect her."

Theo dragged his hand down his face and exhaled. "I'm trying, but she's proving quite difficult to deal with."

"She had the bravery to run away from all she knows. Where's yours?" She stepped closer and sneered. It was now Theo who was at a loss. "What happened to Nate?" Adelaide's words were sharper than the sword at her side. She might as well have taken her weapon and sank it into his chest.

His voice cracked. "Adelaide—"

She raised her hand. "No one will tell me. We received a missive of his death, but that was it."

Theo's head spun. He couldn't do it. Not now...probably never. He'd fought the panic from his nightmare only an hour ago. He didn't have the strength now to fend it off. He gripped the hilt of his dagger, dragging his thumb over the raised crest. *I fight and I live.*

"Did you know his sister ran away?" Adelaide's voice droned in his ear.

Nate's sister? Theo hadn't seen Elizabeth in years. He'd heard she'd been sent to live with her aunt sometime during the war, but he hadn't had the courage to find her or even write to her. *Why would she run away?*

"Their aunt sent the duke a letter after they received word of Nate's death. She said Elizabeth became inconsolable and left in the middle of the night. Their family may never know what happened to her, but they deserve to know the truth about Nate. You can continue to lie to the duke,

Esaias, and even me, but quit lying to yourself." She paused for a breath. "When you came home and I saw you walk up those steps, I thought I'd finally have my brother back. I knew you'd survive and come home because I needed you to. You were the one person who believed in me and stood up for me." She fought tears. "But, Theo, I don't think you came back at all."

Theo chased after her as she ran toward the western doors, to take her hidden trail down to the beach. Everything was slipping through his fingers, pooling down his arms, even though he was holding his fingers together as tight as he could. Adelaide was right. A part of him hadn't come home. Theo sucked in the sob waiting in his throat. He was failing Adelaide. He'd failed Nate.

Adelaide gained distance, and Theo's legs slowed their efforts. The sting of the wind brushed aside the tears that had formed. The breeze stirred through the grass, causing it to sway in the moonlight. The sky was more beautiful than anywhere else. He missed the ability to lie upon the sand and gaze for hours at the endless array of stars shining overhead.

He breathed in the briny taste of the bay, using it to briefly mend what he could of his cracked soul. He didn't want to deal with it all anymore. Esaias had nearly died from an illness, of all things, after going into battle. Adelaide was growing more distant every day, and his father still wouldn't see her for who she truly was. His best friend's sister was missing. His mind was cracking, as if the small bits of his sanity were fraying away. His realm was falling to pieces around him. He was tired of it.

A bouncing brown speck caught his eye in the distance. Amaris was jogging through the garden toward the stables. She was making a run for it. He'd left her alone several times now but didn't think she'd attempt an escape. She'd cured Esaias. Did she even know? When he told his father in the morning, it could end up in her favor. Why was she ruining it?

He'd remembered to lock her door. How had she escaped? His puffy eyes followed overhead and spotted the open window leading to her room. She was braver than he thought or just foolish. She'd stood against men who wished death upon her, and now she'd taunted death and had scaled out her window.

Theo took a breath to collect himself and ran after her, grasping his sword to keep it from alerting anyone to his presence. She likely didn't know about the guard patrolling the stables. His knees ached as he raced down the steep dirt path, dust kicking up around him. She slid through the rolling doors of the stables, allowing them to shut behind her.

As Theo drew near, footsteps came running around the corner. He dropped into the long grass, peeking through the tall blades to spot Alan running around the corner. *This just became more challenging.*

Theo would enter through the back entrance and grab Amaris before Alan had a chance to find her. She was so close to her freedom. If his father found out, he'd send her back to the dungeons, or worse. Theo couldn't fathom what his father would do, whether he would hang her or send her to Elric Prison. Theo shuddered at the mere thought. He'd been to Elric once, and it was enough to learn he never wished his worst enemy to be forced to spend even a night there.

He slipped inside, closing the door behind him without a sound. A banging ensued down a few stalls, and Amaris made a desperate attempt to hush the horse.

She's terrible at this. Theo heard the forbidding roll of the stable doors and Alan's daunting steps as he followed the chaotic sounds. Amaris darted around the corner. Theo hid in an empty stall, waiting to grab her as she came closer.

"Hello?" Alan shouted.

Her feet shuffled a few stalls down, and her breaths panted at an alarming pitch. Each crunch brought Alan closer. Hairs pricked along Theo's skin as Amaris inched closer to the stall. One more step. He reached outside the stall and grabbed her around the mouth and waist. Dragging her back, he pulled a discarded blanket over them to further hide in the darkness. She struggled against his hold, her nails drawing blood from his arm.

"Don't make a sound," he whispered in her ear.

She froze. Her hair tickled the tip of his nose. He was thankful for her signature scent of vanilla instead of the stench of the dirty horse blanket. Alan's steps drew closer.

Through a hole in the blanket, he spotted Alan staring down the row of stalls, his daggers drawn. Theo pulled Amaris closer as he felt her fighting the urge to squirm in his arms. Alan released a sigh and retreated. His footsteps quieted and the rolling of the doors rang through the stables.

Theo tossed off the blanket and released her. "What are you doing?" He brushed past her, reaching for the nearest lantern. With his flint and steel, the candle flickered to life, growing brighter as he swung the lantern toward her. "Were you planning on stealing a horse?"

"No," she stammered, crossing her arms over her chest as she bit her lower lip.

"This is a poor escape attempt. You won't make it by yourself."

"What do you mean by that? I'm a capable woman," she shot back at him.

Theo refrained from grabbing her arm and dragging her back to the manor. "I never said you weren't capable," he replied as he directed her toward the back entrance. "Have you even thought any of this through? Esaias's fever broke, and his rash is gone."

"Good for him," she said, but then scoffed. "And I *have* thought this through, and I'm leaving tonight. I'm not staying another night in this damn prison."

She had no idea what a real prison was like. One where a person was thrown into the dark and all they heard were the screams echoing through the halls, never knowing which day would be their last.

"You aren't leaving, not tonight," Theo said.

Alan was a close enough call as it was. Ward and Gris were also on patrol, and Ward wouldn't take his post lightly. Theo had caught a few younger soldiers falling asleep toward the twilight end of their shifts.

Ward would be stalking through the night, catching any bit of movement beyond the walls.

"I'm not listening to you. You've done nothing but lie to me."

Theo closed the door behind them as she stepped toward the edge of the woods. "Lie to you?"

"Don't play dumb with me," she seethed, her teeth baring as she jabbed a finger into his chest. The woods behind her were a menacing shadow at her back. "I heard you tell Adelaide your father has ordered you to get to know me on a *personal level.* Is that why you've been nice to me all of a sudden, telling me you don't think I'm the murderer? You've been playing with me."

She'd been the one hiding in the alcove.

"Amaris, you were never meant to hear that."

"Save it," she snapped. Navy pools darkened her irises, ripping away all the light. She threw her hands against his chest, shoving him into the wall as she ran around the corner.

"Amaris," Theo whispered urgently after her. Alan could still be lurking.

"Go to hell!"

Theo never understood half her insults, but with the emphasis she put into them, she meant to wound. Theo sprinted after her, grabbing her by the waist.

"Put. Me. Down."

He covered her mouth and carried her toward the kitchen.

"If you don't keep quiet, someone will find you and throw you in the dungeons," Theo said into her ear, not bothering to lighten his tone. He tore open the kitchen doors and threw her inside, shutting them behind him.

Tears streaked her face, ones of anguish. She could hate him all she wanted, but he wouldn't have an innocent woman condemned.

"You're no different from your father or Bennet, you bastard." Her voice cracked. "I can handle myself."

"You almost got yourself caught. You have no idea where the sentry stations are, do you?" he scolded.

She didn't balk but instead pulled her shoulders back and clenched her hands into fists. She was the most stubborn person he'd ever dealt with.

"I have everything figured out."

"Do you?" he shouted, his hand dragging through his hair. "Because it looks like you're making this up as you go. There are guards stationed all throughout the grounds. You never would've made it beyond the wall."

"I've escaped one prison. What's another?" she blurted out. Her hand instantly slapped against her mouth. All traces of anger dissipated. Her shoulders dropped, and the navy flakes in her eyes dispersed.

Theo's gaze sharpened on her. "You...what?"

"Fuck, not an actual prison," she said, throwing her hands over her eyes. "It's a figure of speech." She stumbled back into the wooden countertop. Her head whipped as if she was expecting the black cabinetry to be someone waiting to drag her away. She turned to race out of the kitchen, but Theo grabbed her hand, pulling her back.

"You escaped a prison?"

Amaris pressed her hands against his chest, her eyes once again glistening with tears. "Forget I said anything. Let me go back to my room."

"Tell me." Theo's voice came out in a growl.

She wiggled from his hold and scrambled back, her hands flat against the red brick of the hearth set into the wall. She slid along it, her hands pressed against the masonry as her breaths grew shallow.

"Please," she cried, tears spilling down her cheeks. "Forget it, please."

"Does he hurt you?"

She pulled her satchel to her chest, her eyes darting toward the hall. "Leave Derek out of this."

"I'm not stupid, Amaris," Theo snipped. "Does he hit you?"

"You don't know anything about me or my life!"

She darted out of the kitchen, but Theo couldn't find the ability to run after her. He crumpled to the floor, his legs giving out. His cheek pressed into the cupboard as he leaned against it to keep his bearings. He choked out a breath, digging his nails into his palms.

What is wrong with me? He was an animal, the monster slipping from where it was buried inside him. The war was over. There wasn't a threat. He was no better than Bennet or his father demanding that information from her.

His body trembled. His sanity further slipped through his fingers, unraveling the stitch in his mind. The man he used to be was only a hollow shell, and he didn't think anything left in the realm existed to mend what had been ripped from him.

CHAPTER 23

Amaris

AMARIS'S HEART RACED against the wind biting at her cheeks. She could hardly breathe. Her throat was dry and burning against the warm air. She panted, but a powerful surge continued to propel her forward, whispering to her to keep running. She followed its command without question and no fault. All that surrounded her was darkness, but her feet kept moving until she blinked.

The scene shifted before her eyes, distorting the world around her in a watery haze.

She stopped abruptly, nearly causing her to fall and skid across the pavement. She whirled in circles. A road, a real asphalt road. Even through the rippling vision, she knew she was on her street, only a few blocks from her house. She sprinted home, her arms pumping at her sides. A smile spread across her face as the front porch light flickered against the night. Her heart was about to leap from her chest.

"Derek!" she shouted and didn't care if it woke the neighbors. She didn't care what time it was or who would hear her. She was home.

Derek's head popped out with widened eyes, and his lips parted in a gasp. The rickety porch bowed beneath his weight. His hair had grown, and stubble scattered his face in a rugged beard. She wanted to leap into his arms and kiss that beautiful face, feel his arms hold her as she told him she was sorry for running away.

"Derek, I'm home!"

She wiped her eyes, but her vision still held the murkiness. Her feet bounded up the steps to embrace him. She closed her eyes, waiting for their bodies to become one, but she was met with the hard ground as she slammed into the hardwood foyer.

"Amaris?" he shouted, sounding muffled.

She rolled onto her back, propping up on her elbows. "Derek," she whispered, unable to comprehend what was happening. He towered over her. "Can you not see me?"

With defeat in his eyes, he came back into the house, ramming his shoulder into the door to get it to close. He sulked past her into the living room, where clothes were discarded across the couch and empty takeout boxes piled on the floor.

I'm dreaming. Reality caved.

Amaris's body ached from the tumble, but she picked herself up to follow him. Something crunched beneath her boot. She pulled back to find a shard of glass. It was all over the foyer and scattered into the carpet. Her eyes followed its trail. Where their coffee table used to be was a pile of splintered wood and larger chunks of glass. She swallowed the lump forming in her throat.

She scanned the living room, assessing the damage as she navigated the disaster. Empty bottles of scotch and beer cans littered the side table shoved into the corner. Her vision faded around the edges like her world was tunneling.

Her hand hovered over the swinging door. The last time she'd passed through it, her heart had been cleaved in two. She bit her lip, debating whether to open it again. Theodoric had seen the signs before she'd recognized them herself. With a single mark and a name, he knew what had happened.

Amaris reached out to open the door, but her hand passed through. With a single breath, she stepped into the kitchen. Derek leaned against the counter in his usual stance beside the sink, swirling the scotch in his glass. She expected her feet to carry her to the fridge for a beer, to jump on the counter, but she didn't move. She was glued to the entrance of the kitchen, forced to watch from the outside as the fight that ruined her life unfolded again.

Derek's phone rang, startling her.

"What do you want?" he snapped, the veins in his arms puffing out. "I told you to take care of it." An inaudible voice whispered on the other end, and Derek's brows furrowed. "That bitch is crazy. Why the fuck are you dicking around?" He grasped the edge of the counter, throwing back the remainder of his glass.

Amaris was thankful it was only a dream, and she couldn't breathe in the nauseating scent of his scotch.

"Because if I go near her, I lose my job! You owe me this." He hung up the phone and tossed it on the counter.

Amaris jumped as it skidded to a halt against the fridge.

A knock thudded on the door, and Derek bounded toward it. He passed through her, and an icy sting surged through her. It brought her to her knees.

"What the fuck!" Derek shouted.

Each movement was excruciating, but she pulled herself up. It wasn't unfolding like she thought. Something was wrong. Her body passed through the door, becoming transparent, as if she were a ghost in her own home.

"I told you we aren't through!" Viv's voice rolled through the house.

Amaris ran for the hall and tripped, falling through the recliner in the living room. Crawling the rest of the way to the entry hall, she poked her face over the edge of the carpet.

"Get off my property, Viv." Derek reached behind his back, gripping the gun in his waistband.

Her heart caught in her throat, but she couldn't move. Her body was pinned to the ground.

"Where's Mar?" Viv snapped.

"You're fucking crazy." His fingers flipped off the safety, but he kept the gun poised behind him.

"I found her phone, and a video recorded the whole thing. I know she went into those woods, and it recorded you later that night. Where is she!" Viv's chest heaved and sweat dripped from her brow. She wasn't even wearing any makeup, which wasn't like her.

"Give it to me," Derek seethed.

"You think I brought it with me?" She smirked. "I gave it to your sergeant. He watched the whole thing."

"I didn't find her in those woods!"

"You're lying! I know what goes on in this house. Mar may have kept her secrets, but I grew up with a shitty-ass mother and know what it's like to live with someone like you."

"Fuck you!" He slammed the door. It creaked as it hit Viv's boot, not even making a dent in her steel toe.

Amaris closed her eyes. *What kind of nightmare is this?* She wanted to wake up and didn't care if it was in that cell, the mystique tower, or that uncomfortable bed. She needed to be rid of this dream.

Derek shoved the door against the wall, drawing his gun and aiming the barrel at Viv's head. "You don't deserve to live," Derek spewed, his hateful words ringing through Amaris's ears. It wasn't him. "You're nothing."

Viv fought back, her fists balling at her sides. She stepped over the threshold, pressing her forehead against the gun. "Do it," she raged, lightning arcing across her eyes.

§

244

AMARIS CURLED INTO a ball, forcing herself not to close her eyes but to stare at the last dying embers of the fire as her nightmare flickered behind her eyelids. Her back was still slick with sweat and tears clung to her cheeks. Derek and Theodoric's voices jumped in tandem in her head.

Does he hit you?

You're nothing.

After her fight with Theodoric, she'd run to her room to find it locked, forgetting she'd escaped through the window. She stumbled to the mystique tower, where she'd thrown herself onto the cot and fought through the night against the nightmare severing her existence.

The tower door opened, and a pair of footsteps crossed the room. They stopped at one of the chairs seated across from her. Theodoric's shallow sigh threatened to send her spiraling. She refused to meet his gaze, but her tear-stricken face was laid bare for him to see.

Her heart ached, shredding in two as the perfect image of her future disintegrated behind her eyes. Derek hit her. The one man she'd trusted with everything in her life *hit* her. Her mind sought to show her by conjuring up the worst-case imaginable—Derek threatening Viv.

"Amaris," Theodoric began.

I don't want to talk. She turned her head toward the far wall. Not about last night, about Derek, her life. She was done.

"I only want to help." His stern voice was gone, replaced by the voice of that small boy who'd kneeled before her in the hallway.

"I didn't ask for it," she snipped.

"I can't entirely help myself," he breathed, attempting what he could at peace.

But I don't want peace.

Amaris sat up, whipping her braid over her shoulder as she glared at him with swollen eyes and snot dripping down her nose. "Then, you better learn to." Her world had imploded. The one person in her life who loved her struck her. Every fight spun through her mind, every insult, and every flinch at the wave of his hand.

"Do you wish to not be protected? Should I let you try another escape attempt?"

"You're the reason I'm here in the first place!" she shouted.

He slid his hand down his face. "You're insufferable at times, you know that?"

"*I'm* insufferable!" Fiery rage simmered below her skin. "Why don't you take a good look in the mirror, buddy? You're the one who's demanding, controlling, and can't seem to keep his nose out of other people's business!" Amaris ground her teeth, scrunching her lips together. "If you would have let me run—"

"I apologize for how I treated you when we first met, for bringing you here, and not listening to you, but I won't apologize for last night. You would've been caught if it wasn't for me."

Amaris stood, frustration, fear, anger, everything fueling her movements as she jabbed her finger at him. "You owe me a huge apology for last night." She narrowed her eyes into thin slits. "You were out of line."

He stood from the chair. He was huge, almost a foot taller than her. Burly shoulders and strong hands. Her body wanted to cower, but she forced herself not to tremble. He stepped closer until her nail pressed against his chest. His hand encircled her finger.

This is it. He was going to yank her hand back and dislocate her shoulder. He'd slap her across the face and apologize and blame it on the scotch.

"I'm sorry," he whispered.

Amaris balked.

"I'm sorry, Amaris," he whispered again as he released her finger. He lifted his hand, hovering over her cheek. His thumb brushed along her cheekbone, taking away a line of tears.

The door slammed open, and Bennet stormed the tower with a vicious smirk. Another figure emerged. It was the monstrous man from the riding party with dark and beady eyes—Gerard. Amaris had steered clear of him since that first day. He was larger than both Theodoric and Bennet, and she couldn't imagine what would happen if he got one of his gigantic hands around her neck. Instinctively, she put distance between them until her back was against the far wall. Bennet stalked closer, but Theodoric shifted in front of her.

The impending doom circled around her. *They know I tried to escape.*

"What do you want?" Theodoric asked, using his soldier voice.

"It would seem she's struck again," Bennet growled.

Theodoric inched back until his warmth and scent of brine and worn leather overpowered Amaris's other senses.

She peered over his shoulder. "What are you talking about?" she asked.

Bennet stopped at the worktable as he gave the room a look of pure disgust. "One of my men was found dead in his bed," he snapped. "Scrying fever."

It wasn't about the escape attempt. Theodoric grabbed ahold of her, keeping her behind him as he pressed his back against her.

"We didn't know of another case of scrying fever. We would have made a tonic." Theodoric said. "She cured Esaias."

"The man is dead due to her negligence, and she'll pay for it," Bennet threatened.

Amaris's chest wrapped tight around her heart and lungs. She held onto Theodoric's back, scrunching the fabric into a ball as she steadied herself. "I...I didn't know," she said, but every bit of courage was gone. *Someone died.*

"This isn't Amaris's fault," Theodoric growled.

"Step aside, Theodoric," Bennet ordered. "Gerard will be taking her to the dungeons."

"No," Theodoric snapped. "Not until my father gives that order."

"Step aside," Bennet repeated.

Theodoric held his stance. "We will speak with my father first."

"Gerard," Bennet barked.

Instantly, Theodoric set into action. His fists slammed into Gerard's jaw, spewing blood across the floor.

"Don't," Amaris said, grabbing Theodoric by the arm and attempting to hold him back, but he pulled from her grasp.

He moved on Gerard with his fists as if on instinct. With blood dripping from his lip, Gerard retaliated and delivered a blow to Theodoric's abdomen. His grunt filled the tower. He hunched forward, leaning against a chair and gasping for breath.

"Stop!" Amaris screamed, but Gerard sent his fist into Theodoric's face with a loud crunch. He fell back with a groan and grabbed his nose. Blood leaked between his fingers. "Please, stop!"

Theodoric tried to get up but was too late. Bennet came up behind Amaris. She didn't hear or see him move, but he had his dagger pressed against her neck.

"This ends now," he yelled.

Amaris eyed Theodoric, begging him to stay down. Why had he jumped in for her, risked himself to protect her?

Gerard rolled up his sleeves, and his monstrous legs took a thundering step toward Theodoric.

"I'll go with you!" Amaris shouted.

Bennet sneered at her but grabbed a tighter hold of her arm and led her toward the steps. They stopped at the threshold, and Bennet turned to Theodoric. He was using the chair to get himself off the floor, panting and spitting blood.

"Clean yourself up and be in your father's study in twenty minutes."

Bennet shoved Amaris through the doorway and carted her off through the manor. He took odd hallways, tighter ones she'd never passed through. She didn't dare fight him with his dagger pressed against her back as they walked. Gerard followed in tow behind them. Amaris took deep breaths to prevent the meltdown waiting behind the mask she'd thrown up and clung to with every last fraying fiber of her sanity.

They stepped out into the misty morning with a few raindrops pelting from above. The bay was a gloomy sight, and each daunting step down the dungeon stairs sucked the life from her. He threw her in the same cell and locked the door behind her, but there wasn't the flicker of a candle anymore.

Amaris was left to what little light shown through the bars in the never-ending pit of darkness threatening to pull her to the verge of tears.

CHAPTER 24

Theo

A NERVOUS ENERGY skittered through Theo as he plunged his hand into the water streaming from the faucet. He breathed in, a glob of blood instantly shooting down his throat. A cough tore through his chest. He bathed away the blood, feeling the bridge of his nose. The outer edges were already starting to grow puffy.

It was all his fault. He kept her preoccupied with healing Esaias and didn't recognize anyone else coming down with the disease. He released a shaky breath and stared at his reflection. His father had to see reason. Amaris had cured Esaias. She didn't deserve Bennet's treatment.

He left the safety of his room and rapped on Esaias's door. He needed him and couldn't face Bennet and his father alone.

Esaias's stomping feet carried through the hall as he pulled open the door. "What in the bloody realm are you bothering me this early for?" He rubbed the sleep from his eyes.

If Theo's muscles weren't about to jump from his skin, he would've stopped and gawked at his rapid healing, but he pushed past him.

"By all means, make yourself at home." Esaias stepped toward his wardrobe. He threw on a clean set of clothes and crossed the room to draw back the curtains.

Theo grasped the hilt of his dagger as he took a seat on the edge of Esaias's bed, his thoughts spinning out of control. *I fight and I live.* He inhaled deeply and attempted to stifle the beginnings of his panic.

"What happened?" Esaias leaned against the back of a chair, letting out a cough as he hunched forward.

"I need you."

Esaias's eyes widened against the dreary morning soaking through the window. "What's wrong?"

Theo rubbed at his eyes. "I did something foolish."

"That's hardly new."

"With your recovery, I shouldn't ask this of you, but I need you to come with me to my father's study."

"Theo, what did you do?"

Each pulse of his heart threatened to slice at the stitch in his mind, tearing it open inch by inch. "What I needed to. I'll explain later, but my father and Bennet are already waiting."

Esaias narrowed his eyes. Theo pushed off the bed and headed out into the hall before he could further pry.

"What happened?"

Theo stopped. "Bennet is furious with me." Gris was usually the one to accompany him in meetings, but not now. Once again, he tried to stamp out the growing anxiety within him, but it seeped from him, crawling up his neck. "I need someone who has my back."

"Why?" Esaias asked. "And why do you look like you were in a brawl?"

Theo's feet were silent as he strode through the halls and bolted down the stairs.

"If you're asking this of me, at least tell me why," Esaias shouted from the top of the stairs.

Theo stopped at the bottom. He needed to control himself, his panic, the beast. Bennet wanted him to get worked up, using it to his advantage. Theo turned over his shoulder and gazed at him, his cousin, the one who he saw more as a brother than even Luther or Jeremiah. "Because I came between Bennet and Amaris."

Theo tore through the last few halls with Esaias in tow. He came to a stop outside his father's study. His palms were slick with sweat as he reached for the handle. He pushed open the door, and his chest tightened.

His father sat with his hands laced over his stomach, glaring at Theo and Esaias. The door closed behind them with a slam, but it wasn't only Bennet and his father in the meeting. Gerard, Ward, and a couple of Bennet's most loyal soldiers stood around the room with Sephardi posted in the corner.

"Theo?" Esaias whispered in warning.

Theo gave him a stern look. He stood before his father, crossing his arms over his chest. There was nowhere for him to face besides him. He didn't have the luxury of controlling the room and keeping his distance. Five of Bennet's soldiers were all within an arm's length. Any icy chill creeped up his back as his father cleared his throat.

"I hear you interfered in Bennet's arrest?" he said, his voice dark and gravely.

"Yes, sir." Theo gave his father the respect he wanted. There wasn't room for games.

"Why did you interfere?"

Theo forced a breath as his body attempted to shake. "Amaris cured Esaias of his scrying fever. Bennet is wrongly accusing her of killing one of his men. He claims she—"

"I'm aware of this incident with scrying fever," his father interrupted, eyeing Esaias beside Theo. "What I want to know is why you felt the need to attack one of your officers?"

Esaias went rigid, and Theo felt his eyes straining on him. All the eyes in the room were, and it made his skin crawl. His hand twitched. He balled it into a fist to fight the monster. He didn't know why he'd attacked Gerard, why he'd felt the need to throw Amaris behind him.

"It isn't Amaris's fault. She didn't know." Theo kept the bite from his tone as sweat dripped down his back.

"Are you certain?" his father asked, his voice rising. "I asked you to learn who she is, and you defend her instead." He slammed his fist against the desk, rattling the vase of dead snowdrops. The decrepit stems shook and scattered wilted petals.

"She couldn't defend herself. Someone had to."

"I won't have this among my soldiers," his father rasped.

"Sir," Sephardi interrupted.

The room fell silent as everyone focused on where she stood strong in the corner.

She inclined her head and passed a glance to the others in the room. "The soldier Bennet speaks of never came to Miss Carter about his condition. He was only showing signs of a simple illness for days and sprouted the rash last night. He was on sentry duty with me, and I tried to send him to Miss Carter. He refused and said he wouldn't be treated by the likes of her. He died in the night."

Theo's stiff spine belied the shaking in his legs. He refused to allow himself to buckle before his father.

"Then, Corporal Salter, will you escort Miss Carter from the dungeon to the gardens."

"The gardens?" Theo stammered.

"Twenty-five lashings," his father declared.

Theo's heart skipped a beat.

"For both of you. Do you really think you two were careful last night?" He dragged his finger along the desk, rubbing at the accumulated dust. "Were you planning to help her escape?"

"No, I—"

"She's lucky a lashing is all she'll receive for—"

"I'll take her punishment."

Stunned, his father's eyes narrowed, and their mismatched nature was demonic.

"You can't—" Bennet began.

"According to the law, I can. *If a penance shall be bestowed upon an individual, it is the right of a tenant to accept the punishment of another,*" Theo recited the law, knowing it like the back of his hand. He had it memorized for the purpose of one day getting Adelaide out of trouble with her constant rebellion.

"You'll take all fifty lashes?" his father growled.

"Yes," Theo said, drawing back his shoulders. He'd never received more than ten before.

"You feel a duty to protect her? A murderer over your own people?" his father yelled.

"That sounds like treason to me." Bennet's voice radiated through the room.

Theo's head whipped to the side. Bennet resided in the corner, leaning against the bookcase with his hands gripping his belt. Theo started, "You can't believe—"

Gerard stepped toward Theo with a raised hand. Theo snapped. The beast crawled from his bones, taking over. Without thought, his hand retrieved his dagger and flourished it against Gerard. Two pairs of strong hands gripped Theo's arms and yanked him to his knees. He managed to free himself from one of their holds as the monster reached for Gerard's throat. A third took hold of his hand, bending it back and pinching his shoulder.

"Is this seriously how you want this to go? Throwing your life away for a woman?" his father bellowed.

The soldiers tugged at Theo's arms, and a shout escaped. Their hands were like iron shackles against his wrists. Their heavy respirations were like the whistling wind of Mosfelkov against the prison walls. Darkness crept into Theo's vision. He fought it. He fought them. They pulled harder, like the chains when they'd stretched his arms.

"I won't go back," Theo cried, but he didn't know who could even hear him as the chamber in Rongstad Prison appeared around him. Once again, he was their prisoner, forced to his breaking point. A cry rippled from his chest, and tears burned behind his eyes.

What is he talking about? a distant echo asked.

Theo gasped as the chains pulled at his arms and footsteps thumped down the steps. His world was obscured in the red haze of his blood as it dripped down his forehead from his last session. A single lantern hung in the corner above the table of instruments, taunting and reminding. The steps grew louder, and Theo's body trembled, knowing what was to come. He couldn't do it anymore, feel the bite of the blade as it cut into his skin, carving out every bit of his soul.

You need to get him to Amaris, a voice cracked.

A hand squeezed Theo's face, but it was only his imagination as his interrogator skulked closer, hiding within the shadows. Theo didn't know his name. He was a phantom, instilling fear in Theo's heart. The chains pulled tighter, and he let out an agonizing cry, tears spilling down his cheeks.

What's wrong with him?

He wanted to drop his head, to allow his body to crumple to the ground, to lie in his own blood and piss, but his restraints held him tighter. The dark boots brushed the edge of the poor illumination of the gray-stoned chamber. A knife glinted from the darkness. The phantom stepped forward with a menacing grin. He stretched his long fingers out, setting the other lanterns ablaze.

"No," Theo shouted, his feet attempting to scramble beneath him, but he couldn't move. "Just kill me."

The phantom gripped his face. He was nothing more than an evil smudge against the realm, placed there for one purpose, to torture the living. The chains pulled tighter as Theo tried to fight and pull himself from the interrogator's hand. The scent of blood leaked through his nose, along with the damp smell that permeated every pore of Theo's body.

"What do you want from me?" he breathed, his voice growing hoarse.

The phantom smacked Theo across the face, the bite of his hand stinging against his burning flesh. "To find what breaks you."

Theo's body shook violently as the phantom dragged his knife across his chest, spilling his blood onto the floor. He knew how much to spill and how long to wait until Theo's body was ready again.

He was fucking tortured, you bastards!

The phantom grabbed Theo's hair and pulled back his head to face him. He dragged his knife along his skin but didn't break the barrier to kill him.

He needs a sedative! Another distant echo sounded from a dream of a life he'd known.

Theo tried to tear his head from the phantom's gaze as black drool spilled down his chin. He screamed as the knife dragged across his abdomen.

Take him outside!

The burning smell of his flesh flooded Theo's nose. The blood dripped down his temple and smeared across his eyes, further coating the room around him in a crimson hue.

"Please," he begged, his voice a raspy cry. The shackles chafed against his wrists as they spread his arms farther apart. His body shook with the pain. He wanted to die. If he passed out, his torturer would only inject his concoction into Theo's blood to rally his mind.

He had no concept of time in the dark-infested room. Days, seasons, or even years could've passed. The fact Theo had little strength within his body proved it'd been at least longer than only hours.

The phantom stepped behind him and a hot iron rod pressed against his back. Theo screamed, but it was no longer a bloodcurdling cry. It came out only as a hoarse whimper.

I fight and I live.

"I wonder when your father will beg for your release." His voice was like a serpent's hiss. The phantom thrusted his fist into Theo's abdomen, taking all the breath from his lungs.

Theo needed to keel over, but the chains held his body. His head hung, the blood dripping to the floor and filth at his knees. "You don't know my father well if you think he'd negotiate for me." The rod smacked against his back. The pain from the intense contact and heat threatened to pull him into oblivion.

"You cannot leave so soon, Lieutenant. There is much to discuss."

He jabbed Theo's arm with his vile mixture. Theo's heart raced to his ears, his blood boiled to the surface, and his eyes widened.

A thin lash whipped across Theo's back, a cry escaping him. "Kill me and get it over with," he cried.

"You are more valuable than you realize." The phantom took his jagged dagger and dug it into the flesh of Theo's arm.

He screamed, and whatever resided in the tonic kept his senses alert and his chest moving. *I fight and I live.* The phantom dragged the blade down Theo's arm, eliciting a cry he'd never heard come from himself before.

CHAPTER 25

Amaris

SOBS EVISCERATED AMARIS'S throat as she fumbled with her knife in the lock. Her hands trembled and the tears clouded her vision. It was useless. She returned her knife to her boot, fighting the urge to hurl it across the cell as she crumbled to the floor. She was never getting out of here. She'd never hear Viv's laugh or the blare of a siren again. Charlie's smile as they raced to a call would only ever be a distant memory, and Derek—she needed to know if what she saw would be her future. Were she and Derek destined to always fight?

The gate at the top of the stairs flew open, and footsteps ran toward her. There was a rattling of keys and then Sephardi standing in the open door. She kneeled by Amaris's side, scanning her for any injuries.

"Bennet didn't hurt me," Amaris whispered.

"Good," she muttered. "I need you to go to your room and stay there. No matter what you hear, promise me you won't leave."

"What's going on? Where's Theodoric?"

A deafening crack resonated off the stone walls of the dungeon. Amaris had never heard anything like it. It was a sharp snap like a gunshot. Sephardi winced.

"What was that?" Again, she heard the thundering crack.

"Amaris," Sephardi breathed.

"What is that?" she demanded, standing and heading outside.

A cry of agony followed another piercing clap. It carried through the grim morning air as storm clouds shrouded the bay in a gloomy rain. Another one sent Amaris's pulse racing. She sprinted toward the sound. It couldn't be. She'd never heard him cry, but the wail hit her hard as he cried out again. She stopped dead at the edge of the garden where a small crowd of soldiers gathered around to watch.

Theodoric was pinned against the short stone wall wreathing the garden. He thrashed against the soldiers locking down his arms. Blood spilled down his back. Red welts were open to the damp air. Behind him, Gerard stood with a whip in his hand. He released his wrist, and another lash shot through her ears as Theodoric's left leg buckled beneath him.

Amaris gasped. *No.* Another flick and another scream.

"He's flashing back, you idiots!" Esaias screamed as two soldiers fought to hold him.

Another line of blood dripped down his back, but it wasn't the red welts or flayed flesh that caught her attention. Lines ran across his skin, wrinkly indents and jagged scars.

All the pieces to the mysterious puzzle were falling into place. His panic attacks, his missing time during the war. Flashbacks. *He'd been captured, but had he been...?* Amaris couldn't hold the thought back. *Tortured.*

Amaris took a step forward, but Sephardi grabbed her arm. "I have to stop this," she insisted, daring a look at Theodoric as another lash came down on his back. Blood spurted across the soldiers struggling to hold him. He released another cry.

"You'll only make things worse for yourself and for him. He's doing this for you," Sephardi whispered as she pulled her to hide in the back of the crowd.

Amaris took in the sight of Theodoric's blood dripping down his back, staining the back of his pants. His body trembled, and his right knee shook. She tugged at her arm, but Sephardi tightened her grip.

"Amaris." Pricilla's soft voice came from behind her. "Oh my." Her expression paled. Pricilla's hair was damp with the morning rain, and her dress clung to her hips.

Gerard's hand came down, and the whip met Theodoric's back. It tore away another piece of flesh. His other leg gave out, but the soldiers tried to heft him up and keep him standing.

"Stand up!" Bennet roared, but Theodoric was lost to his nightmare, his body mindlessly thrashing against the men restraining him. "Hold him still!"

"He can't help it!" Esaias's voice cracked as he fought to run for his cousin.

Alan stood off to the side, his face pale as his fingers hovered over his daggers, his features laced with something resembling dread or fear.

Why won't anyone help him?

"This is what happens when one disobeys orders! Everyone must follow them, even the son of the duke. Fifty lashes, Gerard!" Bennet yelled.

Fifty lashes? Why? All of this because he stood up for her? Desperately, she scanned the crowd, her eyes stopping on the duke himself. He stood away from the others under the shelter of the protruding roof. His arms were crossed, and no expression of emotion overcame his face. Gerard raised his hand to unleash another lash.

Theodoric had stepped in for her, fought against them dragging her to the dungeons. He risked his career, his life, all for her. Being a firefighter and paramedic was all she'd ever known. It was all she had left in her crumbling world, but even that had turned into a disaster after she nearly got herself, Charlie, and Viv killed. She didn't know who she was without her badge.

You don't sit back and play it safe. Charlie's words after that fire rang through her head.

"Help me," Amaris mouthed to Pricilla and eyed Sephardi's grip around her arm.

Pricilla nodded and shoved with the weight of her body into Sephardi's side. Amaris slipped free of her hold and sprinted through the mud. She slid, halting herself in front of Theodoric. She raised her arm and the whip came down, encircling her forearm.

She'd received burns from fires, but nothing compared to the pain as the whip latched around her arm, leaving a spiral of raised red welts behind. She fell to her knees, the mud splashing up at her. Bennet ripped the whip from Gerard's hand. She couldn't stop the sting of tears even if she tried. But they were camouflaged by the raindrops streaking her face. She placed one foot underneath herself and stood to meet Bennet's furious glare. He held the whip, ready to unleash his rage on her.

"He did nothing wrong." She held her stance.

"Get out of my way, you little *bitch*." Bennet was more than angry, more than furious. There wasn't a word to describe the hell about to erupt.

"No."

She stood her ground, hugging her arm to her chest, her voice strong. Theodoric raged behind her, but she didn't break her deadlock. Over Bennet's shoulder, Adelaide pushed to the front of the crowd. She was covered in sand, her face red with exhaustion and her hand readied on the hilt of her sword.

No. Amaris's eyes shot to her. She wouldn't allow another Fastrada child to face Bennet's wrath on her account.

"Restrain her!" Bennet shouted.

"No!" But it was too late.

Gerard had Amaris in his clutches, and he dragged her away from Theodoric. She squirmed in his hold, but he only tightened his grip on her arms. Theodoric turned to her as she opened her mouth to scream, but nothing came out. Black storms filled his eyes.

Another lash, and he grimaced. "Please," he pleaded. Rain battered his face, but Amaris knew tears leaked from the corners of his eyes.

Bennet unleashed the whip again and again, tearing open his flesh. Amaris flinched, but she didn't turn away. It was because of her. With each strike of the whip, her muscles grew taut.

"Please, stop," Amaris begged. "I'm the one you want to punish, not him!"

Bennet chose to ignore her. He flung the whip back, administering lash after lash. Sephardi grabbed ahold of Adelaide, dragging her into the manor with her feet kicking.

"You're going to kill him!" Esaias screamed, getting one arm free.

"Then he should have thought about that before his actions!" Bennet wouldn't stop.

Theodoric's wails grew hoarse and soon died to breathless gasps. He'd risked everything to keep Bennet and his father at bay, and now she couldn't do anything. Bennet's teeth ground together as he raised his arm, ready to unleash another blow.

"That's enough." The duke's voice broke through the clamor. It wasn't a yell of anger but a loud bellow of authority. He stepped out into the rain, away from the protection of the manor's roof. Taking one look at Bennet, he jerked his head toward the kitchen doors. Bennet stormed after him, taking Gerard to follow in the duke's wake.

Amaris ran to Theodoric, stopping to stare at his back and the blood spilling from his wounds. His head hung limp against his chest. She held his chin in her hands. There wasn't a flicker of an eyelid, only shallow breaths. As Alan rushed to replace one of the soldiers and Esaias the other, Amaris swallowed and took in his chest. More burn marks and scars spread across his skin.

"Get him to my tower," she ordered Alan and Esaias, struggling to keep her composure.

Neither one of them hesitated to follow her leadership. They hoisted Theodoric and began the trek to the tower. His feet dragged behind. Amaris kept ahead of them, watching his chest rise and fall. He woke once they entered the library and fought against Alan and Esaias. They sped up their pace.

She raced up the tower steps with them following close behind her.

They set him on his stomach on the cot with his head near the edge. Esaias kicked a bucket below his mouth. Theodoric's groan echoed off the vaulted ceiling. He fought passing out, his hands clenching the cot.

"Alan, start a fire," Amaris ordered, another demand he briskly followed.

Theodoric tried to sit up, but Amaris had no idea how he even had the strength to. Esaias forced his shoulders down. An awful gag erupted from Theodoric, and he hurled, luckily aiming into the bucket.

Amaris drew a candle closer, examining the skin of his back. Red welts covered his back, but even more were bloody gashes. She reached to touch one, to see how deep it was. Theodoric jerked and yelped.

"He needs a sedative!" Esaias shouted, gritting his teeth as he fought to hold Theodoric down.

Amaris dropped the candle, extinguishing it. Theodoric latched onto her wrist, his skin cold and clammy. His eyes met hers, again filled with swirling darkness.

She leaned closer without thinking. "Theodoric," she whispered.

His erratic breathing began to slow, but his knuckles didn't let up from their grip around her arm.

Her fingers twitched at her side, but she held her other hand back from reaching for him. Instead, she closed her eyes and took a breath before saying, "You're safe."

His fingers loosened their hold, and she opened her eyes. The storms settled, and bits of golden specks filled his irises. "Amaris," he breathed. He winced and clenched down instinctively as his back muscles spasmed. He let go of her and dropped his hand to the floor. "I'm sorry."

"You have nothing to be sorry for," Amaris said.

"That was the worst lashing I've ever seen my father give," Alan whispered, his face blank.

Gerard was Alan's dad. *That explains so much.*

"What in the realm did you do?" Alan asked.

"He tried to stop Bennet," Amaris uttered.

She hustled toward her worktable. She'd never seen a flogging injury before, but she knew his wounds needed cleaning, probably stitching, but that was off the table. She threw open the mystique journal but gripped the edge of the worktable. She paused. Her heart shouldn't race like this.

Inhale. Exhale.

She hated the feeling settling over her. The panic. Theodoric was just another patient. She couldn't allow herself to get worked up, but for fuck's sake, it was all because of her. He was lying there with some of the worst trauma she'd ever seen, and it was all her fault.

Her hands shook as she read through the pages and found *flogging* scribbled at the top. A groan from Theodoric had her skimming faster, settling on pain management on the next page. It said to take dried leaves of cudweed and brew them into a tea and steep for desired effect.

"Alan, make yourself useful and boil some water." He didn't protest.

Amaris went to her shelves, reading each label. *Fade chicory, uppaway, izaseed...cudweed!* She thought she'd arranged them alphabetically. It appeared someone had been messing with her herbs. The jar of cudweed held small basil-like leaves. She set them in a cup, ladling the now boiled water to allow the tea to steep.

The old mystique often strayed from page to page with his thoughts. Amaris thumbed through the next few pages to find something she could use to treat the wounds. Theodoric let out another moan, sending Amaris pinching the corner of the page and sucking in a breath. She closed her eyes, holding the air in her lungs. *He's just another patient.*

Dragging her finger down the page. She found what she needed. She searched the shelves and found a large begregane leaf wrapped in a cloth. *Produces cooling, numbing, and inflammation fighting effect for wounds, burns, and sores.*

Amaris pulled the knife from her boot, thankful she hadn't tossed it across the cell. She cut away the edges to reveal a light pink paste.

Theodoric hurled into the bucket. Her hands trembled against the hilt, but she squeezed it tighter and plowed through.

"Where did you get a knife?" Alan asked, his eyes flashing to the dark blade in her hand.

"It was my parents'." Her response was short, and she didn't bother sparing him a glance or elaborating further. She strained the leaves and sat on the floor beside Theodoric. Her fingers gripped his chin, raising his head. His eyes were bloodshot, and snot dripped from his nose. He tried to pull away, but her grip tightened. "Drink this." She pressed the cup to his lips.

He smelled the wafting odor, his nose cringing as he raised a brow. "Cudweed?" he gasped.

"It'll help with the pain." Amaris tilted the cup to his parted lips. "Small sips to avoid further upsetting your stomach."

"You won't have to worry about him throwing it up. The brew you made is strong. He won't have time," Esaias chimed in.

Theodoric's shaky hands held hers as they grasped the cup. A muscle contracted in his back, and he winced. His cry made Amaris's attempts at steady breaths falter. He grasped the edge of the cot, his knuckles leaching of color. Instantly, Amaris reached for his shoulder. A wrinkly burn scar slithered from his shoulder down to his heart. She pulled back as his eyes tracked her movement.

She cleared her throat and lifted the cup once more to his lips. He took a sip, and with each swallow he grimaced in pain. It tore at Amaris, each audible gasp. When he'd finished the tea, his head slumped back to the cot.

"Thank you." The next thing she knew, his body went limp.

Amaris stared in awe at the empty cup and Theodoric. She couldn't allow herself to stop and think about him or the effects of the cudweed. All she needed to do was bandage his back.

Alan and Esaias refused to leave his side while she worked. Esaias perched on the table, lost to his own thoughts. She had Alan fetch a basin of water, and when he returned, he leaned against the window, watching her every move.

She began cleaning out his cuts, blood instantly soaking the rag and her hands. It turned the water a dark shade of crimson. Alan and Esaias started a cycle of fresh water every few lacerations. Amaris kept to a rhythm, silently humming a song her mother had sung to her a dozen times over. It aided her quick pulse and soothed her trembling hands. The room was otherwise silent.

She dragged the back of her hand against her forehead to wipe the sweat dripping into her eyes. She didn't know whether to be thankful for the silence or spiteful. Basic first aid was all she had to go on. She cleaned the mud from his cuts, but she didn't know the lasting effects of flogging injuries. He'd have more scars to add to the collection across his back. She kept going, continuing to move her hands and clear her mind. It was all she could do.

After she'd cleaned out each wound, she applied the pink paste, moving gently in case he woke abruptly. Cudweed had been one of the herbs she'd skimmed over but tabbed to read about later. She was kicking herself for not further digesting the material. She'd briefly read a line about injecting the herb. It was good to know needles and syringes had been invented. She moved to the fleshy parts of his skin. The cuts weren't as deep as she'd thought and were already beginning to clot.

She forced her body to relax, deeply breathing. It was startling to feel like this, protective. Maybe it was the guilt. She was the reason for it. Her fingers moved over the ridges of his back, covering every injured part with the paste. Her hands continued to shake as she secured clean cloth over the open gashes, but she positioned herself to keep Esaias and Alan from noticing.

She trudged to the last clean pitcher of water and poured it into the bowl to wash his blood from her hands. It seeped like ink off her fingers and the tendrils swirled in the water. Her hands wouldn't cease their trembling. It infuriated her, but she knew it was only the effects of the adrenaline leaving her body. She dried her hands and used the remainder of the paste on her own welt. The spiral of red stung as she rubbed the begregane paste over her skin.

"That was a brave thing you did," Esaias said, breaking the everlasting silence between the three of them. He and Alan lounged in the chairs on the other side of the fireplace.

"I did what anyone else would've done."

Amaris didn't bother to look at him. She was too exhausted from the lack of sleep and the commotion of the morning. She bound her forearm in cloth, tucking in the edge to tighten it. Kneeling at Theodoric's side, she monitored his vitals. His breaths were regular, his back slowly rising about every five seconds. She held his wrist, her fingers searching for the beating pulse of his heart.

"What was that?" Amaris breathed, coming back to her disbelief about everything that happened.

"Your punishment," Esaias whispered grimly as he dropped his face and a shadow painted his features.

"My what?" She turned to meet his eyes.

"The duke knows about whatever happened between the two of you last night and sentenced you both to twenty-five lashes. He took all of them, at least before the duke stepped in."

"Why did he step in?" Alan blurted out.

"I don't know and don't fucking care. The duke can burn in After," Esaias growled. He leaned forward, resting his chin in his hand. "Has he told you anything about the war?"

Amaris swallowed the lump forming in her throat and whispered, "Barely."

"Bennet called Theo's actions treasonous. Gerard made a move to grab him, and Theo reacted."

"He wasn't committing treason. He protected me when Bennet tried to blame me for another case of scrying fever."

"Luckily, Sephardi stepped in to confirm the truth, but he should've known. Bennet has his eyes set on you, and Theo is stepping in the way."

Everything was turning into one big dumpster fire. She'd never asked to be thrown here, to be sucked from her life.

"Theo was imprisoned for over two seasons. He was captured during a mission at the end of Crimsonreign. With the bitter cold and snowstorms, we couldn't get him out until Stormreign. I fought for a rescue mission, but our superior officers said it was too dangerous. Gris and I gathered a few from our squad willing to make the trek to Rongstad to break him out." Esaias paused then sighed. "I don't know the details, but I do know he was tortured. Today, the soldiers in the duke's study went to grab him, and he flashed back to what I'm presuming happened during his imprisonment."

"How do you know that?" she asked.

"He has nightmares and fits of panic. He was the sole survivor."

"He dreams about it?"

Esaias nodded, reclining back in his chair, crossing a foot over his knee. "He doesn't talk about it."

Her eyes drifted behind her. Theodoric's dark strands were soaked with rain and sweat as they clung to his forehead. He tried to warn her, but she didn't listen. He only wanted to protect her from Bennet and his father.

"Why did you take the whip?" Alan asked, pulling Amaris from her thoughts.

"I don't know." She sighed and leaned back against the wooden frame of the cot. Theodoric's even breaths brushed her neck, calming her growing nerves. It was a reminder of his stable state.

Alan took a swig from a flask he withdrew from his jacket. He offered it to her. "You look like you fell into the cracks of the realm."

"Thanks," she muttered, snatching his flask and taking a drink. Rum coated her dry throat, burning and leaving a spice to tingle her tongue.

"Is that—"

"Cinnamon," Alan answered flatly. "Imported from the Vukubua Islands."

She took a long swig, her hands continuing their shaking. She drew her legs tighter.

"Why do you think he stepped in?" Amaris asked.

"Do you mean for your lashing?" Alan asked.

Amaris nodded. "And in the tower. He'd protected me when Bennet came for me."

Esaias reclined back. "He's selfless."

"I was cruel." She took another sip. Esaias extended his hand, and she tossed him the flask. "I didn't listen to him and look what happened."

"You can't control what Theo does," Esaias said.

"But I can control what I do. I was trying to get away the other night, but Theodoric stopped me. He warned me what would happen."

Alan's hand gripped his outer thigh, his fingers inches from his dagger. "That was you in the stables?"

"Yes," she breathed. "He stopped me, and we argued. This is all my fault."

She never wanted this, any of it. She'd only wanted to get away from Derek, to escape that room, that fight. As Alan and Esaias's grumbles drowned out, she lifted her shaky hands before her eyes. She didn't know what terrified her more—what Derek had done or that she'd lost her composure on a call for the first time.

CHAPTER 26

Amaris

A SHARP PAIN in her neck jolted Amaris awake. She'd fallen asleep on the floor beside Theodoric's cot. Alan and Esaias were nowhere to be seen, and she didn't bother to check if they'd fallen down the stairs in a drunken stupor.

She massaged the angry muscle of her neck while she ventured toward the open window. The crackling hiss of a dying fire and the smell of herbs hung in the air. It wasn't the smell of diesel fumes or the smoldering scent the fire engines had after a fire, but it was familiar. The scent of blood tainted the air from the bowl she had yet to discard, but that was recognizable too.

Her stomach growled. The bay was still shrouded in a haze of clouds, but she was willing to bet she'd missed dinner. Scavenging the tower, she hoped to find a slice of bread or a magical cheeseburger, but she found a jar of peanuts in a small cabinet of the worktable.

"I wouldn't eat those if I were you." Theodoric's muffled voice carried across the room.

"And why not?" she questioned with her hand digging in the jar.

He smirked. "They're poisonous, causing hallucinations followed by paralysis and then death."

Amaris's throat made an audible gulp as she threw the peanuts back into the jar and wiped her hands against her pants. She grabbed a few logs from the corner and threw them onto the embers within the fireplace. Reaching for the flint and steel, she set to work making a new fire.

"How long have I been out?" he asked, trying to sit with a grimace. He stopped mid-rise, his eyes sweeping to his exposed chest.

"You shouldn't move. I only bandaged you this morning," Amaris said, busying her hands as she lit the fire.

"That's all it's been?" he whispered. "The amount of cudweed you gave me should've allowed me to rest for days."

She glanced over her shoulder and caught his eyes straying to a blanket folded beside the fireplace. She bent forward and picked up the wool fabric, smoothing it down as she then kneeled before him.

"Can I check your wounds first?" she asked, offering him the blanket. He wavered but nodded, and she set to work, prying at his bandages.

"I've received punishments before. I'll be fine by next morning." The gritting of his teeth as she checked beneath the cloth said otherwise.

"I highly doubt that. Gerard practically opened your entire back. He could've killed you." She eyed him, but he turned away to face the newly kindled fire.

"What happened?" he whispered.

"What do you remember?" She continued checking each bandage to see if any of his wounds had started bleeding again.

"Pain," he breathed. "Arguing with my father."

"Your father put a stop to it before Bennet could finish."

He closed his eyes, taking as deep of a breath as he could. The lazy strands of his hair brushed the side of his face as he released it.

Amaris stood from the cot, clearing her throat. "I'm putting you on mandatory bed rest."

"That is quite the formality." His scoff jerked the muscles of his back. His jaw tightened.

"As I'm the one who bandaged you up, I make the decisions." Amaris folded her arms.

"You are a stubborn woman." He tossed the blanket over his back, sliding it past the jagged scar on his arm.

She rolled her eyes and began cleaning after the morning fiasco. She wiped down the worktable and placed the various jars back in their homes.

"As you've saved me not only once but twice now, will you finally tell me your secrets?" he asked.

Amaris froze with her rag wound tight. "What kind of secrets?"

"Cornelius was a brilliant mystique, but not in the way you are. Gris told me I wasn't breathing when you pulled me out of the river."

"Did she? I hardly noticed." Amaris draped the rag over the windowsill to dry and dug her fingers into the grout between the stones.

"Amaris," he whispered, and a shiver swept over her. "Please."

She chanced a glance over her shoulder. He may have been from Magoria, but he sure knew the effect of puppy dog eyes.

She leaned against the window and folded her arms. "Fine. Yes, you stopped breathing."

Theo hesitated, unsure. "How did you heal me?"

"Your heart was still beating, so you had that going for you." She pulled a stray hair from her face, tucking it behind her ear. "I performed CPR. Compressions and rescue breathing."

"Rescue breathing?"

"When one is giving rescue breaths, you pinch their nose and put your mouth around theirs, and you breathe for them. For adults, you want to do it about every five seconds until they start breathing again. For kids, it's more like three."

"And if they don't start breathing?"

"A story for another time," Amaris sighed. By the quizzical expression settling over Theodoric's face, the rescue breaths might have been too much. He'd likely never understand compressions.

"How do you see it and not..." His voice broke, and he tugged tighter at the blanket. "How do you still carry on healing people?"

Amaris moved to the worktable, a light shuffle in her step to avoid the flutter his question brought to her chest. She'd seen a lot in her career but had never panicked in the middle of a call before. Her thoughts meandered toward the mystique journal instead of her bounding heart from the morning. "I've been around it all my life, and you get used to it."

She decided to busy her hands, flipping through the pages and avoiding his lingering gaze. Her cheeks flushed, and she set her eyes on the open window. *Would it kill the gods to offer a breeze or a signal gust of wind?* Amaris hadn't deciphered the extent of their religion, but she'd seen statues and paintings of the different gods and goddesses throughout the halls.

"Can we not have a simple conversation where one of us isn't busying themselves or screaming?"

"I'm a member of your staff, aren't I? I'm supposed to stay diligent, especially in the company of someone of your status." It was harsh, but it kept her from saying anything she'd regret. Why did she want to sit beside him and ask him about his world, his life, what his favorite color was?

"Do you take me for the kind of man to look down upon you for your status in society?"

"I don't know what I take you for." Her mind told her one thing, that he was a nosy asshole, but his actions spoke something different.

"As I said earlier, I'm truly sorry."

She finally lifted her head. He bore an expression of remorse deeply felt. Amaris twiddled her thumbs, digging the blood and dirt from her nails. She'd spent so much of the last year of her life being angry. It was exhausting, but she didn't know how to act anymore. Her first instinct was to defend.

She forced herself to sit in one of the chairs across from him. He'd saved her twice. He'd stepped between Bennet and her, and he took her lashings. What could she say to him?

"But I'm truly sorry for how I handled this morning," he said, playing with a stray strand of the blanket. "It was reckless."

"I'm not a stranger to recklessness." She kicked off her boots and curled her legs onto the chair. After several moments of his breaths being the only thing filling the silence, she whispered, "Thank you, by the way. Esaias told me you took my punishment. You didn't have to do that."

"You didn't deserve it." His voice was low, angry.

"But it wasn't because of the scrying fever. It's because I tried to escape, wasn't it?"

He didn't respond. "Tell me something," he said, his muscles slackening as the stern tone faded from his voice.

"Like what?"

"Anything. What did your days look like before?"

She grasped tightly around her legs. "Not that interesting. In fact, compared to everything that's happened today alone, you'd find my daily life to be completely and utterly boring." She dropped her head to her knees.

"Sometimes a boring life is not the worst thing to have." His eyes softened. "I could go the rest of my life without another war."

"Could it happen again?"

"I pray to the gods there won't be another one in my lifetime. My father sent me and several of his other soldiers to aid in the war efforts." His throat bobbed as he swallowed. "When I returned, it seemed all of Luana heard of my war stories, a warrior against the fight in Mosfelkov is what they would whisper." His eyes tracked Amaris as she dragged the sleeve of her shirt over her hand.

"After the war was over, I returned to Soyenia to oversee the disbursement of troops, which took a season to accomplish. The worst part was, Esaias had been sent home, and I was forced to remain in the unfortunate company of some of the king's men. Thankfully, Gris was by my side, but the captain of the Royal Guard is a real piece of work."

"I take it you two never became friends." Amaris rubbed at her wound through her sleeve.

"Gris and I stayed no longer than was required of us, if that tells you anything. That was the last several years of my unfortunately exciting life. Now, tell me about your boring one."

"Why did you step in?" she asked, gripping her thighs tighter to her chest.

"You're evading my question."

"Answer mine, and I'll tell you one thing about me."

"Even after I already revealed something of my own?"

Amaris squinted her eyes. "Humor me."

He dropped his head back to the cot, shifting his gaze to the fire. The pops and crackles were the only thing she could hear besides his slow and steady breaths.

"I'm a soldier," he answered.

"My best friend's name is Viv."

"Tell me about her."

"Viv? She's the fiercest woman I know. She reminds me a lot of Adelaide, only Viv is probably twice the size of her in muscle." A smile spread across her lips as she recalled how she'd dropped Amaris's boot at her feet after the fire. Viv had practically hurled her from that bedroom. "She's never afraid to tell me when I'm wrong or to speak her mind. I miss her. She's one of the few people I have left."

"What do you mean?"

Amaris forced back the tears. "My parents," she breathed. "When I was eight, we went for a lunch on the water. A storm came out of nowhere."

The night flooded behind her eyes. Lighting arced through the sky; the wind blistered her cheeks. "Amaris, don't let go, alright, honey?" Her father stashed her in the stairs leading below deck and guided her hands to the railing. He assessed the security of her life jacket before running to her mother's side where she worked the ropes, straining to keep the mast from being sucked into the wind. They tried lowering the sail, but the winds came quick and were too strong.

Thunder boomed overhead with another flash of lighting, sending Amaris screaming, "Mommy!"

Her father took the ropes from her mother's hands. "Hold her, Ann," he said. "Don't let go of her."

The waves grew violent, splashing water over the edge and rocking the boat. Her father was barefoot and shirtless and struggled as he wrapped the rope tighter around his hands. Amaris clung tightly to her mother, who pressed her lips to Amaris's forehead, muttering under her breath. She couldn't hear her. Maybe it was a prayer to see them home safely.

A crack filled the air, and the mast snapped in half. "Russel!" Her mother screamed, but it was too late. Her father no longer stood in the center of the sailboat with his feet braced against the decking.

"Where's Daddy?"

Her mother turned to her, her eyes puffy and raindrops streaking her face. "Sit right here. Don't move till I come get you, alright?"

Amaris didn't have time to nod before her mother ran across the deck, screaming for her father. Her heart raced in her chest, but not because the ice cream truck was down the road or a butterfly landed on her nose. Fear wrapped around her heart.

Amaris let go of the railing and crawled onto the deck. Ocean water sprayed her cheeks, but she squinted and called out, "Mommy! Daddy!"

Her only answer was a bright light, but Amaris made out her mother standing at the edge of the ship. Before Amaris could crawl closer, her mother was running toward her. She took her in her arms and squeezed the life out of her. She matted down her hair and rubbed her thumbs against her cheeks.

"I need you to be brave, sweetie. It's going to be cold, and you might be scared, but I need you to keep your vest on and keep swimming. Can you do that for me?"

"Swim?"

Her mother kissed her forehead and wrapped her arms tightly around her. Amaris felt her legs lift from the deck, and then frigid water soaked through her clothes. She screamed when she bobbed to the surface. Amaris flailed her arms and legs, attempting to grab onto something, anything.

"Swim, Amaris!" Her mother dove into the water. She lifted parts of the broken sail and followed lines of rope.

A piece of driftwood bumped Amaris's shoulder. She dug her fingers into it and steered from the wreckage. *Mommy said swim.* She kicked her little legs but took one last look over her shoulder as her mother sucked in a large breath and dove beneath the surface.

She could see it all flash before her eyes.

"They both died in the shipwreck."

"I'm sorry," Theodoric whispered.

"Don't be. It's fine." Amaris wiped the snot dripping from her nose.

"You don't need to lie to me."

"I didn't lie." She bit her lip as the waves from the night rolled through her head. She'd grown exhausted and didn't know if she'd ever make it to land. She'd never looked back to see if her mother had found her father before they inevitably drowned. It was a moment she didn't know if she regretted or was grateful for. Her last images of her parents were of their undying love for each other, sacrificing their lives for one another.

"You're a terrible liar," Theodoric said with a small laugh.

Amaris wanted to snarl at him. "What makes you say that?"

"You bite the corner of your bottom lip when you're lying."

"It's a nervous habit," Amaris stammered. "Hardly indicative of someone lying. Besides, what would I have to lie about regarding my parents? It's been seventeen years. I should be over it by now." A twinge sharpened in her chest.

"I was only five when my mother passed away." The deep violet circles beneath his eyes grew. "I miss her every day."

"What happened?" Amaris asked, before she thought better than to pry.

"She died in childbirth."

Amaris had gathered there were at least three Fastrada children after Ms. Borstad had spoken of Luther the other day, but there had also been the boy named Jeremiah, who seemed important to Theodoric.

"Adelaide," he began, answering the pondering look upon her face. "Jeremiah is a half-brother. After my mother's death, my father eventually married Genevieve, my mother's sister."

"Your aunt?" Amaris blurted out. "So does that make you and Esaias cousins and half-brothers?"

He laughed. "No, Esaias's father is my mother and stepmother's older brother, but it's not uncommon, especially for families of nobility. I didn't understand when I was younger, but now I realize it was for the good of both our families."

"Aren't they allowed to marry for love?" Amaris was startled by her own question.

"Of course, people do. It happens every day. But as the duke, he's expected to fill a certain role."

"What about you?"

"I don't have such a burden as my father or Luther."

"Do you plan to marry someday then, or are you like Adelaide?"

"She says that now, but we'll see." His laughter was short-lived as it shifted the muscles in his back.

Amaris rather enjoyed the sound of his laugh, its warmth. "Looks like you're the one evading questions now."

"As you so often do." He sighed. "I have no plans to marry anytime soon. My stepmother, however, sees the Conjugation as a fine occasion to find me a suitable wife."

"You'd let her?" She couldn't imagine marrying someone she didn't pick and love.

"I don't have a choice in the matter," he whispered. "I live to serve my family." He closed his eyes. They squished tighter at the slight feathering of his back muscles.

"I can brew you more cudweed."

"Please," he said, not meeting her gaze. Instead, his eyes lingered on her boots.

She pressed from the chair, kicking her *highly futuristic* shoes under her chair. She hadn't come across a zipper here and likely wouldn't. To keep her heart steady, she set to brewing the tea. Theodoric's eyes still bored holes into her shoes. Amaris bit her lip, her hands moving mindlessly. He couldn't have noticed the zippers. No one had said a word about the jingly little things yet.

She crossed between him and her boots to set the kettle over the fire. She watched the steam build around the spout and counted the seconds and then the minutes, praying he wasn't about to ask where she'd gotten such shoes. As she turned back, her blood ran cold. He wasn't staring at her shoes at all, rather the drawing and plastic bag poking out from their hidden pocket.

"You said you used to draw."

"Yes." She jumped as the kettle whistled behind her. Pouring his tea, her eyes pinned themselves to the single picture poking out and its crinkled corner.

"Can I see?"

"You want to see my work?" She snapped her attention to him, spilling the scalding water across the counter. She yanked back her hand, sucking the burn on her thumb.

She strode over to her boots, shielding them from his prying eyes. She pulled out the picture she'd drawn so long ago from the plastic bag. The small picture had only ever seen two pairs of eyes. Hers and Viv's. She blew out a short breath and offered it to him.

"Is this your family?" he asked, his fingers tracing the image.

Luckily, Amaris had been feeling artsy and sketched it on a decorative piece of paper that was meant to look like old parchment.

"Yeah." She kneeled beside him, grasping the other side as she pointed. "That's my mom and dad, and that's Gran and Grandad."

"Were you raised by your grandparents then?"

"Yep." She sniffled, wiping the corner of her eye. "But it's only me now."

"You're incredibly talented. You even captured the single-dimple smile you share with your mother."

She blushed, grabbing at the picture. "Really?" The flush spread down her chest and stirred a small laugh. "I drew that so long ago, I forgot."

"These are the people you've lost?"

Wow, way to put it like that. Filed away in old boxes in her attic were thousands of pictures of her with her parents and grandparents, but her drawing had always been special. She even had several pictures from birthdays growing up of Gran and Grandad visiting Ivory Beach in North Carolina, but she was always center on the page. The drawing was of them.

"Is my pouch up here?"

"The leather one around your belt? I think Esaias brought it up with your stuff." Amaris moved to the other side of the cot and rifled through his belongings. She unraveled his shirt, and his belt clanked to the ground. After untying the strap, she handed him the pouch. He rummaged through it, coins pinging off one another. A small painting was in his hand. It was well done enough that it could've been a photograph. "Is that Adelaide?"

He laughed again. Amaris held back her grin. She could get used to his laugh.

"No, that's my mother, Giselle."

"Holy shit, Adelaide is like a carbon copy of her."

"A what?"

"I mean twin. They look identical."

He smiled, his thumb brushing over the small picture. "Yes, Adelaide and I have taken on more Burchard traits."

"Then why don't you and Esaias look more alike?"

"The red hair pops up every now and then. One of his nephews has it, and my stepmother does as well." He replaced the picture in his pouch. "I think that should be strong enough," he said, eyeing the tea.

"Right," Amaris sputtered, striding to the worktable and straining the leaves.

Theodoric took the cup this time, not needing her assistance. Before he had a second to say anything else, she slipped into the tower stairwell and closed the door behind her. She didn't know why she needed to step away. He would pass out soon enough, and there was no way she planned to escape now. Theodoric was on that cot because of her. It wasn't only the paramedic within her choosing to stay and see to his healing, but Amaris herself.

She grasped the picture of her family to her chest and slid down the door, replaying the night over in her head, her parents' bravery and the words she uttered until her voice was hoarse and her legs numb. "Mommy said swim."

Amaris nestled her head on her knees. She no longer had a life jacket to keep her afloat, only her mother's last words. But Amaris would swim and keep herself afloat. She'd heal Theodoric as she had Esaias, and one day she'd find her way back home.

CHAPTER 27

Amaris

AMARIS POKED AND prodded at the flesh of Theodoric's back. He'd passed out from another dose of cudweed. She'd read up on the herb, and from all she'd gathered, one couldn't overdose on the stuff, even if it was injected with a needle. Besides the poisonous nuts and the flesh-eating herb, the medical aspects of Magoria hadn't ceased to astonish her. If she didn't have a life waiting for her back home, she'd contemplate staying and setting up her own mystique business, far away from the duke, though. It'd been six days since Theodoric's whipping, but his wounds had already begun to scab over. She could barely believe it. Each morning as she checked, the progress seemed to speed up.

"How is our patient today?" Esaias grinned, setting a plate of eggs and mystery meat on the worktable for Amaris and a bowl of broth for Theodoric.

Esaias had taken over for him in his state, but unlike Theodoric, he didn't leave for hours at a time to train. Esaias had at least toned down the provocative comments and brought her food every few hours. She'd begun to notice the increasing presence of soldiers throughout the manor. Esaias had taken to posting downstairs at night while she slept on the floor. The first few nights Amaris had been worried for Theodoric, but now Esaias felt it was safer for her to sleep in the tower.

"He was in a lot of pain and asked for some cudweed as soon as he woke up."

"That isn't like him," Esaias said, taking a spot in a velvety, turquoise chair. He'd brought them up a few days ago, after complaining that the upholstered ones were *frail and absolutely uncomfortable.*

"Try getting nearly fifty lashes and see how you feel," Amaris said, placing the last dressing over Theodoric's wound. She'd started using yuxiway leaves on the lacerations to prevent an infection from taking over. With how weak he was, she doubted he could handle one.

"The Conjugation is coming up. I know he'll want to be at full strength for it," Esaias said.

"Why's that?"

"I would say to drink and be merry, but knowing Theo, he'll want to be on alert." He rested his narrow face in his palm, the indents below his cheekbones shadowing against the fire. There was a hint of resemblance there, not much, but he had the tight jawline like Theodoric.

"So it'll be like a big hoopla?"

"I've never heard of a Conjugation referred to as a hoopla, but if you mean an elaborate party with people from all over Godwin, then you're correct." Esaias rubbed at his temples, his lips smacking together.

"I'm assuming I'll be up here," Amaris muttered, wadding up the old bandages.

He stood and headed toward the wall of shelves. "You don't have to be." He reached for the highest shelf, pulling out a jar of amber liquid.

"Are you the one who's been messing with my herbs?"

He turned over his shoulder, raising a brow and giving her a sinful smirk. "I'll mess with your herbs any day. All you have to do is ask."

Amaris groaned, crossing her arms. "What is that?"

"My own beautiful concoction," he said, reaching back up and pulling out a silver tin.

She furrowed her brows, jumping onto the counter beside him. He gave her a side-eye but continued with whatever he was doing.

"What's in it?" Amaris asked.

He popped open the tin to reveal a needle and syringe.

"Oh, hell no! You're not doing drugs on my watch."

"Drugs?" He inclined a brow, drawing up the dark liquid.

"Whatever you call it, you're not injecting that into your system to get high." She leaned over, reaching for the syringe, but he held it in the air.

He pushed against her forehead with his free hand. After reading about cudweed, she'd scoured the tower for needles, but the one in Esaias's hands was way more extravagant.

"I'm not about to be taking uppaway, if that's what you mean by high. Besides, you smoke that, not inject it."

He lifted his shirt and pinched whatever bit of fat he had and injected the liquid into his abdomen, wincing as the needle broke his skin.

"What's in it?" His eyes pierced her soul, but she narrowed her gaze. "I'm the mystique. It's my duty to know what herbs people are taking."

He groaned. "I have difficulties regulating the sugar in my blood."

"You're a diabetic?"

"A what?"

"How are you not dead?" Without modern medicine or insulin, people usually didn't live past twenty in the olden days, and whatever he'd injected into his abdomen sure wasn't insulin.

"I don't know what you refer to it as, but it's usually referred to as *mamat*."

Amaris flattened her gaze. "Ma-what?"

"*Mamat*. It's Gorrin for sugar." He tucked in his shirt and grabbed another jar of a clear liquid, using a cloth to clean the syringe and needle.

"Regardless," she began, "how are you not dead?"

284

He tapped the jar with the amber liquid. "My parents are filthy rich and pay their mystique well. When I was six, I developed the disease, so he set about making a cure. He came up with this."

"I haven't read anything about it in the mystique's journal."

"And you won't. Cornelius was a short fellow, so I hid it on the top shelf. Oakheart's mystique came up with the recipe. I make it myself."

"Why didn't you tell me when I was treating you for scrying fever? That's kind of an important thing to tell your provider."

"Speaking of scrying fever, why is it that I healed so quickly?"

"What do you mean?"

"It took weeks for Gris to heal overseas." He raised an inquisitive eye.

Cornelius never wrote the names of his patients down, but she must have been the single survivor.

"I don't know." Amaris shrugged. "I followed the instructions from her care." At least, she thought she had. She followed the recipe he'd written down and the rest of the treatment plan. Her fever and rash had lasted for two weeks according to the journal, while Esaias had healed in about a week.

"Her survival was a miracle in itself. The tonic is likely useless. It didn't work for anyone else."

"But it worked for you," Amaris added, contemplating the curiosity. Maybe the herbs in Luana were stronger than overseas. "With your *mamat*, you should've had it worse, but maybe it helped. How did you manage? You were barely conscious at times."

"Onika," he muttered. "She assists me."

"Why didn't you tell me? I could've done it."

No matter how many different diseases separated Magoria from Earth, their bodies' anatomy all seemed the same. She shouldn't have been surprised, but it made her wonder what other diseases or ailments she could stumble upon.

"Not everyone knows. It can be inconvenient at times, but it's easier if only the people that need to know are aware of it," he said.

"Wait, this medicine could change the lives of so many people. Why haven't you shared it?"

He replaced the tin and jar, obscuring them from view. "To be born with *mamat* is a death sentence, and it requires rare herbs to make it. I'm not to share the recipe, because if I did, the herbs would run out. There are only a few patches left in Godwin that even grow the main ingredient."

"You'll sentence other people to die so you have more time?" She couldn't believe what she was hearing.

"I'm sworn to secrecy!" he shouted, extending his palm, revealing a white scar lining his skin. "Several others in my family have been diagnosed over the last few years. My father has sworn us all to secrecy of the formula so we may all live, or would you prefer I sentence my young nephew to death?"

She dropped her shoulders. Maybe their realm wasn't much different from hers. "No, but it's still awful you aren't allowed to share it. It really screams privilege."

"I didn't ask to be born into my family or with *mamat*, but I've taken the hand I've been dealt." He sat in a chair beside Theodoric. "Has he told you why I'm here and not in Mount Juniper?"

"No, I don't know where you're from. Contrary to popular opinion, not everyone enjoys talking and spilling secrets like you do."

He scoffed, rolling his eyes. "My father is the Duke of Oakheart. I was born in Mount Juniper but traveled here every Sunreign."

"So, you decided to stay?"

He gave her a slow blink, and she swore if he wasn't so goddamn annoying, she'd find it attractive.

"One does not simply decide anything of such magnitude. I renounced my heritage when I was eighteen and became an official soldier of Luana."

"Let me guess." Amaris grinned, taking the seat beside him. She rested her elbows on the armrest. "Mommy and Daddy didn't take it too well?"

"Hardly," he said, brushing off her joke. "My brother, Ricard, will take my father's place. For an heir to assume the title, the one who holds it either dies or resigns. Theo's father is growing older and has no intention of holding his title until he dies. However, my father will likely sit on his throne until he becomes a pile of bones."

"Were you close in line or something and it pissed you off?"

"No, I would've never seen a position like that. Sabina, my older sister, will be the next chief and then train Ricard's second born, Kazamir to take her place when he's ready. She has a daughter of her own and doesn't want to hold the title forever."

"But she didn't want to pass it along to you?"

He turned his gaze toward the window. "I didn't want it, therefore resignation of heritage."

"But—"

He hovered a finger over her lips. "That's enough about me, unless you would like to divulge your deepest, darkest secrets." She pursed her lips, and he smiled. "Good girl."

"Really?" she scoffed.

He shrugged, leaning back in his chair. "Give it time, Amaris. They all fall for my charm in the end."

"Fat chance," she snapped. "There's no way in the realm I'd ever be caught dead with you, *and* I'm engaged!"

A knot formed in her stomach. Her chance at proving herself had dwindled with her first escape attempt. She didn't know when she'd be able to try again or if Theodoric would even help her, but a part of her didn't feel pressed anymore to run down her street and cross over the threshold into her house. Did that make her a terrible person, wishing for more time away?

"Not even if I could get you into the grandest party of the year?"

That pulled Amaris back from her thoughts. "What do you mean?" She glared at his taunting gaze, the way he raised his brows and bit his lip.

"Go with me to the Conjugation?"

Amaris laughed. "Yeah, right." She gestured around her. "Prisoner, remember?"

"What if I told you no one would even know it's you?" His sultry voice was so annoying.

"How?"

"The theme for the Conjugation is a masked ball."

"Of course, it is." She rubbed her face, releasing an obnoxious groan.

It hadn't been long ago when she was sure she wouldn't be in attendance. However, with Theodoric's healing, she'd still be lingering. Again, something in her chest lifted at the thought of going to the party, as if a feather of relief had been plucked from her.

"So, you'll go as my date?" Esaias asked.

"As your friend," she corrected.

"Splendid! I'll send your measurements for a dress."

Her jaw dropped. As he stood and circled her, she burrowed within the cushion. "The fuck you're picking out my dress. You'd pick some skimpy cloth!"

"If I had a choice, you wouldn't be wearing anything besides a pair of heels, but we must all make sacrifices."

She was going to regret it. He was going to put her in a tight-fitting, boob-busting, and ass-hanging-out dress, and everyone would know it was her.

"You can wipe the disdain from your face. The key is to blend in. You're not the first woman I've dressed. It'll be modest."

She scoffed, "And I thought you only knew how to take a woman's clothes off."

"Oh no, I will have no need to undress you. You'll be ripping your clothes off after the night I show you."

CHAPTER 28

Theo

NATE'S BODY HUNG decapitated in front of Theo, the hint of decay wafting from it. He'd already been dead when they'd severed it, but they'd placed his head at Theo's feet for him to stare at for days. No food or water, only the lifeless eyes of his friend. He shouted a frustrated cry. An insect crawled through Nate's sinuses. Theo couldn't take it anymore. He should've been the one to hang there and be mutilated. He should've been dead, not Nate.

"Theodoric!" Amaris's scream pulled Theo from the pain, the dungeons, his head.

Theo shot up on the cot, tears running down his cheeks. Pain instantly overcame him, and his vision faded. Sweat dripped from his hair, soaking his sheets. He gasped as his heart sped. He dropped to the cot, reaching his hand out for the bucket in the dark. He gripped the rim. He coughed and gagged at each memory, sensation, and smell.

Amaris lit a candle, coming to his bedside with a blanket wrapped around her. A few more were on the floor, along with a pillow beside the empty hearth.

"It was only a dream," she whispered as he continued to spew his guts out.

He felt his branded skin stretch with each retch. Maybe the new scars from the whip would cover the burn marks and cuts scattering his back.

Theo hadn't known her faint whisper was what he needed to sooth his racing thoughts. He gripped the edge of the bed, waiting for the nausea to subside.

He sensed her hand hover over his cheek and leaned into her touch.

She dragged the back of her hand over his forehead. "You're hot."

She pulled away, and instantly, pain raced up his back. It wasn't like what he'd first experienced, but it had his jaw clenching. She returned with a basin of water and rag. She dragged it over his face and down his arms. "The evaporation will help cool you down."

He tried to speak but couldn't as she pulled back his blanket and peeked beneath the bandages. He was too exposed, but she only sighed and relinquished herself from his side. She retreated to a small pitcher on the table and poured a glass of water. There wasn't a hint of fear in her eyes over his panicked outburst or the ugly scars marring his skin. His eyes again trailed to the blanket and pillow upon the floor. Why was she sleeping in the tower?

She kneeled beside the bed, her long waves brushing his arm. He wanted to take one of her curls and wind it around his finger. Their eyes met as she brought the cup to his lips. Another wave of tears burned behind his eyes. He wanted to turn away so she wouldn't see the anguish in his heart, but he couldn't pull himself from her gaze. His hand shook as he reached for it, but she batted it away. There wasn't pity in her eyes but understanding.

The pain from Rongstad had vanished once he'd woken, but his breaths were still labored as his body sensed the danger. He took another sip and watched her eyes linger on the jagged scar on his bicep, its contorted line, each cut and stroke.

"A reminder," he croaked.

"Of what?" she breathed.

"My failures." He released a shuddering sigh, his back pulsing with pain.

Her hand hovered over his twitching muscles. He bit back a scream as she laid her gentle fingers along the muscle, and a sensation of pins and needles sprinkled through his back. She didn't remove her hand. He didn't want her to. The pain was ripped away as he focused on her and the feel of her hand against his skin. Why did he want her near? He knew she belonged to another, even though he was a vile bastard for daring to strike her.

She pulled back, his mind fracturing as the pain surged with intensity. He gripped the edge of the bed as she got up and grabbed more supplies. She pulled back the bandages. The paste she began lathering onto his wounds was ice against his skin. If she'd been the mystique to tend to him during the war, would he still have the scars? Would his nights still be filled with the hauntings of his past?

"Why did you save me?" His voice was raspy.

Concern flashed over her features, and she withdrew. "How did you...? You mean, your back—"

"No, in the river," he cried, a tear slipping down his face as his friend's severed head refused to relinquish itself from his mind. "I've cheated death enough in my life. Why did you bring me back?" A sob rattled his chest, but she was there. Amaris slid her hand over his, and he clung to it.

"We don't get to decide who lives or dies," she breathed, her voice cracking. She fought back a string of her own tears.

"I should be dead, Amaris. I should have died weeks ago. I should have died years ago."

He hid his face to shield himself. He couldn't help it—everything was pouring out of him. Ever since she'd come into his life, he couldn't breathe. He hadn't a moment of peace. She was haunting him and forcing him to relive what he'd lost. She'd opened an endless well of emotions within him that he couldn't contain, and her face and the beat of her pulse in her wrist were the only things that had brought him back from his nightmare within Rongstad Prison.

"Why do you taunt me with your existence? Every day I see you, I'm reminded of the second chance I've been given that I don't deserve."

"Everyone deserves a second chance." She didn't hide the tear staining her cheek. "You're still alive because you were meant to be here. I'd be dead or imprisoned if it weren't for you."

"I failed my squad, and now I'm failing you. I can't protect you like this."

She wiped her tears, sucking in a breath. "I don't need you to. Esaias is at the bottom of the steps, and Adelaide checks in. You aren't alone."

"I lost my entire squad, my friend! I can't lose anyone else, no one ever again." Her thumb caressed the back of his hand as he sobbed into his sheets. He didn't care about the pain in his back. The agony he felt in his heart was worse. "I can't stop it," he whispered. "For the last two years, I'd been able to stifle it, but I can't anymore."

"And you shouldn't." She let go of his hand, lifting her fingers to his face but hesitated.

He wanted her to brush back the strands of his hair clinging to his forehead, but her hand fell away.

"Feel, Theodoric. Don't push it away."

"What if it's too much to bear?" He stifled his cries.

"Allow others to help shoulder your burden." Her breaths faltered, and she sniffled. "Don't stuff the feelings down." Her gaze drifted to the candle. "I know what that's like. I think I'm losing myself."

Theo reached to cup her face and brush aside her tear, but she pulled away. With the single candle, the tower felt entirely too small, but she couldn't have been farther away. He wanted to pull her closer.

"I'm not who I used to be. I wish I could blame this place, your father, or even Bennet." She wiped the fluid threatening to drip from the tip of her nose. "But I can't. My world has been turned upside down coming here, but I'm beginning to think it wasn't right in the first place."

"Amaris, you don't—"

"I need to tell someone," she said, raising her voice as she fought more tears. "The night I ran away, Derek and I got into a huge argument over my work." Her voice grew airy as she rubbed the heel of her palm against her eyes. "But that's how it goes now. He drinks because he's stressed, and I fight back because I can't help it." She dropped her head, breaking into a sob. "For a whole year, it's been nonstop fighting, and it's all over stupid shit. I risk my life every day, but that isn't what scares me. That's what fuels me. I'm terrified every day I go home, because I don't know which Derek I'm going to get. I don't know if he'll be baking me breakfast and telling me how much he can't live without me or if he'll be screaming at me for leaving my shoes by the door."

Theo again tried to reach for her, but she fell back against the chair.

"That night, I snapped and punched the mirror because I hated who I'd become, and I ran because Derek backhanded me. He's gotten close or gripped me, but he's never hit me. I egged him on, and he hit me." Her muffled voice turned to cries as she sobbed. "But the scariest part of all is I'm going to go home and walk through that door and attempt to move forward as if nothing ever happened, because I'm terrified to see what else could be out there."

She'd escaped one prison to find herself trapped in another.

"You don't have to go back."

She lifted her head, her face blotchy and her eyes swollen. "What about your father? He'll never grant me my freedom now."

"We can find a way," Theo said. "You don't deserve to be with someone who treats you like that."

"But I've been with Derek for six years."

She hardly saw what anyone else did, that she was an incredible woman capable of taking on whatever the realm threw at her. She'd stood against his father and Bennet and didn't cower.

He wiped his tears from his cheeks and said, "Amaris, you drive me absolutely insane at times, but you're strong, capable, and stubborn." He pulled himself from the bed, ignoring the searing pain in his back as he sat beside her. "Please see what I do, that you're fierce and powerful. You do what's right, regardless of what others think. You jump first to save someone. Don't think for a second that you belong in a life where you're trapped in your own home feeling worthless. You deserve better."

Her puffy eyes welled with tears again. She leaned her head against his arm and sobbed. She trembled against him, but he didn't dare move.

"It'll be alright," he whispered. "I'll make sure of it." Gods be damned if each breath she took didn't send more pain down his back, but her single touch against his shoulder was like shooting stars along his skin. He'd find a way. For her sake, he'd find a way for her to be free.

CHAPTER 29

Theo

"YOU'RE A BLUNDERING fool." A stern voice cut through the grogginess of the cudweed.

Theo rolled his head, his vision coming into focus as he rubbed the sleep from his eyes.

"What do you want?" he groaned.

Luther sat beside him wearing an all-black ensemble and a short red vest. He plucked a stray hair from the turquoise chair. Theo still hadn't a clue how the chairs had gotten up here. It would've been a struggle for Amaris to carry them up the steps.

"I've come to make sure you don't do anything rash," Luther muttered, eyeing the tower with his dark eyes and a grimace. He sat on the edge of the chair, his legs spread as he leaned forward. "You nearly destroyed your life."

"I did what I thought was right," Theo snapped, the extra emphasis in his tone shifting the muscles of his back. The pain had significantly improved, but he had yet to attempt to move beyond the tower.

"If it wasn't for Esaias acting a buffoon, Father likely wouldn't have stepped in."

"And where were you?" Theo asked.

"You asked for Miss Carter's punishment. You brought this burden upon yourself." Luther played with the sapphire ring upon his hand. It'd been passed down throughout their family, given to the next heir of Luana since the declaration of the province.

"She didn't deserve that, to be made a mockery and brutally flogged, or have you forgotten she's the mystique. She's the only person for one hundred miles with her abilities."

Luther extended his hand, picking at a speck of dirt under his nail. "And soon she will be the most capable person in Elric."

Theo's breath halted. "Luther, Amaris didn't kill Freville. It's a mistake to send her there."

"Perhaps she should've considered that before she attempted to sneak away in the night."

"We've already paid for that." Theo's back would always bear the scars from the actions of that night, but he would gladly wear them. He'd driven her to escape.

"It would seem Father contemplated that. It took him some convincing on Bennet's part, but her fate is decided. Lord Freville's family is calling for blood, and they'll have it."

"He can't be serious. She ran to protect herself."

Luther ceased his grooming and inclined a thin brow. There was no denying the resemblance between him and their father. The dominant traits of the Fastrada line ran deep within his veins, and the pretentiousness he flaunted could only have been birthed by their father.

"Do tell, brother." He grinned. "Where was dear Miss Carter running from?"

After she'd shared about her wretched betrothed, Theo couldn't pry further. That was all he'd wanted to hear, not that he'd wished for her to endure it, but for her to be honest. He'd seen the signs, but he needed to hear the truth for himself. Maybe their father would understand and be merciful.

"She was running from her abusive betrothed."

"Abusive?"

"He hits her."

"That's convenient." Luther reclined back, his sneer sending Theo's blood to curdle as he studied a stain on the armrest.

"Convenient? She's lived with this man while he berates her, and when she finally got the courage to run, we automatically deem her a murderer. There's no evidence to suggest she killed that man. Father has asked me to get to know her, to learn her truth, and I have. Why doesn't he trust me? Is it because he's blinded by his arrogance?"

Luther prodded at the inside of his mouth with his tongue, bulging his cheek. "You of all people should know when he has his mind set that he rarely falters. You should consider yourself lucky he isn't sending you along with her. I suggest you take what the gods have offered you and move on with your life."

"I won't stand for this," Theo snapped. "Amaris is innocent!"

Luther jumped from his chair, crouching before Theo. "It looks to me like you can hardly stand at all, let alone protect her."

There was no arguing with him or their father. Their minds were made up, and they'd send her to a prison that sucked every bit of a person's existence and turned them hollow and cold. He'd suffered for years with numbness in his heart. Amaris didn't deserve that.

"When?" Theo asked, his hand tugging at the hem of his shirt, assuring it covered his back.

"After the Conjugation. Lord Godfrey is to accept her as a prisoner and deliver her to Elric."

Theo had to put a stop to it. "Why tell me?"

He smirked. "Because there's nothing you can do. She'll be gone soon, and we'll all forget about her. Father has even begun preparations for a new mystique to be sent from Lockwood."

Lockwood was a fortress of learning and knowledge. Many stayed within its walls, honing their skills and building their wealth of knowledge. Most mystiques serving a province had come from their teachings.

"The sooner you accept this, the easier it'll be to continue with your life. Think about your future and your people's future. Don't throw it all away for a common servant."

Theo couldn't snap back at him. If he was to formulate a plan, he needed his brother to believe he'd gotten through to him. Their father would've seen right through it, but Luther was still young. Even though he'd been by their father's side for over a decade studying and learning his role, he was naive.

"Has Genevieve spoken of the Conjugation?" Maybe if he were to bring someone his stepmother approved of, he could show a semblance of normalcy.

"That she has," he said, standing and lacing his hands behind his back. He walked about the tower, studying the various books and herbs Amaris had left out on the worktable. "She said you haven't returned her list of suitors."

Theo needed someone who'd be on his side and play the part without asking any questions, and he knew one woman who'd be in attendance and owed him an incredibly huge favor.

"I've selected someone, and I'll send word to intercept her travels immediately."

"Might I ask who you plan to escort to the Conjugation?" Luther asked, flipping through a book on the worktable, pulling out a piece of parchment.

"Helen Canon."

He balked. "You intend to escort the Duchess of Ebonmaw? She's hardly in the realm of suitors Mother has selected for you. It isn't appropriate."

"Helen fought valiantly during the war. We are two sides to a piece of silver."

Helen had left her home to fight in the war, disguising herself for her first few seasons. She'd revealed her identity sometime during Theo's imprisonment. As she was an incredible fighter, her officers couldn't risk sending her back. She was the only child of the late Duke of Ebonmaw. She'd only finally been pulled from the fight when her parents had perished in a dreadful fire. They'd been on holiday, and the cottage had gone up in smoke before they could get out.

"Mother won't be happy."

"She'll learn to live with it," Theo said.

"At least you're willing to try. I hear Esaias will be escorting a common merchant's daughter. He still portrays his wealth and class, but he's now no more than a simple soldier. Who would ever step from their birthright and renounce their heritage?"

"He doesn't care what you or the other members of nobility think. As far as he's concerned, he would say class and society can burn in After."

"Class and society are what keep this kingdom in check," Luther sneered, his face twisting in disgust. "It's what reminds the lowers of where they belong. We cannot be associating ourselves with someone far below our class. It's likely why he gave his life away in the first place, so he can be free to fuck whomever he wants."

Luther eyed Theo's hands clenching, and a smirk crossed his face. He was lucky Theo wasn't at his full strength, or he'd make sure Luther was the one upon the bed, unable to get up.

"Once I'm to be wed to Petra Godfrey, Mother will wish to spend her time moving on to her next child. She selected a fine match for me. I presume she's already started spreading your bachelor status among the other nobles of Godwin."

"I won't marry someone just because they're of noble blood," Theo said, lowering his voice. "I don't care what she does. I won't allow her to make decisions about my life."

What Amaris said the other night had stayed with him. She'd asked if people married for love. Every day, people met at the temples across Godwin and said their vows. Why should he be any different?

"Do you forget you don't have a choice in the matter?"

"We all have a choice." Theo attempted to sit up.

"That is a fantasy. You don't have a choice in who you marry, you didn't have a choice that you became a soldier, and you didn't have a choice when you went off to war."

Theo stopped his shifting, his hands gripping the edge of the bed. *How dare he!* While Theo had been living a life of misery for three years, shut up in a prison for two seasons and tortured, Luther had been home. He'd gotten to see Adelaide become a woman and Jeremiah race around the manor. He'd learned about political structure and how best to send his troops to die.

"Don't speak of the war to me," Theo seethed, refusing to face his brother, to give him the satisfaction of seeing the anger in his eyes.

"There's no need for dramatics. You lost a few good soldiers. There will always be more to follow you. You even brought Esaias and your friends Gris and Sephardi home. There's no need to go on acting sour."

Acting? He gritted his teeth against his flinching muscles screaming to attack, to lunge at him and pummel his face into oblivion. That Fastrada face. Theo didn't feel he deserved his last name. He and Adelaide were far more Burchards than Fastradas. They acted and looked the part of their mother's bloodline, unlike Luther.

"You don't get to speak to me about who or what I lost. You have no idea what it was like."

"All wars are the same, people fighting for power. People die, Theo. It's a part of life."

The only person Luther had ever lost was their mother. He'd been eight when she'd passed, but he'd never been to battle or war. He'd never looked death in the eyes or watched someone he trusted his life with die.

"You're blinded and arrogant," Theo growled.

"And you're severely misplaced. Maybe when I take my place as Duke of Luana, I'll appoint my own chief."

Theo didn't stop to allow him to see the relief settling over him. "You'll drive this place to ruin."

"You're doing a fine job of that all on your own."

The door swung open, followed by laughter, warming Theo's heart. Adelaide and Esaias passed over the threshold, but their movements ceased as they spotted Luther at Amaris's worktable. Adelaide's smile faltered, but she regained her composure, putting up a front.

She grinned, coming up beside Luther and nudging her fist into his shoulder. "Have you come to wish Theo a quick healing?"

Luther turned to Theo, his face shrouded from their view as he flashed a look of warning. "Of course, I would hate to see what could befall Luana without his unrelenting protection." He closed the book and darted down the steps, his shoes clacking.

Esaias slammed the door, muffling the sinister echo. "It still perplexes me how we're all even related to him," Esaias grumbled, jumping up onto the worktable. "He's dreadful."

"You didn't have to sit beside him at supper for the last three years, hearing him complain about how much longer the war would last." Adelaide reclined in the chair closest to the hearth, studying her jacket sleeve and brushing off an invisible piece of lint.

"We have a problem," Theo blurted out. There was no sense in dancing around it. "The duke is planning to send Amaris to Elric after the Conjugation."

Adelaide sat up, and Esaias clenched his fists.

"What happened to proving herself?" Esaias asked.

"He never planned to let her go," Adelaide cut in.

"What about her *betrothed*?" Esaias began, adding extra emphasis as he rolled his eyes.

"He beats her." If he made an appearance, Theo would ram his dagger through his gut.

Theo had mentioned Derek to Esaias, in the case he came looking for Amaris while he was confined to his bed, but he hadn't shared further about her circumstances. Any intelligent person, though, would've been able to put it together, but the whites of Esaias's eyes expanded as his lips gently parted. He was a stronger fighter than most, but he hardly paid attention to detail. He'd be one to forget his head if he had to put it on every morning.

"Lord Freville's family wants answers and for someone to pay for his death." Theo leaned back against the stone. He winced, but he forced himself to lean into its cooling touch through his thin shirt. Amaris had removed the bandages since all the wounds had finally scabbed over.

"Then we'll help her escape. If she stays here, she's as good as dead." Adelaide took the lead, pulling a dagger from her boot and twirling the tip and hilt between her fingers.

"I won't allow either of you to be associated with this. I'll sneak Amaris out during the Conjugation. If I'm caught, it's my burden, not yours."

"Sorry to squash your act of heroism, but you aren't doing this alone. Amaris is our friend too," Adelaide said, draping an arm around the back of the chair.

Theo gave them a heated stare, but neither of them backed down. "This is going to be incredibly dangerous, and we're going to Elric if we're caught."

Esaias clasped his hands together, rubbing them back and forth. Theo could already see the plan forming within his eyes, and he waited for him to say the dreaded words.

"Alright, hear me out," Esaias said. "Amaris will be accompanying me to the Conjugation."

"I highly doubt she'll consent to that," Adelaide retorted, twisting her blade in her hand.

"She already has." Esaias gave Theo a dreadful smirk and a twinge settled in his gut. "This will allow her to be free of the tower or anyone else's watchful eye."

"Luther said you're bringing a merchant's daughter."

Esaias's eyes gleamed as he laced his fingers together. "I am. Ann Lawson will be my escort, the only daughter of a widowed father who owns a small jeweler's cart."

"I have to give it to you. That's not a bad idea," Adelaide added, not even bothering to give Esaias a glance. "Where did you get Ann Lawson?"

"Her idea."

"What if someone recognizes her?" Theo asked.

A mask wouldn't be able to hide Amaris's features. Her bright-blue eyes and head of curls would give her away instantly.

"I have her gown and mask already in the works. Adelaide, you'll do your part with hair and makeup to disguise her."

"I can try, but she's hard to hide. She's quite beautiful."

"Isn't she?" Esaias sighed. "If only she could stay. I'd love—"

"Too much detail," Adelaide groaned.

"I haven't even said anything."

"Your intentions permeate the very air we're breathing."

Theo rolled his eyes as they both sent each other darting grimaces of mockery, but Adelaide was right. It was still a risk. They'd need to plan each moment, prepare for the unexpected.

"Toward the climax of the party, Adelaide, I want you stationed on the beach," Theo said, the rest of Esaias's plan forming in his mind. "All the other entrances will be heavily guarded. The bay is our only means of escape."

"Where do you plan to go?" Adelaide asked.

"We'll make our way to Duncaster, and I'll see she's safe." Safe was a broad statement. She may have wished to find other accommodations outside Duncaster, but for now, it was their best option. She'd have access to a ship if she preferred or the safety of a large city to hide in. The missing tenants were still a frightening issue, but Theo could stay with her until she was safe or headed for somewhere new.

"You're forgetting a fatal flaw in this plan. If you aren't here the next morning, the duke will know you aided in her escape," Adelaide began.

Theo's head fell back against the wall. If they were both missing, it wouldn't take anyone smarter than Esaias to put it together.

"I hate to say this, but either someone doesn't come back, or Amaris has to venture herself."

"I'll gladly volunteer," Esaias said, jumping on the opportunity to follow Amaris into a small boat, where there would be no one but them and the ocean for days.

"That I know she won't agree with," Adelaide snapped.

Theo grasped his jaw, rubbing at a nick Amaris had left that morning. Theo had insisted he shave himself, but after a few failed attempts, she'd ended up doing it for him.

"I don't disagree, but I'm inclined to go with Esaias," Theo said. "If he doesn't turn up the next morning, everyone will believe he's taken an extended holiday with this Ann Lawson."

"It wouldn't be the first time." He grinned.

For once, Esaias's lifestyle would be useful. "Esaias, will you grab Gris for me? I had her looking into Freville's death, and I want to know why she hasn't come to me with anything."

Esaias and Adelaide both eyed each other, passing hesitant glances.

"What is it?"

"Gris isn't here," Adelaide began.

"Where is she?"

"No idea," Esaias added. "She's been having Sephardi cover her sentry duties the last few weeks."

"When was the last time you saw her?" Theo attempted to stand from the bed.

"What do you think you're doing?" Adelaide grasped his waist, guiding him back to the bed.

"I've rested enough. I'm tired of being cooped up here. Besides, evidently, I need to find Gris."

"No, Theo, it's not that she isn't working. She's gone. As far as we know, she's left Luana Bay," Adelaide said.

That would explain why she hadn't checked in, but he wished she would've told him before traveling to Duncaster.

Adelaide leaned into him, forcing him back on the bed. She braced her hands against his shoulders, her face pinching tightly as she scowled at him.

"Wait, if Amaris isn't with Gris, where is she?"

"Sephardi is watching her." Esaias jumped from the worktable. "She's held up with Pricilla in that small alcove of hers, and we figured she's the safest person to have watching over her, since Bennet feels she's neutral in all of this. We don't want to risk him sending one of his inner circle."

"I hope she is." Theo recoiled, forcing himself onto the bed. He wanted to see if he could tolerate the walk down the steps, to see Amaris with his own eyes.

"Don't worry. Sephardi's our friend foremost, but she also tried holding Amaris back before she jumped in front of the whip," Esaias said.

A ringing formed in Theo's ears. "She did what?"

"You don't know?" Esaias questioned. "She jumped in front of you and took a lash around her forearm. She tried to get them to stop, but Gerard held her back before your father stepped in."

Theo owed Amaris for too many life debts. She'd now saved him twice by putting herself at risk.

"I'll let Amaris in on the plan," Adelaide said, disappearing down the steps.

"I'd be happy to assist." Esaias smirked and steepled his fingers.

Before Theo could protest, Esaias followed her. He sighed and reclined. In a week, the Conjugation would be upon them, and they'd smuggle her out. But he couldn't stop the growing ache in the pit of his stomach at the thought of sending her away.

Theo was only pulled from his troubles when a pile of books caught his eye. There wasn't much for him to do with his bed rest. Reading was a nice comfort, but he'd devoured countless novels secluded in the tower. The stack beside his bed, however, was new. Amaris brought him a variety every week, but her stack hadn't even been touched yet on Theo's other side.

He bent over and picked up the first tome. It was an old Gorrin sailing book he'd read many years ago. Amaris had only selected Akaric, and many of them were romance novels. He initially believed her to think she was torturing him with steamy books, but he'd begun to realize she might have caught on to his guilty pleasure.

A note slipped from the first page written in Pricilla's curly hand.

Amaris told me about your curiosity with the phrase aslorn per de eclahard *in The Merry Sheridan. I recalled your questioning of its meaning and took it upon myself to research the phrase. Here are a few tomes I think will please you.*

Theo flipped through the pages, stopping where Pricilla had inserted a bookmark. His finger scanned the page until the phrase came into view. Theo spent the next few hours reading through Pricilla's notes and thumbing through the books she'd left him. All of them had the same conclusion and led back to the *Serpent*.

Not a single mention excluded the pirate ship. Theo pondered the idea, but the ship had sunk nearly fifty years ago. Pirates hadn't been a problem since. They'd caused significant damage to the port cities and set to raiding merchant ships. What if they were the ones stirring the mayhem in Duncaster?

Theo brushed aside the thought. It was impossible. They'd taken refuge deep in the Black Sea. With their dwindling numbers, pirates wouldn't stand a chance against Godwin's armada.

He set aside the books and rubbed at his eyes. He hadn't received a letter from the governor in weeks regarding any more disappearances. He'd hoped their extra soldiers had been enough to cease whatever plagued the city. Theo shuddered. He couldn't allow himself to think on Duncaster's issues.

He had minimal time left until the Conjugation. Amaris's safety was a pressing matter. Duncaster, missing persons, and pirates could wait.

CHAPTER 30

Amaris

AMARIS RECLINED IN the brass tub, absorbing the bubbles from Adelaide's inventory of soaps as the warm water soothed her chilled body. As she dragged a rag over herself, the warmth released the tension she held in her muscles. She dipped beneath the surface. Her hair stretched through the water, and she combed through the tangled tendrils.

With jitters regaining their hold, she stepped from the tub. Her gaze swept the ground, avoiding the haunting reflection awaiting her. Mirrors had been a constant battle. She'd avoided them, taking only small glances to fix the occasional stray hair.

As she reached for her towel, she caught sight of something out of her periphery. What she spotted in the mirror wasn't the woman she'd feared she'd find. Her cheeks weren't sunken, nor were her eyes puffy balls of gloom. Brightness spread across her full cheeks. She dared a step closer to the mirror, hovering a finger over the small pink scar on her cheekbone. Forever she'd carry the reminder of what Derek had done to her.

She extended her scarred hand out before her. Similar tiny scars littered her knuckles, and her spiral welt was almost gone. The rapid healing of her hand shouldn't have been possible, but each day, her stiffness waned and her strength returned. Amaris had never seen the healing timeline for a flogging injury, but she'd guessed Theodoric had experienced a similar rapid healing. He'd been on his feet for a week now and only grimaced once at breakfast. It seemed a remarkable feat.

She brushed away the curious thought for later and emerged from the bathroom. She padded on bare feet through Adelaide's room, wrapped in only a towel, stepping over clothes, weapons, and what she was hoping was only moldy food. Water followed in her wake, leaving small droplets on the floor.

Adelaide had already donned her dress, and her makeup was perfection. She was only missing her mask. Her hair was released from its tightly wound ponytail. Its glossy shine spread through the straight, dark strands, appearing to have a blue hue. She wore an elegant long-sleeved gown, black of course, hugging her hips. The neckline plunged to the bottom of her ribcage.

Amaris almost didn't recognize her. She even wore eyeliner and red tint on her lips. In all her time with her, Amaris had never seen Adelaide wear any makeup.

"You look wonderful," Amaris admired.

Adelaide raised a seductive brow. "I know." Then she smirked. "I have your dress."

"Oh great," Amaris said, full of sarcasm.

"I must say, I'm impressed with Esaias."

Amaris tried to imagine what waited for her. Judging by Adelaide's gown, she was even more terrified of the possible revealing nature. She had a feeling they both had different meanings of the word *modest*.

"Here it is."

Amaris turned, expecting to find a flimsy piece of fabric. What Adelaide held in her hands wasn't flimsy at all, but an extravagant gown. It was a cream-colored tulle dress decorated with red roses, connected by dark vines. Lace outlined the sweetheart neckline and plunged past the shoulders to form three-quarter lace sleeves.

"Holy shit," Amaris breathed.

There were few words to describe its sheer beauty. She wanted to hold it and most definitely wear it. She stepped in, and Adelaide assisted with lacing the corset built into the bodice, tightening the strings, while still allowing Amaris to breathe. The dress hugged and outlined her waist before spilling out into a bouncy skirt trailing to the floor.

"Shall we go over the plan once more?" Adelaide asked.

They'd gone over the adrenaline-inducing stunt every day, and Amaris still found her palms growing sweaty with the fear of getting caught. She also wasn't thrilled with the idea of sharing a boat with Esaias for days. The worst part was the twinge in her chest that the discussion brought. As the night of anticipation had loomed closer, it'd only grown. It felt as if a rubber band had wrapped around her and slowly squeezed each day.

Amaris had lost track of time, but she guessed she'd been gone over a month now. It was hardly any time at all, but it felt as if she'd been gone a lifetime. Thrown into a new world, kidnapped, near-death experiences, and being whipped, all with the threat that she'd be sent to a prison that was apparently worse than any nightmare she could concoct.

She'd been so preoccupied with trying to escape that she'd barely contemplated what to expect or if she could even make it back. Esaias was to take her to Duncaster, but from there, she had to figure something out to find the tree in the woods or even venture to Charibert. She hadn't told them of either destination, fearful of their questions. How could she explain it?

Please drop me off at the nearest willow tree. It didn't make any logical sense.

Thankfully, they were setting her up with some money, which she planned to use to hitch a ride on a ship if necessary. When Theodoric had handed her the small silver and gold coins, she'd wanted to shove them into his palm and force him to take them back. She wasn't scared for the journey, having already accomplished the impossible, traveling through space, but she feared what she would be going home to. If Derek had hit her once, would he do it again?

Amaris twisted the band of her engagement ring, the single ruby sparkling in the rays coming through the window from the setting sun. Theodoric hadn't brought up what they'd shared, and she hadn't found the courage either.

How did he hold himself up after what happened? Amaris was falling apart at the seams because Derek hit her once. Theodoric had been tortured. Even through his anguish as he'd poured his trauma out to her, he'd still wanted to protect her and had offered a different life.

What if I stayed? It felt incredibly selfish, but maybe that was what happened to some missing persons. They fell through a magical portal and woke up in a different world.

"At midnight tonight, most everyone will be too drunk to walk straight. Esaias will take you out to the beach. As everyone believes he's escorting Ann Lawson, no one will think anything of it. They'll think you two are attempting to find someplace private."

"Are you sure you can ready the boat yourself?" Amaris asked. "What if someone finds you?" After all she'd heard and seen, she wouldn't fuck with Adelaide, but she wasn't that familiar with anyone's actual fighting abilities. For all she knew, Adelaide could be mediocre.

She smirked, pulling back the slit of her dress to reveal several daggers strapped around her thighs. "I'll be more than prepared."

"Why do you always conceal your weapons? Is it because you're not a soldier?"

Adelaide bowed her head. "That, and only a few know of my abilities. I can hold my own if it comes to it."

"Why hide? Don't you want everyone to know you're a badass?" Amaris countered. "Why can't you be like Gris or Sephardi?"

"Class and societal rules," she seethed.

Amaris expected words like that to be followed with a pompous tone, but her voice was monotone and trailed with a sigh as if she regretted her birth.

"Doesn't that give you more freedom?"

"The opposite, actually," she huffed, her green eyes reflecting an onyx hue. "The duke disapproves of my training. He forbids me from joining his army and refused to allow me to train with Bennet as a child."

The truth enraged Amaris, if that was even more possible. How could such an asshole have been related to Adelaide and Theodoric? Adelaide rolled her shoulders back, scooping the curls of Amaris's hair into a bun.

"Then how did you learn to fight?"

"Theo." The soft smile on Adelaide's face beamed as she appeared to mull through the memories. "When I was young, I would chase after him and Luther with sticks, wanting desperately to join them in battles. Luther told the duke, and that was when he formally forbid my training."

As she hung her head, a grim shadow passed over her. With her fighting spirit, it weighed heavily to be born into a family like hers.

"Why does he forbid it?"

"My mother," she said. "I think it's because I look like her, but Theo is different. He felt apologetic for how Luther and the duke treated me. When I was eight, he finished a grueling training session and spotted me watching from the kitchen. That night, he came into my room and pulled me from my bed. He brought a couple swords and took me out to the beach. With only a few candles to give us light, he taught me how to hold a sword."

She pulled out several pins and flowers, arranging them around the bun atop Amaris's head like a crown. "He gifted me his first one. It was large for my small hands, but I've grown into it. I keep it hidden because I know the duke will take it from me the moment he sees me with a weapon. Every night, I slip out to the beach to train where no one can hear me.

When Theo can't join me, I practice the movements he taught, ingraining them into my mind. When he went off to war, he entrusted Alan to continue my training."

"That's why you're on the beach so much." Amaris recalled her first night and the arms that had wrapped around her and choked her out. "The night when I escaped...was that you?"

"Which time?" She grinned, but the smile didn't meet her eyes. "I'm sorry for knocking you out that first night. I was terrified my secret would get out, and as for the other night... I would've let you steal every horse in the stable to keep it. Only Alan and Theo know."

"Your secret's safe with me."

Adelaide gave her a wry smile. "It's mine and Theo's secret...going to the beach. I fear what the duke might do to him if he ever found out, especially after what happened. I never thought he'd sentence his own son to a punishment of that severity."

"What happens when Theodoric becomes the next chief?" If he'd trained her, maybe he'd allow her to fight one day.

"When Theo assumes the title of chief, it'll be under Luther's rule. He could very well allow it or hold to the duke's wishes. Luther is more like the duke than Theo or me. I'm not holding my breath."

Slumping, she gripped the handle of the brush. She pulled a few shorter strands along Amaris's face, and their curls bounced against her cheeks. She hadn't seen curls like that since she'd been a kid. She'd missed how the salty air caused her waves to turn to spirals.

A single tear rolled from Adelaide's cheek. She let it hang on the edge of her face. "When I was younger, I tried to fight this." She gestured to herself, her knives discarded across the room. "But I couldn't." She gripped her elbows and retreated to her disheveled bed. "I want to fight alongside everyone else."

"A real woman will fight for her true self without caring what others think."

Pressing the wrinkles from her dress, Adelaide wiped the tears from her cheeks, not even allowing them to ruin her makeup. "I'm beginning to wonder if I'll ever be able to have the life I want. Each day passes, and I'm still training in hiding. I cannot wander the manor all day and train at night forever." She adjusted the holsters around her thigh. "With Luther's engagement, I fear I may be next. Theo doesn't have to marry or produce heirs or anything. Well, neither do I, but I don't have many options as a lady of Luana. I can either become a soldier or marry another pathetic noble. As the prior is not on the table, what else am I going to do with my life?"

"Fuck tradition," Amaris blurted out. "Or run away."

Adelaide's look of complete disbelief was almost hilarious. Amaris didn't know it was possible to render her speechless.

"If you want to be a soldier, go make a name for yourself somewhere else. Who says you have to stay here all your life? If you want your parents to arrange a marriage for you, then stay. But honestly, you should marry someone you love and trust, not some stranger off the streets."

She pictured Adelaide in full military camouflage. Her soul yearned for a life far from her own. Amaris had no doubt in her mind if Adelaide could truly wield one of those large swords that she could easily become a soldier wherever she went. She didn't deserve to be sheltered.

Amaris considered sharing the truth of who she was and where she came from, but she swallowed it. "What if you came with me?"

Adelaide relinquished the death grip she had on her sheets, her eyes finding Amaris's in the vanity mirror. "You mean leave Luana Bay?"

"Why not? Come with me, and then maybe Esaias won't have to risk leaving. You could be a soldier in the King's Guard or somewhere else." Amaris held her tongue. If she decided to leave with her, they'd have a long enough journey where she'd eventually find a way to tell her where she was from.

"I can't." The few silver specks around Adelaide's irises fizzled out. "I just got him back. I can't leave."

"Theodoric?" His name came out in a whisper.

Adelaide nodded. "I've missed him so much, but he's changed. After his flogging and learning what happened to him." Adelaide paused, taking a steady breath. "I want to help him find himself again." She reached for her makeup, pressing her finger to the red pigment and brushing it along Amaris's lips and cheeks. A black paste was used for mascara as Adelaide dragged it over her lashes. "All done," she uttered, a dead cadence in her tone.

"It takes time." Amaris inhaled a deep breath as Adelaide threw her makeup into the drawer. "What he went through, people can learn to live with it, make sense of it all, but he needs time."

"I hope you're right," she choked, grasping Amaris's hand and heaving her up. "But in the meantime, I need to be here for him. He's spent much of his life protecting and taking care of others. I think it's time someone else stepped up and showed him the same gratitude."

Adelaide turned to her wardrobe and pulled out a pair of silk flats. Their connection had Amaris wishing she had siblings. If her parents had lived, would they have wanted more kids? Viv was the closest thing Amaris had to a sister. She wouldn't know where she'd be without her. She'd hopefully still be a paramedic, but would she have been brave enough to take the lieutenant's test? Would she have even passed the academy to become a firefighter?

Adelaide stepped in front of her mirror, fussing with her dress to cover the knives. She was willing to sacrifice what she wanted most in the world for her brother. Amaris bit the edge of her thumb. If she left, she'd never see any of them again. No more conversations about books and magic with Pricilla, gossip sessions with Adelaide, or teasing Theodoric over his love for erotic novels.

She stood behind Adelaide, catching a glimpse of herself in the full-length mirror. If she stayed, she'd be a prisoner. But if she returned home, wouldn't she still be a prisoner trapped in a relationship she didn't know what to do with anymore?

CHAPTER 31

Theo

THEO RAPPED UPON Adelaide's door. Immediately, he noticed the scandalous nature of her dress and threw his sister a disapproving glower. Her intentions were likely to enrage their father, but Theo's eyes were lured to Amaris swishing her dress before the mirror. All matters of Adelaide's dress left his mind.

Their eyes locked in the mirror, and Theo could have sworn his heart stopped. She was beautiful. His instinct to suppress the feeling in his chest arose, but he compelled himself to allow it to grow. His dagger was strapped to his belt, but his hand didn't tremble or shift to grab the hilt. No, a warmth spread through him. He even smiled back at her.

The kohl around her eyes enlightened their deep, oceanic color. In all his travels through the Nebulous Sea, he'd never seen a blue so incredibly enchanting.

Amaris strode toward him, hands swinging and brushing the bouncy fabric of her dress. Tulle poured from her waist, wrapping her in an exhibition of elegance. She exchanged his assessment as her eyes drifted over his own appearance, his golden waistcoat fashioned from silk imported from Soyenia and his navy frock coat. But her eyes stopped on the brass buttons and the Fastrada crest etched into each one.

Before Theo could speak, Esaias stepped out from behind him. His cousin had chosen a dark-green frock coat with golden buttons and a crimson waistcoat to match the roses sewn into Amaris's dress.

"Amaris, you're breathtaking," Esaias said, attempting to further deepen his voice.

Theo rolled his eyes. Nearly every woman sought Esaias's affections, but not Amaris. The humor of it all was the only thing keeping him from dismissing his own escort and spending the evening with Amaris in the center of the ballroom. The last few hours he'd likely ever see her.

"I could punch you in the gut and further cease your efforts to breathe." Amaris smirked.

The pang of never hearing another one of her quips would be unbearable. He'd gotten used to her jokes and the whistling laugh she belted through the echoing tower.

"You can put your hands anywhere you like." Esaias's smug grin was malicious.

"How in the realm did I get stuck with you? And green, really?" Amaris asked.

Esaias patted down his coat, as if assessing for tears or stains. "What's wrong with green?"

"Nothing for you, apparently, but it washes me out."

"I don't think anything could wash out that beautiful face, but if you're worried, I have this for you."

Esaias pulled out a red mask with feathers accentuating the corners. Theo's gut writhed as Esaias fixed the mask to her face, covering every bit of Amaris's beauty. It hid the spiraling curls around her crown and shadowed her eyes.

"Can you tell it's me?" She smiled, revealing the two things left to be desired, her rose-tinted lips and that single dimple.

"Hardly," Theo said, fastening his own mask. He'd elected for a partial one to cover only a quarter of his face, so as not to be mistaken. If their plan was to work, he needed to be seen often and by many eyes during the event. His father would look to him as the first suspect when Amaris turned up missing the next morning.

Esaias's mask was a replica of Amaris's, and Adelaide fastened on an angling black mask fashioned to appear fractured. Dark gemstones reflected around the single string of rubies depicting a line of blood slashing across her face.

"Does everyone know their part?" Theo asked.

Esaias sighed. "We've been over this plenty. I'll take Amaris to her bedchamber to gather our bags and change at midnight."

"I'll prepare the boat and be ready for you," Adelaide said.

"I'll keep to one drink to keep up the part," Amaris added.

"We all will," Theo said. "One drink, but appear as though you never allow yourself to be without one. We must be careful if this is to work."

Conjugations weren't only a time to celebrate future lovebirds. Excessive liquor consumption was expected. If any of them declined a drink, speculation would arise instantly.

Esaias gripped his shoulder. "Everything will be all right. I'll get Amaris safely to Duncaster, and I'll be back well before Whitereign."

He better be. The plummeting temperatures of Whitereign would halt most traveling, and the longer he was away, the more suspicion he would gather. He'd likely be home before mid-Crimsonreign, but Theo worried what would happen if anything went wrong.

"Shall we?" Esaias asked, extending his arm for Amaris.

She dropped her shoulders and groaned, but it was only an act as she took his arm and giggled. "We shall."

It was a vast change from the woman Theo had met in the forest. She'd had a peevishness to her that had annoyed him more than Esaias's snoring. Her guard had been fortified, but this was the real Amaris. She'd lowered her shields. He wanted to be grateful, but it was precisely what his father had asked of him.

He hadn't spoken to his father since the day he'd lost control. After Luther's announcement of Amaris's fate, an audience with his father wouldn't have changed the outcome. While he washed and dressed for the Conjugation, he'd battled with himself over whether he should've gone to his father and demanded Amaris's freedom. It wouldn't have done any good.

"Be sure to save a dance for me, Theo," Adelaide shouted behind them. Theo smiled back at her, but she narrowed her eyes and mouthed, "Watch your back."

Theo would, indeed, need to watch his back, Amaris's, Esaias's, even Adelaide's, but their best opportunity to send Amaris to safety was tonight. The manor would be flooded with people, and the sentries would most certainly relax in their positions to partake in the celebrations.

As they walked the upstairs halls, Amaris and Esaias bickered behind him over whether he was allowed to kiss her to further deceive them. The idea of sending them both away was not at all pleasing. In fact, it sent a fury over Theo. He should've been the one going with her. His father was punishing both him and Amaris for his actions. His father may have tied their hands, but Theo had given him the rope.

An audible gulp stalled his strides at the edge of the grand staircase with the bustling laughter of the guests already reaching his ears. Theo glanced over his shoulder. "Are you alright?"

Amaris's scarred knuckles drained of their color, gripping tighter to the sleeve of Esaias's coat. "A little nervous," she admitted with a wry smile, attempting to hide the shaking in her voice.

Theo stepped toward her. His hand hovered in the air before he placed it on her shoulder. The touch of his skin against hers through the lace was a warmth he wasn't ready to let go of. "You're hardly recognizable. This will work."

It had to. His cheeks flushed at the straight-out lie he'd given her. To someone who didn't know her, she was another passing local. But not to him. He'd be able to spot her from across the ballroom. Her chocolate-brown locks. Those deep-blue eyes. That single-dimple smile. All were Amaris.

She straightened her spine and raised her chin. "Let's do this."

Her assurance for herself not only carried her to the steps but lifted a weight from Theo's shoulders. If Amaris could brave the single night of agony where a single slip of her mask would have her sent to the dungeons, then he could force himself to breathe.

They emerged from the shadows of the hall. Not a single spot wasn't taken at the end of the staircase with people from all over Luana and parts of Godwin there to celebrate. The caravan had arrived a few days ago with the hoity-toity nobles of Eastbury, where Lord Godfrey resided.

Amaris's hesitancy vanished as her eyes lit with wonder. They descended the staircase, but she didn't take notice of the gaping eyes glancing her way and trailing down the skirt of her gown. Her eyes only found the garland decorating the walls, the lanterns dangling above her head, and the blood-red wildflowers littering every surface.

"It's like a fairytale," she whispered, "like some beautiful, magical fairytale."

Theo refrained from rolling his eyes. It was hard to believe someone with her knowledge and skill believed in something like magic. He hadn't asked her about her beliefs, but on several occasions, he'd found a few books on mythology in the mystique tower. If it was a new hobby, Pricilla was likely to blame.

"I imagine it's more like a forest," Theo said. "The black tulle above us is the canopy of trees." A canopy indeed, strung in waves from the coffered ceilings. The dark color squashed any chance of a bright affair. Shadows swirled in the corners with iron-caged lanterns and torches along the walls providing the only light.

Amaris turned and gave him a flat look. "So logical and—"

"Realistic," Theo interrupted, giving her a smirk and arching a brow. He found himself regretting all the times he'd suppressed his laughter when she made a joke.

"I was going to say *annoying*, but fine, we can go with *realistic*."

At the bottom of the staircase, a woman stood with tawny skin the color of a bronze sword. A golden dress hung off one shoulder and hugged her hips before draping into two slits. Her shoulder-length hair had a deep side part revealing silver eyes glowing back at Theo.

The Duchess of Ebonmaw ruled with a kind heart but cunning wit. Helen Canon had no doubt marked each exit and assessed the state of the sentries at the main doors. A dagger or two would be found somewhere under the tight-fitting fabric of her dress.

"Helen." Theo smiled as the duchess cocked a hip and flashed a grin over the rim of her silver goblet. If anyone else hated titles any more than Theo, it was her.

"Theo, it's been too long." She flung out her arms and embraced him in a warm hug, taking care to refrain from spilling her drink.

"I only wish you were there till the end."

"So do I. Believe me, I much prefer running across a battlefield, wielding my sword and shield, to sitting in meetings discussing trade."

The extensive trade cities and towns littering the coast of Ebonmaw had direct access to the popular trade route within the Nebulous Sea, ferrying goods to the islands and Soyenia. The city of Col was the most populated city second to Valencia, where the king's palace resided, and it boasted the largest port in all of Godwin.

Helen grasped the arm Theo offered, but those silver stars widened as she gaped behind him. "Esaias, is that you?" She released her hold and charged up the steps, enveloping her arms around him. "By the gods, it's only been a little over a year, but it feels a lifetime."

Amaris raised a brow at Theo, her eyes flashing back and forth between Esaias and Helen. Theo only shrugged, offering a brief smile before taking

Helen's hand and leading her through the manor. Theo would spare Amaris the details of how deeply acquainted Helen and Esaias were. He was lucky she hadn't produced an heir sporting his fiery red hair.

The throne room was their destination, the main spectacle for the night. It served as a ballroom when his father bothered to arrange such affairs or when he removed himself from the throne.

Helen whistled as she took in the tulle continuing to swath the ceiling into the throne room. It shrouded the chamber in a mysterious and dark tone. Amaris balked at the doors. Theo followed her gaze, shooting to the dais.

How could he have been so careless? Only weeks ago, she'd been forced to her knees before his bastard of a father and made a spectacle of in front of his soldiers. He turned to spare her from reliving that dreadful day, but her chest lifted with a large inhale. Her back straightened, and she took a step forward, dragging Esaias along with her.

Theo hadn't been able to set foot in Oystein Castle since the night he'd been rescued, and he wasn't sure he ever would. Amaris emanated confidence, with her chin held high as she walked through the chamber. She even hummed, off tune and out of rhythm, but she still sung along to the music coming from a small quartet positioned in the corner.

They went through the ballroom, swiping goblets of wine off the refreshments table. The room already reeked of cramped bodies perspiring their weight in liquor.

Esaias took a sip from his goblet and grimaced. "Would anyone care for a real drink?"

Theo displayed his criticism with a stern set of narrowed eyes but then contemplated the idea that kusu would better suit Esaias's condition than the sugary wine. He would also be playing the part of a drunken, lovestruck fool to keep others from asking his whereabouts after the Conjugation.

"Yes!" Amaris said all too eagerly as Esaias departed for the kitchen.

Theo leaned in to whisper in her ear. "Do you not care for wine? This is some of the finest in Godwin."

She took a sip, smiling with those perfectly straight teeth as she pulled the goblet back. "I don't mind it, but kusu should certainly be required for every party, meal, bath...really any occasion."

Theo's body shook with his laughter.

"I'm serious, that stuff is to die for!"

"I would have to agree with you, but Eastbury is known for their vineyards. Lord Godfrey will say it was brought as a wedding gift to bestow upon my brother, but it's really because he's a snob and finds any other drink repulsive."

She batted his arm with the back of her hand. "Who is this great Lord Godfrey?" she mocked, eyeing the vast crowd around them.

Theo couldn't explain why his stomach twisted as her attempt at his accent rolled off her tongue. He wished she could stay and pick it up entirely. Her voice was exquisite as she extended her vowels.

"Do you see the man beside the duke?" Helen interjected, pointing her finger to where Lord Godfrey engaged in a deep conversation with Theo's father.

"The pasty bald one with the silk robes, appearing to act way more important than he actually is?"

Helen erupted into a thunderous laugh. "Yes," she roared, wiping a tear from her eye, still unable to contain her fit of laughter. "You are an exuberant woman."

"I really try." Amaris wryly smiled. "Who's that in front of him, seated at the head table?"

Theodoric squinted. Sitting with her shoulders pressed back and her hands laid gently on the table was Winifred Godfrey. Her deep complexion was complemented well by the gold and red gown she wore. Her curls were done up in a crown atop her head, accentuating her tight jawline and sharp cheeks.

"That is Lady Godfrey," Theo replied.

"How did he land a beauty like that?" Amaris scoffed, but before Theo could explain the title and status that came with Lord Godfrey, she rolled her eyes. "I know, noble birth, titles, gold, power, all the shit." She raised her hands in silent surrender.

"Would you not marry someone if it came with a title?" Helen asked. "The man you're with tonight could very well hold one someday."

Even though Esaias claimed to have renounced his status, there were no formal documents to prove it. If something were to happen to his siblings, he would assume one of their titles.

"I wouldn't marry someone for the title. I would be saddled with someone like..." Amaris's voice strained, but Theo knew she wished to say *someone like the duke*. "Well, if they happen to have one, I'd consider it."

"Theodoric, there you are." The voice came from none other than Genevieve.

"Mother." Theo smiled.

It felt wrong to refer to her by anything else. She'd raised Theo since the age of ten, but he felt he was wronging his real mother for using her name for another woman. He'd once referred to Genevieve by her first name, and she burst into tears. Ever since, with great reluctance, he'd called her *Mother*.

"Your Grace, it's a delight to see you." Genevieve beamed, grasping Helen's hand. Her red hair fell over her shoulder, the top pinned back with a diamond-studded comb. "This must be the lovely Miss Lawson."

"Ann," Theo said, motioning to Amaris and clearing his throat as he forced the unfamiliar name from his lips. "This is my mother, the Duchess of Luana."

"Your Grace, it's a pleasure to meet you." Amaris dipped into a small curtsy, which Theo's stepmother waved off before embracing her in a hug and planting a kiss upon both of Amaris's cheeks.

"I do hope you will allow me to commandeer Theodoric and Helen for a few moments," Genevieve pleaded to Amaris.

"Of course, he's your son." Amaris faked a smile and took a drink from her goblet.

"Allow me to leave Ann in Esaias's company first—" Theo began.

"It'll only be for a few short moments." Genevieve captured Theo in her clutches and whisked him and Helen toward her throng of noble friends.

Amaris stood alone, but there wasn't fear behind her gaze. Theo tried to pull from his stepmother's talons, but she held firm to his arm. Anyone could recognize Amaris, but she gave him a smile and motioned for him to follow along.

"Theodoric, I'd like you to speak with our guests," Genevieve said.

He reluctantly followed her to the dais, where he'd be forced to play the part of his bloodline. As a captain, he was thankful to refrain from using the courtesy title of "lord." He might have still been one, but his military rank was distinguishable enough to overtake it. His conversations would likely be skewed toward security efforts or other topics relating to their forces. He reminded himself to act the part for Amaris.

They approached the long table, decorated in a lacy tablecloth with red wildflowers planted in the center. Lord Godfrey was still busy in conversation with Theo's father and had pulled him from prying ears.

"As you know, this is Lady Godfrey," Genevieve said, gesturing to Winifred as she came around the table in greeting.

Theo bowed, and Lady Godfrey extended a curtsy before nudging the young woman beside her to follow suit. Petra was a near replica of her mother.

"How do you do, Lord Fastrada?" Petra said with a bold expression. Her golden-brown eyes drifted between the people scattered around the dais waiting to congratulate her. She breathed a sigh.

"Captain," Theo corrected her.

"Oh?" Petra questioned, snapping her thin face and high cheekbones toward him. Her eyes weren't warm like her mother's, only cold silhouettes.

"Theo cannot stand to be associated amongst the upper class. He prefers his military title," Luther crooned. "Your Grace." He reached for Helen's hand and planted a kiss on her knuckles.

She pulled away and sent Theo a cringe.

"Congratulations, brother." Theo didn't offer Luther a smile.

There was a time when they were younger when he would've called him one of his best friends. That was before Luther had been called inside for his political training. Theo's days had then grown longer, and he'd developed a bond with Nate, after hours of sore muscles and fresh calluses. Now, Luther was another noble to sit among the wealthy elites of Godwin and another member of high society for Theo to despise.

"Thank you." Luther forced a smile before he took Petra's hand and escorted her through the finely decorated throne room.

Theo took it as a means for an exit and linked Helen's arm with his and began leading her off the dais. He scanned the room to find Amaris, but before he could take another step, Genevieve's eyes lit with excitement. She pulled him toward the throng of her noble posse seated on the other side of the room.

"I would like to introduce you to someone," she said, beaming.

Theo was wary of her expression and could only guess who she was excited to introduce him to.

"I want you to meet Adelaide's betrothed."

CHAPTER 32

Theo

THEO HALTED IN his path, startled. "I'm sorry. Did you say *Adelaide's* betrothed?" he questioned.

Genevieve's smile didn't falter. "But of course."

"When was this decided? Does Adelaide know?"

"The arrangements have been in preparation for seasons but were finalized tonight after meeting with the prince."

"Prince?" Theo asked. "Who are you intending to marry her to?"

"The prince of Mensnet," she said.

Luke Gavell? Theo immediately loathed the tall and lanky man standing with such despicable poise. He bowed and kissed Genevieve's hand, his dark eyes attempting to enchant her. It worked, because her cheeks blushed a shade darker than her hair.

Prince Luke was younger than Theo expected. As the sole heir to the kingdom of Mensnet, he was the talk among members of society. Apparently, his age had merely been passed by. He couldn't have been any older than twenty.

A smile tugged at the corner of the prince's lips as he offered a brief bow of his head to Theo. It was as if all color drained in his presence. The prince wore an entirely black ensemble, and even his hair was a shade of midnight settling to his shoulders.

"It's an honor to finally meet the great Captain Theodoric Fastrada. I've heard of your valor during the war. I must say I'm impressed that, at such an age, you've accomplished what you have."

"Thank you, Your Highness." Theo returned the prince's gesture with a bow of his head, as it was only proper.

"Please, Luke will do fine." He smiled. "As we're to become family soon enough, I see it only fitting. Helen, a pleasure to see you again." Luke nodded to Helen instead of kissing her hand, already seeming to know she had an aversion to court formalities.

"Your Highness." Helen smirked, taking a sip from her goblet.

"Have you met my sister?" Theo asked, knowing full well he hadn't and the wrath that would ensue.

"I haven't had the pleasure. I hear she is a remarkable woman, and I look forward to it," he said.

"Any man would consider themselves lucky to have the honor of simply knowing my sister." Theo's voice was cold as his eyes narrowed on the prince, watching his expression grow cautious.

"Adelaide is indeed—" Genevieve began.

"She is intelligent, cunning, brave—"

"I don't doubt those things," Luke interrupted Theo. "I've heard of her...skills." He hesitated.

Theo wasn't fond of such implications. Hardly anyone knew of Adelaide's skills with a blade or her ability to gather any secret she desired. He contemplated further questioning the young prince but thought better of doing so in Genevieve's presence.

"She's more than that," Theo snapped. "She's a better person than anyone in this room, including you." The thrumming of his pulse reverberated toward his ears, drowning the party around them.

"Mensnet is known for their fierce warriors and courageous leaders. She'll do well by my side," he calmly stated, but Theo saw the shadows brewing within his navy eyes.

"I thought they were known to hide within the Dark Mountains. Many would call that cowardly," Theo snipped.

Genevieve threw him a glare, but Theo persisted. He couldn't stop, not when it came to Adelaide.

Helen turned and pressed her lips together to contain her laughter. She played the part of Duchess of Ebonmaw well, but occasionally, her true self showed. She would prefer to be sipping swigs of kusu out by the stables and having a betting match at who could throw their dagger the farthest.

"That was my father's choice to remain neutral in the war," Luke replied, his voice still unwavering.

Godwin and Mensnet have had a treaty regarding peace and trade for resources for the last several hundred years, but it didn't speak to aid in times of war. The kingdom had elected not to assist Godwin or Soyenia in the Trade War.

"Do you envision a different future for Mensnet?" Theo asked. If Luke thought he could come into his home and steal his sister, he was mistaken.

"I do," he answered. "My father, as most know, is unwell. I'll be assuming the throne sooner than expected. But I've prepared for the moment and decided what I'll do differently. The Duchess of Ebonmaw and I are already in discussions regarding reopening Mensnet's mines. I intend to begin mining the onyxbone and using the resources Ebonmaw offers to begin trade negotiations for the material."

"You refused to come to our aid and now wish for our trade resources? The mines haven't even been operational for hundreds of years. Is there any onyxbone left?" Theo had heard rumors of the strange material but had never seen a piece of armor or weapon fashioned from it. If the mines had been closed hundreds of years ago, it would have been for good reason.

He shot a look of disdain toward Helen, but her smirk faded, and she returned his glower.

"Luke and I are excited for this new venture to bring our kingdoms closer together, and the kings have already bestowed their blessings," Helen stated.

"Your father's people won't allow change as easily as you presume they might," Theo threw at Luke. "It takes years to build trust."

"As his heir," the young prince finally snipped, "I've been by his side my entire life, and I've gained my own following. This, however, is a celebration. We should be enjoying the festivities instead of squabbling over politics."

Theo turned to Genevieve, ignoring Luke's attempt to sway the conversation. "When are you planning to tell Adelaide?"

She waved him off and emitted a nervous laugh. "Oh, Theodoric, there are always formalities to deal with first. We'll inform her when it's time. I would like her to get to know Prince Luke first."

"You don't plan to tell her?" Theo sent her an accusing glare. Their betrothal was nothing more than a political stunt to strengthen the ties with Mensnet for the onyxbone.

"When the time is right." Genevieve smiled, like a queen knowing full well the implications it would cause for all of them.

Theo would either be forced to keep it from Adelaide, knowing she would be walking into a trap set by their parents, or he would tell her and risk further retribution from his father.

"If you'll excuse me," Theo muttered.

He was going to be sick. The mere thought of hiding the betrothal from her was unbearably nauseating. Once she wed the prince, she'd venture to Mensnet and become his queen. His stomach lurched. He couldn't fathom what Luana Bay would be like without her. He'd always hoped, one day, she'd finally stand beside him as a soldier, but now that dream might never come to fruition. *But she'd be a queen.*

Lost to his thoughts, it took him a moment to notice Adelaide standing beside him after he'd stormed to a nearby corner in an attempt to bring himself back to reality. He jumped once he caught sight of her.

"She's over there." With a knowing smirk, Adelaide pointed to Amaris, who was in the unfortunate company of Alan. Theo turned, but Adelaide placed a hand on his arm. "I don't think Alan knows it's her."

As neither of them had a knife pulled or fists balled, he could only presume Alan didn't. "Thank you," Theo said, but his voice wavered.

"Is everything all right?" she asked.

The moment had come to decide—defy his parents and tell Adelaide everything or face the consequences later. His back throbbed at the thought of another lashing. "Yes. I was only forced to face the absolute boredom of meeting some of Genevieve's friends."

It could wait for one night. They needed to see to their plan to smuggle Amaris out first, and then he'd deal with the betrothal situation. He'd never killed someone out of pure enjoyment, but he didn't think Adelaide would mind if her betrothed ended up missing after the Conjugation. Bennet already claimed treason once, what was another accusation?

"In that case, here." She handed him a glass of kusu.

He hadn't the charisma to thank her properly, so he answered with a simple nod before taking a long drink.

"I've been dodging Mother for the last hour. I have no doubt it's to see if I find anyone suitable. Do you think she'll be annoyed or see it coming when I roll my eyes and flatly decline anyone she sends my way?" Adelaide laughed.

He almost spit out his drink. His chest ached at her laughter, knowing the situation was unlike the other parties Adelaide had been forced to attend to see who she deemed a likely husband. The wheels were set in motion, and Adelaide was about to be dragged into a rough political landscape.

How could he get her out of it? It wasn't like he had any true power against his father. Would he be unable to stop it? What if none of them truly had a say in the matter of their lives? His shred of hope for something different when Luther riled him up last week slowly seeped away.

What life did he want? Did he want to be chief or to even pick up his sword again? His eyes trailed to Amaris, who bit the edge of her thumb as she appeared more bored than angered in her conversation with Alan. What did he want?

"Theo?" Adelaide's sharp elbow landed between his ribs. Even through the makeup and wardrobe, he knew what Adelaide was, a warrior. She likely had a few weapons strapped underneath her dress. Once she was married, her dream of becoming a soldier would be gone forever.

He took her hand, as he once did many years ago. Back then, he'd pulled her from her bed late in the night. He'd been thirteen at the time and had been in the awkward stage of beginning puberty. His voice had broken, but Adelaide had been most eager to follow him.

"Where are we going?" Adelaide had asked.

Theo slinked around the next corner but turned over his shoulder and gave his sister a wide smile. "Your first training lesson."

A shrill escaped her as she clapped her hands.

Theo cupped her lips and darted his head back and forth. "Keep quiet."

"Why?" she whispered.

"Father can't know about this." He kneeled before his sister and wound a loose hair clinging to her rosy cheek behind her ear. "If you truly want to learn to fight, I need you to keep this a secret. No one else can know."

"Alright." She grinned, eager to begin her first training session.

"Swear it."

Adelaide's eyes widened and her shoulders slouched. "You mean..." She pointed above them. Swearing to Zias was no mockery. The God of Oaths took them as binding. "I swear by Zias himself to keep our secret."

Theo pulled his dagger from his belt, and Adelaide extended her palm.

"I swear by Zias to oversee your training." He slid the blade across her palm.

She winced as her tiny hand dripped with blood.

"To come to your aid whenever you should need me and to never let harm befall you." He grunted as he dragged the dagger over his own palm. They clasped hands. "By witness of Zias himself, I pledge as your older brother to do everything in my power to always protect you."

Theo rubbed at the thin scar across his palm as he stood before his sister, now fully grown and stronger than he ever thought possible. She'd always been a fighter at heart, a cunning, brilliant, and smart woman. "Would you care to dance, Addie?"

Adelaide's playful expression softened. He hadn't called her that in so long, partially because she'd said she'd destroy him if he ever did. This time, she didn't threaten to gut him or pierce his eyeballs. She took his hand and pulled him to the dance floor.

CHAPTER 33

Theo

AS SOON AS Adelaide and Theo headed to the center floor, they were interrupted by the clinking of a glass. He turned to spot Amaris still chatting with Alan, smiling even. He squinted. Alan had one, too, but where was Esaias? Theo didn't see his hair poking out among the members of the crowd. They only had a few hours left and needed to be ready.

Theo returned his gaze to his father standing above the crowd with Lord Godfrey at his side.

"It's with great honor that I present Lord Caratacos Godfrey."

The crowd erupted in cheers and applause but was quickly silenced with a single raise of his father's hand. A commanding presence was what he was, nothing more.

"Tonight, we celebrate the future union of Lord Luther Fastrada and my daughter, the Honorable Petra Godfrey," Lord Godfrey began. "It has been quite a time since we had the opportunity of such a union to bring together two families as one. May it bring prosperous trade and long-lasting bonds between Luana and Ebonmaw."

Theo's father raised his glass. "To the groom and his bride to be. *Amyamam!*"

The crowd raised their drinks in unison and shouted, "*Amyamam!*"

Everyone in the room threw back their goblets in one swig, and the entire room exploded in applause. The small band resumed their lively chorus, and a throng of people flocked around them to the floor. Theo gripped Adelaide tighter and pulled her along to the music.

"I would've thought you'd forgotten how to dance," she said.

"You don't think I had the opportunity while away?"

She raised her brow, and the edge of her lip curled. He pushed her out and spun her to the cadence of the song. She flung back into him, grasping his arm and following his lead.

"I see you've become an exceptional dancer," he noted as he dipped her.

She flourished her arm in a dramatic arch. "I've always been the better dancer."

Theo narrowed his eyes at her, but a smile poked through his demeanor.

She leaned in, lowering her voice. "Keep that smile, and don't allow your face to show what you're about to feel."

"And what am I about to feel?" His head snapped down to her.

"Look back up and smile," she ordered, not averting her eyes as he lifted her. "Bennet isn't here."

"What?"

"Eyes up and smile. I haven't been able to track him."

"Why—"

"Theo, you changed while you were away, but so have I. I'm not a child anymore. I've been keeping tabs on him since your flogging."

He gripped her hand tighter, but kept his face composed as he whispered, "Why are you trailing him?"

"Something is happening under my nose that I can't quite figure out. Alan has been keeping an eye out as well. He's been listening to the duke's meetings."

"He's been what?" He could hardly hear what was coming from her lips, but at least it explained how she knew the secret goings-on of the manor.

"Theo, you need to think critically. We're in the middle of what could very well be the beginnings of an internal war."

He glided Adelaide across the floor, neither of them faltering in their steps to the song they knew by heart. Genevieve had insisted on regular dance lessons. Adelaide dipped back, her hand grazing the floor.

"If you keep doing that, people will start watching," Theo snapped.

"Let them. It'll keep their eyes off Amaris."

Adelaide's eyes shifted, and he followed her gaze as she stared at Luke dancing with Amaris.

"Who's dark and mysterious?" Adelaide asked.

Theo's eyes flared and his teeth clenched at the sight of him. "I thought you didn't want to get married?"

"Who said anything about marriage? Besides, I can admire."

How could she care about eyeing a man now? Bennet was nowhere to be found, likely putting a knot in their plans, and they had only a few short hours.

"I don't wish to hear about men you find attractive or your intimate relations. As your older brother, I'm already obligated to kill any man who looks your way."

"You're so dramatic," she groaned. "But who is he? He seems awfully chipper with Amaris."

He spun Adelaide around to get a better look at them. Amaris was following him, not perfectly, but she wasn't tripping over her feet either. Luke grasped her waist and spun her out. He laughed as she stumbled back into his arms. Theo's jaw tightened.

"Are you jealous?" Adelaide prodded.

"No," he snapped. "She can dance with whomever she likes, and that is Luke Gavell."

"As in Prince Luke of Mensnet?"

"One and the same," Theo answered.

"That would explain the guards I saw in the gardens."

Theo glanced around the edges of the room and spotted the prince's guards in their black tunics and their faces shrouded in hoods.

"We're about to switch. Grab for Amaris."

Theo counted the beats until the switch at the end of the song. He spun Adelaide, who twirled straight for Luke, and Theo waited as Amaris spun freely through the ballroom. If he hadn't been desperate to cling to Amaris, he would've pulled Adelaide back and as far from Luke as possible. He, instead, took hold of Amaris's hand, and she slammed into his chest. Her breath escaped her.

The song ended on its whistling tune, and a slow drum began the next melody, a soft lullaby his mother often sang to him and Luther. Amaris leaned into him. The warmth of her penetrated through his clothes and coated his palms in perspiration.

He grasped her tightly around the waist, pulling her over the dance floor. She emanated serenity. He couldn't help but smile, at least one of them was calm. It was as if a trance had fallen over her as she closed her eyes and felt the room around her. A soft smile curved on her lips.

Was this what it was like to truly feel? A bliss transcending over a person? For days, he wondered what it'd be like to embrace her. Now, with her cheek pressed to his chest, her fingers interlaced with his, and her other hand resting on his shoulder, he didn't want to let go. He allowed himself a moment to breathe. Why did it have to end? In a matter of hours, she would be departing for Duncaster. He pulled her closer and allowed himself to feel. To drink in every last moment with her.

"Are you lost in thought?" he finally asked, his steps carrying them to the drum's steady cadence.

"I'm happy," she breathed, "truly happy."

He felt her smile, and he pulled her tighter, the smile overcoming everything as he glided her through the dance. She leaned into him, relinquishing herself to his guidance. He braced her hip and spun her to the steady increase of the beating drum before tugging her back once more. His hand fit perfectly along her waist, conforming to her curves.

Her chest met his, and her heartbeat fluttered against him.

What if he left with her?

"Amaris," he breathed.

She gazed up at him, her eyes lost in a cloudy haze. She was striking, utterly beautiful. His lips curled into a smile at the sight of her wide grin and that single-dimple imprint on her cheek. She sank into him, her body growing heavier in his arms. His brow furrowed, and he gazed into her dilated pupils. She was drunk.

His hands clutched her waist, and he led her out into the hall. They passed small gatherings of people scattered about, but most everyone was in the throne room having an extraordinary night. She squinted against the dull lights emanating from the candles they passed. He assessed her balance, carefully guiding her through the manor.

"Where are we going?" She grinned, leaning against his arm.

"We're going to get you some water and bread," he whispered back, trying not to let his anxiety show.

She wasn't in a state to think properly, let alone continue dancing. He opened the door to the kitchen, but she pulled from his grasp and stumbled through the door, giggling to herself. He reached out, picking her up and setting her on the counter. Her brows rose, and her eyes flared.

"Viv was the only one who used to do this for me," she said while he scavenged the cupboards for some bread. Ms. Borstad would have made extra loaves for the occasion. "She once sat with me on the bathroom floor for an entire night while I puked my guts out."

"She sounds like a true friend." Theo filled a glass of water and returned to her side with a small chunk of sourdough bread.

"She is."

She swayed as she reached for the glass, but he grasped her hand instead, pulling it to the counter. The pads of her fingers drew soft circles under his palm. He brought the cup to her lips, praying it would aid in sobering her and shifting his focus from her hand caressing his own. This had been reckless. She'd known she was supposed to have only one drink.

She took a sip, slurping the liquid as a shimmering smile gleamed in her eyes. Pulling back, she bit those rose-tinted lips. A drop spilled down her chin. His hand mindlessly grasped her jaw, wiping it away.

"Do you love her?"

"Who?"

She grabbed the lapels of his coat, tugging him closer. He gripped the counter to keep from falling into her chest.

"Helen."

Theo raised a curious brow, and a small laugh escaped. "We're simply friends."

Her eyes softened. She curled her fingers deeper into the fabric and pulled him closer, planting a kiss upon his lips. Water spilled from the cup in his hand as she released his jacket and shoved him away.

A smirk grazed her lips. "Good."

His chest burst into a thousand scorching suns. His eyes drifted to her lips then back to those sparkling blue eyes. He discarded the water cup and caressed her jaw, their lips meeting. A gasp escaped her, but her hand slid into his hair. It wasn't a short peck or one of a deep longing. It was ravenous. She toyed with the strands behind his ear, pulling at his mask's string to discard it on the floor.

He tipped her head, kissing her deeper, needing to taste that sweet scent of vanilla and wanting to wrap himself in it. She nibbled his lip, a groan rumbling in his chest. She tossed her head back and guided him to the slender curve of her neck. He should've been attempting to sober her, not tracing his lips over her skin, but he couldn't help it. He didn't want to help it. He wanted to take her thrumming pulse between his teeth.

He trailed along her jaw, brushing her ear with the tip of his nose, releasing a warm breath. She wrapped her legs around his torso, pinning him against the counter. His cock throbbed for her, but he sucked and kissed along her neck, savoring the small moans escaping her.

He paused, his chest panting. "Amaris," he breathed, "why...what...?" His mind was jumbled with every thought, but he couldn't string together a simple sentence with her hands wrapped in his hair.

"I wanted to know what it was like."

"And?" he gasped through a shaky breath.

"I don't want to leave."

His heart stuttered. "Then don't."

He didn't want her to go. He wanted to fix the mess his father had created. He wanted to take her to his other favorite shops within the city to see her smile and experience joy. A spark had formed in her eyes then, and he wanted to see it every chance he could.

He planted his lips on hers. Stars danced behind his eyelids at the soft touch of her kiss. He pulled her deeper, dragging her along the counter until her body was flush with his. He grasped her waist and pressed her against his hard length, letting her know how much he wanted her to stay.

He forced himself not to rush but to explore every beautiful aspect of her, because she deserved to be caressed with a gentle hand, to be shown mercy.

His tongue brushed across her lips, and hers met his in their exploration. His hand slipped through her curls, pulling her hair from its pins and removing her mask. Her nails dug into his back. A shiver rippled down his spine. *Gods*, she was beautiful, and he wanted more. He shouldn't have wanted to pull her closer. He should've given her time, but he couldn't stop himself.

"But..." she panted, "what about...your father?"

He gripped her waist, his teeth nibbling on her bottom lip. "We'll figure it out," he groaned. He knew it was more complex than that, but he couldn't find it in him to care in the moment, with Amaris wrapped around him.

His lip tingled, going numb as he drew back from their kiss. A kiss that tasted so right but was completely wrong. He took a step back, staring at her flushed cheeks before leaning back in and sniffing her breath. "Amaris, what did you drink?"

"A little wine." She grinned, pulling her hand to her lips. "I promise I only had one. Not even a sip of kusu." She flashed him a cheesy grin as she leaned in to kiss him again.

He gripped her shoulders. "I need you to think. What did you drink? Did you take something from someone?"

Her brows knit together. She relinquished the hold her legs had around him. *No*, he didn't want her to let go. He didn't want it to stop, but the sensation spreading across his lips had his heart stalling.

"What's wrong?" she asked, leaning forward. She lost her balance, falling into his chest.

He pulled her face into his hands, dragging the back of it along her cheeks. "You're burning up. Are you sure you only had one?"

"Positive," she whispered, her hands bracing against his chest as her voice became airy.

"We're going to the tower," he said earnestly, attempting to pull her to his chest.

"No," she yelled, pushing off him and jumping from the counter. She teetered, but his hand around her waist caught her. "We're not ruining this moment. I'm fine." She strained against his grip, but he held her tight.

"You aren't fine."

She buried her face in her hands. "Why are you doing this?" she cried. "I...thought you..." Her chin quivered. "What am I doing?"

"I don't understand," he began. "But—"

"I know. How could you possibly even begin to understand? Because I sure as hell don't."

Her fight to keep from crying turned to a small chuckle. It grew and she began hysterically laughing and wheezing as she slipped from his arms and sank to the floor. "Wow, even the sky is more beautiful here," she said, continuing to laugh.

His heart skipped a beat. *Hallucinations.*

"Amaris, we're going, now." Worried, he kneeled beside her.

"No, I think I'm going to lie here for a minute actually," she sang, placing her hands behind her head and smiling up at the ceiling.

"Amaris, we need to find Pricilla."

"What for?" she scoffed. "I'm perfectly content here."

He didn't care if she was upset with him later. They were leaving now. They didn't have time. He dragged her to her feet, restraining her arms as she fought his hold.

"Shit!" she yelled, her face turning an ashen gray.

She turned her head and threw up. His heart held a moment of relief that maybe she'd thrown it up. She wiped her mouth with the back of her hand and looked down to see the contents of her stomach all over her dress. Theo hefted her into his arms, her head bobbing against his chest.

"How do you feel about me?" she asked, her fingers playing with a frayed spot in his waistcoat.

He hesitated in his steps toward the library. *How do I feel about her?* Weeks ago, he'd been ready to incriminate her as a murderer or let her slip down those death traps for stairs leading from the tower, but now he didn't know. He didn't want her to leave, and he'd wanted to kiss her. *Gods, I still do.*

He turned his focus from his thoughts. Pricilla's help was the only thing that mattered right now. He could sort out his feelings later.

"I... Amaris, you're—"

"Staying," she giggled against him.

He closed his eyes, hearing it again. She wanted to stay. He slipped through a servants' passage to avoid the crowds of the party.

"You said that already," he breathed, needing to keep her talking. If she was still able to speak, then the poison hadn't taken hold yet.

"Yes, but..." she muttered. They passed the wall lining the throne room, and the muffled tune of the fiddle and drums grew louder. "Theo, I..."

He stopped in his tracks, not because the sound of his nickname on her lips sent his heart stumbling over itself, but her words came out as a gasp. Her fingers fell from his waistcoat, and she took an agonizing breath.

"Amaris?"

He shook her in his arms, but she didn't respond. His chest constricted and his breaths grew shallow. She took a forced breath, gulping a bit of air. *Paralysis.* He couldn't stop all the thoughts swarming in his head. She tried to breathe and let out another gasp, then her chest ceased moving. *No.*

She wasn't breathing. He nearly dropped her in his panic. He sank to his knees and drew her closer, feeling for a bit of breath on her lips.

"Amaris?" he choked.

She didn't answer as she stared lifelessly at him with her eyes glassed over and her chest still. He dropped his head to her chest, feeling the slow beat of her heart. He dragged his hand through his hair, his breaths growing erratic.

What would she do? Amaris was the mystique, not him. She was the one who healed and always found a way. She'd brought him back from death and cured Esaias of a deadly disease. *What do I do?*

Rescue breathing, that was what she'd called it. Her beautiful voice repeated in his head. *When one is giving rescue breaths, you pinch their nose and put your mouth around theirs, and you breathe a breath into them.*

He lifted her head and forced a breath through her lips. He further tasted the herix, the poisonous nut Cornelius had been foolish to keep in the tower. Pulling her to his chest, he lifted her off the ground. She'd survived the woods, Bennet's anger, and his father's cruelty. Theo wouldn't let the herix take her.

He sprinted through the passageway, only stopping every few seconds to give her another breath. He came out into the hallway lined with the portraits, and he kicked the library doors open.

"Amaris?" Pricilla's voice echoed ahead of him as he raced toward her. Alan was perched on a desk beside her.

"Pricilla, come with me upstairs," he demanded, breathing against Amaris's lips.

He carried her up the stairs and laid her on the cot. He gave her another breath as his own were becoming more frantic. He sank to his knees at her side, grabbing her face between his hands, but her eyes remained glassed over.

"Amaris, can you hear me?" His voice was ragged.

"What happened?" Pricilla's voice came from across the room.

"I think she was poisoned. Alan, show me that jar of herix." There was a loud shuffling of glass, but then Alan produced the jar of deadly nuts. "Several handfuls are missing, Pricilla. Someone must have laced her drink." Theo tugged at his tight collar, his heart squeezing in his chest. He panted between the next breath.

"Those are strong accusations," Alan said. "Who do you think did it?"

"I don't know. I tasted it on her lips, and it made my bottom lip grow numb. Someone, make an antidote or a tonic!" Theo ordered.

Alan started a fire, and Pricilla grabbed whatever herbs she needed. His fingers combed through Amaris's hair, holding her face as he slid his lips over hers and continued to breathe for her.

He needed them to hurry. He was at his wits' end, and he couldn't stop his chest as it beat rapidly and squeezed around his lungs. He gave her another breath.

"Take this. Hold the smoke in your cheeks and blow it into her lungs. Then cover her mouth so it doesn't escape," Pricilla said, her own breaths were rapid, with tears sliding down her cheeks.

Her hands trembled as she held the pipe to Theo's lips, and he inhaled the burning essence into his hollowed cheeks. He pinched Amaris's nose and quickly encircled her lips, forcing the smoke into her lungs. His hand covered her mouth, and he fought back tears.

She had said an adult needed a breath every five seconds. These were the longest five seconds of his life.

CHAPTER 34

Theo

"IT SHOULD BEGIN working immediately," Pricilla said, her jaw quivering. "Come on, Amaris."

Theo turned to Pricilla, and Alan had his arms wrapped around her as tears fell from her eyes.

He focused his attention back to Amaris and gave her another breath. He leaned back on his heels, praying to Kedes and Kata to spare her. He asked for nothing else. He wouldn't cheat death anymore. He'd gladly accept his death when it came, only if the gods would spare her.

Amaris's chest heaved. He collapsed back on the floor, leaning on his elbows. He tried to release his own breath as he threw his head back, but his chest tightened. A slithering crept behind the stitch in his mind.

"It's working." Pricilla stepped over him and settled beside Amaris, grasping her hand.

With Amaris out of immediate danger, Theo bolted from the floor. He grasped his dagger and brandished it over Alan's neck, slamming him into the wall.

"You did this!" he shouted, his teeth clenching as spit flung from his mouth.

Alan gripped his wrist around the dagger.

As if he could ever withstand my strength. The stitch in his mind parted, unraveling the thread he'd desperately thrown together.

"You told the duke she tried to escape and poisoned her fucking drink!" Theo barked.

Alan's head tipped back to give him as much space as possible as Theo's dagger pressed to the lump below his skin. He released his hands, raising them in defeat.

"Theo, put the knife down," Pricilla said.

"You tried to kill her!" Theo screamed, his breaths coming in short, panicked bursts.

"I knew someone was in the stables," Alan began, "but I didn't know it was you two. I wasn't the one who told the duke. You should be holding that dagger to whomever else was on sentry duty that night."

"Liar!" Theo shouted.

His hands trembled, and his dagger slipped from his fingers. He tried to massage the aching muscles but could barely move his other hand. He tousled his hair, fighting against the constriction around his chest. He fell to his knees, choking on his breath.

"Theo, what's wrong?" Pricilla asked.

"Esaias," he muttered, his hand shaking as he grabbed the collar of his shirt. He couldn't breathe.

"I think he's with Onika," someone said with a muffled voice.

A ringing swarmed in his ears as the room cascaded itself in a red hue. Theo clawed at whatever was constricting around his throat, threatening to suffocate him. He dropped his head to the ground, trying to force a bit of air into his lungs.

"Esaias." He released a single agonizing breath.

"I'll find him."

Theo couldn't tell who said it, but the tower door slammed shut. His vision grew spotty as his breaths increased. Someone kneeled beside him.

A hand bracing against his back caused him to jolt and nearly smack them.

"It's all right."

Nothing's all right! Amaris had almost died and had poison running through her veins. Someone had tried to kill her. His father wanted her dead or sent to Elric—he couldn't even remember which, and his collar was too damn tight!

He tugged and pulled, trying to rid himself of the strangling garment. A pair of hands pulled off his coat and whatever was strangling him. His hand ripped at his chest, trying to take in a breath. His vision darkened, and his hands grew completely numb.

He gasped. His eyes pinched together, and his body trembled. He forced a breath, holding the air in his lungs. A weight pressed on him, threatening to stop his heart.

This is all my fault. He'd stepped away from her for too long. Anyone could've laced her drink. *Where was Esaias? Where is he now?* Theo was going to kill him for leaving her. He clenched his hands, searching his waist for his sword. *Where is it?*

"What happened?" a voice asked.

"Something's wrong with Theo." A hand grasped his, but he could barely make out the edges of their face.

He couldn't focus. It was all his fault. *Amaris is... Fuck, I can't breathe. She's...She's fine. No...breathe. She was poisoned. It's my fault.*

"Is Amaris alright?"

"She is now."

"It's...fault." Theo choked.

"Theo, it's me. Take a deep breath for me."

He sucked in a breath, attempting to hold the air again.

"That's it. Now let it out."

He released his breath, but his chest still felt as though a rope were tied around it, and his head thrummed with every possible thought. He'd ruined everything. She wouldn't be escaping tonight in her state, but did she even want to? She'd said she wanted to stay, and she'd kissed him. Was it only an illusion from the poison and alcohol?

"Breathe, Theo."

He couldn't breathe.

"Maybe..."

Theo shook his head, his hand trying to reach for his nonexistent sword as the swarm of voices filled the room.

"Everyone out, now!" a voice demanded. "Come on, Theo. Take another breath."

Theo battled against every fiber in his body to breathe, but the ever-swarming emotions within him held their grip.

A hand circled his back. "Amaris is fine. You're fine. Take a deep breath."

He sucked in, holding it and pursing his lips. He followed several more cycles, the voice coaching him through each one. Swirls of color flourished in his vision, pulling him from the darkened tunnel. The feeling swept back into his fingertips. He scrunched them, dragging his nails across the firm hand that held his in its grasp. He blinked, willing his world to come back into focus and for his breaths to slow. Esaias was there.

"Inhale, exhale."

Theo breathed again, but the sight of Amaris on the bed was too much. His breaths were ragged, increasing in a faster cadence. "Amaris was poisoned."

"By the gods," Esaias muttered.

"Who did she talk to?" he shouted. "Where did she get her drink?"

"It was the one she picked up off the table." Esaias sat back on his heels.

Theo hung his head and wrapped his arms around it, curling himself into a ball and gripping his hair at the roots. "What are we going to do? My father still wants Amaris sent to Elric, and there's no way we can get her out now." He lifted his head, but even Amaris's even breaths couldn't pull him from the panic wrapping tightly around his lungs. Nothing could aid him in the rapid pounding of his heart.

"First, you need to try to calm down."

"I can't!" Theo shouted.

"I can't have an unconscious Amaris and you doped on cudweed. Try and breathe," Esaias demanded.

No. Theo wouldn't allow him to jab him with a needle like they'd done in the infirmary. Amaris needed him. He scrambled back. "Don't!"

Esaias gripped his shoulder. "Then, for Amaris's sake, pull yourself together."

"Not again," Theo muttered. "Not again." He dropped his head in his hands.

"What do you mean *not again*?"

"It's all...Amaris...not again," he muttered.

"Theo, what's going on with you? You're panicking. You haven't done this since..."

He couldn't do it. He knew if he told Esaias the truth, it'd rip an entire hole in his chest. But his body defied him. His hand trembled as he found his dagger and dragged it over the wooden floor. His thumb found its comforting place along the crest.

"Is this really about Amaris or—"

"Esaias," Theo cried, too ashamed to even look at him. He forced his eyes to stare at a loose nail pried from the floorboard as a tear leaked from the corner of his eye. "I can't let anyone else die. Not on my watch, not because I failed."

"Theo, it wasn't your fault."

"You don't know that," Theo snapped. "You weren't there."

"No, but I read the reports, and I was on the team that extracted you." Esaias sighed, and Theo met his solemn expression. "I saw you hanging there, nearly dead. My best friend, my brother." It was Esaias now who fought tears. "I was forced to guard the door while Sephardi and Gris cut you down and dragged you through the chamber. I could barely watch my post when all I saw was your blood covering every tool, every crevice, the floor."

Theo sucked in a breath. "I'm sorry."

"You have nothing to be sorry for. You were the one who was captured. You were tortured, while we were forced to wait. It killed me every day not knowing if you were alive, but I can't imagine what it was like for you."

There weren't words to describe what Theo had experienced. He doubted the cracks in the realm had torture like what Mosfelkov was capable of.

"They gutted Nate in front of me," Theo began, hiccuping between his panting breaths. "They strung him up, and I was bound and forced to watch as they cut him open, bit by bit, bleeding him." A wave of nausea rippled through him as the words slipped from his tongue. "Our friend... Nate was mutilated."

"Theo—"

"Nate is dead because of me. They killed him, not me," Theo cried. "When Nate couldn't take it anymore, they beat me and made me feel so much pain I wanted to die. I wish I'd died that night in Oystein Castle or in Rongstad Prison, because I don't deserve to live. They're all gone, because I failed as a leader. I failed to bring them home."

"You didn't fail. You were betrayed."

"I should've seen it, been smarter. We were ambushed from the start," Theo yelled, grasping his dagger and attempting to bring himself back to reality, to wash away the tint of red.

"You may not believe it now, but you did what you had to. You didn't give in, and Nate knew that too. Nate didn't die in vain. You both didn't break," Esaias said.

"They did break me! They didn't want information. They wanted me to suffer. Nate is dead, and now someone tried to kill Amaris." His body shook with his lament.

"No one else is going to die." Esaias let out an agonizing exhale as he placed a hand on Theo's shoulder.

Everything welling within Theo was overflowing, and he couldn't stop it. Amaris had told him to feel, not to bottle it up, but he couldn't contain it, no matter what he did. Why had he opened himself up to it, to feel the burden and agony of the loss of his friend?

"Nothing we do will bring them back or make ourselves forget, but we can honor them and remember them. You can honor Nate by fighting for Amaris," Esaias said. "What you went through made you a stronger leader."

"It made me a monster." The stitch in his mind frayed, the slithering creature of who he became seeping into his bones.

"You survived. Don't be ashamed of becoming the person you needed to be."

"But I am ashamed," Theo breathed.

"You have to forgive yourself."

Forgive myself? Theo had survived while every member of his squad had been slaughtered. "How can I? I still breathe, unable to make it a few days without a nightmare or a moment of panic."

"You have to learn. Remind yourself it wasn't your fault. No matter who led your squad, their fates would've been the same."

Esaias was right, but it didn't stop the wave after wave of emotion as it hit him harder. But as the sobs filled the tower and all of him was exposed for Esaias to see, Theo found himself not wanting to stop it. For once, he didn't want to push it away or restitch his mind. He wanted the pain to seep through his blood.

Could he learn to forgive himself? To ask the question was a weight lifted from his shoulders. A burden so heavy he'd allowed it to crush him. The rope around his chest loosened, and a natural cadence of breaths resumed. He could breathe, truly breathe. His back rippled as another wave of tears streaked his face.

Esaias stood and reached out his hand. Theo gazed up at him, the man who'd always been by his side.

In the infirmary, Esaias had sat by his side each day, getting leave until Theo was healed. But even after his body had mended, he couldn't get himself out of bed. Esaias had reached a hand into the darkness and stayed by Theo's side until he'd been ready to grasp it.

When Theo had been in the darkest part of his life, flashing back each second into that torture chamber, Esaias had been there to pull him back. To remind him what waited back home, that Adelaide and Jeremiah waited for him.

Theo reached out and grasped his hand.

"To the end," he whispered.

"To the end." Esaias smiled.

CHAPTER 35

Amaris

AMARIS OPENED HER eyes, feeling a small throb in her head. A warm light emanated through the room from the glowing fire beside her. She shifted her eyes, squinting. She was in the mystique tower.

What the hell! She sat up, feeling the immediate effects of a hangover. Her hands at her sides felt sticky, and through the foggy sleep lining her eyes, she made out red vomit stained into her dress. She dropped her head in her hands. *Did I seriously black out?*

A shrill scream alerted her she wasn't alone. Amaris rubbed at her sleep-filled eyes and pulled back to spot Pricilla running from one of the chairs beside the fireplace. With tears in her eyes, she curled up on the cot and embraced Amaris.

"You're alive," Pricilla cried.

"Of course, I'm alive." Amaris assessed the vomit stain ruining her gorgeous dress. "What happened? Did I do shots?"

"You don't remember?" She drew back.

"Getting ready with Adelaide, but that's about it." Amaris groaned. "I haven't blacked out in years."

Pricilla shook her head. "No, it wasn't the alcohol. You were poisoned."

Amaris's eyes widened. "I was what?"

"Poisoned." The smack of her head into her palms echoed through the tower. "The captain came rushing into the library with you."

"Wait, Theodoric? What about Esaias?"

"I'm not sure. Everything was chaotic. You weren't breathing. I don't even know how he kept you alive."

Rescue breathing. It had to be. Pride swelled in her chest, but the reason for the lifesaving maneuver swam to the forefront of Amaris's mind. "Who?"

"We don't know. Is it because someone is crazy enough to believe you're responsible for the soldier who died from scrying fever? Or is it because you tried to escape?"

A dark shiver settled over her, and Amaris wrapped her arms around herself. "Wait? How do you know?"

"That's what you're worried about?" Pricilla asked, confused. "I told you someone poisoned you, and you're wondering how I knew you were being kept under guard?"

Amaris only shrugged, contemplating whether she was growing accustomed to the idea of someone wanting her dead or if she was numb. It was an unsettling thought. "When did you find out?"

"I've known for a while. It doesn't take a lot of brains to decipher why you had a guard trailing you everywhere. I consulted my own sources and learned the truth. I also attempted to visit you in your room one night and found your door locked."

"You still wanted to be my friend after you found out?"

Pricilla wiped the tears from her cheeks and took Amaris's hands in her own. Her platinum hair was mussed, but old ringlets curled around the ends, and a few flowers were woven through the strands. At least her lavender tulle dress remained unscathed. "You've been kind to me."

Amaris only wished others thought the way she did, but her line of thinking was also naive. Pricilla was lucky she remained within the safety of the manor walls. The outside world was a cruel place, at least in her world.

"Do you think it was the chief?" Pricilla asked.

Amaris was pulled from her thoughts and shoved back into reality. She rubbed at her neck, not that it would aid the dryness of her windpipe. Someone had tried to kill her, but why? She was already about to be sent to Elric.

Amaris froze. "What if it's something else?" Her voice was frail. Pricilla would believe her; she'd be about the only person who would. What if someone had learned she was from a different world and that was why they tried to kill her?

"Why else would someone want you dead?"

She swallowed hard. "Do you remember what was in that journal you lent me?"

Pricilla tilted her head, studying her. "Yes...why?"

"What if I told you that it was true, all of it."

Pricilla's silence settled through the air like an ominous fog rolling through the dark on a humid morning. Immediately, Amaris wanted to hide within the ruffles of her dress.

"Are you saying it's possible to travel between realms?"

Amaris bit her lip, stopping herself from taking it all back. "I wouldn't be here if it wasn't."

Pricilla's gasp rung through the tower.

"I know you may not believe me," Amaris continued. "I can barely believe it myself most days. I come from the world Wineman described, a different part of it, but the same one." She swallowed a shaky breath. "The night they found me in the woods was when I fell through whatever portal he described. It's why I've been trying to escape, not only to get back to my life, but to my world."

Pricilla didn't reply. She sat with her lips parted and her eyes wide.

"Please say something."

"Do you still plan to go back?" Her whisper carried through the tower in a loud echo.

Amaris dreaded her words, fighting the sting they brought to her chest. She hadn't told Theodoric what his words meant to her. He'd offered her the choice of a different life. Not that it mattered now. The duke wanted her sent to Elric, and someone wanted her dead.

"I don't belong here." The words felt like a lie. She may not have remembered the Conjugation, but she remembered the question she'd asked herself while getting ready with Adelaide. *What if I stayed?*

"But what if you do? Maybe this is all supposed to happen. What if it wasn't a coincidence?"

Amaris felt as if the world was dropping onto her shoulders. "Is it a coincidence that, for a whole year, I've been verbally abused and berated at night to wake up to a completely different man who wants nothing more than to love me?" She coughed, attempting to keep her composure. "I only ran because he hit me."

"Amaris," she breathed, "I didn't know—"

"No one did, because I hid it. I was too afraid of what it would mean if I gave it true meaning. I faded away until all I had was healing people. I stopped drawing. I stopped living. I lived for others, risking my life, my friends' lives. I haven't been able to stop it. My life has spun out of control, and every time I look in the mirror, I fear the coward I'm becoming."

Pricilla took her hands in hers, not even knowing it was everything Amaris needed. She didn't have her mother to hold her after her fights with Derek or to tell her it was going to be all right.

"I may not know what your realm is like, but I understand pain. You may feel the burden of the realm on your shoulders, but it isn't yours to bear alone. You were brought here for a reason," Pricilla said, squeezing her hands tighter. "Everything happens for a reason."

"I don't know what to do." The fear lingering in her heart screamed to run, but something else tugged and whispered for her to stay.

"Do you truly want to go back?"

"I don't know what I want anymore." The truth liberated her, and she sighed. Who was she? All her life she'd wanted to become the next firefighter legacy. She wanted to help people and enjoyed being a paramedic, but what was she living for? For a year, she'd been lying to herself that she could fix her relationship with Derek, and now she'd pulled back the veil. She saw Derek for who he'd become, and it frightened her.

"Then stay," Pricilla said.

Amaris's eyes drift through the tower. The worktable was cluttered with opened jars of herbs, and a pipe sat on the corner. The sheet beneath her was no longer a foreign fabric, instead soft and warming. The tower was hers. Derek couldn't walk up the steps and demand she unlock the door or use the key he kept hidden.

All the signs had been there. For how long had she believed her relationship was normal when everyone around her had seen something different?

"But what about Viv? Is it selfish to leave her?"

"Only you can answer that." Pricilla rubbed a hand over Amaris's back. "But fight for the life you deserve."

Amaris wiped the snot from her face. "But the duke—"

"The captain and Esaias want to help you escape and build a new life. Allow them to do that for you here."

But what if the life she was beginning to envision for herself wasn't possible? What if she stayed and was caught? A life on the run was no life at all, but trapped in her own house was no different than being the duke's prisoner. Getting her fix for freedom by risking her safety at work was a different kind of reckless. It was suicidal and one she no longer wanted a part of.

Amaris hugged her legs to her chest, battling the tear ripping a hole in her chest.

CHAPTER 36

Theo

AS THEO STOOD guard of the tower steps with his dagger in hand, he waited for Esaias to return with the bags for their journey and his sword. Each second sent a drop of sweat down his back, and not even the coolness of the library could contain the heat building within him. Amaris wanted to stay.

Esaias's panting breaths came from down the way. He handed Theo his sword, which he promptly tied to his belt before racing up the steps. All thoughts eluded him. Should he embark on the journey with her or beg her to stay and find a way to resolve everything?

Someone tried to poison her! Theo reminded himself. Luana Bay wasn't safe for her anymore. The walls of his childhood home felt wrong. It was where he'd grown and expected to live his entire life.

He opened the tower door and saw Amaris sitting up on the cot with Pricilla at her side. He didn't have time, though, to send a prayer of thanks to the gods.

"We need to get her out of here now. Adelaide is waiting for us with the boat," Esaias announced. He threw Amaris's bag to her.

She caught it, pausing as she slid her hand over the fabric. With a sigh, she stood and stepped behind the worktable, rummaging through her pack and beginning to get dressed. Theo averted his eyes but caught the subtle shake of her hands.

He turned, and Pricilla was there. She grabbed him by the cuff of his shirt and pulled him to the other side of the room. Her arms folded across her chest, and she pouted. "Are we going to discuss how you *tasted* the poison on her lips?"

There was an easy answer for that. "Another time."

Amaris came back around the worktable. Before Theo could run to her, Pricilla snagged his arm.

"She doesn't remember," she whispered, offering a sympathetic look.

His heart plummeted. *The Conjugation? Our kiss?*

"What do you mean?" Theo asked, struggling to hold himself together.

"She doesn't know who spiked her drink or even what happened during the Conjugation, whatever happened." Pricilla raised a brow. "But I think she doesn't want to leave."

Theo turned to Amaris, who sniffled as she folded her ruined gown and set it on the bed. She rubbed the tulle between her scarred fingers. "Do you want to go?"

She turned over her shoulder, her lips slightly parted.

"What are you talking about?" Esaias cut in. "Of course, she wants to leave. Your father—"

Theo closed the distance between them. "Amaris, if you want to leave, we'll take you out to the boat right now. But if you want to stay, I'll find a way."

"Are we forgetting—"

"How?" Amaris cut Esaias off.

Theo desperately clawed at his mind, deciphering anything that could work. Amaris was a brilliant mystique and had proven herself ten times over. "I'll speak to my father."

"Because that worked so well the first time," Esaias interjected.

"Not since she stepped in when Bennet whipped me." Theo straightened up. "If it wasn't for you, I would still be on that cot, barely able to move. You healed Esaias of scrying fever and brought breath back to my lungs. They only want someone to blame. Luther said my father took convincing. That means there's still a chance."

It was a small chance, but one Theo was willing to take. To have Amaris stay and give her the chance to remember what they'd shared sparked hope in him. If she wanted to stay, he'd defend her with his last breath. He would be dead if it wasn't for her. He owed her his life.

"I..." Her voice was raspy.

He wanted to move, to pull her to his chest and show her what their kiss had meant to him and hopefully to her. But before he could reach out, an explosion shook the tower.

He threw himself at her and pinned her to floor. She winced beneath him as the walls shook.

"Was that—" Esaias began.

"Cannon fire," Theo called, poking his head up. Esaias was crouched over Pricilla, dust and debris raining over them.

Theo pulled Amaris to her feet. Another blast sounded, shaking the ceiling and sending more bits of dust falling around them. His blood filled with the rage of war. The monster within him slithered to the edge of his mind without a hidden stitch to hide behind. Theo breathed and allowed the creature from the depths of his mind to wait. He couldn't unleash it.

"Did you say cannon fire?" Amaris asked, the whites of her eyes overtaking the oceans.

"Both of you get downstairs and barricade the door. Don't let anyone in, understand?" Theo ordered.

"But, Theodoric—"

"No, Amaris," he shouted. "Lock yourselves in and don't leave until I come and get you."

His gentle composure was gone, replaced by the commanding officer. She took a breath but nodded. He wanted to pull her to him and give her a moment to remember what they shared, but this was his home, regardless of what he told himself. The surviving memories of his mother resided within its walls. He forced himself to turn away and headed down the steps.

Theo and Esaias sprinted through the library and into the hall. Chaos ensued around them. Another cannon blast sent the walls shaking and the portraits shattering as they hit the ground.

"What in the bloody crack in the realm are you two still doing inside? Get your asses out there now!" Bennet snapped from down the hall.

He stormed toward them, two swords drawn and a look of brutal conquest in his eyes. Theo gripped the hilt of his sword, mainly to hold his composure as he stalked closer, but also to show he wouldn't be afraid. Bennet had been testing him ever since he returned home, attempting to break him, to see if he'd truly become a soldier or if he'd cower under his thumb.

Bennet stood before him, their noses inches apart. There wasn't a whiff of alcohol on his breath. "Are you ready to defend your people or are you planning to hide that *bitch* who killed one of my men?"

Was he the one to poison her?

Theo leaned in, forcing Bennet to balk. "Amaris didn't kill that soldier, and I'll defend my people, not to show you my loyalty, but because that has never been in doubt. My allegiance is to Luana, my home. You and my father can throw whatever you wish at me, but I'll protect everyone of Luana Bay, and that includes Amaris. She saves people, and you'll see that soon enough."

Bennet released a snarl. "Gather a few soldiers and defend the western entrance," he grumbled. "Several are already positioned along the gardens, but we need more. Grab them from the southern doors. They're making their push along the coast."

The metal of Theo's sword dug into his palm. "Who?"

Bennet flared his nostrils and said, "Deavopan." His tone grew colder. "Esaias, stick with him, and both of you try not to get killed." He took off at a sprint for the northern entrance.

Another blast echoed through the hall, and Theo rolled to the side as a large portrait attempted to squash him.

Esaias bent forward, resting his hands on his knees. "What in all of Magoria is going on? Why would they attack us?"

"I don't know," Theo breathed. "My father has been obsessed with incriminating Amaris instead of focusing on Duncaster. What if they killed Freville and left his body as a diversion?"

Drawing his sword, Esaias twirled the silver blade with a smirk. "Look who's thinking like an officer again." He reached out his other hand, waiting to pull Theo along.

Theo didn't have time to further ponder the implications. He grasped Esaias's hand to fight for them, Amaris, and his people. He hauled him to his feet, and they once again went into battle.

CHAPTER 37

Amaris

AMARIS LATCHED ON to Pricilla, dragging her from the shaking tower and into the safety of the library, or at least where she'd thought they'd be safe. Amaris gaped in horror at what had befallen the library. Bookcases had tipped over, spilling their contents and scattering pages across the floor. Silent tears spilled from Pricilla's eyes, but Amaris squeezed her hand and pulled her along.

Gone were the swirling emotions building within her. Her only focus was on how to survive the night. She held tight to Pricilla's hand. They needed a safe space to hide from the enemy soldiers and the swaying shelves threatening to topple over. A shriek froze them in place, and Amaris's heart leapt from her chest. Lying crushed beneath a pile of rubble was what had once been a person. Blood pooled around the stone. Only a single leg was exposed.

Another blast rung through the air, and Pricilla threw herself into her, but Amaris couldn't take her eyes from the pool swelling with each of her passing breaths. She had to do something.

"I'm going to help the wounded."

"But—"

"Find anyone who's willing to bring my supplies from the tower to the kitchen."

The first thing in a mass casualty situation was to begin tagging the wounded and creating a triage. The sheer size of the kitchen would accommodate her needs, along with having access to fireplaces and water, but the real necessity of the kitchen was its proximity to the bay.

"Amaris, mystiques don't go into battle."

She took a sharp breath. "This one does."

Pulling from Pricilla's grasp, she took off with a force of pure determination toward the kitchen. The manor had been ripped into complete confusion and chaos. All around her, soldiers spilled through the halls with their swords raised and piercing gleams in their eyes. But Amaris could only focus on the beating of her heart and the possible number of bodies piling up beyond the manor walls.

Amaris squeezed through the crowds of people, cold sweat beading down her back. Another blast shook the walls, extinguishing several torches.

"If you can't fight, head to the library for safety!" she shouted, confidently.

A few people nearby watched in horror as she charged against the swarm toward the battle. Others heeded her warning and bolted for the library.

She didn't know what she expected to find or how she'd even begin setting up a triage for a disaster of this magnitude, but she was going to try her damnedest to save as many people as she could. Fuck the duke and Bennet. No one deserved to die because of them. She'd fight to stay and help, even if she paid for it later.

Once in the kitchen, she leaned into her knees, choking back the taste of iron. The doors leading to the gardens were barricaded with tables, chairs, anything to keep out the enemy, *and the wounded soldiers.*

Amaris immediately began pulling at chairs, but a sharp voice halted her movements.

"Get away from the barricade!"

She spun on her heels to face Alan with his sword clutched in his hand, ready to pounce. Screams broke out on the other side of the doors. The hairs along her arms spiked.

"Someone could be injured," she snapped back, stepping closer and forcing Alan back.

Pounding came from the barricade and a muffled scream. As Amaris ran to begin dragging tables away, another explosion blasted against the manor wall. Dust fell from the ceiling, and the chandelier rattled, sending candles to the ground to extinguish and further wrap them in the darkness of the dimly lit kitchen. Even more screams came from the other side, and fists beat against the door.

"I'm moving these tables with or without you."

Alan didn't latch his arm around her or drag her back as she threw chairs out of the way and shoved tables to the side.

"I was instructed that, under no circumstance, should this barricade to be moved!"

"Someone's hurt and could be dying."

Alan took several agonizing heartbeats, as his hand tightened around his sword. His eyes swept over Amaris and shifted to the continuous shouts of the soldiers on the other side, growing with their anxiety to make it inside.

People needed Amaris's help, and all she had to do was move the stupid barricade. She threw her back into a table and grunted as she slid it across the floor. As she leapt toward the barricade to grab another, Alan gripped the other side of the table and dragged it away. She balked but pressed forward. Her time to stop and think was over. She could only act.

Soon, a path was formed, and Amaris removed the wooden plank holding the doors closed. They busted open, and Gerard barreled into the room with a man slung over his shoulder.

"Where's Ms. Borstad?" he shouted, setting the man on the nearest table

Ms. Borstad? Amaris questioned why he would be calling for her when a useful paramedic was standing right in front of him.

At the sound of her name, Ms. Borstad came running, but at the sight of the blood, she stopped, and her eyes widened. "What can I do?" She peeled her attention from Gerard and swung her gaze to Amaris.

Gerard leaned over the wounded man, pressing his hand against the blood seeping from a gash in his leg. "This man needs attention."

Ms. Borstad's eyes lingered on Amaris as she stood with her hands balled into fists at her sides. The audacity. Gerard shot Amaris a disdainful glare before he sneered and pounded his fist on the table. The man's near-lifeless body shook upon the impact.

Amaris stood with her spine erect and her heart beating against the cavity within her chest. Adrenaline coursed through her body, her mind tunneling. "Ms. Borstad, I need as much cloth as you can muster, and I need the tools and herbs brought down from my tower. Pricilla should—"

"I'm here," Pricilla announced with a large basket in hand.

Amaris ran and threw her arms around her. "Thank you," she said. "Now get back to the library."

Onika stood behind her, her golden-brown eyes shrinking as she took in the scene. "We're not leaving," Onika said, swallowing and shaking her head. "We're here to help. All of us."

Amaris caught movement behind them, and dozens filed into the kitchen with baskets and trunks full of herbs, cloth, and tools.

I have a team.

"What we need is a real mystique, not you," Gerard spewed.

He was cruel, but Amaris had dealt with much worse in her career. She'd been spat at, puked on, and shit on. Gerard's bullshit was nothing compared to what she'd seen or dealt with in the field.

"You listen to me." She stuck out her finger and shoved it into his chest. "I am the mystique. This man needs medical attention, and I can give it to him." She leaned closer, narrowing her eyes as she ground her teeth against his ugly sneer. "Now get out of my fucking way."

Amaris felt alive, fighting the nervous energy skittering through her at her defiance. Gerard didn't budge, but he eyed the others around her, willing to risk their lives to stand on the edge of the line.

"This man die if pale girl don't help," Ms. Borstad said with such authority and intimidation that it startled Amaris. She was glad she was on her good side. "You may not see what pale girl did for Theodoric when you sliced back open, but he did." She pointed a crooked finger at Alan. "She will save him."

Gerard stood tall and puffed his chest out. His glare shifted to Alan. Amaris waited for Alan to agree with his father and drag her to the dungeons.

"She's more than capable," Alan said.

Amaris was stunned. Had the gods of the realm finally answered her prayers?

"If anything happens to him..." Before Gerard finished his threat, he charged through the door.

"Get in line," Amaris shouted, bolting to her patient lying on the table.

His complexion was a gravely pale color, and he couldn't speak past a moan. She grabbed her knife and cut open the tear in his pants. He had a large laceration to his right lower leg, with heavy bleeding, but Amaris sighed with relief to see no spurting blood. *It's not arterial.*

She grabbed a handful of cloth and exerted pressure on the wound. A scruffy-looking man with the reek of fish hefted the man's leg up while she bound a strip of cloth around it to keep constant pressure and control the bleeding.

Amaris faced her helpers, braiding her hair back tightly, readying herself for what was to come. "I know some of you might be scared." *She* for sure was and would be lying to herself if she considered the knot in her stomach only indigestion. Instead of casting her fear aside, she embraced it. The surge of adrenaline wrapped itself around her heart, and she used it to channel her words and movements. "We're all they've got. We must move swiftly and quickly."

She pointed to several of the men and women with baskets. "Keep the fires going and begin boiling water. Alan, gather as much alcohol as you can." She'd need some form of an anesthetic to aid in the pain. She doubted she had enough cudweed. "Pricilla and Onika, start organizing the herbs and make baskets for everyone. Place a bottle of alcohol in each, bandage squares, linen, and several belts."

They both nodded and began following Amaris's instructions. The remainder started righting tables and took over attending to their first patient. Amaris closed her eyes to breathe. She'd never been a part of a mass casualty situation. They'd done table discussions at work to prepare for the insurmountable odds that would be stacked against them. But she'd never hung a tag over someone's neck and left them for another paramedic to continue their care. Before the chaos had even begun, Amaris knew she never wanted to experience it again.

She watched as a makeshift triage formed. Ms. Borstad tended to the fire, and she sent someone to grab every bit of cloth they could find. Alan returned with more than enough bottles of liquor, but Amaris sent him again to procure belts, in case she needed to fashion tourniquets.

Esaias barged through the door carrying someone in his arms.

"Put him here." Amaris gestured to the next free table space. The young soldier was unconscious but breathing. "What happened?"

"I don't know," Esaias began, panting as he leaned against the table. Blood dripped from his face and splashed a single dot on the table. His shirt was soaked with it.

"Esaias, where are you injured?" She scanned him head to toe, looking for the source of the bleeding.

He almost laughed. "It's not mine."

"Is—"

"He's fine, but you shouldn't worry about him. It seems you have enough to deal with." He gathered himself in one large breath and charged back out into the night.

Amaris returned her attention to the young soldier and took a breath to compose herself, repeating what every paramedic knew by heart. *The smoother I move, the quicker I'll be.*

She attempted to rouse the soldier and rubbed her knuckles against his sternum, but he didn't move. A large goose egg poked through the scraggly locks of his hair, but he had no other signs of trauma. His pupils were equal and reacted to the candlelight, and a strong pulse beat in his wrist.

"Peter," Alan cried, racing over to their new patient. His hands shook as he took the soldier's face between them, brushing back the sweaty strands of his hair.

"He'll be alright," Amaris whispered, landing a gentle hand against Alan's arm. "He's only knocked out."

Alan collapsed beside him, but Amaris didn't have time to deal with anything other than physical wounds.

She turned to the door in anticipation of her next patient, but there was no one. She should've felt relieved, but the knot within her stomach tightened. Returning to her first patient, she assessed the bandage. His eyes fluttered open, and she obliged him with a glass of kusu for the pain and his anxious nerves. The pallor of his skin worried her, but Magoria seemed given to quick healing. Maybe he'd be back on his feet in a matter of days.

Without a wound to wrap, bleeding to control, or a patient's hand to hold, her nerves took over. She grabbed the mystique journal Pricilla had graciously brought down and rifled through the contents. She'd briefly read about an herb with coagulation properties and its ability to deal with blood loss.

Fade chicory. Ground leaves into a powder substance. Coagulation properties to staunch heavy bleeding.

She raced for the table of herbs and found numerous jars already ground into powder. "Pricilla, make sure a jar of this goes into the baskets."

"Already on it," Pricilla called back, offering a wink as she filled a basket.

Another explosion shook the building, sending Amaris into a crouched ball. A few others followed suit, but Alan paid no heed to the quaking, as if he had no doubt the structure would hold. Amaris had her doubts as the chandelier swayed above their heads, threatening to rain more candles on them.

The garden doors remained open, but not a single soul stood on the threshold. There had to be more injured. Too many screams filled the empty void. Amaris grabbed a satchel and filled it with squares of cloth, belts, and a dozen rolls of linen. She rechecked the security of her knife, taking a deep breath as her fingers ran across the ribbed hilt. No one paid her any attention until she was at the doors.

"Amaris, no!" Pricilla shouted after her.

Amaris wrapped her hands around the strap of her satchel and took off through the doors. She drowned out the cries behind her, knowing they wouldn't dare chase after her, not with what she was running into.

CHAPTER 38

Amaris

LANTERNS SWUNG AS the wind picked up, and the fires within hissed and extinguished as the beginnings of a storm filled the sky. The first drop was gentle, then a stream of rain poured over Luana Bay.

Clinks and gunshots rang through the air as blades clashed and pistols were fired. Amaris slipped through the smoke of gunfire billowing in a lazy cloud around the gardens, obscuring herself. She didn't allow herself to stop and think. If she did, she feared she'd turn back.

She waited for someone to burst through a shrub or come barreling down one of the garden paths, but it was eerily empty. She'd heard the whispers when she'd run through the manor. *Deavopan? Bazrath? Deavonian Accord?* None of which she knew the meaning of. It wasn't until she slid to a crouch behind the half stone wall circling the gardens that she allowed her mind a moment to consider. *How will I even know who Luana's soldiers are versus the enemy?* She doubted anyone had had time to change into their uniforms.

The reek of iron filled her nostrils. Poking her head around the wall, the chaos of the battlefield unraveled around her. Navy tunics with swashes of red scattered the grounds, breaking past the defenses. Amaris immediately spotted what was likely the Luana forces—the men and women dressed in fine attire. The hems of dresses were ripped, and coats and vests were thrown to the ground. Duels broke out, and cries were silenced with the slash of a blade. Soon enough, bodies would begin to scatter across the grounds.

Her eyes scanned the terrain. Not twenty yards away, a woman in a black tunic lay in the grass. She was still alive, her chest moving erratically with rapid breaths. Amaris stayed low, moving into a crawl through the mud and long grass. The soldier's breath grew shallow when Amaris reached her. She fought the voice in her head shouting that she wouldn't make it. The soldier would live if she had anything to say about it.

"Where are you injured?" she whispered as best she could over the sound of battle and the thundering overhead.

"My leg," the soldier cried hoarsely.

Amaris slipped a finger over her lips, her eyes wandering to the fighting around them. She needed to be quiet, or they'd both end up dead. The soldier nodded, crinkling the hood spilling around her auburn locks. With only a few remaining lanterns scattered in the night to guide her, Amaris followed the woman's leg down to her foot, at least where her foot *should've* been. All that was left was a bloody stump with frayed tendons.

"What's your name?" Amaris whispered as she pulled a belt from her satchel and secured it around the soldier's thigh.

"Ediva." She winced but bit down on her screams as Amaris tugged against the leather.

"Stay here. I'll find someone to bring you inside."

"Don't leave me," Ediva begged, fear in her eyes, not of death, but to be alone when the end came.

More people were out there who needed her help.

"I can't," Amaris muttered.

Before Ediva could latch on to her shirt, Amaris rolled away and crawled deeper into the chaos. After getting out of her earshot, she bit her sleeve, forcing back the tears. She couldn't think about her. All she could do was tag, treat, and move on. She shouldn't have asked for her name. She'd never left a patient before, always seeing their care to the end, but not tonight.

Amaris froze as a fight broke out with a navy-dressed soldier charging up the slope. The ring of metal through her ears sent her teeth chattering as he met his opponent, a woman with her teeth bared and blood spilling down her bare shins where she'd torn her skirt. Amaris kept moving, looking for someone else to help.

They'd practiced mass casualty events when she'd been in school. The goal had been to save as many as possible but to know one's limitations. Amaris had tried saving everyone then, but tonight she was the only mystique for miles. It had to be her.

A man lying sprawled out in the grass caught her eye. He was face down, but she watched his chest rise. She got him on his side, turning him onto his back. She let out a small yelp and fell back. His navy tunic was sliced down the center, with blood smeared into the fabric.

She swallowed, but nagging guilt built up as she started to turn away. With a breath, she went against common sense telling her to move on. She opened his tunic to reveal a large gash, exposing his intestines. *An evisceration,* she noted, but before she could dress the wound, his eyes shot open.

He lunged, pinning Amaris's arms as he straddled her. His guts spilled from his abdomen. Yards of gooey organs poured onto her chest. She fought the urge to vomit as they rolled onto her neck. She tried to let out a scream but only managed an awful gag.

The man leaned into her face, completely unfazed by his bowels between them. Amaris wiggled and attempted to break free from his grasp, but for a dying man, he was strong as hell. A line of bloody spit dripped down his lips to land on her cheek. Her eyes widened, but he took a single breath before more blood spilled from his lips and his eyes rolled back in his head. A sword had skewered his body, and Amaris shrieked as a boot kicked him off her.

"Amaris?"

She was still in the grass, blood and intestines scattered across her shirt as her vision focused in on Theodoric's face. His hands reached around her, pulling her to her feet. Her throat dried, even as raindrops pelted her lips.

"What are you doing out here?" He was angry, storms immediately filling his eyes. Gone were the golden drops of sunlight, taken over by the soldier within.

He's alive. Amaris displayed her bloody hands before them.

"Are you hurt?" he asked, but she couldn't speak.

She only stared at her hands, the blood seeping into the chapped ridges of her knuckles and the lines of her palms. Her gaze didn't move as Theodoric's fingers grasped a stray hair coated in blood clinging to her cheek. His thumb grazed her skin, wiping away the red before it stained. Amaris stared at the blood dripping down her forearms, her heartbeats drowning out all around her.

Theodoric kneeled, untucking her shirt as he slid his hands around her abdomen to feel for cuts. His hands were rough with calluses and strong as they wrapped around each limb and felt for injuries.

"Amaris!" He shook her.

She dragged her eyes to meet his. *He's alive. I'm alive.* His shirt was ripped in two, and blood splattered across his face and chest. She swallowed, the gravity sinking into her bones. He wasn't a soldier as she knew him, none of them were. An assault rifle wasn't slung over his shoulder. He was only several inches from a man when he took his life.

Her hands ceased their trembling, and they began searching for any visible injury. She brushed the hair from his forehead, coated in sweat not blood. She was rendered speechless, unable to form a thought as she scanned his bare chest for any life-threatening injuries. Her fingers scoured every inch of his chest, arms, neck, and face. There wasn't a single cut. She tried to gaze at the wounds on his back, but he stopped her and grasped her shoulders.

"I'm not wounded," he whispered.

Amaris shook her head, snapping back to reality. "You better not be wounded." It was like earmuffs were ripped off her ears and everything hyper-focused. "Fuck, if I'm running out here just to see everyone splattered dead in the grass, I'm unleashing hell on this realm," she said, fire turning to rage in her eyes.

She was focused. She was a paramedic.

"Not that it isn't a joy to see you alive," Esaias called, "but we have more pressing matters." He jabbed a thumb toward an incoming horde of navy-suited soldiers fresh from the beach.

"You shouldn't be out here." Theodoric pulled her closer.

She could barely smell his salt and leather, masked by the reek of sweat and blood. "We removed the barricade and—"

"You did what?" Theodoric burst out.

"People are out here. I can't leave them to die!"

The cry of battle loomed closer.

"Theo," Esaias warned.

"Get back to the manor."

"I won't," Amaris declared, planting her feet in the ground.

"Theo." Esaias grew more impatient.

"You almost died, and I won't allow anyone else to harm you," Theodoric insisted, but Amaris stood her ground, even with her heart skipping in her chest.

"You'll have to drag me back before I leave this battlefield."

Theodoric's eyes trailed down her figure, making note of her crossed arms and anger in her eyes. She swore he smiled, but the slight feather of his cheek distracted her, and he lunged. Grabbing a hold of her waist, he lifted her over his shoulder.

"Put me down!"

"When you're inside—"

"Theo!" Esaias's yelp was sharper than the blade he plunged into a soldier's chest.

Theodoric tossed Amaris behind him and brought his arm up to shield them. His sword met the next blade. The muscles of his back tightened with his push forward, opening another wound. His blood mixed with the sweat and rain and trickled down, soaking the waistband of his pants. The soldier's white teeth were a vibrant contrast to his deep-umber skin. He gritted against his strength. Theodoric brought his leg up and kicked the soldier in the chest, leaving a muddy boot print across his blood-smeared tunic. But the man only stumbled before swinging his sword again. Their feet were ever moving, circling their prey, neither yielding.

Theodoric didn't tire. His breaths were even as he danced the duel. His eyes met Amaris's. There wasn't worry but a direct order to get inside. She shook her head as he finished the soldier with a single swipe of his sword to the neck.

A booming erupted from the bay, leading to the screeching of a cannonball overhead. Before Amaris could run, Theodoric was on top of her, shielding her body from the blast. It hit the wall and sent several chunks of stone raining down. He grunted as pieces of debris scattered around them and pelted his back. Her breath had escaped her when he'd pressed her into the grass, but his warmth against her further ceased her efforts to breathe. His hand tightened around her middle as another cannon fired. His heart thundered against her, and she knew if she could feel his, then he most certainly felt the skipping and tumbling of hers.

"Get inside," he demanded. "Stay close to Adelaide."

"She isn't there."

As he lifted his body from hers, breath filled Amaris's lungs. Their gazes both turned to the beach. Adelaide was supposed to be getting the boat ready. A startling realization hit. She was either still fighting down there or dead.

"Go back to the manor," he said, his eyes darkening.

Before she could protest, Theodoric spun, and his blade pierced the chest of another soldier, who collapsed to the ground. As he removed his sword, the silver shine was replaced with crimson blood.

Amaris couldn't move. Paralyzed. *Was it fear or shock?* She couldn't pull her eyes from Theodoric's stance. He unsheathed his dagger, and his sword clashed with his next victim. His sleeve ripped and curled around his wrist. The muscles in his arm tensed with each swing of his sword. With another jab, he pierced his next attacker's heart. She couldn't leave. Esaias and Theodoric were both engaged in combat and maybe wouldn't get to Adelaide in time. She could be injured.

Theodoric stayed close as Amaris crept up the path toward the gardens. She'd find a different route to the beach, staying far off to the side so as to not raise suspicion. When she no longer sensed his lingering footsteps, she dared a look back. He was fighting three soldiers, all armed and circling him. One had two cutlasses trained on Theodoric, while the others hesitated in their approach. With a roar, they charged. He parried each strike and hit skin with each of his own. There was no flinch or cry as blood splattered his face. He didn't halt when their bodies fell around him, nor did he stop when more soldiers raced to meet his blade.

Amaris stepped back, her legs jelly beneath her. Esaias joined him back-to-back. They moved swiftly, each an extension of the other. Where one faltered, the other guarded, neither giving up the other's blind side.

Amaris wished for a weapon she knew how to wield, for her bow that remained hidden beneath a tarp in her garage. She gripped her satchel, her mind for medicine the one true weapon she had. She wasn't on Earth anymore or walking the streets of Gainesville. Automatic weapons or bows with a scope had no place in Magoria. She felt utterly useless, but she had to try.

She crouched and crawled through the grass, hiding from view as she went to the side arch she'd passed through what felt so long ago. She'd get to the beach and find Adelaide.

CHAPTER 39

Theo

AMARIS WAS ON the battlefield. Theo couldn't believe it. She'd had the nerve to run out here, unarmed no less. He shouldn't have been surprised, since she was the most stubborn woman he'd ever met. His heart had been set ablaze when he kicked the Deavopan soldier off her and he saw her beautiful face. Seeing her covered in his blood had nearly brought him to his knees. She could've been killed.

Theo shook his head. He couldn't think of Amaris. He needed to find a way to break free to find Adelaide. A sword sliced through the air, but he heaved his own and matched their swing. A face poked out from behind the blade, and Theo stalled, almost dropping his guard.

"Isabel," he whispered.

The woman with her raised sword and freckled cheeks had bright-orange hair poking out from under the bleeding black dye, but he wasn't mistaken. The serpents on her boots glowed against the lightning striking along the skyline. She wore brown leather armor instead of Deavopan's military tunics. Isabel stood before him, but she didn't seem fazed as she moved with feline grace.

A sharp smirk painted her lips. "Hey, big guy. Apparently, you didn't figure out my warning."

Isabel was one of them. The whole time she'd deceived him, *or had she?*

"You?" Esaias shouted over the rain. "I thought you were destined for a long drop on a short rope."

Isabel ground her teeth as she skimmed her sword against Theo's. "Sorry to disappoint," she said but didn't remove her gaze from Theo. The black dye continued to seep from her hair, dripping down her face.

Theo held his blade firm. "You knew of the attack. It's why you stopped me on the docks."

Isabel scoffed. "And you thought me a lonely woman from Duncaster. Some soldier you are."

Theo allowed her taunts to roll off his back as he trained his eyes on hers, their golden hue tightening a muscle in his chest. Why did he know those eyes?

Before Theo could contemplate the origin of such a vivid color, she pulled back and pounced on Esaias. He blocked her lunge, but her feet moved swiftly as she twirled through the rain, grabbing a fallen sword. Her movements were fluid in the downpour, like she'd done it for years. The droplets were her fueling power.

"You can fuck off to your hovel in the Black Sea," Esaias barked, spitting blood into the mud. A split lip trickled more down his chin as he breathed.

"But where's the fun in that?"

Theo and Esaias circled Isabel. How had she escaped the jail? Isabel feinted a lunge and laughed as Esaias stumbled. Twirling her blades, she seemed more amused to toy with them instead of drawing blood.

"Fight us," Theo shouted.

"Maybe I like to play with my prey before I kill it." Her golden eyes burned bright, imprinting deeper into Theo's mind as they flared with her smile.

"Enough of this." Esaias slashed with his sword, but she rolled out of the way, caking herself in mud as she slid to a stop. With a growl, he charged, and the ring of their blades pierced Theo's ears.

Theo lunged forward, hitting her other sword to spare Esaias his left flank.

"You're no fun," Isabel pouted.

"What do you want?" Theo gritted his teeth.

She inclined a brow, stepping back, but she held her guard with both swords trained on them. "Wealth, power, pride. Take your pick."

"Pride in what?" Theo snapped. "Killing innocent people?"

"You call yourselves innocent?"

Caught in the shock in her voice, Theo was too slow to block her foot as she slammed it into his knee. He buckled, falling to the ground in a heap as pain and bursts of agony shot up his leg. Isabel raised her sword to end his suffering, but Esaias was there and blocked her blow.

As Theo cradled his knee, attempting to breathe through the pain, Esaias drew away her assault. He gritted his teeth, looming over her like the warrior he was. His next swing sliced her leg and split open her trousers, spilling blood.

Isabel bit her lip, containing her scream as Esaias stepped closer, going in for another attack. Isabel parried his blow, but her footwork was off as she limped and favored her leg. Esaias spun his sword, blocking her next few swipes as she threw whatever she had into the fray of their duel. With a single move, Esaias disarmed her of one blade.

Theo tried to stand, forcing the pain in his knee behind what was left of his mental shields. With a hiss, he took one step, but his leg buckled again. He couldn't stuff his pain down. Isabel watched his movements but regained her focus as Esaias went in for a kill shot. Isabel ducked, but Esaias clipped the edge of a braid, slicing through her hair.

She reached for the severed end and screamed. "Godwin is falling. While the noble bastards spend their time drowning themselves in luxury, everyone else is left to fend for themselves. People are dying, and you're too proud to see it!"

"I wouldn't think someone from Deavopan would care what happened to the common people of Godwin," Esaias grumbled.

"Who said I was from Deavopan?" Isabel smirked.

"You're from Godwin?" Esaias staggered from his quest of vengeance.

"I see these countries for what they really are. They're run by people who only care about lining their pockets."

"If you truly cared about people dying, then why attack?"

"Casualties are a part of life. These rulers didn't seem to care when they shipped off good people to war."

"Did you know someone?" Theo asked, forcing his leg to hold him up, to push the swelling away as he hefted his sword up and angled the blade at her.

Isabel ground her teeth, and the knuckles around her sword burned white. "You all deserve to burn!"

Isabel slid under Esaias's next attack, but he caught her with his leg, pinning her to the ground. Their blades struck as he pressed her into the mud. She ground her teeth against his crushing strength. Blood leaked from Esaias's lip, dripping along her forehead.

Theo raised his sword to take the final blow. The cold metal between his hands froze. The rain washed the remaining dye from her hair, and her bright orange shown through. Her golden eyes widened as he approached. Theo sucked in a breath, his feet unmoving as he took in the familiar sight, those eyes once again filled with fear before the light faded from them.

Isabel's gaze darted between Theo and Esaias. She took Theo's moment of reprieve and slid her leg out from under Esaias and kicked Theo's knee again. His scream and collapse snapped Esaias's head up, but it was all she needed. She drove her legs into Esaias's chest, grabbed her other sword, and began her stumbling retreat.

"Elizabeth!" Theo screamed after her.

She whipped around, her feet taking slow steps back as her chest heaved. "It's Isabel now."

"Elizabeth, as in Harwood?" Esaias gasped.

Theo didn't know how he couldn't see it before. That same smirk graced her lips, and those eyes, ones he saw for years and smiled and laughed with.

"Nate's little sister," Theo breathed, grasping his knee.

Isabel stiffened at the sound of her brother's name. Her feet continued to carry her back, but she raised her sword and pointed it at Theo. "Don't you dare speak his name."

"You've known. You knew who I was in Duncaster," Theo said. "Why are you with Deavopan, the Accords?"

"Your father sent him to his death!"

Theo didn't need to stand any closer to know tears streaked her cheeks. "Elizabeth, your parents—"

"It's Isabel," she spat. "They lost it when Nate died. Your father destroyed my family. You have no idea what life is like outside the safety of your manor walls, and you never will." She turned and ran.

Theo forced his body forward, limping as he attempted to chase after her. Nate's death had driven her to treason, to desert her own people. Esaias grabbed a hold of his arm, halting him as Isabel disappeared, lost to the darkness.

"She's a traitor!"

"It's Nate's sister, Esaias. I can't leave her."

"You will, because we have greater problems. We need to get you inside," he said, eyeing Theo's leg.

"I'm fine," Theo lied, already feeling his knee swelling against his trousers. "We're going to the beach." Theo needed to find Adelaide first, then he'd track down Isabel.

"Adelaide," Esaias breathed.

Theo took another limp forward, summoning whatever he had left to fight.

"Theo, what if—"

"I won't entertain what ifs," Theo shouted at him. "I'm going to find my sister."

Adelaide could be fighting for her life on that beach or worse. Theo ripped the remnants of his shirt and wrapped it around his knee, biting his lip against the ache. He clawed at the fissure in his mind, begging it to restitch and hold the pain.

Esaias nodded, and they took off toward the beach, taking the empty path along the southern border. A few duels were scattered about, but it wasn't the chaos ensuing past the gardens. Theo stopped upon reaching the sand, his knee threatening to buckle on the uneven terrain. He couldn't force it back without allowing the creature to fully infest his mind.

"Are you sure you're able to fight?" Esaias asked, staring at Theo's swollen knee.

"I can fight," Theo hissed, but the swelling was already pressing against the wrap. He had to keep moving, for Adelaide.

"Is that...?" Esaias pointed to a discarded jacket.

In a mix between a shuffle and limp, Theo dropped before the jacket and grabbed the leather coat in his hands. *Adelaide.* His eyes skimmed the dark surface of the beach, hoping she'd found a place to stand her ground, but all he saw were drag marks in the sand with a trail of blood leading to the water.

"Knowing Adelaide, it's not hers," Esaias whispered with a hand resting on Theo's shoulder. "We'll find her." He sheathed his sword and ran to a longboat.

Adelaide's jacket slipped through Theo's trembling fingers. He couldn't bear another loss or what Adelaide was enduring on Deavopan's ship. It was the war all over again, his squad and now his sister. He took a ragged breath and stood.

As they rowed through the violent waves of the ocean he loved dearly, he scanned the waters for the rest of their fleet. No other ships lurked in the darkness accept the single galleon wading in the bay. They reached the hull, and Esaias grabbed the rope ladder and began to climb.

Esaias scaled the ropes, and Theo followed him, attempting to push the pain deeper with each step. Theo braced himself against the hull, taking short bursts of air through pursed lips. He hefted himself up.

"I'm a soldier," he repeated to himself. "I fight and I live." He wheezed as he climbed. He wanted to crumple to the ground but couldn't. He wouldn't. Adelaide was aboard this ship. *I fight and I live.*

Theo and Esaias climbed over the railing. The emptiness set the hair along Theo's neck to spike, and he gazed eerily around the ship. They moved across the wooden planks, each one creaking below their steps. Not a single soldier emerged to challenge them. The rain pelted their skin, but maybe the roaring of the storm hid their arrival.

He spotted the opening in the floorboards leading to the lower decks. Readying his sword and dagger, Theo moved as swiftly as he could across the open deck to avoid being spotted. He ignored any bits of growing emotions swirling within, but they still lingered in the back of his mind. He needed to control them or they would get them killed.

"What are you two doing here?" a woman shouted through the rain.

They whirled around, ready to fight, but it wasn't Isabel. A warrior clad in black armor flipped her golden hair and twin braids from her face. She stood with a sword still sheathed at her back, a bow and arrow notched in hand. She drew back, her hazel eyes staring them down.

CHAPTER 40

Amaris

THE SHIP WAS worse than Amaris expected. Her imagination rallied with what she'd seen in movies, but nothing compared to the ominous gloom shrouding the ship in darkness. It reeked of damp mold and decaying fish.

Rain continued to pelt against the hull, and some trickled through the floorboards overhead. The continuous bounding of feet and the drop of cannonballs above had her skin prickling and her mind on alert. With her luck, a cannonball would break through the floorboards and hit her on the head.

Amaris stumbled through the dark, her hand sliding over the wooden wall as she snuck deeper into the ship. If those drag marks were Adelaide's, Amaris thought she'd likely be taken to the brig. At least that's what happened in the movies. She hadn't come across Adelaide dead in the sand, so she was hopeful she was alive.

A rickety ladder held together with rope and twine bore her weight as she descended further. Running on a sheer whim, she kept moving. A creak of the ladder had her halting as she clung to the death trap.

This is crazy, she laughed to herself. She was running after Adelaide and was probably going to get herself killed.

She released a shaky breath, steadying her hands against the rail of the ladder. With a few more rungs, her feet touched solid ground. Even with her eyes open, the world was cascaded in darkness. She was used to it. At work, she moved through thick smoke, unable to even see her glove in front of her face.

She released her hold on the ladder and allowed her hands to reach for the walls. Her fingers slipped from plank to plank, following their warped nature. Her feet shuffled across the ground, feeling for furniture or holes in the floor. This was what she'd trained for, moving through deadly, blackout conditions.

Her hand slid off the wall and met the soft, mesh fabric of a hammock. She kept moving, feeling where one ended and the next began. Counting each step, she knew she'd only have to turn around to find her exit.

The ship rocked as a wave crashed against the hull, dropping her to her knees. With her pulse climbing, she latched onto a post. The ship teetered back and forth, but Amaris gripped tighter to keep herself from being flung across the room. She dug her nails into the wood, begging for the ship to right itself.

She'd managed to row an excruciatingly tough boat all the way to the ship and scale the deadly ropes. She wasn't going to lose whatever was left in her stomach to the rocking of the ship.

The teetering stilled, and she released her claws from the post. She pushed farther, moving at a quicker pace. She had to find Adelaide before the fight ended and they were both stuck here.

Her foot left solid ground. She gripped the last hammock, ripping the fabric as she danged over a hole. Flailing like a maniac, she found a ladder.

More darkness consumed her, gobbling her up like that fire almost had. She landed, but a single lantern hung in the distance. It swayed over a table with several weapons littered on it. The ship rocked again, but Amaris was too slow to grab a hold of anything. She flew to the side, smacking into iron bars. She cradled the back of her head, waiting for the nauseating swaying to end.

"Who's there?" a vengeful voice hissed in the darkness.

Amaris was on her feet and reaching for her knife. She displayed the weapon as she stepped closer to the voice, readying her stance as she waited for something to jump out of the shadows.

"Who's asking?" Amaris threw out.

"Amaris?" Adelaide's once dark hiss turned to startling relief.

Amaris ran toward it, grabbing a hold of the single lantern to begin checking through the bars.

"Over here."

Amaris spun around, thrusting the lantern through the bars to spy Adelaide leaning against the back wall, holding her side, as blood leaked from a cut on her temple and dripped from her nose. Dropping to her knees, dread filled Amaris as she took in Adelaide's injuries.

"What hurts?" she asked.

Adelaide winced as she made small movements closer to the door. "Is everything an option?"

Amaris sat back on her heels, her hand gripping the metal bar as rust smeared in her palm. "Yes." She nearly laughed, but the muscles around her chin tightened. Adelaide was alive.

"How did you find me?"

"Later," Amaris muttered. "First, we're getting you out of here."

"Do you have the key?" Adelaide rolled to her side, attempting to get her feet beneath her.

"No, but do you know where it might be? Who locked you in?"

"A woman. I think she's the captain," she said. "They nabbed me on the beach and dragged me down here. The key is probably with her."

Amaris prevented Adelaide from seeing the twitch of her eye. Great, now the captain was thrown into the mix. But with her knife still in hand, she assessed the lock. Maybe she wouldn't have to track her down. She slid it into the hole, twisting and listening for the tumbler.

"Amaris, I don't—"

"It'll work," Amaris said, wiping a bead of sweat from her nose. It had to. She couldn't face a soldier, let alone the captain. Twisting her knife, she prayed. Amaris hadn't been one to take part in religions after Gran had passed, but apparently, Magoria would make a churchgoer out of her again. She had to get Adelaide out of there.

"Is that how you got out before?"

Amaris gave Adelaide a shrug and a small smirk. "No one ever checked my boots for weapons."

"It won't work here."

"It has to."

"But it won't!" Adelaide snapped, dropping back on her heels. "You need the key."

Amaris slid down the bars in defeat. Adelaide was right. The lock was too complex. "I'll find it."

"How?"

Amaris gripped the bars. "I'll come back for you."

"You better." Adelaide dragged the back of her hand under her nose, smearing the blood across her face. "Gods, I spent my whole life training, only to be bested on my own beach. How humiliating."

Amaris pried herself from the cell, leaving the lantern by Adelaide's side as she raced toward the ladder. Gripping the rung, she flinched. A frustrated scream erupted behind her, and Adelaide pounded against the bars. There was no questioning. Amaris would either find that damn key or end up next to Adelaide.

She scaled the ladder, counting as she retraced her steps with the imaginary map she'd configured in her mind. She took each turn faster than she should've, running toward the sounds, the fighting, the screams. She reached the deck housing the cannons, stopping only a brief moment to catch her breath. The soldiers' laughs infuriated her as they lit the fuses and watched as they fired on the manor. She tried prying into their shouting matches, but they were speaking a language she couldn't understand. That was until she heard someone whispering ahead of her. Slinking through the shadows of the ship, she forced herself to shrink behind a barrel of gunpowder.

"This is getting out of hand. Why are we taking orders from a filthy pirate." A dark voice sounded ahead of her.

Amaris's eyes grew wide as she gripped the edge of the barrel. *Pirate?*

"Shut it, Tedric, or she'll hear you," a deep voice said, his accent thick.

She? Amaris leaned closer, maintaining her stance in the shadows.

"Without us, she has no ship," Tedric snipped. "The captain never should've given her command."

"Now that our end of the bargain is complete, he'll resume control when we return."

With her pulse escalating, she followed the voices as they moved down the hall and kept in time with the heavy steps of their boots. They climbed to the next deck while she sat at the bottom of the ladder, waiting for their footsteps to fade. She released a breath and poked her head up. Their shadows turned down the hall.

What if the woman who locked Adelaide up is this pirate? Amaris stifled her groan. Not only was she crazy for boarding the ship, but now she had to find a deadly pirate. They were a thing of cinema or olden sailors swindling merchants for their own gain. She didn't want to know what pirates from Magoria implied. She peered around the corner as their shadows disappeared into a brightly illuminated room.

"How much longer?" the deep voice asked.

"You ask as if you have somewhere more important to be," a woman spoke.

"No," he stammered. "It's only we've suffered heavy losses, and a retreat would be ideal—"

"These casualties are only the beginning. I'm your captain tonight, and you all have your orders." Her voice carried into the hall.

"Captain Hornley may have given you command of his ship for your crusade, but *he's* my captain, not you," Tedric's voice cut in.

A shuffling of steps pursued. "You're a sailor on this ship, are you not?"

"Yes—"

"Then you *are* under my command," the woman said, her voice stern. "And if you ever wish to sail these waters without a storm at your back, then you'll heed my orders."

There was a long and foreboding silence, but Tedric answered with a gruff, "What are your next orders then?"

"We have what I want. Start sending the word for a retreat."

Feet shuffled toward the door. Amaris dove for the first open room, sliding under a desk. Several men stepped from her office and disappeared down the ladder.

Amaris crawled from her hiding place and checked both ends of the hall. *Inadequate* was a complete understatement for her attempted rescue, and she was running out of time. Holding her breath, she forced her heart to calm before she crept up to the door frame.

A woman with brunette hair stood facing the square windows overlooking the open ocean. Her long red nails drummed against her hips. They were a match for the red leather jacket draping her shoulders.

Amaris scanned the desk. It was mainly free of clutter, but her eyes locked onto a large piece of parchment and a compass sitting next to it. Raising to her tiptoes, Amaris stepped into the office. The captain crossed her arms and moved closer to the windows, releasing a sigh. Amaris dared another step and scanned the room for the key. She again sent a prayer that it wasn't around the woman's neck, because it was always around the pirate's neck in the movies.

"How lovely you could join us." The captain's words were pleasant, but her tone was far from it, sending Amaris's blood to freeze over.

A pair of hands seized her from behind. The captain turned, a wicked smile gracing her lips. Golden eyes stared back at her, glowing as bright as the lightning in the sky.

Amaris's chest tightened as the man holding her captive shoved her closer. She was back in the throne room all those weeks ago with Alan gripping her arm and dragging her down the hall, but now she was thrown beside the desk.

The captain came around and grasped Amaris's cheeks, squeezing them as her nails bit into her skin. Without giving her sailor a single glance, she said, "Leave us."

He followed her orders, the door shutting with a subtle click. She released Amaris's face, shoving her back. Amaris tried to remain calm, to keep her breathing under control. How had she thought she could do this? As the captain turned her back and strode behind her desk, Amaris's eyes shot to the back of a picture frame and a leather necklace hanging from the corner.

Too easy, she thought. It was the key.

"Who are you?" Amaris asked, attempting to keep her voice clear and calm, like Theodoric with his stone-faced demeanor. She needed a plan.

The captain folded her arms across her chest, her long nails tapping against her elbow. She had no weapon pulled and didn't have a sword sheathed at her side or knives strapped to her thighs. Her claws seemed as good a weapon as any with their long, pointed ends.

"I see you prefer to get straight to the point. How boring," the captain sighed, glancing over her shoulder as if to be sure they were alone. She raised her hand and cupped it around her mouth. "I'm Drauna." She smiled then angled her nails in front of her, but her eyes studied Amaris instead. "You're not what I expected."

"Excuse me?" Amaris blurted out. "You expected a man to come save Adelaide instead?"

Drauna laughed maniacally. Amaris's jaw tightened, and her body jumped as a clap of thunder boomed overhead.

"I know her brother will try. He most certainly has the spirit to, even if it's tainted." She raised a brow in a teasing smirk as she pushed from the desk to stand before the window.

"What do you mean?" Amaris reached for the picture frame.

"Theodoric Fastrada is haunted by who he is, what he was forced to become. His soul is diseased, devouring him."

Amaris's gaze snapped to her, her fingers hovering over the leather necklace. "How do you know that?"

She turned lazily around. Amaris ripped back her hand.

"The same reason I know what you desperately crave."

Amaris pulled back, her face twisting in disgust. "How could you know what I want?" Nothing could prevent the slight increase of her pulse.

She laughed. "Isn't it what we all desire? To belong. To have the answers." She raised a brow and smirked. "To have a family, Amaris."

Amaris sucked in a breath. The wind forced a window to snap open, sending a breeze to fly over them. Sea water and the subtle scent of singed wiring filled the charged air.

"How do you know my name?"

Drauna smiled, once again turning to face the wall of windows. Amaris snatched the key from the frame.

"Your name is hardly of concern. Where you come from is far more interesting."

Amaris choked on her own spit, shoving the key into her boot. "I... How do you...?" she stammered, unable to hide her panic.

"You reek of another realm."

"But how do you even know of other worlds?"

"That doesn't matter," Drauna said, her voice like a siren's. "Why do you think you're here?"

Amaris stopped breathing. She didn't know why she was here. She'd stopped that line of thought weeks ago. All that had mattered was escaping and getting home. "Do you know?"

Drauna laughed, a flash of lightning followed in its wake. "I cannot simply divulge the answers you seek. Where would the fun be in that?"

"What do you want then?"

"To gaze upon you." Her golden eyes were bright like lightning in a storm cloud. They widened as she angled toward Amaris.

She couldn't move, not for lack of trying, but Amaris felt pinned against the floor. A clear thought came to her. *Where's Theodoric?* If there was anyone she wanted in this moment, it was him. She wanted him to come barreling through the door, lunge with his sword, and take her back to the manor. But he wasn't going to, because she'd fucked up.

"Were you the one who tried to kill me?" Amaris dared ask.

"I've no need of that." She donned a feline smile. "A blade may one day slit your throat, but it won't be by my hand."

What? Amaris wasn't sure how many more of her riddles she could take. "Who then?"

Drauna stepped toward Amaris, latching her hand around her throat, but she didn't squeeze. Her nails drew small circles over her chin. "That is up to you."

"What's with the cryptic phrases? Tell me," Amaris demanded, still fighting the urge to get up and run, fighting against her paralyzing moment of panic.

"There's much for you to learn, Amaris."

She balked against her hand, no longer caring how she knew her name, only caring that she wanted to get as far away from her as possible.

"Diggory!"

The door burst open. Amaris fought her grasp, but Drauna clamped down harder, drawing a trickle of blood to spill down the side of Amaris's neck. A tall man with cinnamon-colored hair and silver eyes stalked closer. He didn't wear the navy uniform like the other soldiers. *Is he a pirate too?*

"See that our guest finds proper accommodations." Drauna relinquished her hold around Amaris's neck.

Amaris gasped for air as Diggory grabbed her arm, dragging her off the floor bucking and kicking. She tried to rip from his clutches, but his hold was like iron shackles with his long fingers.

"Seems Drauna has taken a liking to you," Diggory heckled once in the hall. "She wasn't as merciful the last time she laid a hand on someone."

"Fuck you," Amaris snapped, sending the heel of her boot into his toe.

He cringed, releasing the hold on her arms. Amaris swung her leg, the steel toe slamming into his groin. He reached for his crotch and forced a breath. She turned to run, but he grabbed her braid, yanking her back.

"Captain said to find you proper accommodations. She never said where," he seethed. His fingers dug against her torso as he pressed her to his chest. "You're just as feisty as the other one. Maybe she'll love a cellmate."

Amaris's blood stilled. She shoved her palms into his chest, digging her nails into the material of his shirt.

Fuck, Amaris cursed. *What would Viv do?*

She stared him dead in his cold eyes, pulled her head back, and slammed her forehead into his nose. Blood sprayed, but he released his hold. She ran, throwing barrels and whatever else she could behind her to block his path.

She dared a glance over her shoulder. He charged after her, baring his teeth as blood dripped down his lips.

CHAPTER 41

Theo

GRIS FIRED HER arrow. It whizzed past Theo, meeting the neck of a Deavopan soldier creeping up behind them. His sword fell to the deck with a clank. Theo whirled on Gris as she stood tall atop the deck, another arrow drawn and her hair whipping against the wind in the torrential downpour. Clad in her black breastplate, she practically blended into the night, but Theo knew the shine of her bow and the vivid locks of her hair. Gris had come back.

When he'd needed her most, she was nowhere to be found. But the sight of her in the same armor she wore during the war brought determination to Theo's heart. He had Esaias and Gris by his side once again.

"Both of you need to get out of here." Gris didn't dare lower her bow, drawing it back.

"Gods, Gris," Esaias muttered, "you always have impeccable timing."

"What are you doing here?" Theo asked. Had she seen Adelaide taken?

"I've come for Amaris." Gris took slow, methodical steps down the stairs, her aim still drawn.

Theo startled. A cold wind sent a shiver through him, further freezing his bare chest and reminding him of his shame, laid open for the realm to see.

"Amaris is within the manor."

"No, she's not. I followed her." Gris released her arrow. The sound following it was the slump of another soldier hitting the deck.

His breath hitched. "No," he stammered. "We're here for Adelaide. I sent Amaris—"

"Adelaide?"

"They took her."

Gris drew a sharp breath. "I'll find them."

"Gris, where have you been?"

"That's not important right now."

Theo raised an inquisitive brow, and he gently set the tip of his sword on the deck. "Not important?" He gestured around them. "I sent you to investigate Freville's murder, and the Accords attack!"

"The entire Accords aren't here, only Deavopan. It isn't a full-scale siege."

"Then what do they want?"

"I don't know."

Esaias stepped forward and threw his hands up between them. "It would seem none of us have the time to explain. We have both Amaris and Adelaide to find."

Gris nodded, but her eyes drifted to Theo's knee. "You're injured."

He tightened his grip around his sword. Amaris and Adelaide were here. He swallowed as the monster threatened to break to the surface. Its claws were a subtle reminder, a mere whisper in his head. He allowed a single shred of it to sweep away his pain and slow his heart. No injury would keep him from protecting them.

"Who isn't?" Esaias threw out.

The rain grew stronger, creating sheets around them, narrowing their circle of vision.

"We need to get below deck," Theo said, but as he did, a creak sounded behind Gris.

Theo narrowed his eyes, eyeing a shining blade through the rain, raised and ready to strike. Before he could warn Gris, she turned and launched an arrow through the soldier's throat. His body tumbled down the stairs and jerked like a fish flopping on the deck.

"I'll go after them. Esaias, you need to get him inside," Gris shouted over the rain. "Theo, I tried to find you at the Conjugation. Your father wants to send Amaris to Elric."

"Old news," Esaias said, annoyed. "We were planning to get her out."

Gris only raised a brow before she shook her head. "You both stay here. I'll go after them."

"No." Theo wouldn't leave their rescue only to Gris. She needed their help, and he had to protect Amaris.

Gris worried her lower lip, her hand tightening around her grip. "I know how you feel about her."

Esaias snapped his attention to Theo, but he ignored the curious raise of his brow. He would tell Esaias later. If they survived.

In a split second, Gris released her arrow, but a gunshot went off. Theo dropped to the deck, his body screaming and his ears ringing. He grasped his arm and blood pooled through his fingers.

Esaias turned and stabbed his sword through the soldier's throat, but Gris's arrow already protruded through the man's chest. Another one came charging down the steps, catching Esaias off guard as he tackled him. They rolled in a tangle of limbs through the sheets of rain.

Theo pivoted to his stomach, biting his lip against the stinging in his arm. He stood against every fiber of his being telling him to stay down. Gris cried out. A soldier pinned her, straddling her and sending fists flying into her jaw.

Theo was torn as they both locked in their battles. Esaias grunted as he took a cut across the face, and Gris screamed with another punch. No more. The muscles of his forearm flexed, and his neck twitched. Anger spilled from his marrow, seeping into his blood. He was done with his friends and the people he loved being ripped from his life. The monster flexed through his fingers, wrapping tightly around his sword.

He raised his blade, but a third soldier jumped from where he'd hidden at the helm. He smiled, a silver tooth glinting in the lightning's flash. In a matter of moments, Theo was upon the man. He slashed and swiped, parried and blocked.

The deck was slick, but the soldier, with his feet bare, jumped and moved with ease. Theo rolled to block his next strike, grabbing a fallen sword and raising both against him. The soldier was quick, guarding both Theo's attacks with his single weapon. But Theo was bigger, stronger. He hacked at the soldier's defenses, beating him down until his sword slipped from his grip. Without hesitation, Theo cut off the soldier's head, and it rolled across the deck. He stepped over the man's lifeless body, looking for his next fight.

A *clink* pierced the air, an unnatural sound, causing Theo to cringe. The soldier pinning Gris held a bent dagger against her midsection. Theo furrowed his brow, training his focus through the rain. He'd seen it true. Whatever armor she wore, it'd bent his dagger.

Gris grabbed his thighs and threw him back. She rolled onto her hands, pushing off as she stood, waiting for him. Her fist sailed into her attacks—a jab, a left hook, a kick, but her opponent was swift. He hurled his own attack, landing one to Gris's jaw. She grunted, but it didn't drop her to the deck. No, she spat a line of blood and reached for her sword, her hand wrapping around the leather-bound hilt. With a single thrust, she pierced his heart.

The scent of blood filled the air around them, but so did Esaias's scream. Gris charged, running straight for Theo. He crouched, and she used a barrel to hurtle over his kneeling form. She came down, driving her sword through the soldier's back.

Esaias laid sprawled and panting while Gris leaned over her knees. For a moment, all was still besides their rapid breaths.

"Gris, do you know who told my father of Amaris's attempted escape?"

Theo needed to know the truth. If it hadn't been Alan, it left only a few choices.

"Where is this coming from?" she snapped.

"You were one of the few on sentry duty that night."

"No, I wasn't, but we don't have time for this. We have to find them."

Another soldier descended the steps, two blades trained on them. Theo twirled his sword, and Gris's head snapped up as she readied herself. But Esaias groaned on the deck, coughing and rolling to his side.

"Help him," Gris said to Theo before charging toward the soldier.

Rain pelted Theo's face, like small daggers against his skin. He kneeled over Esaias. One of his eyes was swollen shut, and the cut was longer than he initially thought. It trailed from his temple, down his cheek, and met the split in his lip.

"That fucking hurt," Esaias coughed, blood spilling from his lips.

A breath escaped Theo as he watched the crimson liquid slide down his cousin's chin.

"Don't worry. It's only from my face."

Theo had never felt such sudden relief. He grabbed Esaias's hand and pulled him to his feet. "We need to get you off the ship."

"If you can fight, then so can I," Esaias insisted, but the fresh laceration dripped blood into his eyes and obscured his only good line of sight.

"You can barely see."

"I've had worse odds," he reminded Theo.

Esaias tipped his head back, angling his face upward to clear his eyes. His hands shook as he flung the blood spilling down his cheeks.

The sharp strike of a blade pulled their attention. Gris struck down her opponent, but she was already caught in her next duel. She charged across the helm to meet the next Deavopan soldier. "Go find them!" she shouted.

They didn't wait for her to say more. Esaias descended the ladder into the ship with Theo following behind him. Theo relinquished the hold on the monster within, allowing it to slither back from where it came and give him a moment of reprieve.

They landed with their swords ready, but Theo began feeling the effects of his injuries, the press of his knee against the binding and the blood leaking from his shoulder. He eyed the wound, but the musket ball had only grazed his arm.

"Where do you think they'll be?" Esaias asked.

"If Adelaide was taken, she'll be farther below deck. Amaris could be anywhere."

"Is it true?" Esaias whispered, wiping the blood from his eyes as they began their trek through the ship.

"Is what true?"

Esaias gave Theo a flat look before he checked around the corner. "Love fizzles out eventually, especially with a woman like Amaris."

"I don't love her," Theo snapped. "It was one kiss."

"You kissed her?"

"Technically, Amaris kissed me first, but she doesn't even remember it."

"Whatever is between you two, set it aside. Focus on why we're here. You can sort out who kissed who later."

Theo ground his teeth, but Esaias was right.

A cannon fired, jostling the boat.

Esaias gazed down the next ladder. "Sounds like they're below us."

"Then we avoid that deck. I doubt Amaris would be foolish enough to crawl into Deavopan's nest."

"Do you even know the woman?"

"Excuse me?" Theo asked, lowering his sword.

Esaias forced out a sigh and spat blood from his lips. "She's looking for Adelaide, who will be in the brig. She needs a key."

"Why do you only show this level of intelligence when we're near death?"

"It's one of my specialties." He grinned.

Esaias swung himself over the ladder and scaled deeper. Theo gripped the rung, waiting to descend into the chaos. His thumb brushed against the worn wood from the many hands having climbed it.

Several weeks ago, he'd wanted desperately to know what plagued Duncaster, but now he would've gladly stayed in the dark. He wished it was anything other than the Accords. He wanted to have met Amaris in the market, offering to carry her basket of herbs. He wished Adelaide to be a soldier, learning and training under him. But the life he wanted was only a dream. Amaris's life was threatened, not only by Deavopan, but by his father and someone wishing to poison her, and Adelaide might never again see the end of a sword.

Before Theo could follow Esaias, someone ran into him. His grip slipped, and all three of them crashed below. Theo smacked the back of his head, seeing stars glittering in his vision. The attacker pressed against his stomach, but he gripped their wrist and dragged them against the wall. Theo's vision blurred in and out of focus.

He swayed as he pulled out his dagger and held it to their throat.

CHAPTER 42

Theo

"*SO RIN ESDIL id uldo bere bre flon lod cha ca clol bre cod.*" Theo
seethed Tendasy in the assailant's ear, threatening to drag his dagger across
their throat if they didn't hold their tongue. If he couldn't find Amaris and
Adelaide, then he'd need someone to drag along to show them.

"Please," they begged.

"You speak Akaric?"

"Theodoric?"

Theo pulled back his blade. Everything ceased its spinning, and the
face came into focus as his eyes adjusted. Amaris stood with wide eyes and
her brown, frizzy locks. He didn't care if she didn't remember their kiss.
His arms wrapped around her. Her heart beat ferociously against his, but
she didn't embrace him back. Her arms dangled at her sides, trembling.

He peeled away, assessing the shaking of her limbs. Tears spilled from
her eyes, and her breaths came out as small gulps.

He sheathed his dagger and scanned her neck to be sure he hadn't cut
her. "What in the realm were you thinking?"

Amaris grasped her arms and gazed up the ladder into the dim passage above. "Adelaide needed our help," she said softly.

Where is her fiery spirit? Theo's hands curled into fists.

"Did you really think you'd stand against soldiers?" Esaias snapped, leaning against the ladder and releasing an exhausted breath as he wiped more blood from his eye.

Amaris narrowed her gaze at him. "What happened to you?"

"A story for later."

"We have to go—"

Amaris was silenced as footsteps carried from above. She shoved them against the wall. Her breaths were ragged beside Theo. She bent down, pulling something from her boot and thrusting it into his hands. It was a leather necklace with a key.

"I swiped it from the...captain."

More footsteps echoed. Theo grabbed Amaris and Esaias, and they moved deeper into the darkness, allowing it to swallow them in its infinite shadows.

"We need to go this way." Amaris pointed toward a ladder heading below deck and didn't look at Theo or Esaias before she scurried down to the next level.

Theo grabbed a lantern hanging several paces away. He and Esaias followed her, each turn quick and methodical. She'd gotten herself lost in the manor daily, but now she was able to direct them without hesitation through the ship. Interesting was hardly able to describe the kind of woman she was.

"Where's the brig?" Theo asked.

Amaris jumped off the ladder, stepping out of sight. Theo lifted the lantern. Hammocks hung around them.

"One more deck down," she said.

"Why did you think it was a good idea to go after Adelaide?" Esaias asked. "You aren't even trained. What if someone attacked you?"

Amaris grimaced. "Why are you here?"

"Obviously someone needed to rescue you two."

"I was doing fine on my own," she lied, biting her lip. Her teeth released their hold, and her nostrils flared as she caught sight of Theo eyeing her tell. Someone was chasing after her.

"How were you planning to get off the ship?" Esaias asked.

"I was figuring it out."

"Sure," Esaias scoffed.

Amaris pushed farther, pulling away from the light, from Theo. He wanted to grasp her hand and hold it to his heart so she could feel how it raced within his chest and know she wasn't alone.

"You did that on purpose!" Esaias shouted, crashing to the ground.

Theo quickened his pace, finding Esaias twisted in a hammock.

"You'll be fine, you big baby," she spat.

"Amaris, I can barely see a fucking thing," he seethed, untangling himself and ripping the hammock from where it hung.

She turned on him, grabbing his cheeks and assessing his cut. He winced at her touch. "Stop squirming." Amaris wiped the blood running down his brow and prodded at the swelling around his other eye. "The swelling will go down." She pulled out a roll of cloth from her satchel and wrapped the bandage around his head. "That should hold for now."

"How much farther?" Theo asked.

"It shouldn't be far." Amaris reached out, feeling with the tips of her toes as she walked and sliding her hands along the edges of the hammocks.

Esaias glared at Theo, his eyes swinging between them like a pendulum. Theo crinkled his lips into a snarl. Esaias could believe whatever he wanted to about love, but Theo refused to feed into his delusions that love wasn't worth it.

"Last time—" Before Amaris could get out another word, she and Esaias fell through a hole in the floor with a loud thud.

"Are you alright?" Theo swung the lantern out, feeling with his foot for the ladder.

"Yes."

"No," Esaias whined. "She's sitting on me."

"You're sitting on me!"

Theo found them in a tangle on the floor with Amaris seething as she shoved Esaias off her. Pulling from their bickering, Theo's chest stilled at the sight of the cells around them.

"Amaris?"

"Adelaide?" Theo called out. He limped toward the sound of his sister's voice, toward the dying lantern of the farthest cell. He begged for his body to hold out for a little while longer so he wouldn't be forced to unleash the beast within him.

Adelaide leaned back on her hands, blood spilling from her nose and temple. Her skin was a shade paler than normal, but Theo's breath halted as the light reflected small white scars on her arms.

"Adelaide," he whispered. "What have they done to you, and what are these?" He grasped her forearm through the bars, rubbing his thumb over a small scar. She hadn't had them when he left three years ago.

"You should see *them*." Adelaide pulled from his grip. "You look like shit, Esaias."

"I could say the same for you." Esaias leaned against the cell across from Adelaide's. In the small bit of light, his cheeks appeared sunken with shadows, and his skin resembled a spirit's.

Theo retrieved the key, and Amaris was beside Adelaide the moment he opened the door. They whispered, quickly assessing the state of her injuries.

"She likely has a bruised or broken rib, but I need to get her to the manor to further assess her," Amaris stated plainly. The once-fragile composure was gone, and not a single tear welled in her eyes.

"Then let's go," Esaias answered for everyone, his voice coming in an airy pant as his hand trembled around his sword.

"Esaias, how are you feeling?" Theo asked, stepping toward him.

Amaris's head snapped up from Adelaide, and she eyed Esaias as he started sliding down the bars. Theo rushed to his side, catching him under the arm before he hit the ground.

"Esaias has—"

"*Mamat*, I know." Amaris took hold of Esaias's chin, bringing his eyes to meet hers. "Are you trying to die tonight?"

His answer was a scoff and a roll of his eyes as his body grew heavy against Theo.

"I have to bear his weight." He handed Amaris the lantern.

She snatched a sword from a table littered with discarded weapons and kneeled before Adelaide to offer it to her. Adelaide brushed her fingers over the braided leather of his old sword before winding them tight and gritting her teeth. She stood, wincing and grabbing a hold of her side. Theo reached for her waist, but she held up a hand.

"I can walk."

With the lantern in hand, Amaris led the way. Adelaide followed, and Theo gripped Esaias's waist, assisting him as they made their way through the ship. Adelaide attempted to stand strong, raising her sword at each corner they came upon, but he saw the winces and heard her grunts.

As they climbed the next ladder, Esaias further leaned into Theo. "I...need to...eat something."

"I know," Theo whispered, hefting him up to the next deck. "Just a little longer."

Farther on, Theo leaned closer to Adelaide. "What happened?"

"I was waiting for Amaris and Esaias—"

"Not on the beach. Your arms," Theo demanded.

She stalled on the ladder. "A few soldiers jumped me," she continued, ignoring him. When it was all over, she would have to tell him who hurt her, who cut up her arms and scarred her. "I don't know how it was possible, but the longboats pulled into the bay without a sound. They thumped me on the back of the head. They thought they knocked me out, but I faked it and managed to knock out two of theirs. One of them got a good shot at my nose before he fell."

"What about your ribs?"

"Courtesy of their friends. They didn't appreciate how I outsmarted them and threw me in that cell and got a good kick to my side. They only stopped because she ordered them to."

"Who?"

"The captain," she snipped before ascending to the next deck.

Esaias struggled against Theo as he attempted to get him up the ladder. He often grew angry when he hadn't eaten in a while. They moved faster, pausing around each corner, ducking behind barrels to avoid a fight.

"One more and we'll be on the main deck," Amaris whispered to them.

Esaias slowly lifted his brows, giving Theo a dazed look before his head rolled onto his shoulder. With Amaris's and Adelaide's assistance, they got Esaias up the ladder and laid him on the deck.

Theo kneeled beside him, attempting to rouse him for the last few minutes of their escape, but he only groaned as Theo pinched his shoulder.

"Watch out!"

Theo whirled, but a boot kicked him in the chest. He hit the deck hard. A blade was drawn, and he rolled, narrowly missing its vicious swipe. He wiped the rain from his eyes. Adelaide drew her sword against Sephardi, who spun hers then lunged with a fury. A second sword was strapped to her back, and her twin pistols were sheathed at her sides.

Theo startled. What was Sephardi doing?

Adelaide strained against her attacks, but she blocked each of her hits. The clash of their blades rivaled the thunder's call. Not only was Adelaide defending herself against one of Theo's most-skilled soldiers, but she did so with a smug persistence. Theo could've sworn a smirk graced her lips.

The scars littering her arms were a testament to her strength, her fight. He didn't know what had become of the person who dared cut her up, but knowing Adelaide, they'd gotten what they deserved.

Theo eyed his bulging knee, but Adelaide's quick breaths had him pushing through. Amaris leaned over Esaias, attempting to rouse him.

"Get him out of here," he shouted to her.

Theo turned from Amaris and her fearful expression. He couldn't let his mind wander to the shrinking oceans as her irises filled with darkness. He stood, palming his sword. Theo charged, blocking Sephardi's next strike.

"What are you doing?" Theo pulled back, and she readied her stance.

He stood by Adelaide's side, both angling their swords and waiting for Sephardi's next move.

She scoffed and jerked her head to flip the short strands out of her eyes. "What should've been done the moment you found her."

This was about Amaris.

She pulled her second sword from its sheath and lunged. It was a mix of blades and arms as the three of them battled across the deck. Theo pressed forward and further drew their fight from Amaris and Esaias.

He didn't allow himself to think of the soldiers lurking below or Amaris dragging Esaias across the deck. All he thought about were Sephardi's next moves and anticipating where she'd strike. Nothing made sense. Theo aimed for Sephardi's weaker side, but she parried, gritting her teeth against his blade.

Why was she doing this? His mind thought back to the tower with Esaias and Adelaide. They'd said Sephardi had been working Gris's sentry duty. Had she been the one to tell his father of Amaris's escape attempt?

Theo stepped between Adelaide and Sephardi. "Help Amaris get Esaias out of here."

Adelaide opened her mouth to protest but spied them unarmed and unguarded on the deck. They needed her. With Adelaide at their side, he knew they would get safely off the ship.

Theo threw himself into his next swing. "You were the one to poison her!"

"Should've known a bit of herix wouldn't have been enough to kill her," Sephardi seethed. Her next series of strikes hit hard and strong, weakening Theo's stance. This wasn't her.

The grip he held to keep the beast at bay was weakening. He felt the creature begging to show itself. "Why?" He took a breath and a chance. He twisted his sword and disarmed her of one of her weapons.

Another strike of her sword sent Theo's teeth chattering, but he kept up his guard, breathing through the trembling in his arm from the wound still dripping blood. His knee ached as his feet shifted back and forth.

He needed to get back on the offense, but his mind reeled. Betrayed again. How many more friends would he bury? How many more deaths would be on his hands?

"The realm is changing."

Theo couldn't believe what was coming from her mouth. "Sephardi, please tell me you haven't sided with Deavopan."

"They're willing to do what must be done."

"This is madness!"

She lunged, swiping a gash into his thigh. He didn't wince, but she forced him back, moving with speed. She was older, wiser, quick with her sword. Years of training and fighting were at her back, but Theo had his strength and his will.

"No, what's crazy is trusting a woman you found in the middle of a forest, covered in blood," Sephardi rattled on.

Theo forced the pain growing in his body back and sucked in a breath. He needed to disarm her. She was skilled and deadly with her blade, but he couldn't kill her. She was his friend.

Sephardi didn't let up on her attack. Her breaths were even, and her footing was solid. She wasn't tiring, but Theo felt the fatigue riddling through him. He couldn't keep up.

"Who else wants her dead?" he yelled.

"Not everyone sees what I do."

Theo felt disgraceful for having any bit of relief. She'd acted alone, but why at all? None of it made sense.

With his rambling mind, Sephardi twirled her blade, sliding down his and ripping the hilt from his grasp. She kicked his chest, sending him backward against the deck. She straddled him, pinning his arms to the ground. Her fingers pressed against his wound and a gasp escaped him. The pain in his arm spread up his neck. The cold barrel of one of her pistols pressed against his temple. Now, he really hated guns.

"I don't want to kill you."

"How long?" he gasped.

"You don't know her, Theo. None of us do—what she is."

What she is? What did Amaris have to do with siding with Deavopan? "Amaris is a mystique. She's saved countless lives. She isn't a threat."

Theo let out a cry as Sephardi further pressed her fingers into his wound. To keep his tunneling vision clear, he puffed out short breaths.

"Is she?" Sephardi slid her gun to Theo's jaw, slowly forcing his chin up. A clap of thunder overhead had her grimacing, and her hand trembled. She shook, the muscles in her arms flexing. She didn't want to kill him. Theo saw it in her eyes. She held back.

"Sephardi, put down the pistol," he panted. "We can go inside—"

"Quiet!"

Theo writhed beneath her as her fingers dug into his shoulder. He was going to black out, or Sephardi would shoot him. He wouldn't know if Amaris got Esaias off the ship. He wouldn't live to see Adelaide grow into the woman she was becoming. She would marry the prince, because Luther would never stand up for her. Amaris would be carted off to the dungeons, even after what she'd done, the people she'd saved.

He cheated death during the war. He should've died in Rongstad with the torture he'd endured, the amount of blood he'd lost. The river should've taken him. Once Sephardi pulled the trigger, he would stand before Kedes, but he knew After didn't wait for him. He would be swallowed into the cracks of the realm to be eaten by the burning fires within.

CHAPTER 43

Amaris

AS THE RAIN poured down on them, Amaris took in the sight unraveling around her. Adelaide stood by Theodoric's side as they faced Sephardi. Amaris sat in disbelief. Sephardi had freed her from the dungeon and attempted to shield her against Bennet.

What changed?

Pulled from her internal struggle, she bent over Esaias and assessed his state. Luckily, he was still breathing. She attempted to rouse him, rubbing her knuckles against his sternum, but he only breathed deeper. If she were home, she'd start an intravenous line and give him medication to get his sugar up, but she wasn't in her world. She didn't have her drug box, her ambulance, or even Charlie. But she was more than her tools.

Esaias was her patient. She'd get him off the ship and find Onika. Hopefully, she had an herb or something. With Onika's expertise, she'd get him talking and joking again. She didn't want to think of what Luana Bay would be like without Esaias, without any of them. For weeks, she'd learned the routine of the mystique, sat with them at dinner, walked the halls with Theodoric, but in all of it, she'd felt freer than she ever had.

Her literal freedom might have been gone, but wasn't that what the duke wanted all along? For her to prove herself? She couldn't fight beside Adelaide or Theodoric now, but she could fight for the life she wanted.

Her eyes followed the railing of the ship. How was she going to get Esaias to shore, let alone the battle still breaking out on the grounds? She'd barely dragged the couple more than a few feet in that house fire, but she was all Esaias had.

Closing her eyes, she forced her stammering heart to calm. Each breath through her nose eased her mind. She would deal with each problem as it came. Crawling to his head, she got him in a sitting position with her knee propping him up. She wedged her arms under his armpits and began dragging him to the edge of the ship.

He was heavier than she expected, and his belt and clothes caught on loose nails and uneven planks. A slew of curses followed, but she refused to give up. She didn't have Viv to throw him over her shoulder and scale down the hull like the hero she was. Amaris only had her own strength.

With each gasping breath, she spat rain and sweat from her lips. It continued to pour, drenching her clothes. Lightning lit up the deck, and thunder roared in the sky. She ignored the clashing of blades and the ringing in her ears. She couldn't worry about Theodoric or Adelaide. As much as it killed her to leave them, they were risking their lives so she could save Esaias. They'd trained to fight, while she'd trained to heal.

Each drag was excruciating and short, but she managed to get Esaias to the edge of the deck. A longboat was hoisted to the railing and held with ropes. Amaris blew out a breath and grabbed lower on his torso. As she squatted down, her eyes caught a glint of gold through the sheets of rain.

Amaris squinted, and her eyes found Gris's body lying across the way. With the rain, she couldn't tell if she was breathing. Her sopping heap of hair covered her face. Amaris gently set Esaias back on the deck and sprinted toward her. The deck was slippery under her boots, and she came to a sliding halt. She rolled Gris onto her back and dropped her cheek to her lips and felt her pulse. She was alive.

Amaris slung her bow over her back and slid behind her, angling her face to avoid one of Gris's arrows poking her eye out. Thankfully, she was lighter, and Amaris had little trouble dragging her beside Esaias.

She could barely believe the chaos around her. Adelaide was fighting, and Sephardi had betrayed them. None of it made sense. Sephardi had been the one to watch over her for weeks. They were alone plenty of times, why wait to poison her at the Conjugation?

A surge of footsteps had her lunging over her patients.

"Need a hand?"

Amaris whirled. Adelaide ran up behind her, blood smeared across her face. Amaris threw a glance over her shoulder. Theodoric stood alone against Sephardi.

"He knows what he's doing," Adelaide assured her.

It should've been a comfort, but Amaris's gut still tightened. Adelaide jumped into the longboat, wincing and grabbing her side as she braced herself against the hull. She didn't complain about the blood spilling from her nose or the likely broken rib. Adelaide held her hands out and waited for Esaias.

Amaris hefted him up, shoving him against the railing for Adelaide to assist her in rolling him into the boat. It wasn't pretty, and he would likely have a few bruises. Gris was next. They got her into the boat, and Adelaide arranged them to balance their weight.

Amaris gripped the railing to hurtle herself into the longboat, but a shout froze her to the deck. Sephardi straddled Theodoric, with a gun pressed to his head, her fingers digging into the wound in his shoulder.

Adelaide popped her head up, but before she could draw her sword and jump over the railing, the ship rocked. Amaris braced herself against the railing, her nails once again clinging for dear life. The longboat swung, sending Adelaide to the far edge. Her muffled scream turned to a raging growl, but then her eyes widened.

Amaris lifted her gaze. A rope holding the longboat hung by a few fibers.

Adelaide jumped to grab it, but the longboat tipped as it snapped. She dropped and swung her arms out to keep Gris and Esaias from pitching forward into the water.

"Cut the line!" Adelaide screamed, her face red as she gripped the edges of the boat to keep them all from slipping out. "Cut it!"

Amaris drew her knife and braced it against the rope. She began sawing, frantically trying to sever it. Her arms burned in agony, and the rain weakened her hold on her knife. A scream from Theodoric stalled her hands.

"What are you waiting for?" Adelaide grimaced, tossing an arrow onto the deck.

The weight of Gris's bow threatened to shorten Amaris's spine. One more movement and she'd cut through the rope. But one more cut and she'd be all Theodoric had.

"Do it!"

Amaris sliced her knife across the fraying rope, and the longboat plunged into the sea. She didn't stop to think. She grabbed the arrow off the deck and the bow from her back. Her fingers moved in a rhythm she hadn't used since her days of hunting. This arrow was heavier, sharper. Amaris pulled back the bow and aimed. Her arm strained. She hadn't shot her bow in years. What if she hit Theodoric?

He writhed, his boots shuffling against the slippery deck. If she didn't shoot, Sephardi would kill him. She forced a deep breath and willed her aim. With an exhale, Amaris released the arrow. It sailed through the rain, slicing through wind. It landed in Sephardi's shoulder with a startling cry. She fell to the deck, releasing Theodoric and flinging her hand around her shoulder.

Amaris sprinted into action. She willed Theodoric to get up, but he was flat on the deck. Her feet carried her toward him, but she stalled as

Sephardi shot up. She gripped the shaft of the arrow and pried it from her flesh. Blood stained the arrowhead.

Sephardi tossed it aside and stepped toward Amaris but placed the tip of her boot against Theodoric's neck instead. He latched onto her ankle, but he seemed to have little strength. His legs kicked, and with her single foot, she cut off his air.

"Should I spare him?"

"Please, Sephardi. Why are you doing this?"

Theodoric clawed frantically at her ankle.

"Pity it had to come to this."

His hands slumped to the deck, and Sephardi slipped her boot from his neck. She nudged his cheek with the tip of her boot, and Amaris's chest caved as his head rolled to the side. She couldn't tell if he was still breathing. She bared her teeth as anger swept over her. She dropped the bow at her feet and sprinted. Instinct consumed her movements. She threw herself at Sephardi.

They rolled and slid over the planks. A nail caught Amaris's shirt and ripped it. She came to a halt against the center mast, striking her hip. A grunt escaped her, but she was on her feet in a moment, because Sephardi was already on the move. Amaris turned and ran.

Sephardi wanted her dead, not Theodoric. She'd give him time to wake up, or she'd lure Sephardi to the beach. She didn't allow herself to think of another outcome. Sephardi hadn't killed him. Theodoric wasn't dead. Amaris wouldn't accept anything else.

Her legs carried her in an awkward limp toward the railing. She'd be forced to dive into the ocean, but they were close enough to shore that she could swim to land. A sharp pain shot through her leg, and she pitched forward, slamming hard into the deck. Amaris turned over her shoulder. A dagger protruded from the back of her thigh.

Her eyes widened, and her muscles went rigid as Sephardi approached her. A sword was in her hand as she twirled the blade. The muscles of

Amaris's leg twitched and spasmed as she attempted to shuffle back.

"What did I do to you?"

Sephardi laughed, placing the tip of her blade against Amaris's chest. "I know who you are."

Amaris's lips parted. *What the hell is going on?* One minute a pirate had riddled her into a tailspin, and now Sephardi pressed her cold sword to her skin. It wasn't possible. She'd said she didn't believe in magic.

Amaris forced back the tears waiting to fall. "I didn't kill Lord Freville."

Sephardi kneeled, her eyes scanning Amaris and the blood starting to form under her thigh. "I know that, but you're still an abomination. Wicked sorcery is what you are."

Amaris's hand curled against her thigh, fighting the sting pulsing in her leg. Sephardi wanted her dead because she was from a different world? Why did it matter? Is that what Drauna meant by a blade one day slashing Amaris's throat?

"I don't know what you're talking about." Sephardi couldn't possibly know who she really was. *Unless...* "Are you working for Drauna?"

Sephardi's brows knit together. "Drauna?" Her sword paused as it barely pierced the skin of Amaris's chest. "There is only one god I bow to."

Amaris bit down on her lip to suppress her scream and tried to peer around her to spy Theodoric, but she couldn't see beyond her menacing glare. Sephardi was crazy. What did gods have to do with this?

"Think of Gris and Theodoric. Don't turn on them." She was desperate, clawing at anything to humanize her and bring Sephardi back to reality.

"Do you even know him?"

Amaris paused.

"Has he told you about his time overseas, what they called him?" Sephardi asked.

Amaris didn't care what they called him. He'd survived. Theodoric had lived through the loss of his squad and his friend.

Sephardi bent down and drew her pistol, resting her elbow on her knee as she cocked it and pointed it toward Amaris. "They called him the Hydra."

"Why?" Amaris found herself asking the question, but she wasn't certain she wanted the answer. She'd learned too much in the last hour but had more questions spinning through her head than she could begin to process. But she needed to keep Sephardi talking.

"You cut off one head, and two more will take its place," she said. "When one of our soldiers was slaughtered, he grew more ferocious, cutting down the enemy. With each fall of one of our own, he killed two of them. He butchered hundreds of soldiers. His hands will forever be stained with the blood he spilled."

Amaris swallowed. She knew he was a soldier in a war, for fuck's sake, *but hundreds of people*? Her mind flashed to the montage of duels and fights with the soldiers back on the grounds, the way his body moved without thought or pain.

His soul is diseased, devouring him. Drauna's words repeated in her mind.

"I don't care," Amaris said.

"You should."

Sephardi's eyes widened and she spun. Theodoric was there with his sword trained on her. The look that warped his eyes was one Amaris never wished to see turned on her.

CHAPTER 44

Theo

COLD, HARD RAIN pelted Theo's flushed cheeks. He needed to breathe. His lungs forced the air in, and he choked. His blotchy vision sharpened on the sky. The storms circling above. Had he again been spared, or had Sephardi failed in her attempts to kill him?

Theo regained control of his hands. He slid them until they met cold metal. His sword. He clutched the hilt and pulled himself to his feet.

Sephardi kneeled before Amaris, her pistol pointed at her heart. Fear had no place. Anger simmered. His rage wasn't containable against any predator who dared harm anyone he cared for. Theo had surrendered once in his life, and he never intended to again.

Come quietly or he dies. The words echoed by Mosfelkov's ruthless king, Terje Ottum, a cold and beastly man with hair the color of snow and a heart as brutal as the ice storms swirling outside his castle.

The throne room of Oystein Castle had been a dark chamber lit with torches burning flames so hot they had appeared blue. Theo's tight grip around his sword had faltered at the sight before him. Whatever had been left of the old Theo Fastrada had died that night, consumed by the monster.

Don't do it! Nate had shouted with a blade pressed to his neck.

Theo had laid down his sword, raising his hands behind his head and dropping to his knees. He'd turned from Nate's expression, unwilling to face his failure. Now, he'd give anything to go back and see his face, to have another memory of his best friend because his surrender had been for nothing.

"They called him the Hydra." Sephardi's voice rang in his ears, pulling him back to the fight before him.

Theo breathed deeply. He'd wasted his energy fighting the demon inside him, but no more. He'd never spoken of who he'd become that night. He couldn't face the name his enemies screamed when they met his face on the battlefield.

After his squad had been slain, he'd taken as many of their soldiers, if not more, to their graves. He'd never intended to survive, slashing his blade through each gut and severing their heads from their bodies. He did it because he thought death awaited him, and he'd atone in After. But he hadn't been met with death. He'd been their prisoner, tortured for his transgressions. They didn't care for information, only that he'd suffered for what he'd done to their people, their friends.

He paid in his dreams, forced to relive his hand in being the means to their ends. What tortured him most wasn't the pain when he'd been imprisoned, but the faces of all those he'd murdered in a fit of rage. Yes, it'd been war, but nothing could've stopped him as he barreled through the guards and soldiers who dared step in his path. Upon returning to the war, his name had been muttered across battlefields. Where he stepped, they cowered at it. The Hydra.

"I don't care," Amaris said.

"You should," Theo hissed, the voice of the Hydra ringing out. He felt none of his injuries as he stood with his sword raised. Basilisk was the blade's name. A serpent crafted into the metal of the hilt with an emerald for its eye. It was the perfect weapon for the Hydra.

Sephardi pivoted, firing her gun. She missed. Theo palmed the creature within his grasp, angling the sword. Blood dripped down the once pristine blade. As he jumped for her, Basilisk came slashing down.

His mind was overtaken by the Hydra. The raging calm settled over his once panicked demeanor. He allowed the infestation of the creature. He'd fight and protect. For them, he'd tunnel within himself and let the beast take form.

Sephardi sprang forward, snagging her sword and fighting with a newfound energy. Blood coated her shoulder, but it didn't faze her. Her movements were precise and ruthless. But Theo met her fury with his own.

Theo had been betrayed that night in Oystein Castle. They'd been sent on a mission to retrieve the plans for troop movements that could've ended the war. Once inside the castle, a swarm of Mosfelkov soldiers had fallen upon them. There had been no plans. A traitor had been among their ranks and had sent them to their deaths.

Sephardi moved with impossible speed, but Theo had fought by her side for years and knew her ways. He guarded her blows and slashed with his blade. He nicked her thigh with a vicious jab, and she screamed. Sephardi might not have betrayed him then, but she was no friend to him now. A monster lived within Theo. Placed there by the forces of Mosfelkov when they showed his soldiers no mercy. But whatever Sephardi had become was a monster incarnate. She eyed him with her angry silhouettes.

"Of all people to betray me, I never thought it would be you." Theo glowered.

"You think you can lead again? You've allowed her to consume you."

Amaris rifled through her satchel behind Sephardi. Blood dripped from the cut in her chest, but a pool of blood piled underneath her. Her skin was pale, and her hands trembled.

"I've allowed Amaris to show me the truth of the realm." Theo raised his blade and, with a single swipe, he disarmed Sephardi.

She went for a dagger, but Theo was there with his fists and gripped her wrist, pinning it between her shoulder blades. Her scream was weak. He dropped his sword to wrap his arm around her neck.

"You were supposed to be my friend," Theo whispered in her ear. "My mentor." His arm tightened around her throat, and she dug her nails into his flesh. "Now, you're nothing to me." His arm flexed, and he felt the darkness creeping into his mind. But a breath of a whisper stilled him.

"Theodoric." Amaris slid her hands around his arm.

He faced her as she stood before him while he strangled Sephardi.

"Look at me," she breathed.

Pain, anguish, fear. Every unbearable feeling rushed into him, and he dropped Sephardi. She hit the deck and didn't move. Amaris dropped to her side, but all Theo could see were his hands soaked with rainwater but stained in blood. His knee throbbed, sending stabbing pains up his leg. His shoulder was a dull ache, and blood dripped past his elbow. He teetered and gripped the main mast as his vision threatened to darken.

What have I done? Theo collapsed to his knees.

Amaris scrambled toward him and gripped his shoulder to keep him steady. "She's alive!" Her hair was soaked, her makeup long gone, but she didn't need it. Her eyes were bright against the lightning. Her lips plump and a vibrant shade of pink.

Theo's heart hammered, but he allowed her words to wash over him.

"Sephardi's alive," she repeated. "It's over."

CHAPTER 45

Amaris

THEODORIC CLOSED THE kitchen doors behind them, and Amaris tossed Gris's bow into the corner. After they'd struggled to get off the boat, they'd been forced to swim to shore. Amaris had sunk into the sand, her arms tired and her legs exhausted, but Theo had been weary. His skin was pale, and blood poured from his shoulder. Her own wound had slowed to a trickle. She'd managed a tourniquet around her thigh. The water had been a dreaded sting as the salt seeped into her cuts, but the sand had been no better when they'd made land.

With the dagger still embedded in the back of her thigh, she forced back the pain and limped through the kitchen. The room was in complete disarray, with people scattered on tables and lying on the floor covered in blood. Even more people ran around, while Ms. Borstad attempted to direct them in any way she could. Theodoric leaned into Amaris, exhaustion finding him.

"Hold on a little longer," she whispered, bracing a shoulder under him.

He didn't reply, but judging by his panting breaths, she knew he couldn't make it further. They staggered through the swarm of people.

The ones they'd passed quieted and stilled as they moved through the kitchen. Ms. Borstad directed Amaris through the servants' door into the main hall. What she saw was far worse than in the kitchen. Many more were on makeshift cots or even the bare floor. A few soldiers saw her struggling to bear Theodoric's weight and assisted in carrying him to an open cot.

"Go help the others," he said. "I just need to rest."

"You can be so stubborn," Amaris said, pressing against his chest as he tried to sit up. "Sit your ass down."

They were their first words uttered since they'd stepped off the ship. Their trek up the beach had been brutal and neither of them had words for what hell they'd just gone through.

A servant came over with one of the baskets and set it at her feet. She shifted her gaze and spotted Pricilla working without tiring. She searched the hall for Onika but didn't see her dark curls among the throng.

She scavenged the basket for ude stalk to mix with the yuxiway leaves as Pricilla instructed what seemed so long ago, but there was only the small jar of crushed-up leaves. The servant came back and placed a fresh basin of water and a cloth beside Theodoric. Amaris wrung it out and pressed gently against the first wound. He groaned.

"This is going to be really uncomfortable," she warned him.

"I think it'll be worse than uncomfortable," he added, huffing through pursed lips.

"Alright, it's going to hurt a lot," she admitted, slightly laughing. Her shoulders began to relax. Her nerves were shot. No number of deep breaths could fully ease her jitters.

"Do you enjoy torturing me?" He tried to laugh with her, but he winced and grabbed at the wound in his shoulder.

"No, I just don't ever tell my patients it's going to hurt a lot. It doesn't usually elicit a calming effect."

"I would presume not," he said, "but I can take whatever you throw at me."

"You might want to reconsider that." She grinned, biting the edge of her lip.

She moved through each of his wounds, cleaning as best she could. She started with his shoulder, wiping along the edges and cleaning out dirt and sand. He breathed through each stroke, watching as her hands moved along his skin. She assessed the severity of his severed flesh. It didn't appear deep enough to have penetrated the muscle, but it still bled like a bitch. She pressed her fingers against the cut, reaching for a roll of linen to wrap a pressure bandage over it.

The rest of his wounds were easier. She helped him roll to his side so she could clean the opened cuts on his back. Thankfully, there were only a few. The rain had washed away most of the blood, and a few had already begun to dry and clot.

She ripped a bigger hole in his pants to clean a cut to his thigh and get access to his knee to properly bandage it. She didn't know how he'd been able to even stand on that ship, let alone walk back with her. She ripped off his makeshift wrap. His knee had swollen to almost twice its size. She bound it in a new bandage, hoping it'd help to control some of the swelling while she propped his leg up.

She spat into the yuxiway leaves and began rubbing the paste into his wounds. He winced as her fingers pressed to the cut in his thigh. She gave him a look. His eyelids fluttered, and he nodded for her to continue. A warmth spread through her. She coughed, attempting to rid her body of the flush creeping up her neck before it could show on her cheeks.

She finished binding each cut, and he watched her through it all. His eyes never once strayed from her fingers. She finally stood, but he seized her hand. She swallowed her gasp before it had a chance to penetrate her lips.

"Amaris," he whispered, eyeing her leg.

Her eyes followed his and spotted the belt pulled taut around her thigh. "It's hardly a scratch," she said, trying to pull her leg from where his hands grasped around the knife. For how clammy his skin was, his hands were incredibly warm against the outside of her pants.

She'd apparently shoved the pain so far down she'd forgotten all about it. She let out a small laugh. *How could I forget there's a knife in my leg?*

"You call *me* stubborn," he said, his brows furrowing. "You have a dagger in your thigh."

"Fine," she groaned, grabbing the fade chicory from the basket.

He took the jar from her, giving her a narrow look as he gently held her waist and urged her to lie down. She settled beside him before her mind could protest. He scooted closer, his body almost pressing against her back. He practically radiated heat. She forced her breaths to remain cool and steady. His fingers wedged themselves around the knife, ripping and prying her pants apart.

"These were my only pants," she complained, hoping the humor could distract her.

"That's what you're worried about?"

"Well, duh. I'm not wearing a dress from here on out." She nervously chuckled as she turned her head.

His brow lifted to the slight crack in her voice, but she returned her focus to the dagger still embedded in the back of her thigh.

"This is going to hurt."

"See what I mean?" Amaris began. "Telling me it's going to hurt only makes me more on edge and—"

She yelped as he pulled the knife out. She gripped the edges of the cot, wishing narcotics existed here. He grabbed a piece of linen, pressing it firmly against her thigh. She sank her nails into the thin fabric of the cot. Again, she fought the flush in her cheeks as his hands pressed harder against her leg. His fingers skimmed her inner thigh. She shouldn't have liked the sight of his hand wrapped around her leg or how close he was.

When he pulled back, her body instantly yearned for his warm touch. He trickled the herb over her wound, extinguishing all thoughts as a burning sensation seared through her thigh. She grasped his arm before he could sprinkle more of the burning hell into her wound.

"That's enough," she breathed.

"It'll burn."

"You don't say," she grumbled through the pain, her nails no doubt creating crescent moons in his skin.

He hefted her thigh up, pulling out a string of linen. He wrapped it around and tied off the end before falling back to the cot. "You should rest." He released a deep breath.

Amaris stood, expecting him to grab her again and drag her beside him, but he didn't. He shut his eyes, laying a hand across his chest.

"So should you," she whispered.

She pulled away before she listened to him and curled up beside him on the cot. Pulling her hair behind her ears, she fanned her heated cheeks. *What am I doing?* Her thumb fidgeted with the ring wrapped around her finger as she desperately put distance between her and Theodoric. Once at the edge of the room, she closed her eyes and took a deep breath. She couldn't feel this way. It'd only been a few weeks since she'd run out on Derek, but hours ago, in the tower, she'd allowed herself to wonder. She turned back around, and her thoughts drifted as she assessed the scene around her with all the injured scattered. She rolled her shoulders and cracked her neck. She had a job to do. Everything else could wait.

She limped to the kitchen to gather what information she could from Ms. Borstad and check their inventory levels. Alan appeared as though he'd never left. His sword was sheathed at his back without a single drop of blood, but his clothes were covered in it. He carried an injured Luana soldier from the kitchen doors and disappeared into the dining hall.

She looked down at her own shirt. It was ripped, showing her corset, and covered in blood, most likely from Theodoric and the man he'd rammed with his sword. She braided her hair again. Her hands needed to move through the strands like they always did, preparing herself for the call.

Well, now was the call of a lifetime. She moved to a sink and splashed the lukewarm water over her skin. Blood dripped down her cheeks, sliding along the edges of her lips. She spat out the coppery tang and glanced over her shoulder at the biggest disaster she'd ever seen.

Ms. Borstad caught her eye as she tended to one of the patients. Amaris rolled up her sleeves and approached the woman, begging the pain in her thigh to disappear. It was Ediva.

"Gave her cudweed and placed wrap around wound. Yuxiway should fend against festering. Fade chicory to staunch bleeding," Ms. Borstad said, peering at the wrapped stump of the Ediva's leg.

Amaris's hand braced her shoulder, but she didn't stir. She studied Ms. Borstad's work, taking note of the missing tourniquet. No blood seeped through the bandages.

"Cornelius required hands now and then," Ms. Borstad whispered. "He no like flower child. Need strong hands and no singsong voice."

Amaris wanted to speak, to ask her everything she knew about what a mystique did in Magoria, but that would have to wait. She only smiled at her description of Pricilla. She eyed the belt still wrapped around her own leg. She released the buckle and held the edge of the table as the blood refilled her system. Pins and needles started in her toes and worked its way up her leg, but blood didn't seep from the wrap Theodoric had placed around her thigh.

"Three down, way too many to go," she whispered to herself.

She swallowed the lump in her throat as several soldiers carried over a large fellow. They set him on the ground at her feet. He was pale as a ghost, but she had to confirm what she knew to be true. She lowered herself, but there was no burst of breath on her cheek or a bounding of a heartbeat beneath her fingers.

"He's gone," she said quietly.

The men bowed their heads. One kneeled next to the cold and dead man. He placed his hand over his eyes and whispered something that sounded like a prayer. They picked up his lifeless body and carried him into the hall, where Amaris guessed they had a spot for the dead.

She closed her eyes, pushing the morbid thought from her mind. When she used to have rough calls, they'd sit around the kitchen table, allowing their dark senses of humor to get them through the night, but she didn't have Charlie beside her to look at a pile of intestines and ask if they were having sausage for dinner.

She moved down the line, assessing and treating. It pained her when she'd reached the ones where there was nothing she could do for them besides offer a drink to calm their nerves. Several had already passed, probably before she'd stepped off the ship. A twinge of guilt sprouted within her.

How many more would still be alive if I hadn't left? It was more horrible than she could've ever imagined. Everyone in the fire service wanted to see a mass casualty incident once in their lives, whether they admitted it or not, but it was more than she could handle. She cleared the kitchen and began moving into the hall. She felt as though, the further down the line she went, the more grave the injuries.

All while she stopped bleeding, bandaged wounds, and wrapped injured joints, she looked for Esaias, Adelaide, and Gris. She kept her hands moving; it was all she could do to steady them. She assessed Theodoric when she found him down the line again. He'd passed out, but his breaths were even, and his heart beat a steady rhythm.

Her fingers lingered on his neck, her chest tightening. She forced herself to pull away and continued moving through her patients. Why did she sense she was missing something? His eagerness to see her safely out before the Conjugation had been replaced by something else, but she didn't know what to call it. Did she want there to be more?

She pushed through, fighting the urge to let her leg collapse. Finally, she was forced to cease her efforts when she stood up and swayed as the room twisted and warped around her. A hand caught her arm and pulled her into the kitchen.

Gris sat Amaris in a chair and forced a glass of water and a piece of bread into her hands. "Eat," she demanded. Her eyes were swollen and red. A bandage wrapped her arm, another around her leg.

"I'll be alright," Amaris said, scathing off the dizziness. "How are you?" She tried to stand but Gris pressed against her shoulders.

"You need to rest." Her chin quivered, and her hands clenched at her sides.

"Where are Esaias and Adelaide?"

"They're safe," she assured her. "Ms. Borstad and Onika tended to them both immediately. They're resting in the back corner of the hall."

"I hadn't gotten that far yet," Amaris muttered.

"And you won't if you don't take care of yourself." Gris eyed the bread and water.

Amaris took a bite, her eyes rolling back in her head at its glorious sweetness. "Why were you on the boat?"

The first week, Gris had visited Sephardi while she oversaw Amaris's guard duty, but the ship had been the first sight of her in weeks.

"Why were you?"

"Adelaide needed help." Amaris didn't have the energy to elaborate further.

"I didn't know about Sephardi," Gris whispered.

"She's your wife."

"Everyone has their secrets." Gris's bow had found its home slung over her back. It shifted as she leaned against a table and folded her arms.

"Even you?"

Gris bowed her head and gripped the edge of the table.

Amaris remained silent as the adrenaline began to wear off. She lifted her hands, and they started to tremble before her eyes. She bit into the bread and lowered them to her lap, fending off the shaking.

"Eat, drink, and rest. This isn't only your burden to shoulder." Gris left, heading into the hall.

Amaris finished the morsels and leaned her head back. It *was* her burden to shoulder. She knew what to do, how to assess and treat, but she was so tired. Her limbs ached and grew heavier the longer she sat. She closed her eyes and promised herself only a few moments of rest.

§

A LOUD CRASH echoing through the kitchen startled Amaris awake.

How long did I sleep? Glancing through the window, it still appeared dark out. She drew her gaze around the kitchen, searching for the cause of the commotion.

Bennet strode through the open doors. "Deavopan has fled!" he cheered.

He sheathed his sword and grabbed a large glass of kusu from a barrel. He led a parade of men and women. All of them were stained in blood and covered in dirt, but each one grabbed a glass and joined in the celebration. Amaris couldn't judge them. She needed a shot herself. They dispersed throughout the rooms, finding their fallen comrades or tending to the other injured.

Bennet stiffened when he eyed Amaris. She watched as his eyes moved to each person lying in pain. He faced her, taking several steps, until he glared down at her.

"What are you doing here?" he growled.

She swallowed but didn't shrink into the chair. She stood, forcing *him* back. "My job."

"How many dead?"

"I don't know."

Bennet scoffed, taking a sip from his drink. "How bad are his injuries?"

"Who—"

"Theo," he spat.

She crossed her arms. "I didn't think you cared, since you tried to kill him with that whip."

"The boy is strong," he barked. "It was meant to teach him a lesson."

"He's passed out in the hall, but he'll live," she muttered. She wasn't in the mood to debate with him.

Bennet's hand wrapped around his sword, and her shoulders tensed as she waited for him to draw it. Instead, he pushed past her and disappeared into the hall.

"I don't understand how you can do all this and still remain calm," Alan said, his thumb brushing along the edge of a bowl of broth.

She stared at him, still processing the interaction with Bennet. Alan turned his gaze to Peter, who was awake and upright, fidgeting with a wood carving.

Amaris sighed. "Is it that I can remain calm, or are you asking if I have any fear?" She ambled closer, eyeing over Alan's shoulder at the color peeking through Peter's cheeks.

"Both." Alan let out a huff, mixed with disbelief and laughter as he dragged his hand through his disheveled hair. "I understand how to wield a sword and remain calm in the heat of a fight, but taking a man's life is different than saving it. How do you do it without bearing the responsibility of the realm?"

"It's all still there, the fear and panic, but I've learned to control it. I've tended to dying people before," she confessed. "I can't do anything for them if I'm in my own head about their uncertainty. I'm not the one who's injured—it's them." She gestured to Peter. "I have to remind myself of that."

She excused herself from the room. More hands were scattered about now, and she avoided Bennet as he kneeled beside Theodoric's cot. She walked to the back corner, wondering what she'd say first, but Adelaide was nowhere to be seen, as usual, and Esaias was passed out.

She wished she could rest, but there was still too much to do. She found where she'd left off with her patients and began again—assess, treat, and repeat. It was only when she finally reached her last patient beside Esaias that she curled up on the floor and closed her eyes.

CHAPTER 46

Theo

EVERY PART OF Theo's body hurt as he sat up on the cot. He rubbed his hand against the scars on his chest. How many had seen the marks of his suffering? He had a servant fetch him a shirt and something to assist with his getting around. He'd rested enough for now. There were more pressing matters to discuss. When he was finally leaning against a crutch, he spared a glance around the hall and spotted them.

Through the dimly lit chamber he saw Amaris. She was nestled beside Adelaide in the far corner. Esaias was next to them, likely one of the few snoring.

He wanted to go over and pray she finally remembered the Conjugation, but he knew it'd be futile. Maybe with time, she'd come to remember. He wouldn't allow himself to believe it was a fleeting moment lost to the poison and wine. He wanted it to be more than that. He wanted Amaris to be more than the mystique, more than his friend.

He hobbled through the hall, taking slow strides to put as little pressure against his knee as he could. The binding Amaris had wrapped around it had worked immensely for the swelling, and possibly the hours of rest did too. He staggered past the shut door he could only assume housed the dead. A mass funeral would take place at sunset, either tonight or the next, to burn the victims of the massacre and send their souls to After.

He didn't wish to see who was among the dead, not yet. He wasn't prepared for who he'd find. The light of dawn was building within the manor, flooding the halls in bright light. He knocked once on his father's study before he hollered for Theo to enter.

"It brings me joy to see you aren't dead," his father said flatly, nursing a glass of kusu. His feet were propped on the edge of his desk, crusted blood and dirt coating the soles of his boots. Dark circles hung below his eyes, along with several drops of splattered crimson.

"I would say the same for you. I didn't expect to see you joining the fight." Theo took a seat across from him.

His father poured him a glass and slid it across the sleek surface. "I couldn't very well be one of the few who sheltered within the walls. Besides, a true leader leads his people from their sides," he huffed, taking a long sip. "It would seem we have found the culprits to our Duncaster situation."

The glass stopped at the edge of Theo's lips, his eyes skimming the surface. He only wished he'd seen it coming. They ran into sailors weeks ago, and Isabel had warned him, but he'd cast it all aside. He should've been preparing for a possible attack.

"Sergeant Salter informed me of what happened on the ship," his father said. "Bennet plans to further question Corporal Salter before she's sent to Elric for her treason."

Theo's stomach dropped at the thought of Sephardi in the prison and what she would endure. How could she have turned to the Accords?

"I know it may pain you—"

"She betrayed her kingdom," Theo said, thumbing the edge of the glass.

"I was also informed of Miss Carter's actions," he stated flatly.

Theo's thumb ceased its circling, all his nerves vigilant. "Do you plan to send her to Elric too?" Theo sniped.

His father inclined a brow.

"I'm aware of your plan to have Lord Godfrey cart her off to that wretched prison. I won't allow it, especially after last night."

"Never once have I seen one enter a battlefield. She is far from the old mystique who used to walk these halls."

"She's a different breed." Theo's eyes fell to the vase and the newly added snowdrops.

"And proved to be a valuable asset."

"She's more than an asset," he breathed. "She saved me and many more." He placed the glass on the desk, no longer thirsty for the taste of his father's kusu. "You wanted her to prove herself, and now she has. Amaris entered that battlefield, not knowing if she would live, all to save as many as she could."

His father inhaled deeply, biting the inside of his cheek as he folded his arms. "You may be a leader on the battlefield, but there's a difference when it comes to leading a province," his father said. "I couldn't very well allow a potential murderer to roam about freely, but she most certainly proved her loyalty last night when she tended to each fallen soldier herself."

Theo had fallen asleep before she'd begun treating the wounded. She must have been exhausted to have treated every man and woman, especially with the injury to her thigh.

"I will have a letter sent to Freville's family stating he was likely killed by Deavopan soldiers," his father began, "and I would like you to offer Miss Carter a permanent position as mystique."

"I doubt she'd be willing to accept your proposition after how you treated her."

"Who would turn down an official position as a mystique to a province?"

"Was her healing not enough before?" Theo's leg muscles tightened with his anger, sending spasms around the cut in his thigh. "She risked her life to save me in a river, healed Esaias from scrying fever, and jumped in front of that whip."

His father set aside his kusu, releasing a deep sigh. "Theo," he began, "I don't expect you to understand the decisions that must be made to protect one's people as their leader, but I do implore you to see the rationality of our situation. We have our family and our people to protect. We must not trust just anyone. Their loyalty must be proved beyond a doubt."

Theo picked at a chipped part of the upholstered chair, digging out a sliver in the wood. "I'm well aware of what can happen when trust is placed in the wrong hands."

Twice now he'd been betrayed. He still didn't know who'd betrayed his squad and sent them on a fool's mission to Oystein Castle. Maybe he never would. But at least Sephardi hadn't been successful in her mission to kill Amaris. As much as he wished otherwise, his father was right about one thing. He could no longer blindly trust.

"I'm sure you are," his father said. "I know you have not sought me out only for her freedom, but to discuss what we're to do about future attacks."

"We need reinforcements," Theo began. "We need to ask for the king's aid."

"I agree, but we also need to see if our friends in Westbury have suffered similarly."

"The Grants can suffer every bit of what we went through last night," Theo hissed. "They deserve it."

"I don't like or respect Lord Grant any more than you do, but he is still a lord in Luana, and as such, he's entitled to our security. When we have enough healed forces, I want you to take a small party and journey there. We are to determine whether there are any damages and whether we need to send a part of our army to Westbury."

"We can't risk spreading ourselves thin. They have their own people to defend them. They prefer it that way anyways." The Grants were the last people Theo wanted to help. "We should focus our efforts on making it to Charibert to ask for aid from the king's armada."

"Westbury isn't entirely out of your way. You'll travel there and send a messenger to report back," his father demanded.

"Won't we be sailing down the coast?"

"No, you'll journey through the Scarlet Mountains. I won't jeopardize good soldiers for the sake of efficiency. The waters are no longer safe."

Theo shook his head, grasping his temples. "But it'll add at least a few days if we stop in Westbury, especially if they insist on arguing with us," he shot back. They did as they pleased, however they pleased.

"Much like how you insist on arguing with me?" his father asked, his tone still flat.

"I simply think it's a waste of resources, but if it's what you wish, we'll travel to Westbury before making our journey to Charibert," Theo grumbled.

"Take the time to heal and recover. Deavopan suffered significant losses and likely won't return anytime soon. I also don't intend to send my soldiers wounded. Gather a list of names of who you wish to accompany you."

"Bennet won't be leading this mission?"

"No," his father snipped, his annoyance finally leaking through. "I would think you'd be grateful for an opportunity such as this after your stunt."

Theo ground his teeth together.

"What happened here that morning?"

Theo turned from him, drawing his gaze toward the bay. "I'm bringing Amaris with me."

"Don't change the subject, Theo."

He gripped the armrest, fighting the emotion flooding his system. "Taking a small squadron to Westbury and then all the way to Charibert without a mystique would be reckless. I'll make a list of who I intend—"

"Theo," he said, "I'm aware of what happened in Oystein Castle that night and what followed in Rongstad Prison."

Theo couldn't hold back the tear that rolled down his cheek. His stitch was gone, and his mental shields were in shambles.

"I wasn't sure of it until Esaias said you were tortured when Bennet ordered you dragged outside." He rounded his desk, settling on the edge before Theo, whose hand trembled on the armrest. His father laid his hand over his, wincing as he took a knee.

"Look at me," he whispered.

Theo's eyes dropped. He couldn't pull his line of sight from his father's hand resting against his. He couldn't look into his eyes, but his father cupped his other hand around the back of his neck. Theo fought it, but he finally lifted his eyes to meet his father's. For a moment, he wasn't the duke, but a father aged by the stress and worry of a long life. A flood of tears fell from Theo's eyes. His father pulled him to his chest and wrapped his arms around him as he sobbed.

CHAPTER 47

Amaris

"AMARIS."

She brushed away the faint whisper, wanting to continue her dreamless sleep.

"Amaris," they muttered again.

She begrudgingly opened her eyes and adjusted to the light streaming into the hall.

"Adelaide?" she asked, stretching her arms and letting out a big yawn. She sat up, straightening her back. Sleeping on the floor had seemed like a good idea last night, but she was regretting that decision now.

"You're alive," Adelaide whispered, scooting closer and hugging her.

It took Amaris several more blinks to wake up entirely. Adelaide pulled back, and Amaris instantly awakened at the sight of her crooked nose.

"Your nose," she said.

Adelaide touched it, wincing. She gripped either side of her face and took a deep breath. Before Amaris registered what she was about to do, Adelaide shifted her nose back into place. Grabbing for a ball of cloth beside her, she pressed it to the fresh blood trickling down her lip. Amaris blinked.

"Happens more often than you think," she said in a nasally voice against the cloth.

"How do you feel?" Amaris asked, released from her stupor.

"I just woke up, but I think I'm fine." Adelaide offered a shrug and sat up. She twisted her back but winced and grabbed her side.

"I'm well, too, thanks for asking." Esaias sat up beside her and rubbed the sleep from his eyes.

"No one asked," Adelaide threw at him.

A few steps shuffled toward them, and Esaias slumped back on his cot, groaning. "Onika, your services are not required at the moment."

Onika let out a frustrated huff of breath, completely ignoring him as she shoved him over and sat beside him. She was in a bright-green gown, probably from the Conjugation, but there were tears in the skirt and blood soaked through in large splashes.

"Eat this before I'm forced to stick my fingers in your mouth and rub jam over your gums again," Onika said, handing him a bowl of porridge.

Onika turned to Amaris, sucking in her lips as she offered her a wry smile.

Adelaide brushed aside their bantering and demanded, "Tell me everything. What happened after I saved Esaias from certain death?"

Esaias shot her a scowl, but Onika swatted him on the arm.

Amaris looked around, taking in the decorations for the first time, or at least what felt like the first time. She began with how she'd snuck off toward the ship but was quickly interrupted by Esaias to explain how they'd fended off Deavopan soldiers and then raced to the beach to save Adelaide. With a flat look and then an eye roll, Amaris jumped back in.

She sat for what felt like forever, going over the night. Each of them filled in their own gaps, reliving the battles they'd fought, but Amaris omitted her conversation with Drauna and Sephardi. She assessed their injuries. Esaias's face had stopped bleeding, and he was able to clear the blood from his eye. He also seemed to be in decent spirits. She hoped he paid Onika well for her splendid job of managing his diabetes. *No,* mamat.

She finally pulled herself from their grasps and made her way around the hall. She stopped by some of her gravest of patients, who she'd worried wouldn't make it through the night. Most were faring well, but others weren't as lucky. Soldiers who were awake and uninjured helped carry their bodies away. She stepped from the hall after the last one was brought out, unable to stand the grieving beginning around her.

"Amaris!" Pricilla whisper-shouted from across the hall.

Amaris turned and they collided. Pricilla was covered in dried blood, but by the smile on her face, it wasn't hers. She dragged Amaris out into the hall and secured them in a small alcove. She slammed the curtain closed and shook with what was either excitement or the need to use the restroom.

"What?" Amaris laughed.

"You're from another realm!"

Oh that. "You believe me?" Amaris asked, brushing aside the hair fallen from her braid.

"Are you kidding me? Of all people?"

Amaris's whistling laugh was replaced by a nervous giggle. She swallowed the lump in her throat. *Fuck, here we go.* It all spilled out, everything. She told her about Viv, Charlie, and Derek. She fended off several tears, but with Pricilla's hands grasping hers, it pushed away the panic and anger.

Amaris even tried to describe what it was like being a firefighter paramedic. Pricilla was astonished by the idea of running into a fire and begged for more. She went into as much detail as she could about technology. She even did her best to describe a car, which blew Pricilla's mind, but the entire time Pricilla never once questioned it. She sat with those violet eyes brighter than Amaris had ever seen them.

"You still believe me?" she joked.

"I won't lie, it's quite a lot to digest, but you've experienced magic! You've come from another realm!"

"I don't know exactly how it happened. I mean, I fell through a tree."

"It's most likely a gate that connects our two realms," Pricilla corrected. "I can't wait to start reading more on this!"

"If you can find anything else on it. The journal is probably the only thing. For now, if there's anything you want to know, go ahead and ask, because we are totally secluding ourselves in the library all week so you can teach me everything about this realm. I can't keep running around pulling shit out of my ass."

Pricilla laughed. "I can't imagine what it's like walking around with this secret."

"You're telling me. I've been dying over here!"

"Where do I even start?" She sighed. "Well, you passed through a gate. Does your world have magic then?"

Amaris folded her arms, leaning against the cold stones at her back. "I never thought magic existed until I came here, and that even took a while to finally grasp."

"But one of our worlds has to have magic." Pricilla paced the small alcove, her tulle dress bouncing around her with each turn.

"I'm ninety-nine percent sure that's not Earth, unless you call microwaves magic."

Pricilla gave her a peculiar look but blew off her joke.

"Magic has to exist here," Amaris began, studying the dried blood crusted into her knuckles. "Those books and the myths you've read must mean something. What about how quickly everyone heals here? You mended my hand in three days, for crying out loud."

"Has anyone else experienced anything like that?" Pricilla asked.

Amaris shrugged. "Theodoric seems to heal fast, too, and Esaias."

Pricilla pursed her lips and folded her arms across her blood-stained chest as she leaned into the opposite wall.

"And..." Amaris hesitated. Pricilla knew everything else at this point, what was another mystery? "Something happened on the ship." She rubbed nervously at her arms before Pricilla crossed the alcove and leaned beside her. "There was someone onboard who..." Amaris felt the heaviness of the night, but Pricilla laid her hand gently on her shoulder, and it let up from its unbearable weight. "She knew my name."

"Had you met her before?"

"No." Amaris slid down the wall, throwing her hands over her face. "She knew I was from a different world."

"How's that possible?"

"The question of the hour," Amaris groaned. "How's it possible I'm here in the first place, and how did Sephardi even find out?"

"Sephardi?" Pricilla sat beside her, hugging her knees to her chest. A perplexing expression with soft eyes and pouted lips sat upon her face.

"She was the one who poisoned me. All because she knew I was from a different world. She called me an *abomination*."

Pricilla clung to Amaris's arm, wrapping around it. "You're not an abomination to me." She smiled. "More like a miracle."

"Should we tell anyone about this?" Amaris asked.

Pricilla shook her head vigorously. "No. I'm laughed at for collecting *books* on myth and magic. If you tell people you're from another realm, they might think you to be crazy."

"Sephardi sided with the Accords because of me, and they were working with pirates—"

"Pirates?" Pricilla questioned.

"I overheard some of the crew members arguing about working with the captain since she was a pirate."

"They were speaking Akaric instead of Tendasy?"

Amaris threw her hands up. "All I know is I could understand them, but some had heavy accents. They made some kind of deal."

Pricilla wrung her hands together. "What was it?"

Amaris raised a shoulder. "I don't know, but whatever it was, the soldiers said they held up their end."

Pricilla blew out a breath and pressed the wrinkles from her dress.

"Alright. Now might be more than I can digest. So, this pirate and Sephardi both knew you were from a different realm?"

Amaris nodded.

Pricilla stood and grabbed the edge of the curtain, drawing it back. "I don't know where I'll even begin, but I'll start investigating this. There was a disagreement with a province under the Accords over twenty years ago. Bazrath nearly started a war. I'll start there."

"But what about the pirate?"

"Pirates haven't been an issue for fifty years. They attacked Godwin's coast but were defeated. Any remaining retreated deep within the Black Sea. It's unlikely, but it's possible they sided with the Accords." Frazzled, Pricilla clung to the curtain as if it was the only thing keeping her standing. "I need to go to the library."

"What about me?"

"For now, focus on your patients. I'll let you know what I find."

In a second, Pricilla was gone, striding at a brisk pace toward the library.

Amaris had never seen Pricilla stumped. Part of her wanted to follow, but she was swarmed with all the thoughts and emotions in her head. The strangest and most prominent feeling, though, was elation. Regardless of the mystery aboard the ship, she'd finally done something right, building the triage and helping as many as she could. The feeling settling over her was something she'd never felt before, even as a paramedic.

She trailed through the kitchen instead of racing after Pricilla. Her eyes darted around, scanning her patients, but there was something she needed to do first.

She stepped through the garden doors, instantly breathing in what should've been the fresh scent of the morning. She crinkled her nose as she was hit with the coppery scent of blood and the beginning smell of decay instead of the morning dew.

Thumbing her engagement ring, she took a long breath. A wave crashing off the coast pulled her before her thoughts could start piling in.

She kicked off her boots and limped toward the water. She only halted when she spotted Theodoric sitting in the sand, allowing the surf to graze his bare feet. Settling beside him, she winced as her thigh twitched, but she kicked her feet out and leaned back on her hands.

"How are you feeling?"

He shrugged. "I could be better." His gaze remained fixed on the open sea.

She pushed back her hair, which was threatening to pull from her braid as a gust of wind swept over them. "Does your father still want to send me to Elric?" Since Bennet hadn't whisked her off to the dungeons last night, she had some shred of hope.

"No," Theodoric whispered. "You're free."

Amaris shifted toward the water, watching as a bird swooped down to capture its prey. Finally, something she could understand. She released a well-deserved sigh. *I'm free.*

"He's asked for me to offer you a permanent position as the mystique." Theodoric bent his good knee and wrapped his hands around it. It was such a natural stance for him to sit in the sand with his pants rolled up and water skimming his toes.

Amaris didn't know how to respond. In a matter of a day, she'd felt tugs to go back home, stay, run, and fight. But the greatest tug of them all was her desire to heal. Only last night, she'd thought she'd never be free, no matter where she was.

"I'm not proud of who I became." His voice nearly disappeared within the sound of the crashing surf.

"The Hydra?"

"I never wanted anyone to find out. I thought I'd run from it at last when I came home."

Amaris sat up, grasping her knees between her hands. "You were in a war."

"But how do I lock it away?" He rounded his shoulders. "I need to be a soldier, not a monster. How am I supposed to fight if I can no longer distinguish between the two? How do I keep from losing myself?"

Amaris hadn't known how to describe what came over him when he'd almost killed Sephardi, but now she understood. He'd stuffed everything away to keep back the Hydra, but it'd also hidden who he truly was.

"You became the Hydra to protect yourself, to keep your humanity." A hidden monster within where he could hide his shame and his guilt. "It may be a part of you, but it doesn't have to define you."

Amaris had always believed she'd never kill, but last night, she almost had. She couldn't aim, but she'd begged for the arrow to land anywhere non-lethal. Hitting Sephardi's shoulder had been pure luck.

"Who you saw last night...that's who I've become. A vicious killer."

"I think vicious is a tad excessive." Amaris smiled, but her mind slipped back to that damp, dark ship and Drauna. She swallowed and pushed aside the thought.

"I'm broken, Amaris. I don't know if I'll ever be who I used to be."

"You won't," she replied. "We'll never be who we were a year ago, a week ago, or even yesterday. Maybe we're both broken."

"You're far from broken. What you did in the last few hours is indescribable. You treated every soldier," he began. "You boarded that ship to save my sister. I'll forever be grateful for what you did for Adelaide, for me. You're an incredible mystique."

Last night was possibly the scariest night of her life, not even comparing to the terror she had when Derek struck her. Everyone had put their lives on the line, defending each other. Setting up that triage had given her a purpose she never knew she could find.

Amaris stared at her engagement ring. "We all have our faults."

"I have nightmares about what I did. I feel the panic lingering beneath the surface all the time."

"You won't heal overnight, but opening up and forgiving yourself is the first step."

"What if I can't forgive myself?"

"Only you can answer that."

He rested his head on his knee and closed his eyes. "Will you help me?" He turned his head, squishing his cheek on his knee. Any sign of foreboding storms was gone. His eyes were bright emeralds with golden stars.

She wanted to reach out, to brush back the hairs clinging to his forehead, to further expose those beautiful eyes. Instead, she slid off her ring and twisted the small piece of jewelry between her blood-stained fingers. It was insane that such a tiny piece of metal represented a promise intended to last a lifetime. A promise that could easily be broken.

She stood and stepped into the surf. She pulled her arm back and chucked the ring into the water. "I'm the mystique, aren't I?"

"That you are." His smile was small, but it warmed something in her chest.

She kneeled before him, ignoring the sea soaking her pants and the twinge in her thigh. "And you'll learn who the great Captain Theodoric Fastrada has become. You'll learn to see the man others see. Someone who risked his life in more ways than one for a woman who yelled at him, mocked him, and makes terribly reckless decisions."

"Theo," he whispered, and Amaris raised a brow. "Just Theo."

He was like a shy little kid as he said it with his shoulders hunched forward, and for a second, all she wanted to do was rest her head on that shoulder, because they'd done it. They'd made it out alive. She couldn't stop the smile spreading across her face.

"Do you remember last night?"

"The Conjugation?" she asked.

He nodded.

"No, but I want to." She wanted to do so many things. Her heart, a moment ago a steady river, now beat like the wild ocean behind her, but she only sat beside him and welcomed the breeze drifting from the sea.

Even through the chaos, as she'd run and fallen to that lower deck, she'd been overcome when she heard Theo's voice. For the first time in what felt like far too long, she hadn't wanted someone to let go of her. In that moment, she'd known she didn't want to go back to her old life, where she held onto her anger and grief.

She wasn't the same person who'd landed in those woods. She barely remembered a life without Derek, but in the last few weeks, she'd started to see a different side of herself. She'd held too tight to something that had been lost for too long. She was done pretending. The ache of leaving Viv would remain, but the relief she felt was something she couldn't ignore.

Amaris watched Theo cast his gaze toward the sea. Last night's revelations further proved there was a reason for her hidden desire to stay. She'd felt a call that first night when she stepped toward the bay. Despite her attempts to suppress it, an inkling in her knew Magoria whispered to her, and now she was ready to listen.

CAN'T GET ENOUGH?

For BONUS material and to follow Theo and Amaris's story in book 2 of
The Godwin Chronicles: *A Dance of Fate and Dreams*, sign up for K. M.
Laumann's Newsletter.

WWW.KMLAUMANN.COM

ACKNOWLEDGMENTS

Wow. To be even writing an acknowledgments page is something I wasn't sure I'd ever get to do. There are so many incredible people I'd like to thank. I'm so grateful for the support I've received in making *A Realm of Blood and Mercy* possible.

For starters, I want to thank Jen. You were there from its conception, reading through a mess of a first draft and every draft I put under your nose since. You've encouraged my writing from the very first story I shared with you in that pink spiral notebook. Thank you for making sure I ate on busy writing days and for leaving affirmations on my desk every time you visited.

To Katie—my video chat goddess. Thank you for the hours you let me blab about these characters and the future I see for them. Thank you for being one of the first beta readers and helping me see the flaws when I didn't want to. Also, for being my mini promo team in Scotland. I still can't believe I came down for breakfast to new friends asking if I was the writer. That's when it really started to feel real.

To my writing group for suggesting adding Theo's POV. His character came alive because of that single suggestion and now holds a special place in my heart.

To my copyeditor, Jason, for his meticulous approach and fantastic insight. He not only helped take my book to the next level but taught me new and exciting grammar rules.

To my proofreader, Shannon Cave, for her attention to detail and for making me realize for the first time the true complexity of the world I'd created.

To Stefani Saw at Seventhstar Art, for creating a beautiful cover that had me in tears the first time I saw it. Absolutely stunning! Thank you for your patience with my millions of questions I had while navigating this world of self-publishing.

To Beth. My fellow romance and fantasy lover. Without your insight and questioning of the small details, Magoria wouldn't be the realm it is today.

To all my friends, readers, and community who have followed my writing and publishing journey and continue to cheer me on, thank you. I couldn't have done it without any of you.

K. M. LAUMANN has always had an unrelenting tug toward writing, her early pieces consisting of heaping doses of magic and horror. Now, she still piles on the whimsical but prefers a side of swoony romance. When she isn't writing her next novel, she travels, twirls her sword, or reads anything with a tragic love story.

www.ingramcontent.com/pod-product-compliance
Lightning Source LLC
Chambersburg PA
CBHW020003120726
47903CB00004B/1114

*9 7 9 8 9 9 9 2 3 2 2 2 9 *